WE TOOK THE LONG WAY HOME

WE TOOK THE LONG WAY HOME

A Novel

Marilynn Celeste

Detroit Red Publishing
www.thedetroitred.com
www.detroitred.net

Detroit Red Publishing

www.thedetroitred.com

www.detroitred.net

Library of Congress card catalogue number: 2018905859

ISBN 978-1-7323440-0-6

First Printing: June 2018

Printed in the United States of America

This book is dedicated to the good people of Detroit, Michigan, past, present and future. My memories rise up shiny and golden as only they could through a child's eyes and a child's heart. Detroit has formed everything in my soul—my love of music and art, my citified folksiness, my hardened wariness and the sharp tongue I can't seem to hold. But most of all my optimism that as long as God allows the sun to rise each morning, there's something good coming: love, family, friends and adventure. I wish I had more of all four.

If you are from Detroit, I hope you recognize the places and the feelings this story evokes and if not, I want you to wish you were there during this indelible and special time in history. Real places and traditions of Detroit have been intertwined to revive the vision of the best days, I think, of my city on the river. This story has been buzzing around in my head and heart in one form or another for decades. I'm glad it's finally out of me!

This book is also dedicated to all the girls and boys with parents who have passed away, took a voluntary leave or were otherwise removed from their lives. We are the ones who fight through the dark, run through the fire, only to turn our faces towards the sun—in hope. Always hope! Never, never, ever give up.

Special thanks to my family and everyone I have met, for better or worse, who has touched my life in a way that could be written about. Lastly, I thank a boy from Minneapolis named Prince who was born the same year as I, who made me believe in myself and my talent and my vision.

Prince Rogers Nelson said the creation of something from nothing is in and of itself, a success. Any view to the contrary is just an opinion. I know he would say, "Love God. Believe in yourself." I do. I hope you do, too.

I

Without a sound the snow fell like tiny diamonds from the late afternoon sky. The suddenly sprung to life streetlights making each crystalline flurry look otherworldly as they settled atop the gray mush already enshrouding the ground. How could the delicate simplicity of new snow make Detroit seem so tranquil and expectant? *Damn! Is this gonna be all night long?* the man driving along Woodward Avenue looking for the freeway entrance was thinking, his lips twisting over his teeth. He was clearly not happy about leaving his family tonight, just two days after Christmas.

As he had turned out of his driveway onto the slushy street, he'd smiled to himself peering back at his house in the rearview mirror, admiring his holiday handiwork. The strings of colored lights on the shrubbery in his front yard were buried and unyielding under inches of white fluff, like tiny twinkling rainbows swaddled in cotton. He'd only be away for about two or three hours max, but that didn't make it any easier. Mike Morton wanted to be at home in front of his fireplace with his wife, watching his 5 kids figure out how to destroy their toys in record time.

"The little ruffians," he mumbled to himself.

The car radio was on 800 AM, CKLW, the big 50,000-watt station that had been broadcasting out of Windsor, Ontario since before anyone could recall when it wasn't. Mike travelled all over the Midwest and anywhere he'd drive, he could always count on "The Big 8" keeping him company. He even enjoyed the chirpy jingles sung by the popular Johnny Mann Singers. He imagined the women in the group as being porcelain skinned and statuesque with bouffant hairdos and chic chiffon dresses with mink stoves. *Was it stoves or stoles?* As a child, he'd always told his mother he would be rich one day and he would buy her a *mink stove*. She knew what her Mikey meant.

Mike Morton was a bit of a relic and he knew it. What other man in his thirties listened to AM radio for the music? Certainly no one he knew, and in a few days, it would be 1984. He vaguely recalled some gloom and doom story from high school about 1984, but from where he was sitting, it looked like life was going to be business as usual. Mike never knew when he would be needed, but he was always ready to help with a problem or a special request. Like tonight.

Though he was in a hurry to get up to Ann Arbor, Mike knew he had to drive carefully, making certain to avoid attention that might attract an unplanned stop by the police. They would be more than a little interested in what they'd find inside his car. The woman he was going to see about was an old friend from his school days, who'd likely not recognize him now though they'd seen one another only months earlier. They didn't exactly run in the same circles. *It's probably a good thing she doesn't really know me anymore*, Mike was thinking. *Make it easy on the both of us.*

He caught the flash of his eyes in the rearview mirror, illuminated by the lights of a car about to pass on his left. He looked so different from the old days, anyway. His bright auburn hair, which brought torrents of teasing as a kid, was now dyed black thanks to Miss Clairol, as were his eyebrows. He used his wife's Maybelline Great Lash Mascara on his eyelashes and kept his face clean shaven so there would be no pesky red beard growth. He wasn't "Mike the Moron" anymore. The driver's face gathered into an uninvited scowl.

When he was a kid, Mike Morton's family had a wooden sign over their house address that said "The Mortons," decorated with a small proliferation of vacant eyed mallards heading heavenward. Unfortunately, the "t" on the sign had somehow fallen away, effectively rendering it "The Morons." Mike Morton had to live with this typographical outrage, first spied by a schoolmate who had dutifully taken notice on the way to school one day and decided to share his clever discovery with anyone within earshot.

Mike had been a pale, rail thin kid who was friendly and easily influenced, as he didn't seem to have much by way of his own thoughts or opinions, just appropriations of those that others had come up with. When he spoke, he would often finish a person's sentence, basically repeating what they said as they were saying it, like a clairvoyant mynah bird. People considered him slow, yet most would agree it took some brains to be able to talk when someone else was talking and say the exact same thing they were saying.

As Mike came into manhood, his affability and loyalty made him an "every man," giving him a minor value. He could slip into a situation and not be noticed because he kind of looked like everyone else. People couldn't quite seem to identify him for he was completely familiar yet indistinguishable. A paradox for sure, but an asset for a man in Mike's profession.

It wasn't until the age of 21 that Mike Morton became the dealer of unmitigated unpredictability that was as final as funeral clothes. He was the thing that went "bump" in the night, but in the instant it was heard, time had certainly run out for the unfortunate listener. That bump was usually the cocking of the hammer on his gun, or the muffled explosion of a silencer on the barrel.

The irony wasn't lost on Mike that his profession was tied, in the most tenuous of ways, to the loss of his mother. Mrs. Morton was emptying the family's trash one summer night and when she didn't return after several minutes, her dutiful son broke away from the television to retrieve her from the alley. All he found was trash strewn about the ground as well as his mother's warm and vacant house slippers, stranded on the concrete like small aliens from outer space. Now it was her boy who made families grieve and wonder what happened to their loved ones.

Mike the Hitman was now on I-94 heading West to Ann Arbor. He was warned that there might be more than one target and he knew he could end up dead if he hesitated or failed. He'd have to park down the road, walk up to the house and wait out in the snow before he could make his move. The element of surprise never failed to, well, *surprise.*

Mike reached for a Marlborough from the half empty box on the passenger's seat. He always got a little nervous, but that kept him on his guard and on his toes. He didn't much like the idea of having to stow a body (or two?) in his ride, but what could he do? He'd already removed the rear facing seat and replaced it with a 4 by 8 piece of plywood that he could replace many times over. He patted the dashboard of his 1983 Chevrolet Caprice Estate station wagon. Mike enjoyed looking at the burled wood interior trim that housed his controls. Power everything: windows, door locks, steering and brakes. And of course, the AM/FM stereo with an 8-track tape player included. With that mighty 305 V8 engine powering him along, he felt like he was driving a cruise ship.

Turning down the radio as he came upon the address he was looking for, he smirked to himself. *Why do people turn down the radio when they're looking for an address while they're driving? Go figure.* He felt for the knob again and turned the radio off for good measure. This was business.

He killed his headlights before reaching up under his glove compartment to grab his .44 with the scope. Mike stamped out his cigarette in the overflowing ashtray, pulled up the collar on his coat and slid out of his car.

As the gloaming set in, gently tamping down the last light of the day, Angelica Meadows felt a chill go up her spine as she stared vacantly out of her living room window. She allowed the heat from the cup of hot jasmine tea to warm her hands, though it wasn't needed. She wasn't cold. Angelica took a small sip from her cup and impulsively, blew her hot breath on the frosty window pane. A ragged circle of condensation reached out and as if changing its mind, contracted into itself and disappeared, revealing on the horizon a mere suggestion of a river, now frozen under its coverlet of snow. Winter seemed to come all at once this year, but it made no difference to Angelica. She felt warm, she felt safe. At least for now.

In the distance stood the bare maple trees, their branches reaching skyward as if pleading to the heavens to halt the scenic snowfall. Angelica thought back to when she first saw the Ann Arbor property. It had been a two-bedroom brick cottage then, within view of the Huron River and ringed with a small forest of trees—elm, maple and oak. The real estate agent had pointed to the woods with a sweep of her hand to show Angelica what it had to offer by way of flora. The woman had wanted them to retreat back inside, a bower of low, heavy clouds threatening rain any moment, but Angelica kept walking towards an outlying stand of trees. She stood in silent contemplation for several minutes and when the real estate lady began to call to her, Angelica put up her hand to shutter the woman's voice. Though it was summer, the ground was carpeted in fallen, decaying leaves. Just as she turned to venture back to the house it began to rain and the refreshing scent of the petrichor assailed her senses letting her know there was life there and she belonged to it.

Angelica scraped together her money to buy the ramshackle property that had so much potential. She expanded out and up adding a master suite upstairs complete with a fireplace and lounge area that took up half of the upper level. Downstairs she even had an indoor pool installed--the ultimate indulgence. Growing up in Detroit, Angelica had dreamed of owning a home like this. It took years to finish, but she had to marvel at how fortunate she was. Even her husband Carlton, whose nonchalance made him seem inured of all but the most conspicuous displays of consumption, had given her high praise for her real estate coup.

A tasteful riot of muted pastels, clusters of comfortable soft sofas and chairs, and faithful reproductions of her favorite paintings by Alma-Tadema, Renoir, Cezanne and Monet graced the inside of her sanctuary. But none of that comforted her now as she stood on the cusp of silence that separated the beginning of night from the end of the day.

Angelica was anchored to where she stood as much by the heaviness in her soul as by her inability to will her body to move. Outside two fawns were walking deliberately and unsteadily through the snow, trying to find their way back to the woods. Angelica imagined for a moment that she was inside a snow globe with a miniature living room and that the deer were looking in at *her* wondering why there was no snow flying inside? Angelica could feel her world--lonely and soundless. She turned away and drew the curtains.

She stoked the tentative fire in the hearth and once she was satisfied with its progress, put her slightly swollen feet up on her damask sofa, grabbed a book and a chenille throw. Tonight, her home was a beautiful fortress against the enemies who might come for her now. So much had gone wrong when all she wanted to do was the right thing. How had her life turned out like this?

A year ago, she had been a young lawyer on the rise at her firm. At work, the beautiful Angelica Meadows was known as a smart, feisty, tenacious litigator, who enjoyed the loyalty of her small team and the trust of the senior partners of the firm. She was tireless and diligent for her clients, yet maintained a warm, inclusive personality.

A year ago, Angelica thought she had a fairly good marriage to Carlton Meadows, himself a lawyer and very ambitious man she'd known since childhood. A man who was planning to be the next mayor of Detroit, Michigan, though she couldn't see how that would happen with incumbent Mayor Coleman Young about to mount his 4th bid for the office. A man she now realized she didn't know at all. A man she had no idea had, earlier in the day, given the address of their lovely home to two individuals along with strict instructions. The two killers were told by Carlton Meadows to make it look as if his pregnant, clumsy wife had fallen down the stairs in their beautiful house and broken her neck.

A year ago, Angelica didn't know the man she loved but thought she would never see again, her best friend and the love of her life, would walk back into her life like a loaves and fishes miracle.

A year ago, she didn't know who her father was, as he had remained a mystery in all her 32 years of life. He was just someone she wondered about, fantasized about and knew not to ask too many questions about. She now knew why no one in her seemingly close family would ever offer up a name and doled out few details on who he'd been.

8

Angelica also knew she could not walk back what she had begun, and many well-constructed lives were about to come crashing to the ground, including her own. Who was she kidding? Those lives were built on the sinking sand of lie after lie and it was justice, delayed no more, that would topple every artifice. Her marriage would be over. It was going to fall apart anyway, riven by a belly that simply got bigger month by month.

Angelica began to cry softly. She understood that telling what she knew now, years after the precipitating tragedy had set everything in motion, would not undo the past. She was about to lose her relationship with just about every man in her life. *Those relationships were just lies anyway*, she reminded herself, *atop an even bigger lie*. And now she, Angelica Tanner Meadows, with a soft fluttering like butterfly wings tapping inside her stomach in affirmation that she was responsible for more than just herself, had set the gears in motion to end that lie. She wiped her eyes with the backs of her hands and drew her blanket close to her face. Angelica was utterly alone in her mission and all she could do was wait.

ONE

Detroit is a centuries old city in Michigan abutted by a river between America and Canada. Strategically located and rich in natural resources, not the least of which are its lakes and rivers, a French explorer and fur trader named Antoine de la Mothe-Cadillac settled the area in 1701. Because Detroit is so closely identified with the French, it's surprising the city was captured by the British in 1760 during the French and Indian War. Though the Brits withdrew during the next major conflict of that era, the American Revolution, they tenaciously recaptured the city during the War of 1812, but returned it a year later.

Because it was such a short distance from Detroit to Canada via the Detroit River, the city was an important stop on the route of the Underground Railroad. Though a major Northern city, Detroit was not without its racial tensions and strife. In 1863, a race riot drove blacks from the city. Little more than 100 years later, another riot, devastating and televised, would drive many whites from the city of Detroit, never to return.

Centuries after its founding, the self-sufficient, self-sustaining frontier justice and law of the land was still in practice in many of the grittier parts of the city. The mantra and edict were simple: take care of your own problems. Some people might call it vigilantism, some the will of the streets. Whatever it was called, it was swift and final, and few people found cause to argue with it.

Detroit is where someone can meet a Chinese person, turn away as they speak and honestly believe a Negro is talking. Adaptation. Assimilation. In some of the working-class neighborhoods, immigrants from China, Poland, Germany, Greece and all parts in between moved in to seek a patch of the American Dream for their families. However, the immigrant children, attending school with their majority black peers, assimilated and adopted the language, the slang, and the colloquialisms of the Negro contingent. Undoubtedly, the parents at home struggling with English in their daily dealings with the world, were appalled and confused by how their sons and daughters were speaking. In some homes, the native tongue of the motherland is spoken solely and English only outside of it. It's an uncomfortable dichotomy, but in Detroit, a necessary balancing act.

Ultimately, this adaptation is affected for reasons of survival. Negroes do not respect nor accept those who seem weak. Language is a barrier that telegraphs weakness. If you are weak you are prey. Period. That is the law of survival and the law of the jungle called Detroit.

Just as the opportunity for a good job in the automobile factories lured Southern blacks, it also lured whites from Appalachia. Working side by side was an uneasy chore for blacks who didn't trust whites and hill folk, or hillbillies, who had seldom if ever been around blacks. After all, most of the hillbillies came from generational poverty and had no chance of slave ownership when slavery was common in the South. The two groups shared a love of the same types of food, folkways, long standing Southern traditions, and of course, superstitions and suspicions—mostly of one another. The competition for these "good jobs" and better housing led to racial disturbances in 1943 and the most prolific and memorable one in 1967. However, the reasons for the conflict in the 1960's had other social conditions

11

piled on: poor educational opportunities, a heavy handed, mostly white police force and widespread discrimination.

Summertime in Detroit is generally a hot, hazy and humid affair. Many residents make their way to the Detroit River to enjoy what errant breezes they can while having a leisurely picnic on Belle Isle, watching the big ships floating down the glinting sea green waterway. Kids bet each other, without any real threat of having to pay up or even take up the dare, they can swim across the river to Canada. Optically, the distance is completely deceiving, as are the currents and 53-foot depth of the water.

One of the greatest pleasures the Detroit River had to offer was a trip on the Bob-lo boat to Bob-lo Island Amusement Park, a 90-minute ride away in Amherstburg, Ontario. There were two gleaming white steam ships trimmed in cerulean blue--the SS Columbia and the SS Ste. Claire. The triple decker boats were almost identical with their black, blue and gold smoke stacks belching carbon clouds into the sky and blasting their tremendous horns to announce their departures. The ships resembled a floating straw hat, or a fancy birthday cake tossed onto the water.

Angelica Tanner and her best friend, Sheila Davis, stood on the wide, dark wood expanse of the ship's staircase, their arms entwined in its brass bannisters, contemplating their next move. Just ahead of them on the second deck was the big, open, wooden dance floor where couples and families danced to classic American music. The band played "Anchors Aweigh" as the SS Columbia pulled out of the dock.

"Let's get some souvenirs or a pop," said Sheila.

"And where are we gonna keep the souvenirs while we ride the rides?" Angelica asked. "Let's just get some pop and walk around, 'n see who we know."

They ran up the stairs to the concession stand to get their cups of Faygo Red Pop. A perfect opportunity to stay out of sight from Angelica's aunt and uncle for a while. Angelica glanced at her old gold toned Timex watch with the brand new Speidel band which was a bit too loose for her delicate wrist. Her uncle Ned had given her and Sheila exactly 40 minutes to explore the boat, get snacks and socialize with any other kids they might know on the ship.

After the time expired, the two girls were to meet Uncle Ned and Aunt Ella on deck two, port side, so her 6 and 8-year-old cousins could be passed off to them, so Ned and his wife could go dance. When Uncle Ned suggested she actually let the little ones tag along with her on the island, Angelica just stared at him, her green eyes pleading silently in unblinking desperation.

"Fine," Uncle Ned acquiesced. How could he deny his favorite and coincidentally, only niece? She was a good kid and he could never tell her "no," much to her mother's consternation. She thought Ned encouraged Angelica to be too much of a "free spirit" and reminded him from time to time she "ain't raising no hippies!" Was anyone more uptight than his sister, Liz? If there was, he was glad he didn't know them.

Angelica understood that her excursion on the Bob-lo boat as a reward for babysitting her cousins had conditions attached. She didn't mind because she loved Frankie and Lydia and they were crazy about her. But the deal was once they docked and disembarked, Angelica and Sheila would have most of the day to themselves to ride whatever they wanted without being shackled to little kids. She was determined to have her fun unfettered. It was the General Motors company picnic after all, and everyone seemed to know someone on the outing either directly, through school or work. Detroit was both a big city and a small town where people, it seemed, always knew you or your family.

Angelica and Sheila raced upstairs to the souvenir stand to figure out how much some little trinkets would cost so they could stash a few dollars in their socks. Angelica decided on a golden ring that had small white and coral colored "pearls" floating in a sphere of viscous liquid. It was so cool and so beautiful, surely it was worth much more than a dollar. *Suckers!* Sheila liked the Captain Bob-lo piggy bank but also wanted the plastic "Chantilly lace" fan with the fluttering tassel at the end. Angelica had gotten the very same entrancing little fan her last time on the boat. It broke before she could get it off the ship.

"I'd get the bank," she told Sheila.

The girls ran back downstairs to get a seat facing out toward the river. Standing near the railing, feeling the thrum of the powerful engine beneath their feet and watching the wake of waves nearly upend neighboring watercraft as the big boat swooshed through the river, Angelica felt Sheila's bony elbow in her ribs.

"Dang! What? I'm right next to you, girl! That hurt--"

"Look! No, don't look! Okay, look slowly on your left side. Do it slow!" Sheila said with the clumsy panache of an actor speaking in a full stage whisper.

Angelica semi slowly craned her head left as if someone was twisting it. Her mouth fell open slightly.

It was a boy. Or rather, a young man about 6 feet tall, slender yet athletic in build, with a face that could only be described as beautiful. His skin was a rich, smooth and unblemished cocoa brown. He had large brown almond shaped eyes, framed by long black lashes. His keen nose fit perfectly between his high cheekbones. And there at the finish were the perfectly bowed, full lips of his wide set mouth. He turned his head toward the pretty girl he was with and Angelica could see his wavy black hair

14

hanging in a ponytail about 6 inches down his back from the nape of his neck. She'd never seen a black person, especially a black boy, wear his hair like that. Simply put, he resembled an Indian or someone whose face should have adorned a mountainside.

Angelica and Sheila just stared as if watching a movie unfold just a few yards in front of them. The girl must have said something funny because the boy laughed and when he did Sheila and Angelica grabbed each other's hands digging fingernails into flesh, but not feeling the pain. He had big, white, even teeth. They were perfect, like a small white washed picket fence inside his mouth.

These were two girls who liked to bet each other that they could get close enough to a cute boy at school and with undetected stealth, touch his clothing or hair without him noticing. Angelica always took it a step further and would pantomime kissing the boy passionately or holding his hand in a broad, exaggerated way. She was a clown, she was clever, and she never got caught. Sheila would always double over with laughter as a teacher or hall monitor rolled their eyes at the two silly friends.

The boy must have felt someone staring intently because he looked up at the girls and smiled. What happened next would be debated over the subsequent years of their friendship but, the sudden flash of blinding enamel from the young man startled Angelica and Sheila, and in an effort to turn away quickly and inconspicuously, they slammed their heads together! More precisely, Angelica's head into Sheila's face. They were so mortified they didn't dare look back to see if the boy saw that they were about as sophisticated as Larry and Curly of the Three Stooges.

Once they recovered from the throbbing pain of embarrassment, they went to find Uncle Ned. Angelica hoped she wouldn't see the boy again. The one time had almost killed them! Well, not really, but if you could die of embarrassment then they were the walking dead. At a safe distance from the "scene of the crime," Angelica stopped walking and turned to her friend.

"Dang, that boy was fine! I wouldn't mind having a headache for the rest of the day for him," she said weakly, her head throbbing in agreement.

She wanted to look around to see where the handsome youth had gone but thought better of it. Angelica could feel the warm flush of scarlet on her cheeks; she would have to be content with the memory as she prayed she would never lay eyes on him again after making such a spectacle of herself.

"Well, my face ain't all that happy about it. Ow!" Sheila responded. "Do I have a black eye?"

"Sorry, girl. Naw, you're okay, just a little puffy. Maybe rub it out with your hand. Use your palm," Angelica instructed.

Sheila was probably going to have a black eye, Angelica surmised, but no use giving her the heads-up and letting that ruin their day. She'd be sure to steer her clear of the mirrors at the Fun House.

"You see the girl he was with? My cousin goes to school with her. She's a cheerleader," Sheila offered. "She thinks she's so cool, huh? She can't be *that* smart. I mean, she goes to Mackenzie High. It's not like she goes to Cass."

Cass Technical High School was the grande dame, the historical, storied, premier public high school in Michigan, certainly Detroit.

"Well, neither do *we*, Sheila. She's sure pretty enough. Wouldn't you want a cute boy to be with a cute girl? Otherwise you'd think something was wrong with him. I wonder if they 'do

16

it?"" Angelica asked, knowing she had just shocked her best friend.

Sheila looked stricken, as if she'd just been told the most terrible of secrets.

"Oh, close your mouth, Sheila. There's Uncle Ned and them. Come on."

The roaring blast of the ship's horn announced their arrival to Bob-lo Island. The Sky Tower, the 378 feet tall steel sentry overlooking the island, welcomed all comers as did the 4'-1" Captain Bob-lo, who was waiting at the gangplank. He was a jolly clown who wore full captain's regalia sans makeup and greeted the crowds coming on to Bob-lo Island.

Within a few hours of getting off the boat, Angelica, her family and Sheila had covered much of the park. The girls had met up with Ned and Ella at the big pavilion for the picnic and barbeque at noon. For the families, it was warm and comforting to be ensconced in a big company like GM. All the divisions-- Cadillac, Chevrolet and Pontiac—were as the branches of the same tree offering the cool shade of financial security and the towering strength of the United Auto Workers union.

When the girls were waiting in line to ride the twisting roller coaster known as the Wild Mouse, they saw him. This time the boy, his girlfriend and a small coterie of other high schoolers were debating whether or not they wanted to ride the coaster. The thrilling Wild Mouse offered a small four passenger car, two seats in front and two in the rear, on a narrow steel track thus giving the feeling of being in danger and slightly off kilter while high in the air. Riders loved the feeling that any sudden twist or turn could pitch them over the side to their doom. In the midst of the chatter, the boy's deep brown eyes found Angelica's. She wanted to be cool, like those greaser girls at her school who hung out with Bobby Go-Go, their cigarettes hanging from overly rouged lips.

But that wasn't her style. The boy didn't smile this time but raised his hand in their direction with a small, quick salute. Angelica smiled back in answer and passed her hand in a semi-circle and mouthed, "Hi." The boy kept staring at Angelica as if to mark her face for remembrance in case they ever were to meet again. The pretty girl at his side was smiling and about to laugh at something someone in their group had said when she looked up and caught the subtle and tenuous connection between her boyfriend and the green-eyed girl. She playfully poked him in the chest and he hugged her reassuringly as she now had his full attention. The girl threw her head back in laughter and shot a vicious look at Angelica. Sheila, fully involved with her favorite snack, fried pork rinds, had missed it all.

"Dang! Why did I get these knowin' they ain't got no hot sauce out here?" Sheila complained, oblivious to the life altering exchange that had just taken Angelica's breath away.

The duo rode every ride they could fit into their time on Bob-lo Island, including the traditional train ride around the amusement park. It was corny, but it reminded them of when they were little, and the park seemed so big. They had time for one last ride and the shortest line was for the Model T cars. Sure, the bumper or dodge 'em cars were more fun and exhilarating, but they had already ridden them twice. Nothing like banging into each other to let off a little steam! As they tooled around the track with Sheila driving, Angelica allowed her mind to wander and settle on the boy she saw on the boat and at the Wild Mouse. She was ruminating deeply when she thought she heard Sheila say something.

"What did you say?"

"I said there they go! They right in front of us." Sheila stepped on the gas to try to catch up to the boy and the cheerleader who happened to be a couple hundred yards ahead of them.

"Ooh, ooh, go faster! Catch up to 'em," Angelica urged.

Comically, Sheila floored the old-fashioned steel car's gas pedal only to lurch forward just slightly each time as the car sped up only to level out at 10 mph. Clearly, the couple in front of them would have to slow up somehow for Angelica and Sheila to catch up to them. Sheila was now hunched over the wheel as if that would propel her forward and faster. Angelica wondered what they might say to them if they did catch up? It's not like they were all buddies who wanted to shoot the breeze.

"Sheila, forget it. Slow down, girl."

And with those words scarcely out of Angelica's mouth, they were suddenly, seemingly hurtling toward the blue Model T in front of them. Holy crap! What had happened? The car ahead had stopped because the ride was over. Luckily the couple hadn't gotten up before Sheila and Angelica crashed into the back of their vehicle. It wasn't real hard, but it was hard enough to snap everyone's heads forward and backward. Could their day get any worse?

ngelica awoke on the Saturday following the Fourth of July to the sounds of neighborhood children playing on her block. The tinny cacophony of cicadas rose and fell repeatedly and relentlessly about every 7 seconds like the ticking of an oscillating lawn sprinkler throwing water in a circle. The noise receded into the background, becoming part of the ambient sounds of summer, as unremarkable as a mother calling out for her child to come in to eat. The morning symphony was a preamble to Angelica, telling her today would be hot and humid, a day for a ponytail high on the back of her head to keep her neck as cool as possible as its gentle sway made her feel like she was dancing instead of walking.

When she was younger, the ritual had been to wake up early enough to slip into the living room to watch her favorite Saturday morning cartoons with a bowl of Kellogg's Sugar Frosted Flakes in her grip while her mother slept. After getting her fill of animated hijinks and cereal from Battle Creek, she'd get dressed to meet the neighborhood kids outside for freeze tag, dodge ball, monkey in the middle, "Mother May I," rock teacher and hand games like "Miss Mary Mac" that involved rhymes and slapping another child's hands in rhythm. But now at almost 16, she was more leisurely and purposeful in how she spent her Saturdays, especially on summer vacation.

Angelica turned her face toward the screened in window of her bedroom without opening her eyes. The morning breeze, intermittent and begrudging, filtered through her gauzy curtains smelling of rain and dust and tears. The scent told her that it was truly summertime in Detroit, but more pointedly, she needed to wash her curtains.

Because her house had only two air conditioners, one in the living room and one in her mother's bedroom, the oppressive humidity and heat that settled like a dome over her house in the evenings made getting to sleep a protracted and uncomfortable proposition. What should have taken minutes sometimes took more than an hour of sweat filled tossing and turning in bed.

Angelica yawned and stretched as she put her hand underneath her pillow. She touched her white plastic transistor radio, bringing it out into the morning light. She opened her eyes, finally, and rolled the "off-on-volume" wheel back and forth with her thumb. *Dead.* She fell asleep every night listening to her favorite disc jockey on Super Soul Station WCHB. Even though 'CHB was the first black owned radio station in the U.S., the DJ with the coolest rhymes who played all her favorite jams was a white boy, Rockin' Robbie D.

He was on from 8 to midnight and all the kids at school thought he was the coolest, the smoothest and the baddest that station had to offer. The boys said he was so "boss" and the girls found his voice just "dreamy." "Ooh, Robbie, you got soul!" Or "Ooh Robbie, Robbie D!" were the jingles that sometimes preceded his hip, soulful patter. Angelica always tried to turn off the radio when she got sleepy to preserve her 9-volt battery's life but sleep usually thwarted her plans.

After showering and getting dressed, Angelica came into the bright yellow breakfast room off their kitchen to find her mother sitting at the table reading the Detroit Free Press. Liz Tanner

21

sipped from her cup of Maxwell House Coffee and didn't look up.

"Smells good in here, Mama."

Another rite of passage away from childhood: a hot breakfast instead of cold cereal.

"Good morning. I made bacon and eggs. There's still some bread in the breadbox for toast if you want it. I'm gonna have to go over to the A&P to get groceries a little later, anyway. Spending Saturday at the grocery store is…" Liz said, trailing off, getting back into her newspaper.

Angelica busied herself making a plate of food at the counter. She opened up the refrigerator and saw about a half cup of orange juice in the bottle on the top shelf. Taking the bottle out of the refrigerator and loudly clearing her throat, Angelica shook its contents dramatically. Her mother looked up.

"Oh, shoot! Sorry, honey. The Cook's man will be here today, and he'll have juice on his truck, I'm sure," Liz said, returning to the Free Press. "You look cute, by the way," she said matter-of-factly, not looking up again.

The Cook Coffee Company made home deliveries from a bright gold truck twice a month. They were like a Sears catalogue on wheels. They had the most diverse range of products outside of, well, a Sears and Roebuck store. One could buy anything, from an envy inducing above ground swimming pool to exotica called papaya juice. Liz Tanner loved to shop with the Cook Coffee Company and sometimes, she even purchased coffee!

As Angelica sat watching her mother's right hand absent-mindedly go from her coffee cup to her fork to turning the pages of her paper, she sighed. Her mother was someone who just as soon live alone as with her only child, it seemed to Angelica. She

22

liked her own company and made no apologies for it. Liz had always treated Angelica like a little adult and later, more like her roommate. She felt no natural urge to be overly affectionate or demonstrative.

Angelica sometimes wondered what had happened to her mother to make her this way, but she also knew she was lucky. Her mother trusted very few people, but she trusted her daughter. Angelica was given much more freedom than most girls her age and Liz knew she'd raised a good girl who would never do anything to bring shame to her front door. Angelica had gotten so much love and affection from her grandparents, aunt and uncle, she'd scarcely thought about what was missing in her relationship with her mother. Still, sometimes it felt as though they were part of a truce in an undeclared war.

It was not yet noon and it was already warm and muggy outside. Angelica sat in the glider on her front porch reading "The Outsiders." Even though kids were screaming and squealing and yelling up and down her block, she barely heard them. She had a goal of finishing her book and she only had a few chapters left to go. Angelica hummed along to Jimmy Ruffin's "What Becomes of the Brokenhearted," which was playing on the kitchen radio she'd relocated near the front door to entertain herself. She allowed herself to briefly reflect on how sad and desperate Jimmy's song was. This was a man walking a land of broken dreams saying that happiness was just an illusion.

"Sheesh, mister," she mumbled.

No matter how downtrodden Mr. Ruffin's take on things, it was still good music to her ears. Ever since Angelica could remember, there was music. Always music. Before she could talk, music. Before she could walk she would bounce up and down to whatever song her mother had playing on the hi-fi stereo. As a tot she would take her mother's LPs of Ray Charles, Frank

Sinatra, The Platters and anyone else she could find and arrange them into a vibrant story, her own running narrative on the living room floor. She would entertain whoever would listen, usually her grandmother, for hours.

"Ain't Too Proud to Beg" by The Temptations came on and Angelica put down her book to take a break. Listening to David Ruffin wail was all the inspiration she needed to get up and dance. She thought Jimmy should have a better attitude about love, like his brother David. Angelica put one arm up and brought the other down slightly behind her at her side, fingers snapping, head bobbing, her body jerking like a whip. She even did the Pony, jumping gingerly from one foot to the other. She heard the faint sound of clapping and looked up to see her neighbor across the street, Mrs. Gogolian, clapping and waving. Sheepishly, Angelica waved back.

Mrs. Gogolian was the sweet little Armenian lady who had lived in her house longer than anyone else on the block. Her son Robert, who went by the moniker Bobby Go-Go, was a greaser with bad skin and a Brylcreemed pompadour, a throwback from the previous decade. Bobby Go-Go was not to be trifled with and he wasn't scared of anyone—not niggers, not hillbillies, not Polacks, not Micks, not even Wops. He had a soft spot for kids as he was an only child, and an even bigger soft spot for Angelica Tanner. He always said "hello" to her at school and was never too cool to act like she was a stranger. The other greasers, even the bigoted ones, would nod at her in passing for fear of getting on Bobby's bad side.

In the distance rounding the corner, Angelica could hear the familiarly cloying song like something from a child's toy, signaling that Mr. Softee was cruising its way through the summer haze. Children scattered like marbles only to return in record time, clutching coins for ice cream. Angelica dug into the pocket of her pedal pushers and brought out three shiny quarters. She jumped down off her porch, clearing the concrete steps as the truck wended its way toward her side of the street. She found a good place to stand just a few paces from her driveway. Angelica always got the same thing: a vanilla cone dipped in the chocolate that dried into a crackling shell that was some form of magic!

Walking away with her treat, she happened to see a little girl about 7 years old clutching her even smaller brother by the shoulders at the curb. These kids lived across the alley on the next block. It was clear they were going to be empty handed when the truck pulled away, their hopes evaporating in the air like the truck's exhaust. They were staring hungrily at all the creamy delights the other children trotted away with, when the girl's big brown eyes settled on Angelica. Angelica looked toward the ice cream truck, where Mr. Softee, the ice cream cone in the jaunty bow-tie looking debonair yet goofy, seemed to wink at her.

"Hey, kid! Come here," Angelica said, waving her hand to beckon the two children.

"Here, get something for you and your brother," she said, slapping two quarters into the little girl's hand.

In their excitement, the little boy fell down running the few feet to the truck but sprung back up like a spinning top that appeared prematurely spent, in anticipation of his Mr. Softee cone. He probably wanted to cry, but knew he'd better not distract his sister. Maybe he'd get to it once he got his cone. Within a few minutes and a few licks, the chocolate ice cream had worked its magic and the skinned knee was forgotten. The little girl waved at Angelica on her porch and smiled broadly before sauntering away with her little charge in one hand and a Mr. Softee in the other.

Angelica finished her ice cream and went into her house to wash the dishes from breakfast and lunch. Her mother had already left for the store. Reaching up to turn off the radio now back in its perch on the counter top, Angelica realized she had spent most of her day far too leisurely and resolved to go shopping for some new records at the Shake 'n Spin. She hadn't been up to the 'Spin since school got out and she needed to get away from the house in the likelihood her mother came home with more chores for her.

She ran her fingers over the paperback resting on the counter and decided, reluctantly, the end of her book would have to wait. Angelica dreaded the sad and familiar anticipation of the story's end. Usually, she'd fly through the pages of a book only to pause near the end with the trepidation of saying goodbye to the characters and their dramatic, humorous, adventurous lives. Perhaps it was an unavoidable symptom of being an only child-- no sibling witness to her childhood, no intimately shared memories or experiences of her household.

Angelica ran to her room to get her pink coin purse laying on her nightstand next to her neatly made bed. She frowned at what she saw on the side table—her plugged in radio and a black Panasonic cassette recorder—partners in crime! Oh, how she'd adored this fancy gift from her Aunt Fan. Only one other person at school that she knew of had a cassette recorder. It was the latest thing and it was the bomb as far as Angelica was concerned. She loved recording all of her favorite songs from the radio on it even with the disc jockey talking through the intro and sometimes complete verses of the songs. Some of these guys were so anxious to hear themselves speak again, they would begin talking before the record had even partially faded out. Annoying! New records were definitely the cure.

She ran out of the house and down the stairs, letting the screen door slam behind her. Angelica decided to swing by Sheila's house to see if she wanted to walk with her. The air raid siren began to scream in the distance. To Angelica and her friends, it just meant that it was 1 p.m. on a Saturday. For some of the older men sitting on porches, mowing their lawns or washing their cars, it was an auditory prompt that made them gaze uneasily toward the sky.

THREE

S heila Davis had been Angelica Tanner's best friend since third grade. Sheila was a tall, thick, sweetly mischievous girl with deep brown skin and large eyes. She and Angelica were inseparable and saw themselves as sisters as much as friends. Sheila was the youngest and the last daughter out of three at home. Because Angelica was an only child, she believed it was cosmic kismet that allowed her to find a friend with whom she could share just about everything.

In the story of Angelica and Sheila, there had only been one time they veered off the page. Angelica presumed she should reveal some information she'd discovered to be so shocking, she had to share it with her closest friend. It was her intention to save her sweet Sheila from the potential horror and heartache of hearing it in passing.

Angelica divulged what she considered to be the "Three Traumatic Truths" of childhood: 1. There is no Santa Claus! Your parents buy your presents at the store and hide them until Christmas! 2. Your parents "do it!" They have sex and that's how and why you were born! 3. Everyone, including you, is going to die! No exceptions! Ever!

Sheila's face contorted more and more with each revelation, her eyes filling with tears and her 10-year-old fists bunching up at her sides. She ran home without a word, leaving Angelica confused and wondering what she'd done that was so wrong? Velma Davis called Liz Tanner and Angelica found herself on the receiving end of her mother's belt. Liz said what she'd told her friend was "inappropriate" and it upset Sheila very much.

"I want you to apologize to Sheila next time you see her," her mother admonished.

Angelica sat in her bedroom fuming. She was only trying to help Sheila be "in the know." Why was she the bad guy? She wasn't going to say she was sorry. She was going to punch Sheila in the nose, that's what she was going to do. Mrs. Davis could catch a knuckle sandwich, too, Angelica decided. She knew Mrs. Davis would be staring at her over her eyeglasses the next time Angelica went to their house as if she was a burglar. Luckily, a chance game of hopscotch about 10 days later brought the girls back together. All was forgiven, most was forgotten, and they were happy to be friends again.

Sheila grew to be a pretty, shapely young lady. Because she was so much taller and bigger than most of the other girls, she thought she'd inherited her grandmother's figure. The old woman was a refrigerator wearing a church hat. No, Sheila had turned out just fine and no one was happier about it than her mother.

Velma Davis, petite and wiry, didn't take any sass from her kids or her husband. She loved the Lord and she loved her Maybelline cosmetics. Sheila's mom had eyebrows that were drawn on with a shiny black eyebrow pencil, resembling strands of black licorice crouching above her almond shaped eyeglasses. Her hair was an equally glossy black patent leather helmet of a wig that fooled no one. Occasionally Velma would press and curl her own hair and then wear a halo of pink foam rollers which could barely be seen through the ever-present haze of cigarette smoke. Mrs. Davis carried a double clasped coin purse, a red vinyl rectangular contraption about 6 inches long with a snap close at the top and a smaller compartment, like an after-thought, at the bottom. The larger compartment housed her continually crushed pack of Kool Filter Kings cigarettes, and the bottom her stainless-steel Buxton butane lighter. Her mouth was a scarlet line that served as a clamp for her perpetually burning butt.

Mrs. Davis kept Sheila occupied with church as much as she could but sometimes, unwittingly, she provided uproarious entertainment for Sheila and Angelica. There were the scary but exhilarating car rides on the big couch of a front seat in their Ford Galaxy. Seatbelts were buried so deep within the cushions as to be considered non-existent, and when one could be fingered and dug out of the crevice, it invariably came with some unidentified sticky or crunchy matter. Velma Davis always rode her power brakes all the way up the block in anticipation of a stray ball or errant child. A nervous slap of her foot sent the girls flying toward dashboards and windshields like wet socks at a wall, and then jerked back uncontrollably upon discovery of the accelerator. Desperate glances would pass between Angelica and Sheila as if to silently call out, "Help!" but then their fear would give way to muffled giggles. Giggles inevitably cut short by another introduction to the dashboard or if riding in back, the sturdy upholstery of the front seat back.

Mr. Davis, her husband, was a very jovial man who seemed to be hard of hearing and always in a hurry to get somewhere. Or perhaps away from Velma. He would agree with almost anything said to him, constantly wagging his head, rhetorically saying, "Well, that's okay, isn't it." Not quite a question, more of a statement. No one knew what he was referring to, but he was always smiling, so nobody cared. No one even knew Mr. Davis' first name.

Angelica strode purposefully from her block over to Ohio Street where Sheila resided with her parents. It wasn't a long walk, but at times, her internal reverie was interrupted by a stray dog that had somehow gotten away from its yard. Angelica hated when this situation, literally, reared its ugly snarling head. No matter how cool or cute she was in crisp pedal pushers, a midriff top and Keds, all that composure folded like a deflated accordion when a dog gave chase. One of the constant perils of life in Detroit, the "D," which always stood for "dogs" as far as Angelica was concerned. Today she was in luck because there was not a dog in sight during her walk, not even that Chow that always seemed to come out of nowhere to charge his fence each, sending her into a frantic trot.

Mrs. Davis answered the door in her home uniform: pink foam rollers and a zippered pink quilted house coat.

"Hi, Mrs. Davis. Is Sheila here?" Angelica chirped.

"Come on in, baby," said Velma, pushing open the screen door with one hand, her cigarette in the other.

"Thank you, Mrs. Davis," Angelica responded, careful not to begin coughing or waving her hand as she pushed her body through the cloud of cigarette smoke.

As she passed the living room coming out of the tiny vestibule, she spied Mr. Davis in his green Naugahyde recliner. The only piece of soft furniture to have escaped being enshrined in zippered plastic.

Angelica wasn't going to speak but thought better of it and hurriedly said, "Hi, Mr. Davis!"

31

As if on cue his absent-minded response came, "Yeah, okay."

He was watching wrestling on Channel 9, the Canadian Broadcasting Company's television station. It looked like Bobo Brazil versus The Sheik, and if so, it would be a great rumble. Angelica and Uncle Ned sat in front of the television set many a Saturday to watch their favorite grapplers--Brazil, Killer Kowalski and the fearsome Dick the Bruiser. They'd be on the edge of the couch unable to sit back, so engrossed in every pile driver, half Nelson or body slam, yelling, "Whoa," "Oh man, did you see that?" or "Dang!"

Angelica noticed two portraits adorned one wall of the living room. First, Jesus Christ, with his blue eyes looking upward, flowing flaxen hair just to the shoulder of his white shroud-like robe. Next to him was President John F. Kennedy, assassinated right before Thanksgiving in 1963, his hair perfect with a toothy, youthful smile affixed to his face. In a mere two years the triumvirate of tragedy would be complete with a portrait of Reverend Doctor Martin Luther King, Jr., struck down by an assassin down South in the spring of 1968. His face, with its sad, slanted eyes, was hopeful and burdened.

Mrs. Davis had disappeared into the kitchen leaving Angelica to find Sheila on her own. She hadn't done it to be rude, but more so as a gesture of trusting familiarity. Sure enough, she spotted the back of Sheila's head as she came upon the dining room. Sheila was seated at the big dining room table and though it was daytime, the light in the center of the ceiling was on and it reflected off the rich dark wood of the table. Mrs. Davis, who wore glasses, was always convinced other people couldn't see as well as they claimed, so she was always willing to "burn up" her electricity, just so long as it was her idea and not theirs. Any suggestion by others would always be met with, "No, you don't need to cut on those lights. Y'all can see just fine."

Poor Sheila had a Crowley's bag full of Top Value Gift Stamps, a Sears bag full of S&H Green Stamps, a Hudson's bag full of Gold Bell Gift Stamps and a Federal's bag full of Holden Red Stamps sitting in chairs around the table like unhappy guests at a dinner with no food. She had empty redemption books stacked in four piles in front of her along with a shallow bowl of water and a small sponge. She looked completely miserable. Just about every lamp, small appliance, piece of silverware and dish in their home was the result of Mrs. Davis diligently collecting and redeeming her mountainous cache of trading stamps acquired from a multitude of trips to the A&P, Wrigley's and Kroger as well as from fueling up their two automobiles at Marathon and Texaco gas stations.

"Hi, Angelica," Sheila said forlornly.

"Hey," Angelica said, not attempting to sit down.

She knew her friend was in some kind of trouble. She furtively glanced toward the kitchen door and back toward the living room to ensure they were indeed alone before she spoke again.

"So, I guess you can't go to the Shake 'n Spin with me, huh? I wanted to get some 45s today. What's all this?"

"Shoot," Sheila said, emphatically disgusted, "somebody told my mama that I was outside spraying water on the cars parked on the street and watering the driveway instead of watering the grass."

"Well, were you?"

33

"So what if I was? Why does everybody gotta be in everybody else's business? Somebody called her on the phone and next thing I know, she's running out the house, cutting off the water and making me come in the house."

To the last part of the story, Angelica shot her friend a raised eyebrow. They both knew it could have been so much worse. She'd seen Mrs. Davis charging from that house swinging a belt, a rolled-up newspaper, even a shoe, all in the name of instant discipline. Mrs. Davis didn't care who was witnessing the unholy display. She'd done it with Sheila's two older sisters and certainly, Sheila was not exempt. It seemed one of her neighbors delighted in seeing the girl in trouble.

"Alright, Sheila's got work to do. Sheila, show your company to the door," Velma Davis yelled from the kitchen. "Okay, Mama," Sheila replied, getting up from the dining room table. She stomped her right foot lightly as it had fallen asleep and continued to do so to the front door, walking a few steps ahead of Angelica.

"Dang, girl," Angelica said, shaking her head at her pal's perpetual punishment. "You want me to get you somethin'? Candy or somethin'? Some pop and some skins?" she asked.

Skins or fried pork rinds was by far their favorite snack, especially the kind with the little packet of fiery red-hot sauce that came inside the bag. Sure, everybody dug potato chips—Better Made or Superior—but there was something deliciously decadent about the bubbly crackle of pork skins.

"Um," Sheila considered.

"Girl, hurry up. I don't want your mama mad at me," Angelica said, peering toward the kitchen door, visible behind Sheila's head.

Sheila patted the outside of the left pocket of her pedal pushers, poked her fingers down inside and came up with a dull quarter.

"Just get me some red licorice, Banana Splits, Squirrels and a candy necklace."

"Man, oh Manischewitz, a candy necklace! That's little kid candy!" Angelica chuckled. But just then she imagined herself in deep concentration, reading an Archie comic book while clutching a candy necklace. The glossy glazed smoothness of those multi colored discs on an elastic string beckoned her. A couple of stealthy licks, careful not to wet the surrounding pieces, before biting into turquoise blue heaven or electric yellow sunshine.

"Okay?" Sheila asked, shaking Angelica from her sugary dream.

"Yeah, okay," she said, knowing she hadn't heard a word Sheila said, but mostly vexed that her sweet daydream had been stopped in its tracks. "I'm gonna just put your stuff up on the porch. Just come out and check in a little while, okay?"

Bounding down the concrete steps of the porch, Angelica headed down the block.

"**M**ami, Eddie ate all the Super Sugar Crisp and now there's no more left. See?"

The few lone wheat puffs rattled riotously inside the empty cavern of the cereal box. Before Ana Williams could answer her youngest daughter, Ricky took the box out of his sister Pilar's grip.

"Pi-pi, how about some Sugar Frosted Flakes? That's what I'm having. Don't you wanna be strong like me and Tony the Tiger?" Ricky enticed.

"Yeah!" squealed Pilar.

She couldn't help but think of drinking down the sugary opaque milk that was always left after the corn flakes were gone from her bowl. The best part!

"They're g-g-g-reat!" 8-year-old Eduardo yelled thrusting his spoon toward the ceiling.

Ricky laughed and shook his head. Ana kissed her baby boy's cheek.

"Too much TV commercials," she said in her melodic Spanish accent.

At 40 years old, Ana Torres Williams was a stunning woman. With her honey kissed skin, luminous brown eyes and Roman nose, she still turned men's heads constantly, whether she was conscious of it or not. She would toss her thick mane of shoulder length hair and men would deceive themselves into believing they had what she wanted. Ana never noticed because her children were her life. Her memory of the only man she'd ever loved was kept alive in their faces.

Danny, her oldest, was the spitting image of their dad down to his deep brown complexion. Alecia was lighter skinned than Danny, but not as light as Enrique, who was darker than Pilar. Eduardo was fair like their mother.

"Sit down, Ma, I'll fix you a bowl, too. You want some coffee?"

"No *mijo*, just the cereal is okay."

Enrique Williams moved about the kitchen like he was quietly conducting a symphony. He grabbed three plastic bowls with one hand, flipped open the cupboard and grabbed the big box of cereal with the other. He used the hand that had released the bowls to the counter to open a drawer to retrieve spoons. As he crossed the kitchen to the refrigerator, he began to smile to himself. Ricky, as he was sometimes called, had met the milkman at the side door and paid for four-quart bottles of fresh milk and a carton of eggs earlier that morning. The Twin Pines milkman usually shoved the milk, cream, butter, eggs and whatever was the usual order, into the milk chute on the side of the house. In the winter, if the bounty wasn't removed soon after its arrival, they might end up with cracked and frozen eggs, though slightly icy milk was actually refreshing. In the summer, things could go bad quickly, so it was best to intercept the delivery.

Ricky routinely got up earlier than everyone in the house on Saturday mornings. He encouraged his mother, Ana, to sleep in since she worked the afternoon shift from 4 p.m. until midnight at the General Motors plant. He loved his little brother and sister, but he could get a lot done in that hour or two before they began rambling about the house. Pilar, the 10-year-old, was Ricky's favorite and she knew it. Ricky couldn't resist giving his baby sister anything she wanted. Not to be left out, Eduardo was the youngest and he had their mother rapt and wrapped around his little fingers.

In this summer of 1966, their father Gabriel had been dead for two years. Gabriel Williams had the sad distinction of being one of the early American military casualties of the Vietnam War. Mr. Williams was a career soldier with the U.S. Army and had achieved the rank of Sergeant First Class, top advisor to the platoon leader. From what Ricky could understand, this war seemed strangely meandering and persistent. He had talked to his dad about it before his last tour and it was not certain that war had ever actually been declared, yet here Ricky was at 16 years old dealing with the crushing result.

He and his older siblings Danny and Alecia, 20 and 18, respectively, had a chance to really know and miss Gabriel. The younger kids not as much, so the burden of helping his mother around their house and the responsibility of sharing memories of their dad fell to Ricky. Danny had moved out on his own a year before the family moved to the Northwest side of Detroit from the West side. He'd been in and out of trouble for years, so his absence was mostly a relief. Alecia was graduating and on her way to college.

"Did the paper man come already?" Ana asked.

"Yes, Ma. I paid him. Here you go," Ricky said, reaching for The Detroit News, rolled up in a green rubber band on the floor near his chair.

He started to tell his mother that the paper route had been turned over from the regular paper man to a boy. *A paper boy*, he supposed. The boy was the little brother of a kid named Mike Morton. According to neighbors, one-night Mrs. Morton had stepped out of her backyard and into the alley to put the family's trash in the garbage can and she disappeared.

Even though the Williams family had been in residence a relatively short time, Ricky had heard the story and felt bad for the Morton boys. It was said Mr. Morton essentially acted as if nothing out of the ordinary had happened, as if nothing was amiss or out of order. *White people are strange*, Enrique thought. They handle things differently, unpredictably. A colored person would have been bent on revenge while circumventing John Law. Years later it was discovered that Mr. Morton was involved in a criminal enterprise that resulted in the kidnapping and apparent murder of his wife. It was an ominous message that only needed to be relayed once. Within the black community it was an unwritten law that women and children were off limits, no matter what the transgression. Anyone who would harm either had crossed a line even the most hardened criminal respected.

Ricky peeked at his Timex. Almost one o'clock. He had to hurry if he was to be at work in an hour. He scrambled to finish his last task, watering the lawn, which he didn't find to be much of a chore on hot days. He was already sweating when the air raid siren began to scream.

Though the Fourth of July had been earlier in the week, American flags still adorned almost every house on the block. Every porch had a flag pole and, on that pole, flew an exalted and fluttering American flag. Standing on the lawn at just the right angle and staring down the block, it looked as if Old Glory had sprouted on dozens of spindly wooden arms, hanging languidly in hopes of a breeze. Detroiters were a patriotic lot by and large, cherishing their homes and their jobs. The children pledged allegiance to the flag of the United States of America and their parents pledged allegiance to one of the "Big Three" automakers: General Motors, Ford or Chrysler.

Ricky turned off the water hose at the side of the house and ran his hands over his face, the rivulets of sweat intermingling with what water remained on his hands. He paused before opening the side door to his house and considered how quickly he'd adapted to their new environment. Ricky hoped he'd make some real friends when he began school in a couple of months. He liked the neighborhood and all the people he'd met through his job at the Shake 'n Spin. The owner, Mr. Gilhooley, was so much hipper than he let on and he respected Ricky as a hard-working young man helping to support his family. Gilhooley didn't mind Ricky's long hair as long as it was in a ponytail or braid, accompanied by a hairnet. Ricky went into the house to take a shower. It felt like it had been a full day already.

s Angelica walked the mile or so to the Shake 'n Spin on Livernois and W. McNichols or 6 Mile Road as it was also called, she found herself considering the relationship between Sheila and her mother. Her poor friend always seemed to be in trouble or just getting out of trouble. Mrs. Davis just seemed so harsh at times, but there was no doubt that she loved Sheila, perhaps even more than her two older daughters. Sheila was the last child in their home and Mrs. Davis' grip on her seemed to be tighter, her arm's reach longer. Somehow this, in some perverse fashion, was preferable to the vacuous almost absent-minded thing Angelica claimed as her relationship with her own mother. What had made Liz Tanner the beautiful shell she'd become? Had she been hurt so deeply that the walls she'd erected didn't allow anyone in or her out? Angelica instinctively knew she had something to do with the distance, but what exactly?

Angelica could see the neon sign for the Shake 'n Spin a few yards in front of her. The go-go girl on the marquee never got tired of dancing and was always lit up while the business was open, no matter how bright the day. Angelica's stomach began to rumble, so she made a mental note to pick up a hot corned beef on rye slathered with plenty of mustard and a fat kosher dill pickle at Lou's Delicatessen on her way home. She was tempted

41

to turn back, forgoing the records and candy so she could get her sandwich, but didn't.

It was cool inside the store and brightly lit. Angelica made her way past all of the succulent penny candy on display, deciding to make the candy counter her last stop rather than her first. There were just too many temptations in sight! And the scent, *Oh my.* Angelica wanted to lick the air like a snake to taste the sweet fragrances that hung there, beckoning and taunting her. She wondered if adulthood would make her shut the door on her love for candy? As far as she could see, confections were comfort and the embodiment of all that was good in the world.

Looking past the gossip and teen magazines, Angelica spotted several girls dancing and laughing near the music booth where a disc jockey was playing records. Angelica hadn't been to the Shake 'n Spin since a few days after school had ended in June, and it looked like Mr. Gilhooley must have hired someone to replace the kid who used to work there. Dennis was his name and he'd quit around that time to spend the summer down South with his grandma before he reported to boot camp for the U.S. Army.

As she approached the coterie of giggling teens, the music only got louder. "Cool Jerk" by the Capitols was playing and the girls seemed to be trying to out "jerk" one another in an impromptu dance contest. Once the song ended, the DJ put on "(You're My) Soul and Inspiration" by the Righteous Brothers. Bill Medley's soulful baritone was slicing the air like a knife through ripe summer fruit. By the time Angelica had gotten to the disc jockey booth, nothing more than four wooden pallets forming an elevated platform surrounded by crates of records and a hi-fi, she could see why the girls were so agitated.

There he was, the boy with the ponytail, the boy from the Bob-lo boat. He was writing out sales slips for the 45s he was handing to the group crowded around the DJ booth.

"Just take your records up to the candy counter and pay Mrs. G. Thanks, girls," he said over and over again, flashing his brilliant smile.

The girls didn't realize they were being dismissed, very pleasantly, but dismissed nonetheless. The show over, they trundled toward Mrs. Gilhooley at the cash register near the front of the store, while a few others went to the soda fountain for a burger or a hot fudge sundae. Mrs. Gilhooley was a taciturn woman in her 50s with no lips to speak of and her puffy hair dyed jet black and stuffed into a hairnet like black cotton candy caught in a web. Though the hairnet was a perpetual fixture on her head, growing from her forehead like a gunshot wound, Angelica could not recall ever seeing Mrs. G actually at the grill or behind the soda fountain. Her plump little unshaven legs were encased in thick utilitarian hosiery, imprisoning the untamed hair forest growing from them. Though she said little, Mrs. Gilhooley liked being around the young people from the neighborhood, which sometimes made her feel like a mother hen. She'd watched most of them come into the store as toddlers in tow and now they were practically grown-ups.

As Angelica tried to think of what to say to the boy playing the records, he looked straight at her and smiled. He beckoned her closer with a crook of his long slender index finger.

"Hi there," he said, almost laughing.

"Hi. Um, I wanna buy some records. What's new?" Angelica said.

She couldn't believe how stiff she sounded.

"Oh, I've got something for you. It's not exactly new, but it's perfect for you, uh…" he trailed off.

"Angelica."

"I'm Enrique, but my friends call me Ricky," he said, taking a 45-rpm record out of its dust jacket. "I thought your name might be Jenny," he said pointedly, with a smile.

Before Angelica could reply, she heard the opening piano chords of "Jenny Take a Ride" by Mitch Ryder and the Detroit Wheels. She looked at Enrique, blushing. He was being mischievous and making a joke about their bumper car incident back at Bob-lo. So, he did remember her! They'd known each other less than five minutes and were already sharing an inside joke. Angelica didn't care if he was teasing her. She loved this song and how the booming bass drove the song while everything else just rode on top. She'd seen the group on "Swingin' Time with Robin Seymour" one day after school on Channel 9. Boy, that Mitch Ryder was one cool cat. He sang and carried himself like someone decades older than he was.

Unconsciously, Angelica began to move her body to the music and to her surprise, so did Ricky.

"This song is the bomb," he shouted over the din.

"I dig that crazy wall of sound. The piano doesn't even sound like a piano, it's muted like it has a damper on. And that backbeat with the bass! Man, oh Manischewitz!" she exclaimed loudly.

Without inhibition, Angelica was doing the Pony and the Jerk right where she stood. Ricky couldn't take his eyes off her as she was danced, feeling the music with her eyes closed.

"Hey, I don't hear some kinda wall of sound. What is that? What do you mean?" came the voice suddenly next to her.

44

Angelica opened her eyes to see Carlton Meadows standing there. What was he doing there, and what kind of nonsense had he injected into their happy trance to kill it?

"Oh, hey, Carlton," Angelica said dryly, as all movement ceased.

"So, you know Carlton? He comes by almost every day, right, Carlton?"

Angelica wasn't listening anymore as she busily picked out some records to buy. Carlton Meadows was a boy she had known since they attended Noble Junior High. Initially, she thought he was kind of cute, but for some reason, he never spoke to her. Yet, there were times when walking down the hall with her friends, she'd feel the urge to turn around. Almost every time she gave in to that urge, there was Carlton staring at her. Sheila thought he was a creep. Angelica just thought he was shy. Carlton occasionally accompanied his mother, Mavis, when she collected for the numbers she ran. Did Mavis think her chubby son was going to scare anyone or provide protection for her as she pursued her illegal bookmaking? Mavis thought it made her a more sympathetic figure as a mom and less the money grubbing cold hearted bitch she truly was.

When Mavis Meadows came to see Liz Tanner, Carlton usually sat in the car waiting for his mom. Angelica would wave at him from behind the screen door, but they never talked. She didn't really mind since she always seemed to be busy with chores or homework anyway. One day Mavis appeared at the door with her son in tow. *Jesus*, thought Liz when she answered the door, *Not both of them darkening my doorstep.* She called Angelica from her bedroom to entertain Carlton in the kitchen.

The teenagers sat across from one another at the steel-edged Formica table, the plastic tablecloth flecked with telltale signs of

Cheerios from breakfast. The conversation was slow going with Angelica making inquiries that netted one-word answers. *Why is this kid so shy?* She was beginning to get frustrated.

"Hey, aren't y'all rich or something? That's what I heard," she blurted out, realizing she'd asked yet another question that could be answered with a simple, monosyllabic utterance.

To her surprise, this seemed to light a small fire under the boy.

"We're not rich. Where'd you hear that?" he said, slightly defensive.

"At school. Around. You know how people talk. I figure you can't be too rich if your mama's a numbers runner."

And there it was, impetuous and impolite. How could she take back the words as they lay there crispy and hard like burnt toast on a plate? Carlton laughed, and Angelica began laughing even harder. They were soon easily chatting about school, their teachers and what they were going to be for Halloween. Since it was lunch time and their mothers didn't seem to be coming around anytime soon, Angelica asked if Carlton wanted to have lunch with her.

"Sure."

Angelica ran to ask their mother's permission as the ladies were in the living room, seemingly deep in conversation.

"Do you like Ovaltine?" Angelica inquired. "What about a grilled cheese sandwich? It's my specialty."

"Yeah, that sounds good. You can cook?" Carlton asked, incredulously.

Angelica just rolled her eyes.

"Of course, silly. Boy, I been cooking since I was 8. I'm pretty darn good, too. Shoot, a grill cheese ain't nothin'," she bragged.

The Twin Pines milk man had left two bottles in the milk chute for the family that very morning. They'd even gotten a new frying pan the day before from the Cook Coffee Company salesman. Angelica wiped off the tablecloth and, in a few minutes, served up her famous grilled cheese sandwich—butter on both sides of the bread slices and two pieces of Kraft American cheese. They had their icy cold chocolate milk to wash everything down. Carlton thought it was the best lunch he'd ever had. The crispy, buttery, toasted bread enveloping the gooey cheese, along with the rich, chocolaty Ovaltine—what more could a kid want? The air raid siren revved itself up to punctuate the ambience.

"Ever wonder how you can always hear that horn no matter where you are in the city? Wonder where it comes from? The sky?" Angelica asked, with the innocence and curiosity of a little child.

"I don't know. I just know it's always there on Saturdays, like cartoons in the morning, no matter what."

"I wonder if grown-ups know where to go if we need to go somewhere 'cause we're getting bombed? I'm not sure ducking and covering is gonna be much help," Angelica said, genuinely concerned.

In her mind she saw herself and her classmates ducking under their desks, a huge atomic flash and then a bunch of little charred black skeletons with their hands and arms over their skulls.

"I heard in some cities and where folks live in the country, they have bomb shelters underground," Carlton offered.

"Yeah, I've seen it on TV and they showed us the movie at school. Crazy, man."

They both laughed.

Just then, Mrs. Meadows appeared at the entrance of the kitchen with her keys jangling in her hands. That ever-present fake smile, reserved for children and people she generally considered unimportant, was already in effect.

Once in the car, Mavis matter-of-factly asked her son if he had fun talking with Angelica.

"Yes, she's a nice girl. I always see her in— "

"Well, they're trash, son, so don't get too friendly with that little girl," Mavis interrupted. "I've known Elizabeth Tanner for most of my life. So, I know what I'm talking about."

She looked over at her son's stunned expression and tried to do a quick repair.

"They're nice enough, but certainly below us, honey."

Carlton wanted to tell his mother that she was awful for saying such a thing, but instead he just sat back in his seat, silent. He tried to think about the fact that today they were riding for the very first time in his father's brand new 1963 Cadillac Coupe de Ville. The big plush front seat was like a couch and the inside of the vehicle had an aroma of plastic and vinyl and polyester that excited the senses. It shouted, "New Car!"

"Mama, are we rich?"

When his mother didn't answer right away, Carlton thought perhaps she hadn't heard him. As he opened his mouth to repeat the question, the response came.

"That's none of your business, son."

And then she smiled a real smile for the one person she loved more than herself.

During the ride home, which seemed to take three times its normal duration, Carlton began to feel gassy, his stomach angrily cramping and punching him like a small fist. The more he tried to hold it in for the sake of his mother, the worse he felt. Shifting in his seat, he implored his mother to get him home quickly. Mavis obliged, running every stop sign in her path. However, just as they turned onto their street, Carlton's puckering anus could no longer contain the literal shit storm that was brewing within him. It would be years before Carlton would hear the term "lactose intolerant" used in describing what was taking place in his digestive tract; he only knew it felt and smelled like his intestines had exploded. A brown liquid shit stain was spreading out beneath his pants onto the seat like a shadow someone had painted. He and his mother stared at each other in horrified, stunned mortification.

There were kids playing up and down the street and Carlton knew he couldn't just casually get out of the car for fear they'd see what had happened. What would his father say? He'd be completely disgusted, of course. How could he clean it up and get the smell out of his dad's new car? Mrs. Meadows ran into the house to get Carlton's bathrobe and slippers. It would look strange, emerging from a car with bedclothes on, but, all those things could be washed, including his Keds, which were now streaked with drops of brown.

When Mavis Meadows came back out to the car in the driveway, Carlton could see his father fast on her heels. His heart sank like a torpedoed ship into a sea of humiliation. He would never forget the look of absolute horror and revulsion on his father's face.

"Get your stinkin' ass in the house, boy!" Sidney roared.

Carlton burst into tears as he put on the bathrobe while kneeling on the car's driver's seat. He took off his shoes outside the vehicle, put on his house slippers and took the walk of shame into the house. His father made him use the side door, where he headed to the little bathroom in the basement.

When Angelica saw Carlton at school the next Monday, she waved and smiled, to which he responded by turning and walking in the opposite direction down the hallway. Before, Carlton always just seemed weird, now he just seemed mad. *Bump him! Who cares?* she thought. After a few more awkward and incomplete encounters at school, they intentionally stayed away from each other for the remainder of the school year and eventually, Angelica was able to ignore Carlton Meadows as if he'd never existed.

Angelica heard Enrique asking again if she knew Carlton, just as she saw Carlton half-heartedly wave. She immediately found herself irritated. Were these two friends? Ricky took note of the awkward exchange as Angelica handed him the small stack of 45s, saying, "Yeah, I'll write those up for you." Luckily, Ricky was quick about his task and gave the records back to Angelica, along with a sales slip. She remembered she needed to get the candy for herself and Sheila and take it to her while Mrs. Davis was in a semi good mood.

"Say cheese!" exclaimed Mr. Gilhooley.

When Angelica turned toward his voice, she heard a pronounced *click*. Mr. Gilhooley had a Polaroid Land Camera and he'd been taking candid shots of some of the kids around the store. He liked to put the photos up on the bulletin board near the front door. There were only so many missing cat or dog notices he would allow, and this was a much better alternative. Also, the kids knew somehow if they tried any mischief in the

Shake 'n Spin, they might be more easily identified. Mr. Gilhooley smiled at his own cleverness.

Angelica, Ricky and Carlton clustered around Artemis Gilhooley to see their instant image. He peeled back the emulsion infused covering, the photo revealing the three teens frozen in a nanosecond of time. The instant it took to press a button and for a flash to blind them for a few seconds, signaled the beginning and the end for the smiling teens in the photograph, and the man with the camera in his hands. None of them had any idea their lives were about to be irrevocably intertwined forever.

SIX

C arlton Meadows was the only child of prominent attorney Sidney Meadows and his wife, Mavis. Mr. Meadows had big political aspirations and the biggest home on their block, if only to harness and harbor his wife's delusions of grandeur.

Mavis Meadows was an attractive, short, stocky woman whose tastes knew no excess. She seemed to do nothing but shop for more and more knick knacks and bric-a-brac to cram into every open space in their house. That is, when she wasn't running numbers. The lawyer and the bookie, strange legal bedfellows, indeed.

As a teenager, Mavis began taking bets and collecting money all over Detroit for her mother. She eventually branched out on her own and crossed paths with a local mobster named Angelo "The Snake" Santori, for whom she went to work running numbers. Angelo ran a no-nonsense operation with eyes and ears everywhere, his own hands in every underground criminal venture.

Soon Mavis caught the eye of a young attorney named Sidney Meadows, who also worked for Santori mostly keeping his men out of prison and giving Santori tips on new business opportunities in the colored community. Sidney Meadows' father was pastor of one of the largest Negro churches in Detroit. He'd hoped Sid would follow in his footsteps, but his son had bigger plans for himself. No one knew how or when he met Angelo Santori, but theirs was a long and fruitful union.

By 1965, Sidney had distanced himself from the Santori family. He had real and serious ambitions to be a judge and he believed he could do it on his own without the influence of Santori. Delusional though he may have been, Sidney Meadows felt he had done some good within the black community and had a solid reputation as someone who could make a difference. He knew how to skillfully navigate within and between the worlds of blacks and whites. He saw himself as a bridge builder, even though the black side of the bridge felt he was an Uncle Tom and the white side, an uppity nigger. Yet no one ever refused an audience with Sidney as the common denominator was fear. Fear of Angelo Santori.

Mavis struck Sidney as demure and coy and it took three attempts before she agreed to go on a date with him. As they danced and socialized all over Black Bottom, Mavis never let Sidney get past a kiss on the cheek. For three months she was able to keep up the cat and mouse game as Sidney grew weary of trying to figure out how to get next to her.

One evening he was driving her home thinking of the words he would use to rid himself of her. When they arrived in front of her apartment building, Sidney knew by rote what would happen as they said goodnight. Nothing! His mind feverishly formed the words he needed to scrape her off his plate and into the trash. But, before he could give her the easy let down, Mavis had deftly unzipped his trousers and pulled out his penis, manipulating it with her hands and her plush lips. He proposed to her the next day.

Carlton had been a much wished-for child as Mrs. Meadows had tried for years to get pregnant without success. There would be no other children for Sid and Mavis and Carlton became the focus of the intense floodlight of his mother's attention and affection. As a child Carlton was a bit of a social misfit, trying far too hard for comfort. People found his jokes to be unfunny or cruel and cutting. He laughed too loud and too long and at generally inappropriate times. The elders in his family would whisper that he was "born under a bad sign" and nod as if no further explanation was needed.

As he got older, Carlton discovered he had a usefulness to some adults. He was always "around," quiet and ambient and full of passive aggressive tidbits to pass along to anyone fishing for information. Carlton found he could readily trade on the currency of other people's business as he had no business of his own. He was amused at how easily adults would react to some well-placed but seemingly innocuous remark. They all seemed to be in a secret war with one another and he simply helped load the ammo.

Sidney Meadows, it seemed to Carlton, was always either completely impassive or simmering with anger. He was hard to read and even harder to please. Though Sid was perpetually disappointed with everyone residing in his house, he was resolute about the choices he'd made for his life and he lived with them.

Carlton grew to be a handsome chocolate bar brown boy with strong features. Once he met Ricky Williams and began to hang around him and Angelica, they were virtually inseparable. Carlton imagined Ricky to be the brother he never had. He looked up to him and wanted to emulate him—his ease in his own body, his voice, his temperament, even his kindness. How could a kid with so many bad breaks—dead father, criminal brother and uncle— be so cool and not at all bitter? Yes, he wanted what Ricky had and that included Angelica. Ricky didn't acknowledge it, but it was obvious to Carlton that she liked Ricky. There was a casual connectivity to their relationship, a talking without words, an excitement and knowing when they did speak. He envied that, but was he jealous of Ricky or of Angelica?

SEVEN

The summer of 1966 rolled toward its lazy conclusion with Sheila and Angelica indulging their amusement park preoccupation by taking a city bus up 7 Mile Road to Edgewater Amusement Park. The girls loved the fact that a real, full sized amusement park was right in their midst and only a short bus ride away. They would start out mid-morning and be home by dark.

Sheila's favorite ride was the Himalaya and no matter how she conspired over where to sit on the ride, she would always end up smushed by Angelica as the gravitational pull of the spinning ride sent them into the edge of the safety bar. Angelica would always scream her apologies as they laughed and laughed going around and around in a rotating wave.

Angelica's favorite was another type of centrifuge called The Rotor, where patrons stood inside cages in a huge drum with nothing more than a chain holding them in. As the ride spun around gaining speed and the floor dropped, the centrifugal force would plaster the rider inside the cage, pinned as firmly to the wall as a bug in an entomologist's lab. Spinning wildly, the rider was wise to keep their eyes wide open and focused on a particular object, perhaps their own white knuckled hand, in order not to become dizzy. Daredevils would lift their feet slightly, onto the back wall, but the trick was to not be in that position when the ride slowed enough to release its human quarry. Angelica was always relieved and happy when the floor came back up to meet her gym shoes. Was there really a danger that it wouldn't? She hoped to never find out.

About a month before school began, Mrs. Davis drove the girls up to the Beverly Theatre on Grand River to see "Alfie," an English movie that was rated "M for Mature" because of all the sexy and racy situations the dreamy actor Michael Caine found himself in. It seems he was a chauffeur who serviced rich women and bored wives. Aunt Fannie had seen it with one of her boyfriends and said Angelica should try to get in to see it as well.

Unbelievably, and without knowing the details of what was playing or staying to chaperone, Mrs. Davis dropped the girls off at the theatre. With a title like "Alfie," surely it was a kid's movie, Mrs. Davis reasoned. It was playing with an Alfred Hitchcock film called "Torn Curtain" and Velma Davis knew a double feature would keep the girls cool and entertained inside the Beverly for a while.

The fresh, hot popcorn was irresistible, and they could smell it as soon as the heavy door to the theatre opened. Angelica and Sheila liked that the girls behind the candy counter would put so much butter on the popcorn that every heavenly bite had butter dripping from it down to the last kernel.

While getting popcorn and some Raisinets at the candy counter, the girls spotted Carlton and Ricky.

"Hey y'all!" Sheila shouted.

Angelica decided to be polite as the boys walked up.

"Are you guys waiting for anybody else?" *Like that stuck up girlfriend of yours*, she wanted to say.

"Nope, we just got here. Wait for us to get some popcorn and pop and we'll sit with you, unless you're waiting for somebody,"

Ricky said, hoping there weren't going to be any other boys showing up to beat his time with Angelica.

"Okay," said Sheila, a little too eagerly.

"Hi, Angelica."

"Hey, Carlton. We'll wait for you at the curtain," she said indicating the heavy burgundy velvet curtain framing the entrance to the auditorium.

The Beverly, located in the midst of a busy shopping hub off Oakman Boulevard, was popular with kids of all ages and had ushers who took their jobs quite seriously. Too much noise or horsing around would get a kid a beam in the face by a well-tended flashlight. Outside, its architecture was sleek and modern looking, like a still from a Fritz Lang film. Across and down the street a couple of blocks was The Grand Riviera Theatre, once one of the most beautiful show and movie palaces in Detroit. The inside was over-the-top ornateness with its Greco-Roman statuary, chandeliered rotunda, and entablature topped columns. The place was a cross between a museum and a mausoleum and who needed that? Also, it was now mostly westerns and bad science fiction, like "Billy the Kid vs Dracula," while the Beverly was Elvis and James Bond and "In Like Flint." The Riviera's patrons, mostly creepy old men and agitated teenagers, gave most people pause and like 8 Mile Road, at almost any given point, one crossed the street at one's own peril.

When the boys caught up with Sheila and Angelica, they all ambled down the aisle with Ricky leading the way.

"How about here? It's the middle, pretty much," he said stopping center aisle and pointing his bucket of popcorn at the empty seats.

Angelica slowed down as did Sheila, both trying to be strategic but not obvious. Carlton began down the row as Ricky tapped his shoulder with his cup of cola.

"Naw, man, ladies first."

Angelica's eyes got wide. Did he expect her to go first and be stranded next to Carlton for the next four hours? That wasn't going to happen.

"Go ahead, Sheila," Angelica said matter-of-factly. "Go on, Carlton," she said, a little more sternly than was necessary, as the two friends found their seats.

She and Ricky stared at one another briefly and reluctantly, she followed Carlton down the row, sitting to his left. Ricky sat in the aisle seat right next to Angelica. Ricky smiled to himself. *This girl is bossy!* He liked that.

"Did y'all drive over here or did your parents bring you?" Angelica asked, looking toward Ricky.

"We drove. Or, *he* drove, I mean. He's got a bad ride. A Deuce and a Quarter," said Carlton.

Angelica could barely maintain her smile as the very sound of Carlton Meadows' voice got on her nerves. Was she talking to him? Ricky, ever the quick learner and discerner, could see she was struggling to be nice to Carlton. *Why didn't she like him? He seemed nice enough.* Ricky knew that sometimes only children had a hard time being social with their peers. He hoped he was referring to Carlton and not the pretty girl next to him.

"Gosh, that's a pretty big car. You already got your license?" Sheila chimed in from Siberia, barely heard.

"Yup, I got my license in June, but I've had the car for a minute. My uncle gave it to me last year, but my mother wouldn't let me drive it on my learner's permit."

"Nice uncle. What does he do that he can afford to give a kid a big, fancy car?" Angelica asked innocently.

"Hmm, well, he's a businessman. A successful business man," and with that, the lights dimmed, and the heavy burgundy velvet curtain parted to reveal the shimmering screen.

As previews of coming attractions played and segued into a Road Runner cartoon and before the first feature began, Angelica thought about her driving prospects at this point in her life. She would be 16 next year but she already had her driver's permit. How could she score a car? The idea of her mother buying her a car seemed to be stomped out like a discarded cigarette after the incident with Bobby Gogolian. Well, it wasn't really an incident, but her mother always referred to it that way.

Bobby lived across the street and Angelica could look out of her bedroom window into his driveway and partially, his backyard. Bobby "Go-Go" Gogolian was 18 years old and had a reputation as a tough, leather jacketed greaser who rebuilt engines and raced cars at "The Castle," the street adjacent to the White Castle hamburger joint up in Warren on East 8 Mile Road. But that wasn't how Angelica saw Bobby. She recalled the day she was in Charlie's Party Store, before it was the Shake 'n Spin, buying a pack of Hostess Devil's Food Cupcakes. A little colored girl about 8 years old came in to buy some candy and Charlie yelled at her and accused her of stealing.

"You're with that group that came in here and stole from me last week. I seen ya."

The little girl, her hair in two pony tails with ribbons to match the pink in her pedal pushers, began to cry. She just stared at the large white man because she wanted her candy and she certainly knew she wasn't part of "that group," whoever they were.

Bobby had been on another aisle and took only a few strides before he was at the counter, behind the little girl.

"Charlie, what's wrong with you? This is a little girl. Don't you yell at her," he said sternly. Then turning to the child, he asked, "Whaddaya want kid? Get whatever you want, and I'll take care of it."

The small girl looked from one man's face to the other and when Bobby Go-Go smiled at her, she knew he was serious and she was safe. She got a small bag of penny candy and ran outside after thanking Bobby.

One spring day Angelica shyly came over to see what Bobby was doing to the car in his driveway and they got to talking about cars and engines. Angelica loved fast cars and liked watching the races on occasion at The Castle with her uncle Ned. Her depth of knowledge impressed Bobby. They agreed that the Chevy Nova's 427 big block was the best and fastest engine in an American car and a Corvair, no matter how good looking, was a casket on wheels.

Bobby and Angelica struck up a friendship centered around their love of the American muscle car. She learned everything there was to know about the engines of a Chevy Impala SS, also called a 409, the Pontiac GTO, and her favorite, the 1966 Chevy Chevelle SS, which is what Bobby drove. His was cherry red and just as sweet. Bobby used his tough exterior to his advantage when he raced, by intimidating the competition with his demeanor before ever getting behind the wheel. He seldom smiled and spoke even less, but he always managed a wave for Angelica when he spotted her in the crowd with her uncle.

Eventually, Liz Tanner took notice of the friendship between her daughter and the boy across the street and she put a stop to it. Liz scolded her brother for allowing it to go on, even though there was no "it." "It" was completely innocent and respectful on both the teen's parts, Ned tried to explain. Liz could not be swayed and fumed, saying Bobby was a white boy who could only be interested in one thing from Angelica. In order to keep her mother from embarrassing her, she agreed to stop being friends with Bobby outside of school. She could no longer go to visit his garage in the back of his house. Angelica was completely ashamed of her mother's silly notions and her unwarranted prejudice, but Bobby understood. Nonetheless, it didn't extinguish the infatuation he had for her.

Bobby graduated in June and two weeks ago, at the beginning of August, Bobby Gogolian was drafted into the U.S. military and he was now on his way to Vietnam by way of Ft. Bragg. Angelica prayed for her friend's safe return.

The movie began, and Angelica could feel eyes on her. Glancing to her left, Ricky Williams flashed a smile at her before turning back to the screen. She smiled to herself and looked to her right to find Carlton Meadows staring at her. She quickly turned back to the film and reminded herself not to look that way again. She couldn't believe she used to like that drip, Carlton Meadows.

EIGHT

I n September of 1966, the day after Labor Day, school began all over the city of Detroit. As much as students feigned dread, it was tradition to go shopping at J.L. Hudson's to get new school clothes. Sure, there were other department stores like Sears, Montgomery Ward and Federal's, but Hudson's was the grande dame of everything consumable. Anything a household might need could be purchased in the elaborate, multi-storied downtown department store.

Angelica Tanner, Sheila Davis, Enrique Williams and Carlton Meadows all found themselves in the 11th grade and part of an experiment in integration. Their parents, along with several dozen other Negro families, agreed that their children would integrate the all-white John Francis Dodge High School on 8 Mile Road on the Northwest side of Detroit. When the kids first learned of the location, they were concerned about crossing 8 Mile Road. They needn't have been, since the school was on "this" side of 8 Mile, rather than "that" side. "This" side was a semi safe haven of people, places, and businesses the kids and their families were familiar with. "That" side was like an imaginary nether region of unfamiliar names and faces that had the authority to beat up those who did not belong. There were stories of Negro parents who were fortunate enough to occasionally indulge, unmolested, in the great shopping that was both alleged and legendary across that mile marker.

8 Mile Road had always stood as a physical and psychological line in the sand for Detroiters and crossing it was fraught with peril. Up past Southfield Road one ended up in Southfield, which was more a suburb, but an unwelcoming one, nonetheless. Down near Woodward, one ended up in Ferndale. Ferndale was a bedroom community between the borders of 8 Mile and 10 Mile Roads, Livernois and Woodward Avenues, with all manner of stories about tough white kids who never met a nigger they didn't want to beat with a baseball bat. Exaggeration? Perhaps, but, why find out firsthand?

The very first day of school at Dodge High, the black and white students held one another in wary regard, painfully aware that they must both occupy that unholy ground. The heat of the summer had suddenly given way to a bright crispness in the air, as if someone had turned a page in a child's story book of seasons. Angelica and Sheila rode to school together on the city bus, with Sheila initially standing near the front door so her friend could see her when the door opened, assuring Angelica would board the correct conveyance.

Angelica's first day of school tradition was to be cute--white go-go boots, white fish net stockings, a red, black and white color block mini dress and a black sweater. She had gotten her hair cut and styled in an asymmetrical wedge like singer Tammi Terrell. Oh boy did Angelica wish her mother would let her wear black eyeliner and coral lipstick like Tammi wore, but no dice.

Sheila knew she could never outdo her friend as far as fashion was concerned, especially on the first day of school. She wore knee socks and loafers (damn her mother!), a green short sleeved jumper with a black patent leather belt, and a white sweater to ward off the early morning chill.

Over the Labor Day weekend, the neighborhood was buzzing with word of a black boy being beaten by a gang of whites and taken to Henry Ford Hospital after being caught walking with a white girl on a street in Southfield. No one knew if this had actually happened or if it was a figment of someone's mendacious imagination. Angelica was cautiously eager to see what life was like at her new school. She couldn't wait to see which of her friends had become a part of this integration experiment riding across town instead of going to Mumford, their neighborhood high school.

The day had been largely uneventful with Angelica seeing many old friends and familiar faces, black and white, in the freshly painted hallways. She saw Carlton Meadows, who was his usual haughty self. She'd waved at him and he waved back. *Maybe he was nervous too*, she thought. *How can someone whose mother is a numbers runner act like they're better than you and make you believe it might be true?* Before she could use any more brain space on Carlton, she saw Enrique Williams. This made Angelica stop walking.

As she stood wondering if he would look in her direction, Ricky suddenly looked up and smiled. She felt someone grab her elbow. It was Sheila.

"Ain't he fine, girl? And I see he remembers you, huh?" asked Sheila, always too loud.

Angelica had only been up to the Shake 'n Spin a few times during the summer, but each time she had engaged Ricky in conversations about music. They seemed to like the same artists and have the same critical ears.

"He's beautiful," Angelica replied, dreamily, seriously. She made a face and they both laughed. She didn't care if she sounded silly.

"Girl, the boys are gonna be trying to choose up on you for real this year. You are looking *just* like Tammi," Sheila said.

Tammi Terrell was a beautiful colored Kewpie doll who sung stirring duets with soul singer Marvin Gaye. They were the most boss couple at Motown Records, but Tammi and Marvin didn't "go together." Their natural ease and playfulness, along with the earnest and soulful sexiness of their duets, belied the fact that they were just friends who sang together. Tammi was known for her mod threads, asymmetrical haircut and luminous kohl rimmed eyes.

"Why didn't you wear that eyeliner we got at Kresge's last week?" Angelica asked, feeling a bit uncomfortable that they were only talking about how good *she* looked.

Sheila pursed her lips and stared sidelong at her friend.

"Now, you know my mama. If I had tried to leave the house with eyeliner on my eyes, man, she woulda dug my eyes out of my head."

They both laughed because it was definitely in the realm of possibilities. Somehow the image of Elizabeth Tanner doing that very thing to her, flashed through Angelica's mind. She saw herself crumpled to the ground like a discarded paper bag, using her hands to blindly search the floor for her useless orbs as her mother stood there laughing maniacally. She heard Sheila's snapping fingertips near her ear, bringing her out of the darkness.

"Dang, girl. What happened? Where'd you go?" Sheila asked.

Angelica shook her head slightly, insuring the image had vanished.

"Girl, I'm cool. Trust me. I'll have my eyes looking cute by Friday. I didn't buy that Maybelline for nothin'," she said defiantly.

At lunch time Angelica found herself in the library and it was a perfect time to be there, no crowds, no noise, no rush. She perused the card catalogue and happily hunted down the three books she needed. Looking down at her watch, Angelica saw she had a little time left before class, so she walked out on to the green expanse of lawn to find a spot to sit and eat her sandwich, which was completely squished inside her purse. Maybe she could start one of her new books? The prospect of losing herself in a classic story like Homer's "Odyssey" was exciting.

Almost immediately Angelica noticed that the students were assembled in a clearly segregated manner. The Negro students were on one edge of the campus lawn, congregating in small clusters while the white boys and girls coveted a larger, central portion of the lawn. As Angelica journeyed toward a large shady tree to sit down, she noticed four white youths standing nearby. One was tall, two were of medium height and one was short. Though they seemed to be minding their own business, talking and laughing, something inside Angelica called for caution. She shook it off. Surely, they would see she was no threat to them, just a girl with some books, looking for a place to land with her sandwich.

As Angelica approached, the boys stopped what they were doing, turning toward her. Angelica stared straight at the tree, never breaking her stride. As she went past the shortest boy, he spit a giant gob of saliva onto the top of her right foot. On her white go-go boots. From Hudson's. Angelica's eyes narrowed, and her lips drew in, but before she could react, another of the boys knocked her books out of her arms and onto the ground.

"Pick them books up, nigger. And wipe that shit off your shoes."

They all four laughed uproariously, congratulating each other for disrupting Angelica's lunch.

The laughter made a group of boys several yards away look toward them. Ricky Williams was one of those boys who looked up. *Was that Angelica? What was she doing with those white boys?*

Kneeling down to pick up her books, Angelica said, "Fucking cowards. And they're boots, asshole."

This made the laughter stop like a needle picked up from a record on a phonograph. Angelica was still down on one knee picking up her books when a foot kicked her in the back.

"What did you say, you black bitch? Yeah, I thought so!" came his retort when Angelica didn't answer.

The group of boys turned to walk away, when the tall boy suddenly crashed to the ground, knocking the shortest boy down as well, like dominoes. Angelica had run low and into the back of the kid's legs, knocking him off his feet. With a swiftness she was on his back bashing his head with the heaviest library book. She hit him over and over again, repeatedly, as if trying to drive a stake into the ground.

By now the shorter boy had wriggled free from being caught halfway beneath the other one's body. The remaining two teens grabbed Angelica's arms and lifted her up off the ground, as their friend came to his feet. A large crowd was encircling them as if everyone had suddenly awakened and wanted to see what had disturbed their slumber. People were yelling and screaming, pushing and shoving to get closer.

Enrique broke through the crowd, shouting, "Let her go, assholes! Put her the fuck down!" His homeboys were now beside him, all ready and all business.

"I don't take orders from niggers," the tall boy shouted, his face flushed red with a mixture of anger and embarrassment.

In just a few movements, Ricky was on him, punching him multiple times in his face which was now an even brighter red. Ricky's friends pounced on the others as if they'd been cued. Angelica, free now, scrambled to short-lived safety under a tree. A red headed girl took a swing at her and as Angelica quickly ducked the blow, she almost felt sorry for the girl as she came back up unleashing blow after blow to the girl's swelling welt of a face.

The contagion of violence spread like an ocean's wave. Girls and boys, black and white, all found a reason to join the fray. Rocks, bottles and sticks flew indiscriminately. Carlton Meadows, seeing the precipitating incident, turned to flee when the mass melee began and was hit in the head with an airborne bottle for his cowardice. Rubbing his dome while picking up his pace, he felt a hand squeezing his arm. It was assistant principal Greenbaum.

"Go to the office. Now."

"But, I—" began Carlton.

"Go or I'll have you arrested," said Mr. Greenbaum.

One half hour after the pandemonium had begun, Angelica, Carlton and Ricky found themselves in the crowded detention hall waiting to report to the principal's office. It was hard to calm down because of the adrenaline-fueled excitement of the fight. The black and white students were on separate sides of the room, forced to segregate by school officials. The principal was removing five students at a time to interview, and needless to say, school was over for the rest of the day.

Parents began arriving to pick up their children. Many of them were factory workers at the auto plants who were angry that they had to cut into their sleep hours—afternoon shifts began at 4 p.m.—to come up to the school. Emotions ran the gamut with the parents. Some were glad their kids took up for themselves, some were glad their kids were fighting the integration plan, others were ashamed their kids were at school fighting and still others were concerned about the activities their expelled or suspended kids might indulge in while home alone.

Carlton, Enrique, Angelica, and two other kids received an escort to the principal's office. Passing by pin-drop quiet classrooms, Angelica saw Sheila and her mom, Mrs. Davis. The girls briefly locked eyes; Sheila's growing large at the disheveled, bloody and dirty sight of her best friend.

"What happened?" she mouthed silently to Angelica.

Angelica just shook her head. Right then Mrs. Davis saw her and, shocked at the girl's appearance, began to shake her head as well in disbelief. She had never seen Angelica look like this before. She was a girl Velma Davis would describe as "always so well put together."

The frenetic energy between Angelica and Ricky had dissipated by the time they sat in the anteroom outside Principal Janeway's office. Carlton was called in first. The heavy wooden door closed behind him. The other four youngsters had caught the unsmiling profile of the principal and a security officer named Hollister, before the door clapped shut. Ricky looked at Angelica, finally.

"Are you okay?" he asked softly.

"Yes, I think so."

He didn't look any worse for wear, save a couple of missing buttons at the top of his shirt. Angelica reached out and gently touched his hand with hers. It startled both of them, but outwardly, neither showed it.

"Thank you. Thanks for helping me out there. Heck, I didn't know what was gonna happen once those dudes got me off their buddy."

She removed her hand. Ricky smiled and then chuckled.

"You kicked that dude's ass. I'll bet he thinks two or three times before messing with you again."

They laughed, and the tension was broken.

"Hey, what street do you live on?" Enrique inquired.

"I live on Roselawn, between Thatcher and Santa Clara. What about you? I'm pretty sure I saw your mom at the A&P. You have some little brothers and sisters, right?"

It was clear that they'd been checking one another out from afar and likely each already knew the answers to these questions and more. Formalities.

"Yeah, there's five of us. I've got an older brother named Danny. He went to Mackenzie. We used to live on the West side, but we moved right when school got out for the summer. Oh, and I live on Woodingham, between Thatcher and Curtis."

"Cool. Do you remember my name?" she asked. A loaded question that could lead to deflating embarrassment.

"Angelica, right? Taylor?" he said, hopefully, eyebrows raised triumphantly.

Angelica laughed lightly.

"Angelica Tanner," she said.

For a millisecond she toyed with the thought of pretending she couldn't recall his name.

"And you're Ricky Williams."

"Enrique Torres Williams," he proclaimed pronouncing the Spanish names like a native of his mother's Puerto Rico.

The other two students sat there, sullen and trying not to appear to be interested in what was going on between Ricky and Angelica.

"Well, Angel, maybe I'll come over to your house one day to ride bikes to Palmer Park or something. I got a car, but I still like to ride my bike around the neighborhood sometimes, ya know?"

She noticed he'd called her "Angel," like a secret and special name only he was allowed to utter. Before she could answer him, the door of principal Janeway's office opened and Carlton was escorted out.

Carlton Meadows had been in the principal's office about 20 minutes and during that time he made it clear that he was not fighting, but, rather, trying to keep from being injured. Principal Janeway mentioned that Carlton's father was prominent in his profession and would look proudly upon a son who did the right thing in that situation. Within minutes, Carlton had told the principal that Angelica Tanner had started the near riot and that Enrique Williams was one of the ringleaders. The principal thought it quite fortuitous that both Tanner and Williams were just outside her door.

Angelica and Ricky were sentenced to three days detention for the remainder of the week while the principal reviewed all the facts to determine if they would be permanently expelled. Carlton would suffer a day's suspension to protect against the appearance of him being a snitch, which he surely was.

NINE

Immediately after the roll was taken in homeroom and the
bell rang for first period, Angelica's task was to find her way
to the detention hall. For three whole days! It certainly
wasn't fair since she was only defending herself against those
stupid boys, but she figured it was better than being expelled. *It's
going to be a long day and a longer week*, she was thinking as she
opened the door to the grimness of the detention room on the
second floor.

Angelica gave the slip of paper she'd been carrying to Mr.
Nolan, who was sitting at his desk at the front of the room. She
smiled wanly as Mr. Nolan peered over his pince-nez spectacles
at her. She was happy he was the teacher with detention duty for
that week. Mr. Nolan, a favorite Math teacher among the student
body, was an affable, if avuncular man with a great sense of
humor. He had been a teacher at their junior high school and this
was his second year at Dodge High.

"Welcome, Miss Tanner. Three days with us, huh?" he asked,
not quite believing Angelica Tanner was before him and already
in trouble after only one day of school.

"Yes, Mr. Nolan. I'm surprised to be here myself," she said
noting his disbelief. "All I did was defend myself. Since when it
is okay for boys to hit girls? Anyway, here I am making the best
of it. I'll catch up on my reading, I guess."

"Alright, then. Have a seat," he said, vaguely pointing in the direction of the wooden desks, the square of paper still between his fingers.

Angelica made herself comfortable in her uncomfortable little desk and got out her composition book and some ink pens. She was rooting around in her small stack of books when she heard Mr. Nolan speaking to someone in a low tone. *Wonder how many black kids will be in here today?* she thought. Though Angelica had never been in trouble and was not proud of being in detention, she decided if she had it to do all over again, she might have fought even harder since the end result would have been the same.

"Hi, pal. Is this seat taken?"

Ricky Williams slid into the seat next to her and smiled expansively. "Or should I call you Mrs. Bobo Brazil?"

Their laughter was met with Mr. Nolan's unflinching gaze.

"Nope. Mrs. Cassius Clay is just fine," she said as they both chuckled. "You get three days, too?"

"Yup, but I think it's gonna be more fun with you here. You ever have detention?"

"No, I've never been in trouble…" Angelica said trailing off, not wanting to be seen as a goody two shoes or a square. She was no square, but he didn't know her well enough to know that, so she deflected a bit. "But, Mr. Nolan is so nice. He's one of the neatest teachers at Dodge."

"Cool. I wonder what happened to those guys who caused all the ruckus? They probably didn't even get in trouble. Shoot, maybe they're gonna be homecoming kings or something."

"Ha! They got promoted or maybe graduated without having to go to another single class. That'll teach us colored kids to act crazy on school property!" Angelica said as they both burst into laughter.

Angelica shook her head wildly as Enrique slapped the top of his desk a couple of times.

"Alright, students. Let's settle down. If you have work, go ahead and get started. If you have books, get them out. Thank you."

Mr. Nolan was done talking and opened a leather-bound tome by Hemingway, leafing through the dog-eared pages to find his place in the story.

"Okay, later Gator," Ricky whispered, resting his hand briefly on Angelica's arm.

He got out his English Lit book and Angelica found something to take her mind off of Ricky Williams and the fact that she was practically sitting in his lap--well not quite, but close enough. She couldn't wait to tell Sheila!

On day two, it was clear there would be no more than 10 kids in the detention hall and that Mr. Nolan would let them talk and socialize, as long as they weren't too loud. He really just wanted to read his book.

"Do you know how to play Poker? Wait, no fun without money. Okay, how about Tonk or Spades or Gin?" Enrique asked, shuffling a deck of Red Bicycle playing cards he'd pulled from his jacket pocket.

"Um, let's play Tonk. We can play Gin later. I'll be whipping you one game at a time," Angelica said, a sly smile spreading across her lips.

"Oh! Oh, really? We'll see who gets whipped."

"I hope your card playing is better than your capping."

Capping was verbal one-upsmanship designed to shut the other person down. A good "cap" often made bystanders exclaim, "Ooh, cap!"

"Girl, I'm wearing a brand-new belt and I'm gon' whip you so bad, you're gonna think I used it on *you*," Ricky bragged, throwing down a king of hearts.

Angelica drew a card from the deck on the desk and threw out a jack of spades. She put her finger in the air to signal that she needed a moment. She reached into her red patent leather pocketbook and got out a white handkerchief.

"Once I finish beating you, you gonna turn the belt on yourself, my friend. I don't like to see a man cry so, feel free to use my hanky. Wouldn't want you to embarrass yourself!"

"Wow, you are funny! Ed Sullivan needs you on his show," Ricky said sarcastically, trying to stifle his laughter.

On the third day, Angelica and Ricky assumed their now familiar seating arrangement near the back of the classroom. Ricky knew however long the day, it would be too short. He liked spending time with Angelica Tanner. Angelica, too, did a great job of keeping away the dread of day's end. She'd enjoyed the last 3 days like a vacation, but she knew the sun had to set on their paradise. They'd even incorporated her small transistor radio into their routine. Music made memories, and there were very few disagreements when the conversation had gotten deep. Were the Beatles better than the Rolling Stones? Who were the new groovy groups emerging from Britain? How cool was it to live in the city that birthed Motown and its uniquely recognizable sound? Why was all the great soul music out of the South on Atlantic Records? On and on.

"How long have you lived on the Northwest side?" Enrique asked.

"My whole life. My auntie and uncle live on the West side. Cousins, too."

"It's pretty cool over here, though, more integrated. My people live on the West side, too, more colored over there, I think. I'm over there a lot to see my old friends."

I'll bet you are, Angelica wanted to say. After all, that was where his girlfriend, Rita, lived. Funny, she never came up in three days and Angelica didn't know how or what to ask in regard to her.

"I think I told you my brother Danny still lives over there. He didn't want to move with us." He paused. "He's a drop out. Went to Mackenzie."

Like your girlfriend? Angelica stop it! Either say it out loud or cut it out!

"Is he a juvenile delinquent? Not that he's bad because he dropped out—"

"No, no, it's okay. He's had a few problems, but he's got a job and his own place."

"That's neat, your parents letting him live away from home like that."

"It's just my mom, my sisters and my little brother. Alecia's 18 getting ready to go to Wayne State, then there's Pilar and Eduardo. They're 10 and 8. They fight all the time," he laughed. "They're good kids, though. And, Pi-pi, she's my little star. She's the sweetest kid."

"Um, so, where's your father?" Angelica asked innocently.

She regretted the question as soon as she saw the cloud pass over Ricky's face. Then, just as quickly, it was gone. He forced himself to smile.

"My daddy died in Vietnam two years ago. He was a really swell guy and loved the Army. He was a career soldier and he loved America."

"What was, *is* his name?"

Enrique looked straight into Angelica's luminous eyes. They looked like an explosion on the sun. There was no guile in them.

"Gabriel Williams, Sergeant First Class," his son said proudly. It felt good, like an honor, to speak his father's name. "He's buried in Arlington National Cemetery."

"Goodness. At least you got to know your father. Mine died in the Korean War. Never even met him," she said matter-of-factly.

"Dang, that was a long time ago."

They didn't speak again for a long while and it was okay. They knew they didn't have to. When Angelica was little, back when she used to ask about her father, she imagined him like the heroes she'd seen in black and white war movies. A tough talking guy with a cigarette perched between his lips, who had the admiration and respect of those he led into combat.

As she grew up, she saw the vacant sadness of so many widows from World War II to Vietnam. All of whom possessed nothing of their men but an impossibly folded American flag in a wood and glass case. There was no warmth or comfort to be found against that triangular prison. They wanted their men; the children wanted their daddies. Angelica's house held no such blanket of tears. Her mother said she gave her father's flag to relatives for safe keeping but could never seem to pinpoint who those relatives might be.

Angelica long ago gave up the inquiries to Liz about that flag. One day while flipping through *Life* magazine, she saw a black and white photo showing an undulating sea of white tombstones at Arlington National Cemetery. The words came to her mind without asking and she spoke them quietly.

"Mary, Mary quite contrary, how does your garden grow? With all of the bodies of thousands of boys who will always be 18 years old."

TEN

T hough it took place on the border of summer and fall, the annual Michigan State Fair was a "must go" event for families statewide. The smell of fresh popped corn and roasted peanuts competed with the odor of digestive byproducts left on the ground by horses and cows being led to the stables. One year there was even an elephant on display in a barn.

Sugar crystals mixed with hot air in a centrifuge equipped cart to create great clouds of pastel cotton candy. Little kids, whose enthusiasm was always greater than their judgement, took bites out of the candy floss and whined in disappointment when their pink or blue puff was reduced to a deformed, sticky mess with just a few flicks of the tongue. A highlight was always the candy apples. Bushels of crisp and crunchy Michigan apples were put on wooden sticks and bathed in hot, red-tinted liquid sugar, finally settling on their waxed papers mired in a small blood red glassy pool. The first bite—whether a *tick* against the two front teeth to crack the smooth shell before biting into a fresh apple or a brave break-off of the candy halo that would have a kid furiously chewing and praying that no fillings would need to be replaced—was nirvana. At least until October 31st.

Certain rituals were indelible to the coming of All Hallows' Eve. Kids rushed home after school, blazing through their homework and stuffing their mouths with the snacks their moms left on the kitchen table before going off to work the afternoon shift at one of the auto plants. They could barely wait the two hours until the sun went down to dress up for trick or treating.

For some kids, the late afternoon was spent trick or treating for UNICEF to help the world's less fortunate children with pennies collected from neighbors. But, as street lights and porch lights came on, there was a mad dash with leaves flying about like tawny ghosts, as kids abandoned their humanitarian efforts to get back home to put on their Halloween costumes. The air was thick with the sweet fog of burning leaves, the universal scent of fall, and perhaps the residual smoke of fires lit the evening before on Devil's Night.

Children lucky enough to have parents home at nightfall, had help dressing in their Halloween attire. Usually the costume was a well-meaning though ill-fitting one-piece polyester jumpsuit from Federal's, imprinted with a popular whimsical TV or cartoon character, to be worn over play clothes and under a coat. A bulky and unsightly ensemble, no matter a parent's best efforts. A quick movement or long stride would leave the costume hanging in shreds atop street clothes, or worse, revealing a clandestine winter jacket lurking underneath.

The last piece of the costume was the requisite plastic mask with the single elastic strand joining one side to the other, with perilously sharp edges that cut tender faces. Children could only hope that friends would not be inclined to run as the mask's eyeholes only approximated where actual eyeballs might be and made seeing, especially while running, quite hazardous. Many a child had missed a curb or step because of this manufacturing miscalculation, landing face down on the frigid concrete. The kids with patient and creative parents got cool face make up, wigs and a grown-up's dress or suit to trick or treat in.

Tonight, Angelica was content to be handing out candy to all the little ghosts and goblins trekking up to her house. Porch lights had sprung to life up and down every block, piercing the twilight with promises of candy, pennies or other treats.

Angelica smiled watching from her door as kids approached Mrs. Gogolian's house across the street, stampeding up the steps. Angelica shook her head in futility because she knew the kids would ring the doorbell and Mrs. Gogolian, Bobby's mother, would appear with her famous baked rolls and a handful of pennies year after year. Did she ever deviate or vary the bounty? No. Every Halloween Mrs. Go-Go would clap and smile at the children, telling them how pretty or scary they were in her heavily accented English. Then the short, squat woman with gold teeth and features as doughy as her baked goods would drop a leavened brick in their bags.

Without deviation, the daylight of the next morning would reveal a carpet of rolls adorning her lawn. After Bobby was killed in Vietnam in 1968, the children called a moratorium on discarding Mrs. Gogolian's rolls for two consecutive years. Ironically, no one got a bigger kick out of the annual display of lawn ornaments than Bobby. For him it meant that he, a first generation American, was accepted by his neighbors and that the Gogolians were susceptible to all manner of Halloween mischief, like everyone else.

Each November 1st, for as long as anyone could remember, Bobby would go out in the early morning before school with a big A&P bag and scoop up the frosty rocks and deposit them in the garbage in the alley. In 1970 the neighborhood kids again started tossing the rolls and continued until Mrs. Gogolian moved away. Lord, how the children missed her and Bobby.

Angelica chuckled softly as she closed her front door. A small twinge of regret ran through her because she really felt she wasn't too old to go trick or treating, but Sheila had dissuaded her. They were high school Juniors--how would it look if they ran into their cooler classmates behind unsuspecting doors? *Whatever*, thought Angelica, unwrapping a Banana Split and popping it in her mouth. The sweet tasting taffy filling her mouth was ten times better than any real banana split she'd ever choked down. She poked at the candy in the bowl with her slender index finger and found a pack of strawberry Kits. Forgetting momentarily that she was merely a sweet sentinel, a preserver and protector of candy for hordes of neighborhood kids that had yet to appear, she found herself unwrapping and unloading the entire pack of taffy into her jaws.

The doorbell rang, and she heard "Trick or treat" being called out, cushioned by giggles on the other side of the door. She wasn't sure she could speak with her teeth tacking to one another. Angelica grabbed the bowl as she frantically used her tongue to divide, move and tuck the candy around her cheeks and into the back of her mouth so she could at least greet the Halloween visitors.

Angelica turned the knob and flung open the door enthusiastically, thinking she was taking too long and her porch might be abandoned.

"Trick or treat!"

"Trick or treat, smell my feet--"

"No, Eddie, knock it off. Sorry about that," Ricky Williams said, smiling and looking slightly embarrassed.

He was standing under the porch light with two small children, a boy and a girl.

"Hi y'all! What are you supposed to be?" Angelica asked the little boy who'd sung the cheeky rhyme.

"I'm Batman!" he exclaimed.

"I'm Batgirl," said the slightly taller girl.

"There ain't no Batgirl, Pilar. Why are you such a copy-catter?" the young boy asked, faking exasperation.

"Let me guess…you must be Eduardo and you must be Pilar. You guys are so cute. Here," Angelica said, digging into her candy bowl and dropping the sweet treasures into their decorated brown paper bags.

Nik L Nips, licorice wheels, Now and Laters, and Chunkys, the compact candy bar Angelica felt was far too expensive at a nickel, went into their bags.

"Oh, and I'm trick or treating for UNICEF, too. Do you want to donate?" the beautiful brown eyed girl asked.

She was a mini, feminine version of Ricky. Angelica couldn't help but wonder what his parents looked like.

"Sure," she said, digging into the pocket of her blue jeans. Angelica plunked a dime into the slot of the little box Pilar held.

"Thanks, Angelica," Ricky said as a gaggle of kids came running toward her porch. "See you tomorrow at school."

"Thank you," the two little ones said in unison.

"See ya later," Angelica called after them.

"Is that the Angelica you were talking about?" Eduardo asked his big brother.

"Shut up, boy," Ricky said. He halfway glanced back to see if Angelica had heard Eddie's remark, but she was busy doling out candy to the clamoring horde. Relieved, Ricky kept walking up the block with his siblings. Angelica closed her door and leaned up against it, grinning. She'd heard.

ELEVEN

November first, the day after Halloween, always seemed to dawn gray and cold and bleak. Porches held prisoner the caved in, sooty jack 'o lanterns, their smiles and grimaces frosted with dew. Kids tromped off to school in the dull daylight with pockets overflowing with their sweet loot, evidence of a night well spent.

The next three weeks dragged by for Angelica with book reports and Glee Club rehearsals for the Christmas Pageant. The old veterans from the VFW hall had come, as was their annual rite, to sell crepe paper poppies to the students for a penny each. The flowers would be twisted onto shirt, dress and coat buttons to commemorate Veteran's Day. Though she was glad Thanksgiving had finally arrived, the holiday would likely always remind her of what had happened to the world only three years earlier.

Angelica was assisting the kindergarten class at the elementary school with their Thanksgiving party, making turkeys out of tracings of their tiny hands on brown paper bags. She helped set out the cornucopia and pass out the head bands with feathers, all made of multi colored construction paper. In the middle of doing the Hokey Pokey with her little charges, someone from the office came in and beckoned to the teacher. The girl from the office shook her head violently as if to erase some vision within it and left the room in tears. The kindergarten teacher put her hand over her mouth as her tears flowed over the back of her fingers. She crossed the room to take the needle off the scratchy record that was playing, causing the children to stop moving and look in her direction.

Very calmly she said, "Children, class is being dismissed early. We need to get our coats on, gather our things to take home and we will proceed to the auditorium. Your parents are coming to pick you up today. Let's go. Quickly and quietly, children."

President John Fitzgerald Kennedy, the 35th president of the United States of America, had been assassinated in Dallas, Texas just after lunch time. No one in modern American history recalled having experienced such a loss and it was devastating and dreamlike and on television. Who? Why? Every family sat around the TV set that afternoon watching trusted reporter Walter Cronkite on the CBS Evening News' Special Report, overcome with his own emotions, but giving the facts as they came in. This watershed event depressed the nation and held fast in its collective memory for generations.

Thanksgiving in Detroit meant watching the annual J.L. Hudson Thanksgiving Day Parade on television or in person. The parade of colorful floats and giant cartoon balloon characters wound their way down Woodward Avenue with Santa Claus appearing in his sleigh at the very end. The pageantry and anticipation were exhilarating to anyone who watched, no matter the age or how many times they'd seen it before.

Angelica and Sheila decided to get up early and take the bus downtown to see the parade. They dressed in warm wool pants and sweaters and their heavy coats, and though there was no snow yet, boots to keep the cold of the concrete from seeping inside to their toes. Hats, gloves and scarves finished the bundling, as they would be standing on the street for a couple of hours and no one wanted to be cold and miserable. The bus went to Sheila's stop first and she stood near the front where the driver was so Angelica could see her when the bus came to her stop. In this ritual they depended on one another to be prompt and on time. Sheila couldn't very well be getting off the bus after only a few short blocks, aborting her ride and donating her bus fare, because Angelica didn't get to her bus stop on time.

Once they arrived, Angelica and Sheila folded themselves into the ambling throngs heading for the best views of the parade route. They had just about decided on the best place to stand when they heard, "Hey! If it ain't Butterscotch and Chocolate!"

Angelica suspected someone trying to be funny may have been talking to her and Sheila, but they kept moving forward though the crowd, which had slowed markedly. The next thing Sheila knew, there were three teenaged boys in front of them, walking backwards or sideways like crabs. The boys stopped, hemming in the girls.

"Where's your friend, the greaser? He ain't here to help you now, I see," said the larger boy, the obvious ringleader.

Angelica recognized him. Last spring, she was riding her bike up to Lou's Deli to get a sandwich for her mother, when a group of four boys rode up to her, telling her to give up her bicycle. This one, the leader, had a rat-faced kid on his handlebars and she supposed her bike was going to be his new mode of transportation. Wrong. This was *her* bike, *her* Radiant Coppertone Schwinn Sting-Ray with the banana seat, sissybar and high-rise handlebars. Angelica took off, blowing right through the boys and their bikes without losing her footing, willing her slender legs to pump with all their might.

Angelica had gotten down one block before she was again surrounded. People were on their porches, but this wasn't her block. If she yelled for help, would anyone come down to see what was happening?

"Give me that bike!" the leader snarled. He signaled for the boy on his handlebars to get off and claim his prize. Angelica was frozen, not in fear, but in anger. She knew she couldn't beat them and if she clobbered the one coming toward her it would just be worse for her in the end.

Just then, a revving engine's roar echoed in the distance, getting louder as it got nearer. Bobby Go-Go slowed his 405 down to see why his neighbor was so upset. He quickly assessed the situation and put his car in park and got out. Though these four young men didn't live or go to school in that neighborhood, they all knew who Bobby was.

"You need a ride, Angelica?" he said, looking into her wide, grateful eyes.

"Yes. Thanks."

"Let me put your bike in first, okay?"

Bobby lifted Angelica's bike with one hand and stood for a few seconds staring down the boys.

"Y'all live around here?"

"Nope. What's it to you?" said the visibly disappointed rat boy who would be travelling back home on the hard steel of his pal's handlebars.

"What did you say to me?" Bobby asked, almost amused.

"He didn't mean nothin'. Can we go?" one of the boys asked nervously.

Bobby walked a few steps toward him.

"I better not ever, ever, catch you in this neighborhood again. You understand?" Bobby said, menacingly.

The boys concurred in a simultaneous mumble and sped off down the street. Bobby Gogolian put Angelica's bike in the back seat of his car and she got in the passenger's seat.

"Little assholes. Picking on a girl. You okay?"

"Yeah, I am now. Thanks, Bobby. You were right on time!"

"No sweat," he said, pulling out toward their block.

Angelica's eyes narrowed as she assessed the boys standing in front of her and Sheila.

"There ain't no bikes to steal here, thief, or didn't you notice?" Angelica said defiantly, her breath rising like a smoke signal in the frigid air.

Sheila looked from one boy to another, not sure what to do.

"So, is that Bobby guy your boyfriend or somethin'" the boy asked.

Oh great, Sheila thought. *So, this is what this is all about. This stupid boy likes Angelica and doesn't know whether to hit her or kiss her!*

"Nah, he's my friend. Now let us through, creeps."

Is Angelica trying to get us stomped into the cold concrete?, Sheila thought. The boys parted, and Angelica continued walking as Sheila, momentarily stunned, trotted up beside her.

"Always an adventure, my friend. Always an adventure," Sheila said, smiling and shaking her head.

Angelica rolled her eyes playfully. "*Always*, girl."

Finding a good spot to squeeze into, they positioned themselves in front of a family that was too busy corralling their many children to hold their prime real estate near Crowley's on Woodward. Seeing the giant helium filled floats of Mighty Mouse, Top Cat, Bullwinkle and Rocky and Fred Flintstone never failed to excite Sheila and Angelica. It always seemed extra special, almost a privilege to be there in person.

Arriving back home afterward, Angelica ran into the house and took off her boots, stomping her feet to abate the numbness the cold had inflicted.

"Did y'all see me on TV at the parade?"

"Girl, you know I'm in this kitchen tryin' to fix this food to take over to Granny's. Did y'all have fun?" Liz asked her daughter.

"Sure did. People always let us get in front, so we could see really good. And I might have been on TV, too."

She didn't care that the adults didn't seem to care about her adventure with Sheila, the aromas in the air were distracting her, too. The kitchen was humid with the steam from pots boiling on the stove. Her mother and grandmother usually fixed two side dishes and a dessert to take to her great grandmother's house for their Thanksgiving dinner. She could smell pungent collard greens boiling low, with bits of ham infusing them. Angelica peeked inside a pot full of string beans, bacon pieces mixed in helping the flavor become savory and distinct. There were two perfectly baked sweet potato pies cooling on the counter, awaiting their tin foil tents.

Angelica loved her grandmother's collards best of all, with pepper vinegar and Frank's Red Hot Sauce. The combination of flavors, coupled with the natural tang of the pot liquor gave people what Angelica called "the prickles" --an intense tingling sensation like tiny knife wielding fingers running over the scalp, from the crown to the edge of the forehead. The involuntary response was to tap the head with firm fingertips to calm it. Anything less would signal, rightly, that the dish was a dud.

Angelica sniffed at the spicy and sweet aroma of cloves punctuating their kitchen. "Grandma, is that a ham I smell?"

"Yes, ma'am. And, you know, I think we're going to have too much food! Oh, well…" her grandmother said.

"Dee," her grandfather answered, "there ain't no such-a-thing! We'll just have more left-overs for the week. Suits me just fine," he continued, giving his wife a pat on the small of her back.

Though Angelica's family could seem eccentric and playful to outsiders, the feast at Great Grandma Hattie's house could turn into a perilous undertaking. As usual there was perpetually dating Aunt Fannie, Uncle Ned, his wife Ella and their kids, Frankie and Lydia, and assorted other family and friends who seemed to show up each year. Last year, a friend of Ned's said his rotund wife was as big as a house with air conditioning and a two-car garage. The woman was completely mortified, but not enough to excuse herself from the table or the food.

The conversation was the usual--parents bragging on their children's accomplishments at school, complaints about work and co-workers, and the wagering on the "Big Game" that usually took place on the fourth Saturday in November, the rivalry between the University of Michigan Wolverines and Ohio State Buckeyes. However, the game had been played the prior Saturday, and U of M had won. So animated was the conversation it would seem the men sitting about Great Grandma Hattie's living room had somehow contributed to Ohio State's defeat.

Hattie Mason had many curios in her home and the most curious out of all the old timey furnishings and knick-knacks in her living room was a plushily upholstered ottoman of deep forest green, sitting innocently in the corner near the big Sylvania television. No matter the dearth of seating availability, the family knew not to sit on this piece of furniture. Angelica called it "The Impressionable Foot Stool."

Over the years, many a visitor had made the unfortunate mistake of sitting on the ottoman—an action never to be repeated a second time. It wasn't a matter of what happened when one came to rest on this deviant piece of furniture, but rather what happened when one got up. Once, Angelica witnessed a female cousin rise from the inviting little stool only to look down and see a perfect impression of her buttocks, vulva and vagina as if someone had x-rayed her from underneath the seat.

An old aunt saw the girl's horrified expression and said, "Oh, don't worry about it, chile. It happens to everybody," and proceeded to cackle hysterically.

Unwittingly, Aunt Fan's new man sat down on the seat before all were called in to dinner. There was a small stampede of female cousins and one of the boy cousins, over to the ottoman once he got up. There was the poor fellow's buttocks, scrotum and partial shaft of his penis engraved on the furniture for all to see. The witnesses gave Fannie looks of approval and praise for her good fortune, with one cousin pantomiming applause, as everyone went to the dining room to assemble for dinner. Fannie's date had not looked back to see any of the commotion surrounding his revelation.

For Angelica, the beginning of the meal was where either bravery or quick reflexes came into play because, truth be told, Great Grandma Hattie could not see as well as she once had, and it had been evident for a few years. Each year Angelica's grandmother, mother or other relatives would try to dissuade the old woman from preparing the Thanksgiving repast, but Hattie

Mason felt while there was breath in her body and momentum in her legs, why not have the family to the house for her good food? Last year, there were a couple of unwelcomed surprises attendant to Thanksgiving dinner: an earring in the stuffing, a button in the candied yams.

"My goodness, to-day! How did that get in there?" she'd exclaim.

"That's okay, Gran. No harm done," would come the response by an aiding and abetting adult.

Once, a few years ago, one of Angelica's teenaged relatives started to laugh and was smacked in the back of his head by his father, which instigated a small wave of laughter from a couple of the other kids, which resulted in backs of hands flying all around the table.

Angelica saw her great grandmother moving toward her with a pitcher of iced fruit punch in her tremulous hands. Angelica lifted her drinking glass slightly and tilted it toward her so she could make sure it was clean, but in the bottom of the glass was a small forest of dust. *The old lady hasn't washed these bad boys since last time*, she thought. Before Angelica could turn the glass over or say anything, the pink liquid waterfall was cascading into her glass. A gray flotilla of refuse bobbed atop the ice cubes. Angelica shot a wide-eyed look of panic across the table to her mother, who almost imperceptively shrugged her shoulders.

TWELVE

The Williams family was praying over their Thanksgiving feast with Ana and her children holding hands above the festive dinner table in their dining room. Once the prayers were over, Ana opened her eyes and looked at the empty seat across from her. This was where her husband Gabriel used to sit and where her oldest son, Danny, should be sitting now.

"It's okay, Mami," Ricky said gently.

"I'm okay, baby. Can you carve the turkey?" Ana asked, forcing a smile.

All the other children took their seats as Ricky came to the head of the table and picked up the Regal electric carving knife, an appliance that didn't see much action after Easter. The turkey sliced, the children and their mother passed their plates in assembly line fashion to Ricky, where he layered them with thick slices of meat and passed them back.

As 18-year-old Alecia poured milk for the little ones, they heard the side door open and close. Ana put her palm on her chest and turning toward the sound, strained to see if her prayer had been answered. Sure enough, there was Daniel standing to their right, filling the doorway of the kitchen.

"Hi, Danny!" Pilar and Eduardo shouted.

Ana smiled, relieved. Danny hugged his baby brother.

"You little blockhead," he said good-naturedly. "Hey, beautiful," he said, playfully pulling at one of Pilar's long, dark braids.

He waved at Alecia and Ricky, who were still standing and went straight over to his mother to give her a hug.

"Hi, Mama. Bet you thought I wasn't gonna make it, huh?"

Ana Williams shook her head, "No, son, I knew you would come."

Grinning as he took off his coat, Danny clapped his hands together and said, "Let's eat, y'all!"

Ana felt blessed to have all her children at her table once again. Danny looked so much like their father—tall and chocolate brown with curly black hair—that for Ana, it was sometimes almost too painful to look at him. Not just because of the physical resemblance to her late husband, but because of the life Danny had chosen for himself. She wasn't stupid, she knew her son was involved in some sort of shadowy, illegal activity.

"Lecia, where you going to school next year? You moving outta state?" Danny asked.

"Nope, I'm going to Marygrove, Wayne State or U of D."

"Dang, girl, don't you want to leave Detroit?"

"Nope. This is home and where I want to be. Now, I didn't say I was going to actually live at home, but who knows? I might. Or, I could get an apartment over off Dexter or down off West Grand Boulevard, close to everything."

Everyone in that room, including Ana, knew what a mama's girl Alecia was. Her school could be hours away and Alecia would still find a way back to hearth and home each day.

"What about you, big man?" Danny said, turning his attention to Enrique.

"Well, I'm not really thinking too much about college right now, but I probably should."

"Yeah, you probably should," Danny said, sarcastically.

Seeing her eldest child was becoming irritable, Ana interjected, "Danny, *mijo*, I wish you would go back to school, like the night school, and get your diploma."

"How I look going back to school? That's for squares. There's a reason I left."

"What's a square?" Eduardo asked no one in particular.

"You're a Dodo bird," Pilar answered.

"Guys, school is not for squares. It's cool and it's hip and it's how you get a good job so you can take care of your family and have a good life. It's important," Ricky said, defiantly looking from his younger siblings, straight into his brother's eyes.

"'Scuse the hell outta me—"

"Danny!" Ana exclaimed.

Ana Torres Williams simultaneously bucked her eyes at her younger children to get their attention and stabbed her finger in their direction as if to say, "Eat your food and don't listen to this conversation." Eduardo and Pilar hunched over their plates, studying the porcelain discs and the food piled on top of them as if they were a miniature universe. Each time their eyes flew into their plates, within seconds they'd bob back up like corks in a bathtub, to see what was going on at their Thanksgiving table.

"Sorry, Mama," Danny said, leaning back in his chair. "So, so, you Daddy now? Number one son is now man of the house?

You callin' the shots and makin' speeches, huh? Sitting up trying to make me look stupid—"

"No, I'm not. I thought we were just talking about our plans—"

"So only y'all got plans, now? What I think don't count? Hey, I know I'm a disappointment. Daddy wouldn't approve of me, but it's okay because the future is so bright for his favorite son. As long as he's alright, everything's great!"

"Stop it, Daniel. You will not ruin this meal. What is wrong with you? What crazy things you are saying! You need to apologize to your brother."

"No, Mama, that's okay," Ricky said, unsure of where the sudden vitriol was coming from. He loved his brother and always looked up to him until their father died and Danny began getting into constant trouble—truancy, petty theft, burglary.

"Sorry, little brother," Danny said, saluting his brother grandly with his right hand. He looked at Ana. "Sorry I could never be the golden child for you, Mama. Daddy could be so hard when he wanted to be. I couldn't do much that was right, could I?"

"I love you son, we all do. We are your *familia*," his mother pleaded, sensing Danny was about to run off into the night.

"I gotta go. I love y'all," Danny said, getting up from the table and grabbing his coat. He slammed the door behind him.

THIRTEEN

T he Friday after the holiday meant an additional day off from school. Angelica clutched her bunched-up sheet and blankets to her chin, trying to come into consciousness. Turning over, she slid her hand underneath her pillow and touched her radio. She had turned it off right before sleep had overtaken her the night before. There was a light rap on her bedroom door and her eyes fluttered open with a small sound.

"Come in," she cried out, still groggy.

"Hi, honey."

Angelica could now smell coffee and fried bacon coming from behind her mother's silhouette.

"Hi, Mama. Breakfast time?"

"Well, yes but I'm going to be out most of the day running errands. Do you want to come with me? We can have lunch out."

"Sure!" Angelica exclaimed.

"Okay, come and eat and then we'll get ready to go."

"Okay, Mama," Angelica replied, but Liz was already gone.

Angelica stretched, smiling. She always enjoyed shopping with her mother, though it didn't happen often. When she was a little girl, her mom would come riding down the street while she was playing with her friends, letting Angelica know she was running errands. Unfailingly, the girl would beg to come along. If Liz acquiesced and Angelica was on her bicycle, she'd ask a friend to drop it off on top of her porch for safekeeping until they returned home. Occasionally, her mom would say she could bring a friend, but only if they could go home quickly to get permission.

After the breakfast dishes were cleaned up, Angelica asked Liz if they might take Sheila along.

"I'll give you an hour to get showered and changed and see if Sheila's mom says she can go."

Angelica called Sheila's number from the kitchen, but the line was busy. Those "University" exchanges--86 and whatever numbers followed--could be tricky, and with a party line, her phone could be busy all day. A party line allowed multiple families in different residences to use the same phone line and privacy was virtually nonexistent. She hung up the phone planning to try again after she got dressed.

Angelica moved around the bathroom singing "Good Day Sunshine" by The Beatles. In January of 1964, Angelica had bought the "Meet The Beatles" album and fell madly in love with the four mop-top rockers from England. She was only 13 and though she'd never had a boyfriend, the songs from that record sung by those boys from Liverpool had her mind spinning and imagining what it must be like to be in love. She played the record front and back, repeatedly, entranced by every note and every word John, Paul, George and Ringo played and sung.

Sheila, perpetually estranged from anything fun or exciting, would come over to listen to the album on the Tanner's Sears Silvertone hi-fi in the living room. Sheila and Angelica would alternate "yeahs" on "It Won't Be Long," their heads popping up and down like the clown inside an overwound jack-in-the-box. Sheila had seen the film, "The Music Man" downtown at the Adams Theater with her mother, but she knew Mrs. Davis probably wouldn't approve of The Beatles' version of "Till There Was You," no matter how beautifully and sincerely Paul sang it. Paul McCartney made two colored girls in Detroit think he loved them and John Lennon made them wonder if he really meant it when he sang, "I Wanna Be Your Man."

About a month later on February 9, Sheila got her mother's permission to call Angelica on the phone to listen and watch *The Ed Sullivan Show* together. Practically every family in America observed the after-Sunday-dinner ritual of watching Ed's variety extravaganza on the CBS network. Negro families would call each other on the telephone or invite neighbors over to watch each time there was "Colored people on TV!" The rare occurrence of black people on television was a spectacle, a special event. Ed Sullivan's show seemed fearless in showcasing the talents of performers like Louis Armstrong, Moms Mabley, The Supremes, The Temptations, Nat King Cole and so many others.

A few minutes to 8 p.m., Sheila nervously made the call. Surely there were other families listening in on the party line, but the girls didn't care. Liz Tanner shook her head and rolled her eyes at Angelica standing in slack jawed rapture, starring at the TV set. The teenager would scream and bury her fist in her cheek every minute or so. Sheila on her end, was careful not to seem too thrilled, as her mother might declare The Beatles were "the devil" and make her hang up the telephone. The group played 5 songs, which was unprecedented, however, Mrs. Davis had had enough of her screaming, crying daughter by the third song, "She Loves You," and disconnected the call.

When Angelica was dressed, she tried her friend one last time with no luck. She put on her boots, coat, hat, and gloves.

"Mama, I'll be right back. I need to run over to Sheila's house. Her line is busy."

"Hurry up, girl. I want to get going," her mother warned.

It was a cold and bright morning that found Angelica trotting down the street toward the Davis household. She knew they were up and awake even though not much else was stirring in the neighborhood after the feasts that had taken place only the day before. Full and fat and lazy was how everything felt. Today was the day to watch football all day on the television while the soap operas, or "stories," as all the moms and grandmas called them, were sadly preempted.

Angelica bounced up the stairs to Sheila's house, sidestepping each icy impediment, and rang the doorbell. Surprisingly, it was Mr. Davis who answered the door.

"Um, hi Mr. Davis, is Sheila up?"

"Come on in. G'on in the kitchen. They in there," he said opening the screen door wide to let Angelica in and to scoop up his morning newspaper. It occurred to Angelica that this was the most Mr. Davis had ever said to her and she didn't know what to think about it.

Angelica walked back toward the kitchen catching the scent of something in the air that wasn't food. Hair? Burning hair? Sure enough, there was Sheila sitting in a chair in front of her mother, next to the stove. Mrs. Davis sat on a stool, higher up and behind her daughter. Angelica tried to appear nonchalant as Mrs. Davis performed the beautifying ritual that was unfamiliar to her. She felt like she was witnessing something primal and sacred. Mrs. Davis slapped a wad of white hair grease from the red Royal

Crown Hair Dressing container onto the back of her hand and deciphered Sheila's tangled locks with a big black Ace comb, clipping the unused hair with three bobby pins. She dipped two fingers into the grease, massaging the film slightly with the aid of her thumb and spread it onto the parted off section of Sheila's hair.

The heat in the kitchen was beyond cozy and Angelica was afraid for her friend, whose head seemed perilously close to the electrified eye of the kitchen stove. Smoke rose from the straightening comb on the stove and Mrs. Davis grabbed its wooden handle with one hand, picked up an old, folded dish towel with her other, and rubbed the hot comb within the rag as if to see how hot it was.

Mrs. Davis laid the steel comb into Sheila's puffy hair and a *ssssssss* filled the air like the sizzle from a frying steak as she drew the pressing comb through the hair, leaving straight strands in its wake. Amazing. The small wisp of smoke from the burning hair came up to Mrs. Davis' glasses and mingled with the smoke of her ever-present cigarette. Surely her glasses were so fogged up at this point, she could barely see enough to keep from burning brave ear tips or a defiant nape? The truth was she was not always successful, as Angelica bore witness to the wounds on her friend after she'd gotten her hair "done" by her half blind mother.

"Head down, girl. You know I gotta get that kitchen," Velma Davis was saying to her squirmy daughter.

Sheila's shoulders hitched up, involuntarily. The "kitchen," the delicate hair at the nape of the neck, was no real match for the hefty head of a steel straightening comb. Seemingly without fail, the tips of the comb's teeth would graze the skin as the person wielding it tried to get close to the roots of the hair. That millisecond of contact would cause the victim to jump up or forward, which might cause an even mightier scorching. Sheila's mother rapped her between the shoulders firmly with her bony knuckles.

"Relax or I'm gonna burn you. Relax!"

Reluctantly, Sheila's shoulders surrendered.

Did they even realize Angelica was standing amidst them? Angelica waited until the burning hot comb passed through Sheila's kitchen without incident before she spoke.

"Hi!,"

"Hi," Sheila replied, in a nasally voice.

"Hi, Angelica. What brings you over our way?" Mrs. Davis asked. "Our" sounded like "ow-vah."

"My mother has some errands to run today and I wanted to see if Sheila wanted to come."

"Where y'all goin'?" Mrs. Davis inquired.

"I think we're going to Detroit Edison for new light bulbs and to Michigan Bell to get a new telephone. We might go out to Northland, too. I tried to call, but your line is busy."

Velma Davis reached over to the counter to stab out her cigarette in a clear ashtray.

"Davis!" she called out to her husband. "See if the phone is off the hook!"

Sheila took this momentary respite to look up at her friend. Her eyes were red and puffy, a tendril of snot was creeping out of one nostril.

"I think I got a cold, Angelica. I probably can't—"

"Naw, she can't go out. She sick. I'mma finish this hair and then I'm gonna heat up some Vernors and let her sip that before she lays down," Mrs. Davis said, again heating up the straightening comb on the stove. "Maybe next time."

"Okay, I'll see you at school, Monday. Hope you feel better."

"Bye," said Sheila, sniffling.

On her way back to the house, Angelica wondered why she'd never seen her own mother, whose hair texture was similar to Sheila's, press her hair? Maybe it was because Liz got her hair done at the beauty parlor every other week and during the interim, wore cute wigs and falls like Diana Ross of The Supremes. Even Angelica's grandmother wore a wig, while Aunt Fan wore her hair in a natural—tight little coils that could be combed with a steel pronged afro pick.

Angelica and Liz Tanner had come from the Edison store with a brown paper shopping bag full of new light bulbs after trading in the ones that had burned out. They now found themselves in the telephone showroom of Michigan Bell. The iconic building housing the phone company had a giant lighted Yellow Pages on top of it with a newfangled digital time display, which could be seen from the John C. Lodge freeway. This was the place people went to rent a telephone.

"Why do we need a new phone? Is one of 'em broken?"

They had a telephone in the kitchen and Liz had one in her bedroom.

"Nope. I decided to get you a phone for your room. You're a teenager and you're pretty responsible, so—"

"Thanks, Mama! Wow! Can I get a pink princess phone with the push buttons? PLEASE!" Angelica implored.

"Maybe. I need to see how much it is first."

Liz loved seeing her daughter with a smile on her face and she felt guilty that she seemed to have the power to take that smile away so easily. Liz ordered the pink princess phone with the novelty of push button dialing and illuminated numbers. Michigan Bell would have to come to the house to install the wiring and the phone.

"Looks like you got the fanciest phone in the house, girl!"

"Thanks, Mama. I love it and I love you!" Angelica said, hugging her mother.

Liz blinked back the tears that threatened her eyes. Why was it so amazing that her daughter loved her? These outpourings of emotion from Angelica never failed to surprise Liz, but she was grateful nonetheless.

After a while, the Tanner women ended up in Southfield at Northland Center, once the world's largest shopping center. This was the suburbs and Liz felt she was cheating on downtown and the city of Detroit by being out there. She couldn't have known that Detroit and just about every major city in the U.S. would find their once vibrant downtowns abandoned, shuttered, broken and struggling within 10 years.

They stopped into Himelhoch's, Winkleman's and Bakers Shoes, as well as J.L. Hudson, picking up some stylish threads for mother and daughter. Lunch was at Elias Brother's Big Boy and even though the restaurant, home of the famous Big Boy double decker hamburger, had car service where the waitresses came outside to take food orders, they went inside. Liz always felt more sophisticated eating in a booth and hot fudge cake, their favorite, was the capper to their afternoon. The silky hot fudge sauce blanketing what amounted to a bisected brownie with vanilla ice cream in the center, topped in a whipped cream and cherry hat, felt so decadent. Angelica was chattering away about why Sheila could not come with them and that Mr. Davis had probably been the culprit who left the phone off the hook, sparking Velma's smoky wrath. They laughed, uproariously.

"Does anybody know Mr. Davis's name? His first name? I swear I don't know it," Liz chuckled.

"Nobody knows. Even Mrs. Davis calls him by his last name," Angelica said, barely finishing her sentence before busting into guffaws again.

Then out of nowhere, she asked, "What's my father's last name, again?"

The question hung in the air frozen and shiny and sharp like an icicle on the end of an awning. And just like that, the dark clouds began to gather across Liz Tanner's brow. She shook her head rapidly from side to side.

"Angelica, why do you always ask me stuff like that?"

Angelica immediately regretted turning a rare lighthearted moment with her mother into a dirge of unbidden reflection. Truthfully, she didn't always ask about her father as Angelica made a conscious point of seldom ever asking about the man. She decided long ago that she would rather forgo small but significant details, pictures or stories about the other human being responsible for her bouncing into the world, than see the pain that spread across Liz's face like a mask when she spoke of her Angelo.

"Smith. His last name was Smith. That's a pretty easy name to remember, but for some reason, you can't seem to manage it. Sorry, I don't have any pictures, either. We never got around to it, okay?"

Liz took a gulp from her glass of water. The cloyingly sweet dessert needed a small flush of water to level out the palate. Soon,

Liz was going on about The Ice Capades coming to Olympia Stadium and that they should go. The Olympia was the home of the Detroit Red Wings hockey team and the site of great championship boxing like the defeat of Sugar Ray Robinson at the hands of Jake La Motta. Some folks called the venue the Old Red Barn because of the shape of its red brick façade and it had once been the largest indoor skating rink in the U.S. Angelica harrumphed silently because she had not been allowed to see The Beatles two years earlier, the day after Labor Day ("It's the first day of school. Forget it!"), nor this past summer at the Olympia. The stinking Ice Capades could not compare to John, Paul, George and Ringo!

And yes, she could remember her father's name. Easily. She sometimes just wanted to hear it spoken aloud. Wasn't that the best way to honor the fallen? It didn't seem right that Liz wanted to forget him so completely. Angelica always wondered though, why a white man with a fancy first name would have such a plain last name? Only colored people did that.

FOURTEEN

Elizabeth Tanner, Angelica's mother, was 35 years old with a keen nose, thin lips, luminous brown eyes and deep bittersweet chocolate brown skin. Her mother Delores was slightly disturbed that her baby daughter was so dark, seemingly the darkest child born as far back as anyone could remember. Yes, Liz was a striking beauty, but Delores secretly blamed her husband Henry's bloodline for cursing their poor child with skin the color of a roasted coffee bean. Their other two children, Ned and Fannie, were of medium brown complexion. Dee feared Liz would have a harder life because of the hue of her skin and there was nothing she could do about it.

Liz first met Angelica's father when they were both children playing at his family's home where her mother worked as a domestic. Delores Tanner had been the housekeeper for the Santori family for over 20 years and Hank Tanner was the handy man who kept both the Santori household and business running like a top. Several years went by and they didn't meet again until Liz was 18 and Angelo was a 21-year-old college student. Angelo fancied himself a jazz trumpeter and sometimes sat in with the Negro bands in his father's nightclub in Black Bottom.

Liz had been hired as a bar maid, trying to earn money for college to become a teacher like her grandmother. That was what good colored girls aspired to and her mother certainly wanted her to remain a good colored girl. But Liz discovered she could sing, and she was soon soloing at church. One night as Angelo played with the band, the leader of the group asked Liz to come up and, "Sing a little taste." That night, singing "Candy" and "Stardust," the beautiful brown girl mesmerized the young horn player.

During a break, they shared a cigarette out in the alley behind the club. Liz thought Angelo was so striking with his thick black hair, navy blue eyes and dimpled smile. He was a different kind of white man, it seemed to her. He knew how to talk like a hep cat and could 'sho nuff blow that horn. He was comfortable around colored people and it showed.

Angelo told Liz she should forget about becoming a school teacher and become a singer instead. She was flattered that he'd say such a thing since nobody in her family had ever encouraged her or complimented her outside of telling her to keep singing for the Lord. They acted as if they'd been struck deaf when she casually sang anything but gospel music.

"But, I'm not sure how good them cigarettes are for your pipes," Angelo said.

Liz flicked the ash from the end of the butt, defiantly.

"I'm a big girl and I do what I want. Plus, if I don't go back to teacher's college? I won't have to worry about my voice. My mother will strangle me and that'll be the end of that," Liz said, chuckling and taking another quick puff of her Pall Mall before throwing it to the pavement and crushing it under her shoe. "I gotta get back to the bar."

"See you later, Alligator," Angelo said, smiling.

"After while, Crocodile," she chimed, practically floating as she turned toward the back door to Nick's. *Gee whiz, he's fine!* Liz thought. *We're definitely not kids anymore.*

Back inside, Angelo played another set while Liz cleaned up the bar in preparation for closing. When he saw she was about to leave, Angelo rushed to the door and asked if he could walk her to the street car.

"I'll be back, Pop," he said to his dad, who had been watching the exchange with narrowed eyes.

Mr. Santori shook his head as the door closed behind his son and muttered something in Italian.

The neighborhood could be rough, especially at night. They were being stared at as they made their way down John R. The couple walked in silence for some time and when they got to the corner of Canfield, Angelo pulled Liz into the darkness of a storefront doorway, drew her close and kissed her fully and passionately on the lips.

"Let them stare. I don't care. Do you?" he asked.

She was almost breathless, her head spinning.

"N-n-no," she stammered barely audible above the music coming from the Flame Show Bar across the street.

Angelo slowly, reluctantly let her go as they drifted back onto the avenue, giddy, shocked, and a little bit scared of what each might be thinking about the other, their minds racing into a wall of taboos at full speed.

Angelo and Liz began to meet secretly throughout the summer and when they each came home from school for Thanksgiving and Christmas. They spent time together on the Northwest side of Detroit where no one knew them, and they wouldn't get hassled. A favorite spot was Baker's Keyboard Lounge on Livernois, where the entertainment was top notch, and everyone was friendly and minded their own business. Mr. Santori was happy Liz's job ended when she went back to school, and he would have to find a way to tell Delores that he didn't need Liz at the bar anymore. Nicholas Santori could not have his son involved with a colored girl, the daughter of his housekeeper, no less. It's not like they're still little kids. *Hell, what if she gets knocked up?* He couldn't bear the thought.

During Christmas vacation in 1950, Elizabeth Tanner became pregnant. She kept it a secret from her friends and classmates by wearing loose fitting clothes and though Liz remained in college in Virginia, by spring she had begun to show and when she came home for summer vacation she knew she would not make it back to school in the fall. She didn't know that she would never go back.

Her shocked and disappointed parents, after weeks of discussion, finally told the Santoris. Their reaction was to fire Delores and Hank Tanner and forbid the young couple to see each other. Mrs. Tanner, feeling disgraced and embarrassed, told her daughter no self-respecting colored man would want her now. Ironically, the Santoris told their son no Italian girl from a good Catholic family would want him. Dee Tanner fought bitterly with Liz about putting the child up for adoption before she was born.

"You always cared about those white folks and their lives and their kids way more than you ever did us! You should be happy! Your favorite white folks are part of our family forever, aren't they?!" Liz screamed at her mother.

Angelo was forbidden to contact Liz and at first, he argued defiantly against his parents and their objections, he was an adult, after all. Liz would be scared and wondering where he was, he implored. But his family made him look at things realistically and soon it became the norm for him not to talk to her and eventually, not to think about her. Angelo knew he had no future with a Negro for a wife. He didn't want to think of it like that,

111

but it was the truth—in black and white. He prayed she would give their baby up for adoption as he knew his parents would never have anything to do with it.

Liz Tanner gave birth to a beautiful, blue eyed, blond haired baby girl and the hospital was a-buzz. Could this baby be the child of the dark skinned colored woman? There were eye witnesses who'd seen the birth and were verifying the story to whoever would listen. Each feeding and each visit between mother and child began with a full floor debate and cross check before the disbelieving nurse on duty would roll the Isolette into Liz's room.

Liz was fascinated by her tiny daughter and felt blessed that God had gifted her so. She was so sweet and smelled so good, Liz would just sit and stare at her baby girl.

When Angelica was about 8, her mother took her to see the film "Imitation of Life," starring Lana Turner and Juanita Moore. This was a complex tale about a black woman giving birth to a little girl who looked white and all the heartaches of life that ensnared them because of it. Angelica was completely distraught by the end of the movie, crying hysterically. She seemed to understand the underpinnings of the story and related them to herself and her darker skinned mother.

She clutched at Liz crying, "I'll never leave you, Mommy," over and over again.

FIFTEEN

After bringing shame to her family and her parents losing their jobs with the Santoris, the next insult came at the birth of baby Angelica. Liz was admitted to Florence Nightingale Maternity Hospital, a hospital associated with a home for unwed mothers, though Liz had escaped that indignity by remaining at home with her parents. She was sedated for the baby's delivery, and when she awoke, Liz was anxious to see her child.

The nurse fetched a wheelchair from the hallway and eased Liz into it. Lillian Bankhead had pale skin under heavily rouged cheeks and teased strawberry blonde hair with her nurse's cap deserted in the middle of it like a stiff white island. She ferried Liz to the nursery where there was row upon row of small bassinettes, about 20, all with their tiny occupants safely ensconced in various states of wakefulness. The two nurses on the other side of the glass silently became attentive and aware of Liz and Lillian.

One of the nurses came to the window and asked to see Liz's wrist band with her name on it to match it to the one the baby wore on its foot. Barely glancing at the full name displayed on Liz's band, the nurse turned around and looked toward the two little brown babies in the nursery. She scooped up one of the babies gingerly and brought it to the window. Liz Tanner had not been awake to witness the birth of her daughter, but she was fairly certain that the baby she was looking at was not hers.

Though she was still weak and a bit groggy, she asked her nurse, "Did she check the baby's band? The last name is Tanner. I don't think that's my baby."

Nurse Lillian left Liz's side and went into the nursery and after briefly speaking with the nurse holding the baby, she walked over to the other lone black infant. She unwrapped the swaddle blanket from the baby and he began to cry. The nurse's brow furrowed deeply as she returned the receiving blanket to the baby's body. She had checked the chart when she first entered Liz's room and knew a baby girl, last name of Tanner, had been born just hours earlier. But clearly, this was a little colored boy! Where was the baby?

Liz began to get agitated and knocked on the window, putting her hands in the air as if to say, "Where is my damn baby?" Lillian Bankhead put up her hand silently as if to ask Liz for patience, and soon the three nurses were in animated conversation behind the glass. More than four minutes passed as Elizabeth Tanner began to grow angry. She reached up to rap sharply on the glass with her knuckles. The women peered out at her in simultaneous frustration, which made Liz even madder.

"I want to see my baby, please. Can I please see my little girl?" she asked loudly, her voice bouncing off the green tiles of the hallway walls.

Nurse Bankhead rushed out of the nursery and appeared at her side as if she'd flown there.

"Now, now. You just hold on, Miss. The nurses are trying to locate your baby. Give them a minute or two," her hand pressing Liz down further into the wheelchair.

Like a book opened to a memorized passage, Liz didn't have to look at the women to read her situation. They were searching for a "colored" baby with dark skin like hers. She wished she'd waited for her mother or father to come with her. She wanted to shout at the nurses for hurting her feelings, for making assumptions, for ruining a moment that would only happen once—seeing her newborn's face for the first time. Liz was starting to perspire, her loose hospital gown sticking to her frame as she began to feel the sting of the stiches in her perineum through the thick pad between her legs.

She turned to the nurse now circling in front of her, all thought of helping the new mother seemingly abandoned.

"Please, I just want to see my baby. Please! She's got to be in there!"

"Well, let's get you back to your room and get you settled down. We will bring the baby to you there," Nurse Lillian said, now back at the helm of the wheelchair, trying to pull Liz backward to wheel her away.

Liz put one of her shod feet to the floor to impede the chair's progress. She felt a gush of blood push itself into her thick maternity pad. She was getting lightheaded.

"Now hold on, Miss. Are you refusing to return to your room? Are you trying to give me a hard time? I'm not going to have this, girl," the nurse said as if she'd already answered each question herself.

Nurse Bankhead let go of the handles of the wheelchair and rushed to the shiny black phone at the nurse's station. She picked up the receiver and dialed deliberately.

"Yes, I need help with a patient on Ward 3, Southwest corner, Maternity," she said in a clipped cadence, staring at a confused Liz.

Within minutes of hanging up the telephone, the elevator doors parted and two brawny orderlies, colored fellows, came walking quickly toward the women.

"Please take her back to her room, room 319, and put her in restraints. The patient has become violent."

The young men stared at the nurse.

"It's for her own safety. She's acting in a threatening manner and I won't stand for that. Go on, now," she said dismissively.

The next thing Liz knew she was being tied to her bed in four-point restraints, in terrible pain with her flesh awakening from surgery. As she lay there sobbing, her ears full of her own tears, she felt the blood slowly creeping, flowing up her butt crack and on to her back. She shouldn't have been lying flat, she knew she should be sitting up to keep the blood directed down between her legs and onto the pad. Why was this happening? Where was her baby? The nurse appeared to give her an injection in her upper arm and Liz drifted off into unconsciousness. Liz dreamed of voices whispering, rising in anger and then hushed again. Was that her mother? Was she there?

"Lord God in heaven, Hank, they've got her trussed up like a Christmas goose! What did she do to make them angry enough to do this? What did she do?"

"Why does it have to be her fault or somethin' she did, Dee? These crackers don't give a damn if you just had a baby. You think that means anything to them? Any excuse will do 'cause that's how they operate. They do it 'cause they goddamn can!"

"Henry Tanner, if you don't watch your mouth in here! Liz done got herself in this situation probably because of that smart mouth of hers, and now here you go—"

"Look, I don't give a damn what she said or did, they need to get this shit off my daughter." He looked around the room. "I need a cigarette," he said, running his hand through his hair. "I guess you ain't gonna ever forgive this girl, are you?" Hank said suddenly, looking in Dee's eyes.

"Honey, this is neither the time nor the place. I'm just as frustrated as you are. I didn't mean to say it's Liz's fault she's laying here like this. I—"

"Yes, you did," Henry whispered, harshly.

Delores was shamed into silence knowing her husband was right and before she could speak again, Liz's eyes fluttered to life. The nurse came in and Liz could hear her father talking and asking that she be taken out of restraints and cleaned up. Delores was standing next to the bed having just refolded the sheet over her daughter laying in a blossom of blood. Noticing that Liz had awoken, the older woman touched her cheek.

"Hi, honey. What happened?"

Liz had no idea how long she'd been asleep, but her stitches were screaming in pain and her chest felt like someone was sitting on it. Her breasts were heavy with colostrum for her baby.

"Oh, mama, they won't let me see my baby! Where is she? Why am I tied up?" she said as she began to cry.

Her dad, now standing next to her mother, was leaning over her trying to loosen one of the leather bindings that held her wrists.

"Calm down, baby. They're coming to take this off you and they're going to clean you up," he said. "This is a disgrace and you know it," he said to his wife. He was practically in tears himself.

Mrs. Tanner intervened saying, "After they bathe you, we'll get the baby in here, okay? It's alright, it's alright," she said, watching her daughter's lips tremble as she tried to speak again. Delores stroked Liz's forehead, mixing the perspiration into her unkempt hair.

A nurse's aide came in with a basin, wash cloths and a bar of Dial soap.

"I'm sorry, but if you could step out?" she asked.

Liz's parents had barely moved away from the bed before the aide jerked the curtain on the steel frame above the bed and drew it around in a semi-circle for privacy. Mr. and Mrs. Tanner went down the hall in silence, hoping to see their grandchild, wishing they hadn't left Liz earlier, right after the baby came. But, they had to go to work and Liz was still drugged and sleeping, wasn't she? Dee wondered if there was no end to the well of humiliation and pain her daughter seemed to tap into. Hank fantasized about punching in each white face staring at him, no matter what their reasons. These were still dangerous times for a Negro man and he knew he had to comport himself in a manner that was at odds with his soul.

SIXTEEN

D ecember 1966 came in with snow on the ground, but a week later it was in the mid 60's instead of the usual mid 30's. Though mothers tried valiantly to swathe their kids in buttoned coats, woolen hats, scarves and gloves, the spring like clime could not be ignored. It seemed everyone got sick at John Francis Dodge High School, causing a run on Vernors Ginger Ale at Farmer Jack and the A&P.

By mid-December winter and everything attendant to it was in full swing. Cars went preternaturally slower navigating the snow and slush while people on foot walked faster, pushed along by a hawkish wind. It was 5:30 p.m. and already dark outside with the streetlights casting gentle pools of light onto the crusty snow. Angelica was rushing around her kitchen getting out the Crisco and her mother's cast iron skillet. It was Friday and she'd agreed to cook dinner: fried fish, rice and left-over collard greens.

She hated having to scale the fish and cut off their heads and tails, to say nothing of digging out the tiny innards. Once she swore she'd encountered a full miniature bladder inside a fish and it was awful. Angelica was never happy when their neighbor shared his first catch of the season with them. She frowned looking at her watch, figuring she had about half an hour to get dinner prepared since Liz was just upstairs visiting her parents. Like most homes on the Northwest side of Detroit, theirs was a two-family flat or duplex, and their extended family lived on the upper level.

The doorbell rang and Angelica put her fillet knife on the counter. She was sure they weren't expecting company even though it wasn't late. Quickly washing her hands with warm water after a squirt of Joy dishwashing soap, she grabbed a nubby dish towel as she walked to the vestibule. She opened the door and found Ricky Williams standing there with his little brother and sister. He looked like an apparition or an angel, backlit by the street lights, his cherubim below him. Angelica smiled so broadly, she wasn't sure if she could still hear. It was as if the wattage of her grin created a static white noise that filled her ears.

Ricky and his small charges were soon seated in her living room and he was asking if she might want to go downtown to Hudson's to see the Christmas displays in the store's dozens of windows. He didn't mention that his girlfriend Rita had backed out of the excursion at the last minute, having gotten into trouble when she got home from school. Yes, she was grounded for the entire weekend, and no, it wouldn't be polite to mention that.

"Sure, I'd love to go. Let me go change right quick," she said.

She wanted to inquire about RiRi's whereabouts but thought better of it. It just wouldn't seem cool and well, *I'm the one he asked to go with him. Not her*," she thought. Angelica changed into wool slacks and a matching sweater. She grabbed her Sunday coat and hat because they were dressy and befitting a visit to J.L. Hudson's downtown.

"Ready," she cried, standing in the vestibule where her snow boots were parked. "Let go!"

On the way to the bus stop, Angelica realized she hadn't eaten and what's more, she hadn't prepared her mother's dinner. Liz would be mad, but she didn't care. Eduardo and Pilar had insisted on going on the bus even though their brother's car was parked right in front of Angelica's house. To those youngsters, this night was full of adventure and wonder and they weren't going to be denied their full measure, which included riding a city bus downtown with some of Detroit's ne'er-do-wells.

Everyone, including Angelica and Enrique, thought J.L. Hudson's department store in downtown Detroit was the most massively magnificent place in the world and quite possibly, the center of the shopping universe. It was a 27-story microcosm of consumerism with every good and service imaginable. It was almost as if it sprang from the mind of a fanciful child, especially at Christmastime. The dozens of street level windows featured animatronic holiday and toy land scenes: trains, cars, planes, sleighs, lighted Christmas trees, Santa Claus, stuffed animals, candy canes, gingerbread houses, children by the fireplace, storybook and fairytale characters, all coming to life behind the glass. Enrique, Angelica, Eduardo and Pilar could barely contain their excitement as they "oohed" and "aahed" at each winter fantasy moving about silently inside their crystal-clear confinement, each one more spectacular than the next.

After about an hour of sightseeing, Eduardo whimpered, "I'm cold," tamping his small boots in the snow.

"And I'm hungry," said Pilar. "Can we get a treat?"

Out of the mouths of babes, thought Angelica. She was thankful her heavy coat muffled the reverberating sounds of her rumbling stomach. Enrique looked at the kids and then to Angelica.

"You wanna get something?"

"Sure. I actually didn't eat dinner--"

"Dang, girl, why didn't you tell me? These guys already ate before we got to your house. Where do you want to go?"

Before Angelica could answer, "Sanders! Sanders!" the children chanted in unison.

"Well, they're closed, and I don't think Angelica wants cake for dinner."

Sanders Bakery had the best caramel cupcakes that anyone had ever tasted. They were like eating a Kraft caramel with cake underneath it. The mere thought of it made Angelica's stomach concur loud enough to be heard in the few seconds of silence between them. Enrique and his siblings laughed, knowingly.

"Sorry," Angelica said with a grin. "Let's go to Cunningham's. They can have a sundae and I'll have a hamburger and some French fries," Angelica suggested.

Cunningham Drug had a soda fountain that served tasty and quick meals inside their light green and white art deco stores. Enrique teased Angelica that her food couldn't possibly taste as good, or better than the burgers he served at the Shake 'n Spin.

"How would I know?" she said between bites of her meal. "How many times have you seen me in that place?" she asked, not quite knowing the answer herself, but knowing she'd be flattered that he even noticed.

"Angelica, I know I've seen you and Sheila in there a few times 'cause I waited on y'all."

"Man, I don't be coming in there that much. Your fan club is so big, I can't get any records played or a hamburger served," Angelica teased.

Ricky laughed, "Fan club, huh? You should be a comedian!"

They looked at one another and cracked up laughing. Angelica almost choked on her food, which made both of them laugh even more.

"A lot of boys at school like you, Angelica. I bet you already knew that."

"No, I don't know that. Boys seem to want to get my attention by throwing something at me or being obnoxious. Why is that? What's wrong with y'all?" she asked, half-jokingly.

"Beats me. It seems kinda childish. I don't do things like that," Ricky said, realizing the awkward inference. Then quickly, "Carlton likes you."

"I used to actually like that creep. I guess you could say I had a crush on him a while back, but I think I told you how standoffish he can be. Yuck."

Carlton had confided to Ricky about getting sick after Angelica made him lunch that time, leaving out the graphic details and making it look like he had thrown up. Ricky decided he wouldn't mention it to Angelica.

"Where's your girlfriend? Why isn't she here instead of me?" Angelica didn't care if she sounded confrontational. She deserved an answer from this boy.

"Rita's a Senior and she's got a lot to do before she goes off to college. Sometimes it's just hard to get together."

Angelica wondered if they had sex. *Yeah, they probably do. You'd better stop thinking about that.*

"You two are awfully quiet. What gives?" Ricky said to his siblings.

"Nothing. We're almost done," Pilar said.

"Yeah, and we like her. We decided," Eduardo announced.

Angelica laughed. "It's probably 'cause I gave 'em candy."

"Yeah, that too," said Eduardo, amidst the laughter.

123

"Hudson's is open for another hour and I don't think these two have seen Santa yet," Ricky said.

"Yay! Santa!" the two youngsters exclaimed.

"Can we go tonight?"

"Yes, Pi-pi, we can go over there now.

The 12th floor of J.L. Hudson was Toyland and it was a glorious and breathtaking Christmas fantasy come to life. It was surely as if they had, by some miracle, become miniatures and had stepped inside a scene from the windows downstairs. The ceiling was a twinkling night sky of a thousand tiny lights and a steam train rode the rails high above their heads. There must have been two dozen decorated Christmas trees present, each trying to literally outshine the other. There were real elves, at least they looked the part, helping to keep the children flowing through the line to sit on Santa's lap inside his great castle where he perched on a red velvet throne.

Enrique checked his billfold to make sure he had enough money to purchase a picture of the kids with Santa. His mother would squeal with delight when she saw her adorable children in such a beautiful place.

"Wow," cried Pilar.

"I wish we could live here," exclaimed Eduardo.

Bells were brightly ringing as festive Christmas music played through speakers nestled into alcoves inside the walls. The children had a lot to tell Santa, careful to preface their requests with how good they had been throughout the year.

By the time the bus came down Woodward Avenue to their bus stop, the children were exhausted from the enormity of their evening and practically asleep on their feet, swaying gently in the frigid night air. Snow began to fall lightly, dusting their wool caps like wedding day rice. Eduardo had his arms around Angelica's waist and was snuggled against her coat, while Enrique had his little sister wrapped within his arms. Angelica and Enrique smiled at one another, acknowledging the unforgettable amusements of the now silent night.

SEVENTEEN

The big baby blue Cadillac, a 1965 Coupe De Ville, slid into the parking lot at 20510 Livernois, snow and ice crunching underneath its white wall tires. The man driving turned off the ignition and handed the keys to the woman in the passenger seat who enclosed them in her clutch purse with a snap.

He ran three fingers across the brim of his black Borsalino and asked the woman without looking at her, "How I look?"

"Outta sight, Daddy," she purred.

He opened his car door, got out and shut it with a heavy *thunk* before walking over to the passenger side. The man opened the door for the woman to step out into the night, all the while looking slowly and vigilantly at his surroundings.

They walked inside Baker's Keyboard Lounge not getting more than a few feet before the band went from playing "Satin Doll" to "Don't Mess With Bill," by the Marvelettes. This happened regularly whether he was stepping into Baker's or Phelps Lounge on the North End. Heads and hands flew up in greeting to Bill Williams as he quickly surveyed the subdued opulence and sultry vibe of the dimly lit room. The bass line of the song, made indelible by the nimble fingers of Motown's James Jamerson, seemed to add even more rhythm to Bill's swaggering gait.

126

The way a pimp walked was important because it showed that he was a part of a rarefied fraternity and he wasn't a "square." As a matter of fact, it wasn't called walking, it was called *pimpin'*.

Sometimes the walk was accompanied by the use of an ornate cane. Novices sometimes called a cane a pimping stick, but that was not accurate. Pimping sticks were wire hangers twisted together to form an apparatus with which to beat a whore for her indiscretions. Though if one did not have time to make the pimping sticks, or better yet, have the whore do it, the ambulatory assistant, a cane, could be pressed into service to keep a bitch in line.

Bill felt no pimp worth his shark skin suit would hit a ho with wire hangers as they left terrible and sometimes permanent scars. Yet, many of his peers employed this old school method to punish their hos. Bill prided himself on his bitches looking their best, after all, they were a reflection of him, were they not? If Bill had to beat one of his girls, he did it the old fashioned, familial way—with his big, black leather belt, always careful not to hit the flesh with the buckle, which could break the skin. This did the trick psychologically as it put his girls in the mindset that they had disappointed their Daddy, and they never, ever wanted to do that.

Bill and Mary, his companion, arrived at their usual booth after checking their hats and coats, to find a man and woman already seated. The man rose to give Bill some skin as Mary slid in next to the blonde white girl sitting there. The men sat on either side of the women like bookends.

The cocktail waitress appeared as if she'd materialized from a mere thought of thirst, smiling at the handsome men in front of her. She informally surveyed the face of the black woman sitting at the table and lost her composure. Black Mary, as she was known, stared at the young waitress with a look so cold, the girl visibly shuddered as if hit by an arctic blast. She instinctively looked toward the front door expecting it to be ajar.

"Hi, Sweetness. Y'all's best champagne for the ladies and we'll have Jack Daniels and Coca Cola," Bill said with a slight extension of his left arm indicating Smoke was included in the "we."

"Right away, Mr. Williams," the waitress said, rushing away.

Black Mary gave a sidelong look to the blonde sitting next to her. Martha giggled into her shoulder. Getting to go on a real date with their Daddies only happened once a season and this was their Christmastime night on the town.

Black Mary was Bill's "bottom bitch," his number one ho. She was part of his "Lucky 7," which included 6 other women— Chan (pronounced *Shawn*), Eva, Carol, Denise, Sadie and Terri. Mary acquired her name when she first entered Bill's stable because there was a white girl named Mary as well. Black Mary was a 25-year-old bittersweet chocolate beauty with dark eyes that sparkled like black diamonds. She was petite with small breasts and a large butt and wore her hair in a short "natural" or afro style but would still rock a nice wig on occasion.

Mary had been with Bill 7 years, an exception to his "five years and out" rule. No longer having to work the track, she helped run his two houses, keeping his business and his hos straight. The other wives-in-law respected her position and seldom did a bitch try to usurp her authority with Bill. The occasional ho who was so ill-advisedly reckless and bold paid a terrible price, as Black Mary would beat that bitch with no mercy while Bill watched. Mary had no sympathy for ungrateful hos who had been given a wonderful life by Bill Williams. Her philosophy was, "Be grateful or be gone, bitch!" She was completely loyal to her man and he trusted her with his livelihood.

On a night like this when there was no business being handled, Bill and Smoke were just two friends out with their girls. Bill wasn't looking to add to his stable, so he had no proposals for any ho who might be eyeing him that night. Mary and Martha both knew the code and only looked at one another and their men, respectively.

Rodney "Smoke" Peterson was the closest thing to a friend Bill Williams had. They had known each other since elementary school, but they didn't become close until both discovered the pimp game. Smoke was the only man Bill trusted and the same could be said for Smoke. Loyalty meant a lot to Bill and he liked the fact that Smoke always told him the truth, whether he wanted to hear it or not.

Smoke was the polar opposite of Bill in many ways, beginning with the physical. The powerfully built Smoke Peterson was only 5 feet 8 inches tall to Bill's towering 6'-2" frame. His dark skin, the envy of many a woman and man, was so smooth it appeared to be poreless, while he bore no hair on his face, nor on his head. No process or *conk* could make his hair straight enough to suit him, or provide even a reasonable facsimile of his main man Bill's, so why bother? Smoke found he didn't need hair to attract the ladies, because, well, he was fine.

Watching the reactions of women and men to seeing Bill and Smoke together, never got old. A double take on double time pimping fine and who could resist? Bill Williams was slender and muscular, with a golden caste to his skin showcasing fine features. He was a "high yellow" Creole and looked damn near white. He wore his thick, straight black hair combed into a pompadour with a curl in the front like the movie star Tony Curtis.

Bill and Smoke parted ways occasionally on their pimping philosophy, yet they respected one another's game. Smoke knew pimping was supposed to be a non-contact sport between men. Generally, no pimp was going to beat up or kill another pimp over a ho, just one of the unwritten rules of the game. Smoke wouldn't fight another pimp, but he would beat a bitch's ass.

Bill, on the other hand, seldom beat his hos because he believed brutality did not keep a bitch loyal. Security, safety and love, did that. Love for the game, love for the power they had over their johns, and most especially, love for their man. Bill's stable would do anything for him. He knew the older players would laugh him out of the game if they discovered the intricacies of Bill's relationships with his whores, but Bill also knew what worked for him. And yes, he had killed for a ho, a taboo amongst players. It only happened once, but that was more than enough.

Black people tended to be notoriously and naturally suspicious and superstitious, believing a lot of things that may or may not be fact. This predilection helped solidify Bill's rep, so he never had to defend one of his bitches to that extent again. Danger always threatened when Bill Williams was around, though based on something very few people were actual witness to. His legend was carried like a leaf on the wind and he knew it would make a nigga think twice before fucking with him.

When it came to the women in their stables, Smoke had 5 to 8 girls at a time, but he had a hard time keeping them loyal. Bill always had his 7, and he had a challenge getting rid of them, making retirement mandatory after five years. This edict allowed new blood to come in, assuming he didn't lose one of his hos to the streets. Smoke and Bill had a friendly rivalry but did not knock each other's hustle or steal each other's property.

Even though Martha was Smoke's bottom bitch, he seemed to have nothing but headaches from his hos. The problem was, as far as Bill could tell, the girls didn't respect Martha and most of his bitches were white!

"Ain't that a bitch? I don't know how to fix this shit, man," Smoke would complain.

"Nigga, you need to find a colored girl and move her in, move her up, and move Martha's ass out. She need to be back on the track. Them 'lil white girls you got runnin' around, they gon' be scared of that black one. They gon' mind her ass, too."

Smoke would shake his head and say, "Naw, my nigga, I can't do that. I can't. I need to beat them bitches' ass is what I need to do."

Bill would just chuckle and stare at his friend like he had just returned from outer space. Bill knew Smoke's problem. That white pussy had taken over his better judgement, if he had any left. Having those white girls in his stable meant added prestige and status to Smoke, whether he admitted it or not. It meant something to him personally, in a perverse way. He was a dark-skinned Negro with young white girls calling him Daddy and treating him like a king, usually, when they weren't trying to overthrow Martha's ass.

"Alright, man," Bill would say, resigned to having the same conversation and complaint come back up within a month.

Smoke was a grown man and he had to learn to take care of his business or else his business wouldn't take care of him. Somehow, he tolerated the mutinous bitches living under his roof. There came a time in every pimp's life when he had to protect his property one way or another. Were any of them even worth fighting over?

Bill threw his pack of Kools on the table. Mary picked it up, shook one cigarette out and put it between Bill's lips. She pulled a solid gold lighter from her purse and lit his smoke. Bill watched his friend across the table, whispering in Martha's ear, her platinum blonde hair brushing his lips. Strangely enough, in the dim light, Martha and Bill looked like they might be related. Bill turned and winked at Mary in the smoky candlelight coming from the center of the table. He wasn't given to talking a lot nor was he given to talking loud. That was why when he did speak, everyone made sure they were listening.

Life is strange, Bill thought. *I almost killed this man and now he's my good friend.* Bill drew on his cigarette, exhaled deeply and sipped his drink as the music from the bandstand played. He began to reminisce about his first encounter with Smoke as an adult. They were playing Spades at a private club inside a storefront church on Grand River and Wisconsin. Bill stared unblinking, trying to absorb what he'd just heard and not overreact.

"What did you say to me, nigger?" he said evenly. His blue green eyes steady and intense. Smoke took the bait. He'd said it, everyone heard it and he couldn't see an exit anywhere, literally.

"I said, light skinned dudes like you, got it good and got it easy 'cause white folks look at you and see theyself. Shit, how they gon' mistreat somebody look like them?"

"Just 'cause I can jump high don't mean I done went to the fucking moon! Do you think I feel any less disrespected when a white man calls me a nigger? Do you think I don't see how some white ladies' expression change up as I get closer and she checks my threads while she grabbin' her goddamn purse? Trust and believe that slave masters sold off every bastard they had with their slave women and didn't think twice about the fact that they looked like 'em or had their blood in 'em. Black people need to let go of that light-skin-dark-skin bullshit. We all niggers to them."

Realizing he had his hand on his stiletto by the time he'd finished speaking, Bill was going to kill this motherfucker for the sheer offense of making him talk so damn much. Bill didn't have to explain shit to anybody, let alone this nigger here. He looked down and Smoke's black knuckled hand was extended out for him to shake.

"Sorry, my nigga. That was some profound shit!"

Bill let go of his knife and shook Smoke's hand. In later years Bill would occasionally wonder if Smoke, now his homeboy, knew he was about to die? Probably not and best not to ever mention it.

Bill stubbed out his cigarette in the ashtray closest to him and gazing past Mary's right shoulder, he caught Martha looking at him. His eyes narrowed and then got wide as Martha looked away. He immediately looked toward Smoke, who was oblivious to what had just transpired as he was preoccupied with the new gold watch on his wrist. Was this fucking bitch eyeballing him? Should he start some shit by telling his man, Smoke? Bill was growing more irritated when Martha said something to Smoke and he smiled. *Ain't this a bitch?* Fuck what Smoke might do—he knew what he was *supposed* to do, but would he do it? What would Black Mary do? Probably elbow that ho right in her choppers, like a juvenile delinquent busting out the window of a car.

Bill flicked his ash into the ashtray in disgust. This fake ass Marilyn Monroe ho was running the show over in Smoke's crib. A disgrace to the pimping game! The game was to be sold, not to be told and it looked like Martha was the one doing the telling.

EIGHTEEN

William "Still Bill" Williams was Gabriel Williams' younger brother and Ricky's uncle. He was not Willie, nor Billy, but Bill. He was called Still Bill because of his handiness with the blade of a stiletto, and because when Bill was done fucking around with a nigger, he got quiet and focused. He didn't say much, if anything, after he'd come to that point in the conversation or business proceedings, where there were no more words. The point of no return. People who had the misfortune of noticing he was no longer speaking with them, nervously tried to start him up again like a stalled car engine, saying they were just kidding or they didn't mean it or that they were sorry. No matter, because it all came under the heading of too little and way too late.

Bill Williams was a pimp, and Bill Williams was a killer. Though the latter had happened only twice, it was a stark truth that he lived with. On the occasion where he was forced to take a man's life, he was protecting his business, or his bitches, which were one and the same. Not allowing himself to be disrespected, or allowing anyone to harm his stable, Bill believed in absolution by his own hand. He believed a man had the right and the duty to avenge any wrong that was perpetrated on him. His friend and mentor, Red Allen, always told him to "Trust the 6 and not the 12." For Red, it meant trusting the righteousness of the six lead peacemakers in the chamber of his old school .38 special. Bill's weapon of choice was his 6-inch stiletto switchblade, which was much more personal. In any case, neither man trusted the twelve strangers who were deemed to be a jury of their peers--that was laughable—as if!

Young Bill had been his mother's favorite child, as he took after her side of the family, high toned Creoles from Natchitoches, Louisiana. Mrs. Williams' family name was Bienville and the Bienvilles had been very wealthy as far back as anyone could recall. They were slave owners and Lola Bienville told this "family secret" to her youngest son when he was about 13 years old, both fascinating and repulsing him. Though he loved his mother, he could not reconcile what he saw as a villainous family history.

He watched his father work two jobs six days a week to keep his wife and children fed and with a roof over their heads. John Williams was a good man and a humble man and Bill could see why his mother fell in love with him. Tall, dark, and wiry, he was such an incredibly handsome black man with so much pride and dignity, he easily swept Lola Bienville off her feet. The Bienvilles disowned her when she and John married but Lola's love for her man was stronger than money or bloodlines.

A few years after her marriage, the Depression relieved the Bienvilles of their financial legacy and by then, Lola had moved with her young family to Detroit, settling on its East side. William Williams grew up tall and muscular with straight black hair, greenish blue eyes, thin lips, a keen nose, and pale skin. In his teens, men and women began referring to Bill as a "pretty nigga," which at first seemed like an unmanly insult, but eventually, he came to agree.

For Bill, being a white looking black man in a white man's world was always a struggle. Maybe in Louisiana his skin tone gave him a stratified class, but in Detroit, this was not the case.

From an early age he proved to be blacker and prouder than any Negro he knew because he was fiercely and deeply both. Bill knew that some people, even black people, would look at him and not know exactly what they were seeing. But when he spoke, it was jarring because he could "out nigger" any nigger he knew. He sometimes used this to his advantage around white folks because they were so confused, they put themselves at a disadvantage by underestimating how clever Bill actually was. Still, he'd been called a nigger by more white people than he could count, no matter the caste of his skin, so he had no illusions. He knew on which side of the fence he fell.

Bill felt he had to fight for his place in the world and his rebellious antics landed him in jail more than a few times from age 18 to 21 and kept him from serving his country, not that he would have done so willingly. He objected to killing strangers for the sake of the U.S.A. When he last left the confines of the local hoosegow at age 21, he knew he'd never go back. He knew he had a future--one he'd been preparing for his whole life.

The irony of who his family had been wasn't lost on Bill, when he dared to think about it. He had somehow become a master to benevolently enslaved women who called him "Daddy." Sometimes he'd find himself laughing at the fact that he could run, but fate and destiny always ran faster.

Emotionally, Still Bill could be colder than a dead man on a Sunday morning in January. Yet, he knew how to be warm and engaging to get what he wanted, especially in business. Bill Williams was not just an ordinary pimp. There was an assumption that a whore didn't really worry too much about how her pimp looked in the face, as long as he was able to keep her under control and bringing in his money. This wasn't always true.

Just like a beautiful whore liked to be considered a "bad bitch" and an asset to her pimp, she wanted her "Daddy" to be the envy of all the other hos. But a prostitute was not allowed to even look at another pimp. It was called *reckless eyeballin'* and this could get a bitch beaten or even killed, depending on who her pimp was. Reckless eyeballin' meant she wanted to "choose" another pimp—she was shopping around and about to make her purchase.

Bill was so attractive, in every sense of the word, that he couldn't help it if bitches got beaten on account of him. These women would steal a glance at him any and every chance they could get. This was generally not a problem if they approached Bill and said they wanted to "fuck" with him or "choose" him. But Bill usually had to turn hos down because he only kept a stable of 7 bitches at any one time and it was hard to get them to leave. He would often say, "No man wants a woman that no other man would want, and no woman wants a man no other woman would want." They all wanted Bill.

He would tell his girls, "Between these jealous, backstabbing niggas and these thirsty, raggedy ass hos out here, there are plenty who would love to see your man fall. But it ain't gonna happen. Y'all are the cornerstones, the foundation of my success. Our house is solid and built on that foundation."

While most pimps had to continuously talk in the circuitous and confusing vernacular that stereotyped their trade, usually to keep some dumb ho in line, Bill thought that was beneath him. All the slick talk, when analyzed, was just a bunch of nursery rhymes thrown around by niggers who couldn't put a sentence together with a tool box and instructions. To be sure, most of the pimps he ran into were ugly, thuggish brutes who seemed to be compensating for something by beating up their hos. Yes, when crossed Bill could be brutal with his hands or his cane, but he was a little more compassionate than most of the players out there.

He used his head to get into a ho's mind. He could "peep out" what had gone on in a girl's life, almost just by looking at her. Most of these women had low self-esteem, even the ones who considered themselves high-class hookers, but Bill knew how to play on their weaknesses and exploit them to the point that all they lived for, yearned for, and wanted, was to keep him happy and pleased with them.

Bill would say, "Why work hard every day for some chump who's making you have his kids and keep his house, when you can make men pay to fuck you or even just have a fucking conversation with you?"

These women had the advantage of having someone "manage" their lives and they didn't have to think about much except getting money, and they knew just how to do that. Bill Williams figured anything else was plain stupid. The idea that these same women would give him every dime they stood out on the street to make and never complain did not seem foreign to him at all. Why shouldn't they? He gave them a warm house to live in, a cook to prepare their meals, nice clothes, fur coats for special occasions, and health care. And sometimes, if a girl had been extra profitable, a night in bed with him. Bill didn't have sex with his bitches, he made love to them. These street hardened women would melt like a lit candle, professing their undying love as they clung to Bill's taut body.

He would begin by touching her all over with his strong, gentle hands, evolving into long, passionate kisses. A whore never let a trick or john kiss her as it was considered too intimate, yet these girls craved Bill's kiss, for it was their only opportunity to do something so simple, so necessary, so normal. And when he made love to his girls, he would look them in their eyes. None of that behind the back doggy-style shit for him--he wanted them to *see* him. Bill was different in these moments when he wanted them to understand how deep their connection was and that they needed one another. He whispered, telling them they were beautiful and special, and he could not live without them. They were *his* girls. He meant that he could not live his lifestyle without them, but no matter because the women were mesmerized with love, fear and respect for Bill Williams.

Once, no more than 10 minutes after bedding one of his girls, Bill came charging out of his bedroom with the poor unfortunate ho's hair wrapped in his fist, slamming her straight into a wall. The other girls scattered to various corners of the room as the bitch bounced off the wall as if her head was encased in rubber. Naked and bleeding, the girl lay in a clump on the floor. He calmly asked the other women to attend to her as he strode naked, back to his room and closed the door.

A pimp, in a sense, is a whore because he has to be bought by his bitches. A ho is not allowed to have sex with her pimp until she brings in a certain dollar amount which he has predetermined and once that happens, she's blessed with an invitation to his bed. For Bill, not every blessing was about the flesh.

In what might seem like a personal paradox, Bill Williams enjoyed going to church nearly every Sunday. One of his old partners, a former pimp called "King James," was now a pastor. According to Bill's logic, there was not much difference between a pimp and a pastor as they both were always in the finest custom-made suits, with the sharpest alligator shoes, and hair processed to within an inch of its life. They both made a living using words to inculcate and burrow into people's minds, psyches, emotions, and self-esteem to make them part with their money. Each man possessed the gift of minimal persuasion— James' was his words, Bill's was his looks. King James and Still Bill used to muse that those on the fence always seemed to fall over into their yards, ready to be scooped up and saved.

NINETEEN

Oakman Boulevard is one of the most beautiful residential streets in Detroit. Large Tudor style homes line the wide street, sheltered by stately maple and elm trees. One of the few Negro homeowners in the prestigious neighborhood, Bill Williams owned two homes which sat side by side. If there was any hint that his neighbors knew his line of work, it went unacknowledged and unreported. Each house boasted four bedrooms and two bathrooms with Bill having a private bedroom and bath to himself in each.

It was a few days before New Year's Eve and Bill was taking his girls out for their annual holiday dinner. He took half his women, the top three earners, to Stanley's Mannia Café in downtown Detroit for some of the best Chinese food to be had anywhere. A couple of nights later the other three would dine with him at Checker's Bar-b-que on Livernois near 8 Mile Road. The following year Bill and Mary began going to Chin Tiki on Cass Avenue. It featured a two-level waterfall, celebrity patrons like James Brown, Muhammad Ali and Sammy Davis Jr., and exotic Polynesian food accompanied by tall, multicolored libations.

In Bill's room, Black Mary shaved him with her straight razor sharpened on the strop, then carefully styled his hair and helped him get dressed to go out. The only thing loud about Still Bill Williams was his wardrobe and he flew his pimp flag with pride,

140

wearing custom made suits in every color from turquoise to peach, accessorizing with coordinating pocket squares, shirts and ties. His gators came in a rainbow of hues and his hats were made by the legendary Henry the Hatter. Mary wanted to keep her Daddy looking sharp and clean and make his bitches proud to be with him.

Bill's girls were mostly locals and Chan was the youngest at 18. He'd crossed paths with her by happenstance almost a year earlier while he was parked on Larned Street outside of a downtown club. He was about to pull off when he saw a cop hassling the pretty young girl. Chan was a tall, slender Chinese girl with beautiful long black hair trailing to her waist. He rolled down his window, amused by the exchange between the girl and the policeman. Of course, she sounded like a colored girl because in Detroit, black culture dominated all others if left unchecked.

"Oh, hell naw! Fuck you, motherfucker!" the girl shouted as the cop tried to grab her wrists to put handcuffs on them.

If this girl was scared, she didn't show it. Her eyes were blazing with defiance.

"Great. You kiss your mother with that mouth?" the middle aged white man in the blue uniform asked.

"Naw, I suck your old ass daddy's dick with this mouth, nigger!"

There had been a couple of other prostitutes around when the exchange began but they were now absent, having drifted away like feathers on the wind. *This one is obviously the ring leader*, the cop thought, and he was still gathering his thoughts when he slapped her hard across the mouth.

"See how much use you get out of it now, whore," he said impassively.

Bill opened his glove box and clutched his .38, drawing it out of the compartment. He looked at the cop, who now had the girl subdued and under his control. He carefully put the gun back and slammed the small door to the glove box. Bill knew he couldn't shoot a cop. He had to be smart. He didn't even know if this ho had a pimp and if she did, who was he and where was he right now? He opened the glove compartment again and grabbed something inside, shut it and got out of his car.

"Officer, I see you've got your hands full. Can I be of assistance?" Bill inquired.

"None of your business, sir. Get back in your vehicle, please," the policeman said, sternly.

Bill knew he had to make his case before the policeman got the girl into his patrol car or called it in on the radio.

"Officer, excuse me. I know this girl. She's a family friend."

The cop now looked Bill Williams in the face. He wondered why this white man cared about a Chinese whore? Bill was more soberly dressed than usual in all black from his wool felt fedora to his cashmere overcoat to his black alligator shoes, which the cop hadn't noticed.

"Well, I'm arresting her for suspicion of solicitation. Her friends ran off, so looks like she will be taking the fall all by her lonesome. Not much to say now, huh, smart ass?" he said to Chan, who was staring at Bill.

Who was this nigger and what did he want with her? If he could keep her from taking the short drive to police headquarters at 1300 Beaubien, she'd play along.

"Officer, her father is a rather prominent business owner in the Asian community. I'm sure he would not be happy to know

142

his daughter fell in with a bad crowd. Perhaps I can resolve the situation before it escalates?"

For the first time the cop noticed the wad of $20 bills in the man's hand.

"Well…" said the officer, rubbing his fingers across his lips like he was wiping away an unwanted kiss.

Bill extended his hand in which there was a roll of 10 $20 bills.

"Alright, alright," the cop said, quickly grabbing the loot and pocketing it. "She was probably just gonna get a citation anyway," the policeman allowed, unlocking Chan's cuffs. "Off with you, now. The both of 'ya," he said before getting into his patrol car and peeling away from the curb.

Chan stood there in the yellow glow of the street light, rubbing her wrists, looking into the eyes of the tall, striking man who had rescued her. Chan was an independent ho and though many pimps wanted her to choose them, she resisted. It was getting more and more difficult to work without a pimp and Chan knew she would have to choose sooner than later, or things like this would just keep happening.

She knew the man standing before her was a pimp, but he seemed different. He had class and style, yet she could tell he wasn't a chump and wasn't to be played with.

"So, whatchu want, man?" she asked.

Bill reached into the breast pocket of his coat and pulled out his white handkerchief, handing it to the girl. She ran the tip of her tongue outside the corner of her mouth and tasted blood.

"You always call folks niggers?" Bill asked in his normal vocal cadence, casting aside the "white man" ruse he'd been using.

"Yup."

"Even white folks?"

"*Especially* white folks," Chan replied.

They both snickered as she touched the peppery and masculine scented cloth to her mouth.

"Bitch, you owe me $200 dollars," Bill said calmly.

Chan stared at Bill for what seemed like several minutes, with neither of them speaking.

"I choose you, Daddy. Take me home with you," the girl said.

They swung by the apartment she shared with another working girl, got her clothes, and all the money she had saved. Chan gave it all to Bill, having "broken" herself to be part of his stable. Bill gave her over to Black Mary to be groomed and to learn the house rules before going out on the track the next night. Chan quickly became his number one earner. She was a dedicated and loyal ho and Bill showed his appreciation accordingly.

His number two girl was a voluptuous, long legged cocoa complexioned beauty named Eva. Eva sported a blonde page boy wig that complimented her dusky skin tone so perfectly it looked like her natural hair color. Only 23 years old, Eva had grown up in foster homes being molested by the so-called fathers in those homes. When she fought back or told the so-called mothers, she'd be shipped to a new home and the abuse would begin anew.

When she was 17, she was remanded to juvenile detention for assaulting her last foster dad who had come up behind her with his dick hanging out of his trousers while she was about to fry some pork chops for the family dinner. Eva pushed the man backward, whirled around to the stove and threw the skillet of hot grease on him. Once she was released at the age of 18, she began to work the streets. Boldly, Eva chose Bill in the middle of the Apex Bar one night, leaving her former pimp staring with his

144

mouth agape. But, that was the game and there were no hard feelings on the side of the pimp who had been humiliated in the bar. He knew not to fuck with Bill Williams. The outcome would not have been in his favor.

The rest of his stable consisted of Carol, a raven haired white girl, Denise, Sadie and Terri, all colored girls, all bad bitches. Denise was a plump girl who liked girls but loved Bill. Sadie was tall and flamboyant with her signature red dyed hair teased to within an inch of its life. Terri looked like a sexy librarian with her black rimmed eyeglasses. She was the oldest at 28 and Bill believed her eyesight was a problem to her, but the other girls covered for her when it came to anything from counting her money to reading a restaurant menu. They loved her, and she was devoted to Bill.

Bill Williams had never seen or known a retired pimp, except Red Allen, the man who'd brought him into the game. Most of the old players were either too proud, too greedy or too ignorant to find something else to do with their time and energy. They held on with wizened hands to whatever tattered remnants of pimpdom they could. Bill thought it was sad and he swore he'd never be one of these men. As quiet as it was kept, he had a plan.

7 women were a lot for any man and Bill thanked God he had Black Mary helping to keep his bitches in line. He had to face the fact that there were things, nuances that only another woman in the game would know and understand. He could try to understand as a man, a brother, a lover, a father figure, a businessman, or just about anything else and he still couldn't cover every base with his stable of women. Still, Bill was very different from his peers. He split his income from pimping 3 ways.

A third went to his savings account, money he never, ever touched in anticipation of one day retiring and doing nothing but enjoying what was left of his life. A third went to the upkeep of the houses and the girls, money he invested back into the business. He was one of the few pimps out there, perhaps the only one, who provided benefits like health care for his girls and a housekeeper to come in once a week to clean his homes. Bill took his bitches shopping for their clothes, sometimes nice designer threads from a local booster. He didn't want them getting busted boosting or stealing anything for themselves. He hated thieves and that was a ticket straight out of Bill's stable. The chick he bought clothes from had the hottest shit from California and New York, and he made sure they got their hair done once a month or purchased slick looking wigs like the ones The Supremes wore. Bill loved furs and he had a special closet built to hold the beautiful fox, lynx and mink jackets his girls got to wear when they attended a social function with their Daddy or with a high paying john.

The final third was an allowance divided up amongst the women. This was unheard of and unprecedented in the streets. One of the main rules of the game was to keep a bitch broke. To Bill, that was part of the problem. So many of his short-sighted counterparts were so busy making up ridiculous rhymes to confuse the average ho, they were perplexed as to why there was no loyalty in their ranks and why the cycle of losing bitches always seemed to be on "repeat" for them.

Bill gave his hos an allowance to do with as they pleased—as long as they didn't use it for drugs, he was cool with whatever was cool for them. Some sent money to the folks "back home," wherever that was, some blew it on even more clothes and accoutrements, but Bill always encouraged his stable to save their money in case they ever saw a day when "the life" wasn't for them.

For the most part, few knew how Bill ran his house because the girls knew not to talk about it. They believed in the credo, "Woman be wise, if you got a good man, don't advertise." If they happened to run across a good ho while they were working the track, someone who could be an asset to Bill's business, they told Bill, who might handle the recruitment himself or have Black Mary check the girl out. Bill had little turnover, but when there was a vacancy it usually had to do with the girls "aging out" of his employ. He didn't usually keep any girl over the age of 30.

Bill had a simple philosophy: Love what you do or do something else. Yes, some of the girls had been molested, raped or traumatized by a male family member or friend in their past, but to Bill, a bitch had to get over it. He got into their heads individually, to find out their history and to make sure they weren't crazy. Shit, one of the pimps Bill knew got his dick cut off by one of his bitches while he was sleeping. You couldn't know everything rolling around in a ho's head, but he could always get in and make it a little better by letting her know she contributed directly to their economic rise or fall. After all, it was her duty to put her man, him, first. He always had to look the sharpest, have the slickest ride and the baddest bitches. A pimp was the CEO and his hos were the proud rank and file.

Bill owned a few houses around Detroit, which he rented to hard working families associated with the auto plants. There were unwritten rules that needed no enforcement--the house would be kept clean, grass watered and cut, leaves raked, and snow plowed. Only once did an incident take place where a family up and moved out in the middle of the night, never to be heard from again. The lore that sprung up around it was that Bill had to dispose of them because they were deadbeats. This only added to the myth of Still Bill Williams and he simply shrugged it off with neither a confirmation nor denial. Silently, people would wonder how Bill could be so cold as to rub out an entire family, but their next thought was always that they were glad it wasn't them. This urban legend of some family meeting a premature end due to slow or no payment kept the rent coming in steadily and on time.

TWENTY

1 966 had about 30 minutes of life left before the new year would come to kill it like an executioner would a condemned prisoner. Guy Lombardo was leading his band through American standards and celebratory songs on Channel 2, as adults listened in teary eyed inebriation and kids impatiently waited for the excitement of the countdown to the New Year.

What no one could foresee in the witching hour, whose trembling hand let slip the old year while grabbing hold of the new, was that this year would forever change the history of the city of Detroit and put a halt to its prosperous trajectory. June would begin the "Summer of Love," radiating out like a sunbeam from San Francisco, California in a movement of music, arts and attitude that would continue for more than two years, ending at Woodstock, New York. That summer also saw the advent of Daylight Savings Time in Detroit, a gift of time manipulation to hold back the night for another hour or so.

On Thursday, January 26th, two days after an unseasonably rare tornado swiped the Midwest, snow began to fall. The Great Midwestern Blizzard lasted for 24 hours, unloading unrelenting snow on Illinois, Indiana, Iowa, Michigan, Missouri and Kansas. Winds of over 50 mph lashed and drove the snow into 15-foot drifts, turning cars over onto their sides. 76 people in the Chicago area died as a result of the 23 inches of snow that fell there. 24 inches of snow fell in Saginaw, Michigan and 23 in Flint, paralyzing towns and stranding people for several days, yet somehow Detroit dodged the deluge with rain and warmer air, ending up with 4 inches of the white powder on the ground.

Angelica began her morning watching "Rita Bell's Prize Movie" on Channel 7. The show came on daily at 9:00 a.m. and the host, with her black hair coiffed into a flip, would bob her head to a song as contestants on the telephone guessed what tune was playing over the television airwaves. Rita would smile, ear pressed to her princess phone as the melody played. Angelica called Sheila.

"Dang, were you able to open your side door this morning, Sheila? I mean, can you believe this? I guess the milk man won't be delivering today or the paper man, huh? But best of all, no school!" Angelica squealed into her pink princess phone, not waiting for answers to any of her questions.

"I know! And it's still snowing! Who knows how high it could get. I heard my mother say a bunch of babies were gonna be born in October. What the heck does that mean?"

"Um, well, think about it, girl."

"I thought about it and I still don't know—"

"Okay. People. Grown-ups. Stuck in the house with each other...get it?" Angelica could almost hear Sheila's eyes blinking blankly, completely without comprehension.

"Well, my parents are stuck in our house and they in the kitchen playin' cards and drinkin' coffee with the radio on, so..."

"Sex, Sheila. It's about sex. I guess adults get, I don't know...excited when they don't have to go to work and can't go outside."

"Oh, okay. I get it. Well, not my parents and why would somebody want to do sex instead of read or watch TV?"

"Or listen to music? Beats me. And, I think it's 'have sex' not 'do sex,' anyway…"

Before Angelica could say another word, she heard a commotion on the on the other end of the phone. It sounded like someone muffling the telephone receiver with their hand, clumsily, when she heard Mrs. Davis say, "Why you talking about sex on my phone? Who you talking to about sex on my phone?"

"Nobody, Mama. I was asking a question. Ain't nobody saying nothing about sex, Mama," Sheila pleaded.

Then, the line went dead. Angelica could visualize Velma Davis appearing in her nimbus of cigarette smoke with pink foam curlers attached to her head, looking like a giant ant or roach. Mrs. Davis was no doubt concerned that someone might be listening in on the party line and think her girl was "fast" and she wasn't entertaining that notion. Poor Sheila.

Never far from Velma's mind was that day in 1964, just a week before the start of summer, when the Seniors were graduating from Mumford High School. They had just received their caps and gowns in anticipation of the ceremony taking place in a few days. As was tradition, Seniors all over the city of Detroit participated in a "swing out." This celebration entailed students piling into a car and riding around the city, blowing the horn and promenading through the campus of neighboring high schools, wearing tasseled mortar boards while hanging out of the windows of the vehicle. The girls sat on the edge of the door atop the open window, hanging on to the roof with their fingertips. The driver knew not to make any sudden turns or drive too fast.

Francine Davis, Sheila's big sister, the middle sister of the three siblings, fell out of the window of her friend's car and was run over by an oncoming vehicle. Mrs. Davis was devastated as Francine was the love of her life. She loved her husband and her two remaining daughters, but not with the depth she'd felt for Francine. This girl was sweet and kind hearted and never gave her parents a moment of worry. She wanted to be a nurse and she had a scholarship to Wayne State University. Once Mrs. Davis' depression subsided, her already vice-like grip on the only remaining child in her house, Sheila, became even more unshakable. The truth was Velma Davis dreaded the day her daughter would graduate high school even more than the prospect of her going away to college.

On Saturday morning Angelica got up and cooked breakfast for her mother, deciding they should enjoy being snowbound by the wind-swept snow drifts buffering their house like miniature mountains. Soon, the raucous sound of children laughing and playing took over the insulated sound of silence permeating the outdoors.

The telephone hanging on the kitchen wall rang and Liz picked it up.

"Hi, Daddy." After a few seconds she said, "No, I don't think that's a good idea. We'll be okay. I think the news on TV is telling people to stay inside." She listened for about 30 seconds before saying, "Daddy, there is way too much snow for you to try to dig anybody out. People are having heart attacks trying to shovel this snow. We are fine. Y'all stay upstairs and stay inside, okay? Okay, Daddy. Bye, bye," Liz said, putting the phone back in its cradle on the wall.

"Good old Granddaddy. Always trying to help."

"I know, but he can't help if he's in a snowbank dyin' of a heart attack," Liz said.

They both laughed. Angelica was imagining Monday morning coming and finding them still immobilized by snow. No school! Just then she heard a buzzing sound like the engine of a motorized lawnmower. But how could that be? Angelica went into the living room to look out of the window. She used the sleeve of her shirt to wipe away the condensation that obscured the figure moving about outside her house. It was Bobby Gogolian and he was walking behind a snow blower. She rapped on the window without being heard. Angelica ran to the hall closet to find her boots and her heavy coat with the hat in one pocket and gloves in the other.

"I'll be right back," she yelled toward the kitchen and out the front door Angelica went.

Bobby had plowed a neat row down the sidewalk and was starting on the driveway. She waited until he was making his turn toward her to wave. He looked up and smiled, letting his machine idle as Angelica drew closer.

"Hi, Bobby!"

"Hi, Angelica. I'm clearing some of the walkways. I thought you might need help over here."

"Wow, you sure didn't have to do this, but we really appreciate it. Thank you."

"It's no big deal. I got my shovel over there for your front steps. I wouldn't want you to slip or fall."

"At this rate, looks like I'm definitely back to school on Monday, huh? Geez, thanks a lot, pal!" she teased.

Bobby grinned.

"Better you than me. I'm already out. Graduated last week and just in time too 'cause I got my draft notice."

"Congratulations. I didn't know if you were getting out in January or June."

In Detroit, high school graduation was twice yearly, in January and again in June.

"Thanks," Bobby said, his big gloves sliding along the handle of the machine, unconsciously.

"So, what's this about you being drafted? Are they sending you to Vietnam?" she asked, trying to smile.

"Yeah. I already been inducted and I get shipped off to basic training next week."

"Dang. That seems kinda quick. Can't you postpone it?"

She knew she sounded silly now. She also knew she now felt sad and anxious to remember this day, this moment and her friend.

"I mean, what about college?"

Now it was Bobby's turn to smile. He shook his head.

"Well, I never thought much about going to college, Angelica. But if I wanna to go, the Army'll send me when I get out."

"Hey! Angelica!"

It was Liz standing on the porch with a coat around her shoulders, squinting at the vast expanse of whiteness with her hand at her brow.

"Uh oh. You better get back inside," Bobby said, waving in Liz's direction.

Angelica frowned, indignant at her mother's obvious disregard for the deep conversation she was having with Bobby. She turned toward Liz.

"Mama, look what Bobby's doing. He's cleaning up our sidewalk and driveway for us. Isn't that cool?"

"Yes, very nice. Thank you, Bobby. Angelica, you need to get inside so he can get finished up and get back to his warm house. Come on in, now."

"You better go on, then," Bobby said.

Angelica smiled her prettiest smile and said goodbye, rushing past her mother into the house, furious. Angelica stayed in her room for the rest of the day listening to the radio and reading. After some time had passed, Angelica opened her bedroom door and made her way to the front room. She looked outside to see if Bobby was still being a Good Samaritan to his neighbors with his snow blower. There was nothing but silence and street lights and not even a trace of foot prints in the newly fallen, ever so light dusting of snow. It was as if Bobby Gogolian had been a ghost. She never saw him again.

TWENTY-ONE

Two whole weeks without snow in April signaled the official end of winter and the start of the remaining field trips for the school year. Two busloads of students were let out at the wide expanse of marble stairs leading up to the three arched entrances guarded by the impervious and oblivious "Thinker" by Auguste Rodin. The giant statuary warily welcomed visitors to one of the most magnificent museums in America, the Detroit Institute of Arts. The marble marvel of Beaux Arts and Italian Renaissance architecture was as awe inspiring on the exterior--its fraternal twin, the Detroit Public Library was right across the avenue—as it was jaw dropping on the interior with over half a million square feet of paintings and artifacts.

Enrique, Angelica and Carlton stood in the great entry hall and marveled at the fresco style mural, "Detroit Industry" by Diego Rivera.

"Every time I come here I can't believe how beautiful this thing is. You always see something new, something you missed the last time. It's stunning," Angelica marveled to her friends.

"I read somewhere that when this mural was painted in the 1930's, people were so mad and so offended by his artistic vision, they demanded it be painted over, like whitewashed or something. I'm glad that didn't happen," Ricky said. "I'm glad Rivera stood his ground. That's what a true artist does."

"Well, I want to see some mummies," said Carlton.

"Man, this place is so big, we probably won't get to see everything. We only got four hours, and that includes lunch," Ricky explained.

"Let's make a pact to come back here in the summer, okay? Just something fun to do on a Saturday. We might be able to squeeze in the Children's Museum, too. The planetarium over there is so cool. What do you say?" Angelica asked.

"Sure, I'm game," said Enrique.

"Okay," said Carlton.

"Maybe Sheila can come too."

Sheila was missing in action because her mother forgot to return the permission slip and fee to their homeroom teacher in time, so she was spending her day in the school library. It was like detention with books.

Separating from their assigned group, the three students went from floor to floor gazing at one ancient artifact after another, from gallery to gallery admiring works of art they'd only seen in their history books.

"It's so cool that something a painter or craftsman made to please nobody but himself lives on, sometimes thousands of miles and thousands of years from where it started," said Ricky.

"Some of these guys weren't even famous during their lifetimes. They just created art for art's sake, not knowing what would come of it," added Angelica.

"I think it's time to eat. Looks like they're heading downstairs for lunch. Come on," Carlton said, trying not to let on that he'd become bored with the trip and couldn't wait to get back aboard the bus.

As the group sat down for lunch in the museum's café, Angelica could feel someone looking at her. She looked up and saw a boy she'd seen twice already during the field trip. There were several other schools visiting that day and he must have been with one of them, because she'd never seen him at Dodge High, that's for sure. He waved, and Angelica, out of surprise, looked away quickly.

"What's wrong?" asked Ricky.

"Nothing."

The young man got up and walked over to their table.

"Hi," he said directly to Angelica, ignoring the others.

She quickly swallowed the piece of sandwich she had in her mouth.

"Hi," she managed.

The boy was tall, not quite as tall as Ricky, but still well built and handsome. Angelica ran her tongue over her teeth inside her closed mouth to remove any food particles, just in case she had to speak again.

"My name is Barry. I go to Mumford. How you doing?"

"Um, good, Barry. I saw you upstairs, but I feel like I've seen your somewhere before. By the way, these are my friends, Ricky and Carlton."

"Hey," the boys said in dry unison.

"I seen you before, too. You was at the Valentine's Day talent show at Mumford, right? You and another girl."

"Yup. Me and my friend Sheila were there. Good memory!"

There was a small commotion across the room as Barry's classmates were getting up from their tables and getting ready to leave.

"Can I have your phone number and call you sometime?" Barry asked, smiling at Angelica.

"Sure. Do you need to write it down?"

"Nope. I'll remember it."

"University two…" Angelica said, continuing until she'd given Barry her number.

He repeated it verbatim and said "goodbye" before falling in line with his class near the exit. Ricky didn't return the parting pleasantry, as Carlton did. Angelica excused herself to go to the lady's room. Ricky turned to Carlton.

"That dude is trying to steal our girl. I know that kid. He's the star baseball player at Mumford High. I guess, he's pretty popular."

"Yeah, maybe," Carlton responded.

Carlton, always the slenderest reed in the fickle wind of life, really didn't care at that moment even though Angelica had just been referred to as "our girl." Shoot, he was glad somebody was trying to pull Angelica because as far as he could see, Enrique Williams could use the competition. The relationship between Ricky and Angelica was so confusing. They obviously wanted to be more than friends, but Ricky went with that stuck up Rita Corbin and, no matter how he himself tried to impress Angelica, she only seemed annoyed by him. Tolerated, but barely.

As time went on Carlton noticed that Ricky and Angelica were becoming closer and more independent of him. He wondered what that meant for him and his relationship with the two people he actually cared about. Sure, Sheila Davis was part of their clique too, but she barely registered with Carlton. After all, there were only three Musketeers.

In their Senior year of high school, Carlton would become anxious. He wanted things to stay the same and the prospect of his friends going away to school frightened him. Would they, the three of them, remain close friends or become polite strangers with time? The thing growing in the fetid darkness of his mind was, why were Angelica and Ricky doing things without him and never let on that they were doing them? He had almost run the two of them down in a cross walk one Saturday afternoon as he was driving his mother's car to the store to get her some cigarettes. They ignored the car that had come so close to hitting them, ignored the omnipresent 1:00 p.m. air raid siren that was blaring somewhere in the distance, ignored *him*! Carlton almost blew his horn to startle them into seeing him and saying "hello," but they were too busy laughing and looking at one another as if no one and nothing else existed.

Carlton felt the cold fingers of jealousy grab at his heart, squeezing it until he couldn't breathe. He pushed away the thoughts of what it could be like for him and Ricky if Angelica wasn't in the picture. *Don't think that. Anything but that!* He had to face facts: she was the sun, Ricky the stars, and he was some unnamed planet revolving around them both.

TWENTY-TWO

P astor Roberson led the Mount Olive Tabernacle of Faith Missionary Baptist Church and on any given Sunday there might be a half dozen pimps and twice as many working girls taking up the velvet cushioned pews. James Roberson, or "King James" as he'd been called in his pimpdom, was a fiery preacher who knew how to stir emotions among his congregants by correlating stories, people and parables documented thousands of years in the past to situations people confronted in everyday life. At 6'3" tall and 350 pounds, he was an imposing man who wore his size well and his wardrobe of custom suits even better. Pastor Roberson was boyish looking with a meaty bald head on a thick stalk of neck with a nape that looked like a package of hot dogs was embedded inside. Everyone knew of his past as a peddler of flesh, and though he seldom mentioned it in his sermons, he didn't hide from it either.

Part of a pimp's arsenal is his ability to speak, if he is any good at his craft, and James Roberson was a natural orator, capable of making people believe most anything he said. Once his momentum built and he was "hooping and hollering," his white monogrammed handkerchief would be engaged many times to mop his sweat soaked face and emphasize his fervor for the Lord. James understood his calling once he was saved and baptized, and he was committed to helping young people get on and stay on the proper path. He was proud to be a man of God, a vessel for the Lord's work.

A couple of weeks before the end of school, Mt. Olive had a Youth Day celebration and blessing ceremony for members who were graduating Seniors, Class of '67, and any other kid who wanted to take part. Rita Corbin, Ricky's girl, was graduating and invited him to come to church. As far as he was concerned, they didn't spend nearly enough time together with her living across the city, so he was glad to attend. Ricky invited Carlton and Angelica, who invited Sheila. Ricky knew it might be awkward with both RiRi and Angelica in the same place at the same time, but he cared for both of them and Angelica was one of his closest friends. He convinced himself he'd done the right thing by inviting her. Why, then, was he praying that Angelica hadn't invited her stupid new boyfriend, Barry?

Angelica had gotten a used car for her birthday, a 1964 Ford Falcon, and she had to laugh at how tame and meticulous she was when driving her car, not quite the speeding wildcat she imagined herself to be. The four friends rolled into the church's big concrete parking lot and Ricky told them to go inside the sanctuary while he searched for Rita. The church was filling up quickly as Sheila, Angelica and Carlton found seats in a pew near the middle of the church. From this vantage point, they could see around the inside of the sanctuary and wave at friends and schoolmates they recognized.

Behind the altar was a microphoned podium with a cross deeply engraved on the front, running the length of the dark wood. To the left there was a small amphitheater style choir stand with red velvet seats, reminiscent of the archaic and extravagant clam shell Botticelli's Venus emerged from. On the opposite side of this set up was an organ, piano, drum kit and a guitar stand, along with an amplifier.

162

Angelica, Sheila and Carlton waved intermittently at the many kids they knew, like Dave Lizaro and Mike Morton sitting side by side with their fathers flanking them. There were a few white people in the congregation other than the Mortons. Black churches, in general, would welcome anyone through their doors. It was a strange badge of honor, actually, to have white congregants mixed into the pews of a black church audience. It meant more than simply being welcoming. It meant the pastor's message had universal appeal and his arms were wide enough to embrace everyone.

Carlton had to shoo away a potential family of interlopers to their pew, reserving the precious real estate for Ricky and Rita. Sheila waved at Twin and wondered where his brother was? She had no idea which one of the twins this was, that's why when one was without the other, he was referred to as "Twin." If both were present, then it was, "Twin and them." Thankfully, there was usually only one set of twins attending school at any given time and if there were multiples, the least popular would be called by their actual first names.

A girl slid in the pew beside Carlton and as he got ready to tell her she'd have to find other accommodations, Rita slid in right after her, followed by Ricky, who looked at his pals and smiled. Sheila flicked Angelica on top of her wrist with her nails, and Angelica shot her a look as if to say, "I know, I know!" As Angelica turned to her right to get a better look at Rita, their eyes met. Ricky's girlfriend smiled haughtily, tossed her freshly pressed mane and grabbed Ricky's arm, never saying a word.

"Hi, my name is Carlton," Carlton said to the girl next to him.

This woke up Ricky, who leaned outward and pointed to his friends.

"Sorry, y'all. I was busy looking for my uncle. He goes here. Anyway, Rita and Chris, this is Sheila, Angelica and Carlton." Ricky had observed but a millisecond of interaction or lack thereof, between RiRi and Angelica and realized he should not have invited the girls to sit together because he was stuck in their midst, unable to maneuver, like a barge on the Detroit River in the dead of winter.

"Hi," the girls said, coolly.

Carlton asked the girl to his right, "You go to MacKenzie, too?"

"Yeah, me and RiRi are on the varsity cheer squad together. We know most of the kids here 'cause they go to MacKenzie. Y'all go to Mumford?" the girl asked.

"No, we all go to Dodge on 8 Mile. Me, Sheila, Carlton and Ricky," said Angelica. *Why doesn't this girl know where her friend's boyfriend goes to school?*

Chris was a pretty brown-skinned girl with a dazzling full lipped smile and a slicked back ponytail. Rita was talking animatedly and flashing her dimples at Enrique as Sheila stared at the two of them. Sheila had to admit Rita was a very pretty girl and she and Ricky looked good together, but Rita's pal Chris was prettier than she was, obviously and quantifiably so. Looking back and forth at their faces, Sheila decided Chris made RiRi look almost plain. *Almost.* She tried to push the thought out of her head, but it had its breaks on. *It's about time a regular looking girl, cheerleader though she is, got a fine boy like Enrique Williams.* Why should the beautiful girls like Chris Chambers and Angelica Tanner get all the dibs when it came to boys? There was no better friend than Angelica, but Sheila could not halt the disloyal thought from marching through her brain.

164

Angelica turned left and right in her seat, taking in all of the sunny pastel suits. Yellow, salmon, mint and robin's egg blue, with big brimmed matching hats, some with protracted plumage. And this was just the men! It dawned on Angelica that these fancy peacocks were pimps. She wanted to tell Sheila her discovery, but decided against it as Sheila tended to be easily shocked and who knew how she might react? The array and display of humanity kept Angelica from looking at Ricky and his girlfriend. *What did he see in her,* Angelica wondered?

Carlton was chatting aimlessly with anyone within the sound of his voice, when he suddenly fell silent. He realized he was literally between four girls and none of them was his. His face set in a grimace as he pondered what was wrong with him and would it always be this way?

Ricky was distracted, silently searching for Bill Williams. Just as the choir filed into their shell and the musicians took their places, a short, colored man with an impeccable process stood with his hands up and arms out to direct the choir. The pastor emerged from a throne-like chair and stood up behind the podium. The enormous man discreetly pointed at Ricky, who stealthily, returned the gesture. All his friends turned towards him like they were being posed for a photo, but Ricky was looking back toward the middle set of doors where a tall, light skinned colored man entered with a beautiful black woman walking a few steps behind him. Ricky waved at his uncle, stopped short and then quickly waved at the woman, who smiled broadly in his direction.

Now Enrique Williams was truly, as the expression went, nervous as a ho in church. He hadn't realized his uncle would be with Black Mary. Thankfully, they settled across the aisle and a few rows in front of where the teens were. Ricky exhaled and peeked at his friends who were still staring at him. The choir began to sing "Walking to Jerusalem" and that made everyone look in the direction of the choir.

Two years ago, when Ricky was 15 years old, his uncle decided he should lose his virginity and directed Black Mary to help the boy with the task. Mary had never seen a boy as beautiful as Ricky and she treated him with special care and attention. She had given him some universally practical advice about girls, prefacing it with, "Yes, I know I'm a ho, pretty nigga, but I was a girl first. Take heed to what I say." She showed him the difference between fucking and making love and told him he wouldn't need the latter until he was older and had found the right girl.

Angelica tapped Carlton's thigh and whispered, "Who's that guy who just walked in? He looks like a pimp. Does Ricky know him?"

"I hope so," Carlton answered. "That's his uncle."

The pastor began to preach and after about thirty minutes, he hit his stride and began to "hoop" from the pulpit, taking in deep rattling breaths to exhort the crowd into a "call and response." The "call" was usually a question, accusation or bold statement and the response was answered with "Well," "Amen," "Yes, Lord," "Preach on pastor" or the like. The preacher was almost yelling now.

"You are here to serve God, but religion is made to serve you! Wait a minute now! Understand that the Lord is holy, but religion is a man-made thang! If it ain't servin' you, then something's wrong with your walk! We sit up and look down on folk who ain't like us! They don't pray like us, dress like us, talk like us! We sanctified! We better than everybody else! We always want to say what God would say about this or that situation! We think we can speak for God?! As my mama used to say, 'God be laughin' a lot!' Praise the Lord!"

166

After the service, people stood to leave with many people lining up to shake the pastor's hand and compliment him on his sermon. Bill gave Reverend Roberson some "skin" and Mary waved "hello." Once outside, Bill caught up with his nephew and his retinue as they milled about. Ricky had asked that they all wait a few minutes until his uncle came out of the church.

"What's going down, Nephew?" Bill asked, gliding over to the group.

Ricky introduced Bill to his friends, as well as his "business associate," Mary.

"We looking to grab something to eat. Y'all want to go with us to Diamond Jim Brady's on 7 Mile and Greenfield? I'm buying lunch for everybody," Bill said.

A quick query and assent passed through the group.

"Sure, that sounds cool. We can meet you over there since some of us have cars," Ricky said.

"Cool, baby," Bill said as he and Mary walked toward his ride.

At the restaurant, two tables were pushed together to accommodate the party of 8. Bill indicated with a nod that Ricky should sit at the end or head of one of the tables as he seemed to be the common denominator in this gathering. Rita sat to his right and Mary to his left with Bill sitting directly across from Carlton and Angelica.

The conversation was lively and fast paced as Bill was hip and fun and didn't act like anyone's parent, which, technically, he wasn't. Ricky decided to relax and enjoy being surrounded by women he cared about. What was there to worry about? Any awkward moments had long passed.

After a lunch of burgers and chili, RiRi announced that she and Chris had to leave. Ricky got up to walk her to their car, but Rita gave him a quick kiss on the cheek and insisted he stay with his friends and family.

"Okay, bye, everybody" she said as voices rose up to say "Goodbye" and "Nice meeting you."

"Nice meeting y'all," said Chris as they made their way toward the exit.

For the first time that day, Ricky sensed something was up with Rita. Was she angry with him for having his other friends, particularly, Angelica, there? She knew about Mary because he'd told her about her when they first started dating and before they'd ever had sex. It had just come up in the conversation and he wanted to be honest about his limited experience. He knew she didn't like Bill, not only because of his profession, but because he'd been teasing her the first time they met and he took the joking too far and had upset the girl. Bill only joked with people he liked, so she needn't have worried about him doing it again.

"How much you wanna bet she ain't gonna be home when you call her? She's up to something and her friend knows what it is," Bill surmised.

"She didn't even say thanks for the food, Daddy," Mary added.

"Dang, Uncle Bill, do you trust *anybody*?" Ricky asked, already knowing the answer.

"No, and you shouldn't either," Bill said, lighting a Kool.

Bill saw out of the corner of his eye Mary about to get a light for her man, and he motioned for her to relax and stay put. Ricky

168

could tell by Bill's smile that he was really irritated and was about to start some shit. It was time to go.

"Thanks for lunch, Uncle Bill. We probably need to split."

"Thank you, Mr. Williams, for taking us to lunch," said Sheila.

"Thank you for lunch Mr. Williams," Angelica said.

"Yeah, thanks for lunch," Carlton chimed in.

Bill was proud of his powers of discernment and he was seldom wrong. Not knowing the differences between people and their desires and their motives was a detriment in his profession. It helped him stay ahead of his enemies and the law—either of whom would not mind seeing him on his knees or in a casket.

Bill had observed the exchanges between his nephew, the beautiful girl with the green eyes and the chunky boy. There was something about the latter that was strange and peculiar beyond the usual teenaged angst and awkwardness. He didn't like Carlton and didn't know why since they'd never met and, shit, he was just a kid. Bill looked at Carlton.

"Is she your girl?" he asked, indicating Angelica.

"No, she's just my friend, <u>our</u> friend."

"Oh, so you speaking for my nephew, too?" he asked, eyebrow raised, menacingly.

Here it comes, thought Ricky.

"Um, no. We're all just friends," Carlton said in a voice higher than he'd intended.

"Looks like there's about one person too many, don't it?" Bill chuckled. "Not you, sweetheart," he said to Sheila, who looked confused.

Carlton cleared his throat.

"No, she's got a boyfriend," he said, pointing his thumb toward Angelica like a hitchhiker.

Bill looked at Ricky while still clearly talking to Carlton, and said, "And so do you, Youngblood!"

Bill cracked up at his inappropriate joke at Carlton's expense while Mary laughed too, slapping the table. Ricky had to laugh at his uncle's mischievous sense of humor, shaking his head, and Angelica didn't like being talked about like she wasn't even there, but what could she expect from a pimp? Carlton's face was instantly flushed and he looked like he'd just been punched. Was he thinking of a retort? His mind overruled his mouth and would not allow any come-back to form. He was ready to leave.

"Hey man, I was just messing with you. Don't take it personally. What's your last name, little nigga?"

Another insult, Carlton thought.

"Meadows," Carlton spit, barely moving his lips.

Bill's face changed, his smile now gone. The air seemed to stop moving as Carlton eyed Ricky and Angelica nervously. What had just happened?

"Your father is Sid Meadows. The lawyer, right? I know him and your mama, too. Why you hanging around my nephew, man?"

Bill turned away before Carlton could answer.

"Ricky, walk me to my car."

"Sure," Enrique said, sheepishly. "I'll be right back," he said to his friends who were still trying to decipher what had just gone on.

170

Mary got up from the table.

"Take care, y'all," she said following the Williams men out of the door.

"What just happened?" Angelica asked, staring blankly at Sheila.

"Yeah, that was kinda weird," answered Sheila.

"Y'all think he was just joking with me? Thought he was funny? Maybe even cute?" Carlton asked without waiting for answers and obviously upset.

"Yeah, he was just kidding, like tongue in cheek," Sheila assured him.

"Believe me, that guy is less tongue-in-cheek and more like bullet-in-head," Carlton said, almost whispering.

As they walked, Bill was silent. They'd covered the short distance to the parking lot in only a few seconds when Bill turned to face Ricky.

"That Carlton kid is bad news. His family are a bunch of fake ass squares. They pretend to be on the up and up, but they some dirty bitches."

He began poking Ricky gently in the center of his chest, not to hurt him, just making his point.

"That motherfucker is just like his people, I can see it like I'm seein' you right now. Drop his ass or he's gonna cause you a world of pain one day. I don't know how or when, but it's coming for you with that nigga pushing the cart that's gonna roll over you. Maybe it's that girl he wants. Shit, man, maybe it's you. Take care, my man."

"See you later, Uncle Bill."

171

Bill opened his door and turned back to his nephew as Mary got into the passenger's seat and closed the door.

"Hey, when you see your brother last?"

"Not for a couple of months. My moms is kinda worried about him. You know how she gets."

"I know she is. Tell her he's fine. I saw him just last week. I'm trying to get him on at the GM plant, but he act like he too good for factory work. That's some good paper! I don't know what to do about that nigga. How long we gon' bet on a horse that keep breaking his own legs?" Bill asked in frustration.

"I know, I know, Uncle Bill."

"He keep fuckin' around out here in these streets and the streets gon' put him out his misery. I'm gone."

Ricky knew that Bill understood the economy and weight of his own words and a lot of currency had just been spent. He had a lot to consider and he was perplexed. Bill gave Ricky some skin, got in his Cady and drove away.

TWENTY-THREE

T rue to Bill's prediction, Rita was nowhere to be found when Ricky called her later in the evening, but maybe it was for the best since he had a lot on his mind, deposited there by his uncle. On the one hand, his girl was older than he was, a year ahead in school and there were a lot of miles between Detroit and Northwestern University in Chicago. It was close, but far away at the same time depending on what they wanted and right now he just wanted to fuck his girlfriend as much as possible before she left. On the other hand, the inference that Carlton "liked" him was beyond creepy and it could cast a pall on their friendship if he chose to believe it. Sure, Carlton was strange, but not "funny."

"Uncle Bill been around too many folks of ill repute," Ricky heard himself say.

Weeks later, Ricky escorted RiRi to her Senior prom at the Roostertail downtown, her wrist alight with a white carnation and his tuxedo jacket festooned with a matching boutonniere. Later in the evening, a small group of revelers held court at the Twenty Grand, the site of the after party. Some of the graduates had only heard of but had never seen or been inside either of these two Detroit landmarks of nightlife. The Roostertail was an upscale nightclub on the waterfront, frequented by Americans as well as Canadians coming across the Detroit River for highbrow frivolity and entertainment. The Twenty Grand was its colored equivalent on Detroit's West side, a supper club and showroom that featured nationally known entertainers.

Then there was the *after* after party. The hotel. Rita had made it plain that her mother wanted her home by two a.m., so it made no sense to pay for a night at a hotel when a motel, rented by the hour, would suffice. Ricky and Rita got to the motel on 8 Mile Road at 12:30a.m. and immediately got busy before the hour got away from them. Rita loved Ricky, but she knew once she got away from Detroit, she was leaving everyone and everything behind. Chicago wasn't quite far enough, but it was a start.

Ricky cared about Rita, but didn't want to get too serious because they were so young and Rita seemed to understand this, never acting too clingy. As he moved over her body with his, he couldn't help but think of Angelica Tanner. He opened his eyes and looked at Rita, the face and body he knew so well, to dispel any thoughts of being with Angelica.

A few miles away on a different part of 8 Mile, Angelica and Barry were at the West Side Drive-In taking in the double feature, "To Sir with Love" starring Sidney Poitier and, "You Only Live Twice" with Sean Connery starring once again as James Bond. Angelica could sense Barry had become frustrated at her insistence that they watch the movies and not make out. She found Poitier's put-upon teacher of inner city London teens heartfelt and realistic and what girl didn't want to look mod like LuLu? Everything about her was cool from her go-go boots to her blonde bob. Plus, she could sing! Angelica could not remember ever missing a James Bond movie and this intriguing tale had the secret agent looking as if his number, literally, was up!

Angelica let Barry hold her hand and put his arm around her shoulder, sharing some passionate kisses during the intermission while the animated cup of pop, box of marching popcorn and bun-clad hot dogs took over the movie screen imploring a visit to the concession stand. At some point, Angelica found Barry's hands on top and then underneath her blouse. When he tried to unhook her bra, she stopped him and turned her attention to the big screen, hoping he'd get the message and allow her to enjoy the movie. Her date begrudgingly composed himself trying to be content to have his arm draped across the girl's shoulder. Once the credits finally began to roll and the majority of cars in the lot roared to life, Barry went in for one last drive-in kiss. And, before long, he was grabbing Angelica's hand and placing it on his crotch, where his penis sat firm and swollen.

Angelica jerked her hand away as if she'd touched a hot stove, but Barry became more insistent with his strong fingers gripping her wrists and pulling her hands towards his erection. Angelica shook violently away from Barry and shouted, "No!" An instant later she slapped him hard across the face. His hands immediately flew off hers and curled into fists. He pounded the dashboard twice, scaring her.

"Sorry," he said, suddenly calm.

"Just take me home, Barry. Please," Angelica said, holding back the tears that threatened. There was no way she would let this boy see her cry. She just wanted to get home to her house, to safety.

They drove home with only the radio filling the chasm of silence that buried them. Every song was an eternity, babbling on and on about love. She didn't feel any love at the moment, only anxiety.

Calmly, quietly, she said, "I thought you liked me, Barry."

"Are you kidding? I like you a lot. A whole lot. I thought you were ready to do other stuff, that's all. I'm sorry, okay? I'm really sorry, okay?"

Angelica didn't answer, just kept her head turned toward her open window, breathing in the summer night. He waited to speak again.

"Angelica, we been going out for three months now. I know you're a good girl, that's one of the things I like about you. I just thought...we could...," he stopped as she turned to look at him.

They were turning down her street. She wanted to open the door and sprint the last few hundred yards to her house, but she just waited with her hand on the door handle. He'd barely stopped the car when she opened the door and bolted toward her house. Barry's tires squealed angrily as he pulled off down the street.

"He's got a lot of damn nerve," she said under her breath, jamming her key into the door lock.

Her mother must have been nearby, hearing her struggle with the lock. Liz Tanner opened the door and Angelica rushed past her, heading for her bedroom. Liz looked out of the screen door.

"What kind of boy doesn't walk his date to her door?" she asked, realizing she was talking to herself. She went down the hall to her daughter's room and rapped on the door.

"Hey, kiddo. Are you alright?"

"Yes, Mama. I have a terrible headache. See you in the morning."

"Um, okay," Liz said, reluctantly. *Teenagers!* Emotions as up and down and hot and cold as a thermometer.

Angelica lay in the bed with her street clothes still on. Her head really did ache. What was wrong with her, she wondered? She knew about sex and knew it was inevitably her fate to give up her virginity at some point, but damn, why did everything

176

seem so dirty and so rushed? What happened to romance or, "I love you?" Maybe she was just a big baby. *Immature.* A naïve kid compared to other girls her age, well, except for Sheila, but that was another story. She knew the day would come when she had to "give up the drawers," as the boys would say.

"Not today," she said into her pillow, wiping the tears from her eyes with the edge of the pillowcase.

Across town, Rita Corbin lay weeping in the darkness of her bedroom, her forearms a hard cradle for her head. Why had she been so stupid? How did she end up breaking her own cardinal rule of dating? After she and Ricky finished having sex, he held her in his sinewy arms, muscles warm and bulging from their exertion.

"I love you, Ricky," Rita had said, sincerely and tenderly, almost on the verge of tears.

Ricky looked into her eyes, kissed her lips and squeezed her body to him tightly. They listened to each other's breathing for several minutes before Ricky said, "We'd better go," tapping RiRi lightly on her butt.

On the ride home, she capriciously and nervously filled any silence, real or imagined, with a tumble of words. Ricky knew what she was doing and he wanted to tell her to stop, but that would only open the door, its transom breached, to him having to respond to her earlier declaration. Ricky did truly care for Rita, but what could he do? She was about to go off to college and what sense would it make to make things more complicated? It would be hard enough to say goodbye as it was. Surely, he thought, they both knew the fate of others who laid tenuous claim to long distance romance. A few tearful phone calls and a weekly letter would eventually, always, give way to hurt feelings and recriminations and then, silence.

Rita reached for a tissue in her purse. What did she expect? Ricky was probably shocked at her forwardness, if you could call it that. He did kiss and hold her, though, she was thinking as she flipped onto her back. That wasn't the same as someone saying "I love you," was it? The prattling on in the car may have been worse than anything. Well, she'd just have to act as if she'd never said anything to the boy. If he brought it up, she'd say she was kidding around. Lesson learned: don't ever be the first to say "I love you." The expectation of reciprocation can only crush you underfoot. *Be the one who is loved, not the one who loves*, Rita told herself.

TWENTY-FOUR

"Yes? Can I help you?" asked the plump lady with the eyebrows that looked as if they'd been drawn on by a toddler.

"Hi, um, I'm here to pick up Carlton—"

Before Ricky could finish, his friend was by the woman's side. He saw the resemblance immediately.

"Hey, hey, Ricky, whaddaya say?" Carlton said with forced ease as he flung open the screen door.

"Mama, this is my friend, Enrique Williams."

The swat of the door hitting the aluminum frame punctuated the introduction.

"Hi," Ricky said, throwing up his right hand, which Mrs. Meadows grabbed with her meaty mitts, squeezing it tightly.

"Okay, where y'all goin' again?" she asked, still holding Ricky's hand.

"Skating. We're going to Northland Roller Skating Rink over on 8 Mile."

"Just y'all?"

"No, Mama, we're going with some girls we know from school. Dang!"

"Look, don't get my son in trouble out there with them fast girls, hear?" she said directly to Ricky, releasing her grip on his tingling hand.

Ricky, taken aback, was momentarily speechless. This lady didn't even know him. What was she talking about and why weren't they already headed out of the door?

"Mama, we just going skating. Ricky, come on and sit in the den. I gotta get something out of the basement," Carlton said, leading his friend out of the vestibule and down the hall a short distance.

Ricky sat on the couch and looked down at his hand, frowning. He could still feel her hand on his, the weight of it, vaguely persistent and annoying like a spider web across the face.

"Okay. Had to get my wallet," Carlton said, entering the room.

Ricky jumped to his feet, ready to get the hell out of their house.

"Hey, wait, check this out," Carlton said, standing in front of something that looked like a curio or china cabinet. It was full of guns.

"We need to go, man. Rita and them are probably already there," Ricky said, very aware he was about to lose his temper.

"Wait, wait, check this out. These are my daddy's pride and joy. I bet you never seen a colored man with so many guns, huh?" Carlton asked, opening the cabinet door with feigned reverence.

Enrique rolled his eyes. "Shit, dude, come on," he said. Before he could say another word, Carlton was standing in front of him with a chrome plated .38 laying across his palms like a giant hors d'oeuvre on a platter.

"You want to hold it?"

180

"No, not really."

"Here, just feel how heavy it is, then I'll put it back," Carlton said, thrusting the weapon toward Ricky.

Ricky held the pistol in his hand for a few seconds and instead of giving it back to Carlton, put it back on the shelf and closed the cabinet door. Ricky walked out of the room and found his way to the front door, making his way outside, down the porch stairs and onto the sidewalk.

Carlton came running out of the house, laughing.

"Sorry, man."

Ricky looked at Carlton with a look he'd never seen before and it stopped him in his tracks as if his feet were suddenly shackled.

"Look, Carlton. There are two things I don't fuck around with—drugs or guns. And I don't fuck with or hang around with people who do, you dig? Now, I don't know what's up with you and your dad, but leave me out of that." *I already got a brother with daddy issues and I'm pretty sure he's a criminal. Probably a doper, too.*

"I got you. I'm cool."

They got into Ricky's car and pulled away. If only Carlton had known how hard it was to get Chris to agree to come out on a group date that included him. Carlton seemed to strike out with every girl he met. Ricky's face twisted up thinking about the last 15 minutes of his life, which seemed more like an hour--an hour in slow motion. Remembering what Bill had said about the Meadows family, never mind nefarious, they'd officially become weird.

Sidney Meadows walked slowly down the living room stairs and saw his wife shutting the front door.

"Who was that?"

"Oh, just Carlton's friend. They going to the skating rink."

"That's nice. Glad he's got a friend."

"Yeah, and some old fast girls are supposed to meet them up there at Northland."

"Mavis, not every young girl is considered *fast*."

"Well, I don't think I like that boy. He's an orphan. I didn't like his attitude. It's like he thought he was…"

"Good as us, Mavis?"

"You don't have to say it like that, but, yes. Maybe even better than us. He puts ideas in Carlton's head. I can tell my baby is acting strange."

"The boy is lucky to have this kid as a friend. I've seen him before and he seems decent enough. It's always been hard for Carlton to make friends. You know that."

"Well, that kid's mama is some kind of foreigner or refugee, I think. You know they all crazy."

Sidney Meadows laughed at his wife. She should never dare to call anyone crazy.

"Is he an orphan or does he have a foreign mother?"

"I guess we'll have to ask Carlton when he gets back," said Mavis Meadows, walking into her kitchen.

TWENTY-FIVE

The third week of July 1967, saw Detroit's usual summer swelter replaced with fog and rain and temperatures topping out ten degrees below normal. The summer had seemed to give up before reaching its median. Then, by the end of the week, it was warming up and Saturday was greeted by sunshine and the hotbox harmonies of every insect that had a song.

Angelica spent the morning cleaning up her room, scouring through every drawer and every inch of her closet. She hauled away too small, too old, and non-essential to the basement in boxes and bags to give away to Goodwill. She went back upstairs to wash up and change into something cute. She needed to hit the Shake 'n Spin to pick up "I Was Made to Love Her" by Stevie Wonder. She heard it on the radio all the time and couldn't get it out of her head.

The air raid siren wailed in the distance. *One o'clock*, she thought, frowning. *This Daylight Savings Time is for the birds!* It just made the day extra long, which was not great if chores were involved. Amusement park visits, bowling, block parties and general and sundry fun, that's what time embellishment was for. Angelica figured she'd eventually get used to it and hurried out of the house to find an adventure worthy of the extra daylight.

When Angelica arrived at the Shake 'n Spin, she saw Mr. Gilhooley rushing around like a mad man. His wife manned the candy counter while he held down the soda fountain. She could see it might be difficult to buy records today.

"Mr. Gilhooley, where's Ricky?" she asked the old man wearing a hairnet and a scarf like a gypsy.

"He's at home for a few days. He broke his arm."

"Oh, goodness. I hope he's okay."

"Yeah, he's okay. You getting a hamburger or something? Grilled cheese is good today."

"No, no. I came to buy a record, but—"

"Go up in the booth and see what we got. I trust you," he said pointing his metal spatula toward the disc jockey booth.

"Um, okay. Sure thing."

"Just pay my wife at the front, okay?"

"Yes, sir. Thanks."

Angelica ascended the stairs to the small platform that held the dee jay booth. On two sides of the booth's exterior there were crates of records, 45s and LPs. How would she possibly find Stevie Wonder's gem of a song? Kneeling, she began to see that the crates contained small indexes that had groupings of the alphabet. "A-K" and "L-Z."

It took about 15 minutes, but she came away with Stevie's record and a bunch more, including an album that looked like one of the psychedelic posters she'd seen around for The Grande Ballroom up on Grand River. That's where the hippies and the hip kids hung out to watch live music. This album had a man on it who was obviously the leader of the band and he was colored.

A Negro hippie flanked by two white hippies, one with a huge afro just like his. The album cover said the band was called "The Jimi Hendrix Experience" and the name of the record was, "Are You Experienced?" Angelica picked the record up and put it back at least four times, but the cool black man on the cover with the piercing eyes on his shirt unnerved her.

It was becoming very warm and humid and Angelica decided to detour from her route home and stop by Enrique's house. She ended up walking in the street a few times, the sidewalk abandoned to overzealous lawn sprinklers. She could hear Ernie Harwell's voice on porch bound radios calling the baseball game between the Detroit Tigers and the New York Yankees down at Tiger Stadium.

She bounced up the porch steps and rung the bell seeing that the front door was open and the screen latched. Ricky smiled from behind the screen door as he walked toward her, genuinely glad to see his friend.

"Hi! Whatchu got?" he said letting Angelica inside the house.

"A whole bunch of good stuff. Mr. Gihooley let me pick out my records at the Spin. Man, he needs you, brother."

Ricky took the bag from her arms and peeked inside.

Rifling through the records he announced, "Whiter Shade of Pale," "I Was Made to Love Her," love it. "Up, Up and Away," "Brown Eyed Girl," "Can't Take My Eyes Off You," and what's this?"

"I'm not sure, but it could be good. A black dude playing psychedelic music, maybe."

"Yeah, the distributor dropped that off and told me to check it out. It's not out in America yet. You're such a groovy, chick. You dig everything, don't you?"

185

Angelica was still smiling at the compliment when they went downstairs to his basement where it was nice and cool. Ricky led the way, still carrying the sack full of records like an amorous boy carrying his girl's school books, balancing them on top of his arm cast.

Angelica realized she'd never been down there before, and it made her excited inside like she'd reached a new level of trust with Enrique. The large basement with its light-colored linoleum floor, was divided by a wall with a door. On one side was the laundry area and in the middle was a beautician's chair, sink and dryer with the furnace behind a door in the corner. Angelica didn't know what Mrs. Williams did for a living, but, apparently, she was a hairdresser at least part time. On the other side of the wall where they now were was a wood paneled paradise with a bar, stools, a chair, sofa bed, refrigerator, television set and a stereo. Ricky reached behind the bar and flipped a light switch and with that the ceiling seemed to come alive twinkling and dancing with multicolored lights under a scrim.

"Nice," Angelica exclaimed.

Ricky motioned toward the stools around the bar for Angelica to sit down.

"Do you want to play your records or wait 'til you get home?" he inquired, walking backwards toward the record player.

Angelica waved her hand indicating he should put the records on. Ricky took the 45s out of their sleeves with one hand, careful not to leave fingerprints on the vinyl. He inserted a disc in the middle of each one and stacked them on the spindle in the center of the turntable. Twisting a dial, the machine woke up with the record player's arm robotically lifting and swinging slightly to the right as the record plopped down and then further to the left settling on the record.

Angelica smiled to herself and stifled the start of a giggle as she thought about the two pennies she allowed to hitch a ride atop the arm to her portable record player. As her records got worn from so much play, she needed the weight of two pennies placed just so on the arm of the stylus to play her records properly and keep them from skipping along like a carefree little girl.

A slight crackling sound came through the speakers preceding guitar licks and Stevie's signature harmonica. Finger popping quickly led to Ricky reaching his arm out for Angelica to dance with him. They started out with the *Shing-a-Ling* and the *Four Corners*, but Ricky felt hampered by the plaster encumbrance circling his arm. He pulled Angelica to him to slow drag or "social," and she was surprised at how comfortable she was in his awkward embrace. The side of her face on his chest, she could hear his heart beating so clearly as she became acutely aware of herself and where she was. As the song ended, Ricky led Angelica back to her seat and he went behind the bar.

"You thirsty? You want some pop?" he asked casually.

"Okay. You got Red Pop?"

Looking in the fridge, Ricky shook his head. "Nope. Rock 'n Rye, Tahitian Treat…or Squirt."

"Squirt."

He got soda pop for the both of them and used the bottle opener hanging from a hook on the wall to take off the caps.

"You got a lot of moves for a boy with one arm. What happened to your arm?"

"I fell."

"How? What happened?"

"I fell. Out of a window."

Angelica blinked at him expectantly.

"Hey, if you don't want to talk about it—"

"I was jumping out of a window when I got pushed. So, I tumbled out, and didn't get to brace myself. I hit some bushes and then the sidewalk."

"Dang!"

"Trust me, I'm lucky that's all that happened. I deserve much worse, believe me."

Angelica wondered if Enrique was a criminal. A burglar? A second story man? Then it dawned on her. He was a second story man, alright, just not the kind that stole material possessions.

"Was she married?" Angelica asked calmly, trying to keep her voice even and nonjudgmental.

Enrique pursed his lips and his eyes looked heavenward as if he was reading something on the ceiling. His eyes fluttered back down and he looked at his friend.

"She never told me she was married. It was stupid and wrong, I know."

Ricky fleetingly debated with himself on what, if anything, he should confide to Angelica. He knew she cared about him and even if she judged him, she wouldn't condemn him. Should he reveal that he met a woman about a month ago at Dot and Etta's Shrimp Hut on Livernois, who kept talking to him and flirting with him while she waited for her order? That she insisted on paying for his food, but he wouldn't let her, even though she clearly had money because she was buying two pounds of fried shrimp? That the two of them exchanged telephone numbers and within days he was at her house and in her bed doing things to her and having things done to himself that he'd never even heard of? That the girl was older than him and obviously relished teaching a horny, hard bodied young man what lips and tongues were really for? Or how shocked he was when they heard her front door slam and a man's voice ask his wife's whereabouts approximately three minutes before he was pushed, barely dressed, from her upstairs bedroom window?

No, he'd better not. Then he might have to explain how he could be unfaithful to Rita. Angelica was still a girl and she might not understand that he felt he needed to distance himself from the inevitable goodbye that was looming on the horizon a few weeks from now. He was losing his girlfriend to a new life, new experiences and most likely, a new boy at college.

Angelica made a mental note: boys don't bother ending one relationship before moving on to another. She refrained from asking about Rita Corbin since she'd let him offer up entre into that subject, and he didn't.

Trying to read Angelica's face, he asked, "So, how's your boy, Barry? He treating you good?"

"Yep, we're fine," she said, sipping on her bottle of pop.

It had taken two weeks of Barry calling daily to get Angelica to speak to him after what'd happened at the drive-in. Because he seemed so apologetic and remorseful, she relented.

"If that dude ever hurts you, Angel, I'm going to have to see about him, you dig?"

Angel. That familiarity returned, sneaking in like a playful puppy across a newly mopped floor. Angelica's brows knit together as she stared into Enrique's deep brown eyes, framed in a fringe of black lashes. He didn't blink. He was serious.

"Yeah, I dig."

189

Music filled the basement as the teenagers bobbed their heads and snapped their fingers to the beat.

"Can you stick around or do you have to be home by a certain time?" Ricky asked.

"No, I can hang out."

"As you can see, I'm a little bit, um, incapacitated, right? I need help with something."

"What can I help with, Romeo?"

They both laughed.

"Touché. Can you wash my hair?"

"Yeah, sure. Now?"

"Um hmm. Come on."

They went into the adjacent room where Ana Williams had her home salon. Ricky sat stiffly in the shampoo chair and for some reason, it made them both burst into laughter.

"First time, sweetie? Don't be nervous," Angelica teased, trying to sound like a comforting old beautician. "Seriously, just slide down when I put your head back and just relax."

Angelica read the labels of two nearby plastic bottles to discern what she had to work with and they were a shampoo and a conditioner that promised silken locks to the user. She even found a plastic cape to drape over Ricky in case the water splashed up. Angelica turned on the water and adjusted the temperature, agitating the water inside the small basin with her hand.

Angelica took off the rubber band from the balled-up ponytail at the back of Enrique's head. His black hair fell heavy over and past his shoulders in waves.

"Your hair is so beautiful! I know a boy doesn't want to hear that, but it's true. Most girls would kill to have hair like this."

"Blame it on the Indians," Ricky mused as he scooched down into the neck groove of the wash basin. "You really are my angel today. Thanks."

Angelica gazed at Ricky's handsome face and his eyes were closed. He had a slightly expectant smile on his full lips. She wet his hair thoroughly and the waves relaxed under the pelt of water, like a raven winged waterfall. She lathered up his hair, scrubbing and massaging his scalp expertly with her firm fingertips, her breasts stationed right over his face. *Good he has his eyes closed*, Angelica thought.

"This feels great. It's a lot different than washing your hair in the shower, you know? Speaking of showers, I'm gonna apologize in advance if I'm kinda funky. It's murder lifting this cast up."

They both laughed.

"Maybe I like funky dudes. Ummm, spicy!" she teased, laughing uproariously.

Ricky laughed until his neck began to hurt from resting on that hard porcelain lip.

"No, no. You smell fine. I would have noticed by now, especially from when we danced."

"Okay, cool. Just checking."

Then something unexpected happened. Ricky had opened his left eye only for a second and saw Angelica's shirt practically in his eye socket and when he closed his eyes again he took notice of her hand working through his hair and scalp. It was sensual beyond belief and when he fleetingly envisioned her helping him take a shower, his groin sprung to life with a massive erection. Luckily, his Levi's held it in place and the cape dutifully covered him, but he had to think of something else—diversionary tactics—before he had to get up from that chair.

Angelica was applying the cream rinse to Ricky's clean, silken locks and with every brush up against his cheek or forehead with her breasts, her nipples seemed to harden, sending an unwanted signal, a tingling between her legs. She tried to stop herself from imagining Ricky's strong brown hands emerging from beneath the vinyl cape, cast magically gone, tearing back her blouse and cupping her titties, slipping them from her bra and into his mouth. She could feel his warm mouth sucking and licking her nipples. She had to stop herself from thinking like this. He was her friend. *He has a girlfriend.*

"Hey, where's your mama 'n them?" she managed to say to Ricky.

The question seemed to calm them both.

"They went to Cedar Point. I was supposed to go too, but…this," he said, moving the cast slightly under the black cape.

"I love Cedar Point. My first time on a roller coaster was the Blue Streak. Man, was that ever cool. It had just been built and the line was so long to get on."

"I know. I dig that place. You know how you feel when you see that big red tower in the sky after your mom's been driving forever? You always feel excited like a little kid, ya know?"

"Hey, where are the towels?" Angelica asked.

"If they aren't under the cabinet, there might be some in the laundry basket in front of the dryer."

Angelica retrieved a towel and began to dry Enrique's hair.

"I can comb it myself, but I need you to put a rubber band around it."

Ricky grabbed a black Ace comb that had been sitting atop a mirror on the counter and deftly combed his hair back. Angelica had done a good job as there were no tangles. She stood behind him smiling at their reflection in the mirror.

Once she got his hair situated they went back into the recreation room.

"Let's listen to that album. I'm dying to hear this guy," Ricky said, walking over to the phonograph.

"You need help?"

"I see you didn't help me when I had to stack ten records on a spindle with one arm," he said in mock indignation.

"Okay, I know I'm not helping you now, buddy," Angelica protested with her arms crossed.

They laughed as Ricky maneuvered the album from its cover and sleeve onto the record player. Before he could make it back to the bar, "Purple Haze" had enveloped them with the slightly distorted opening notes of Jimi Hendrix's guitar and Noel Redding's bass. Ricky and Angelica looked at each other and smiled as Jimi's voice insisted from the speakers. They nodded at each other ever so slightly, grinning. This dude was boss.

"Wanna play cards? Or we can play some board games and stuff we got under the bar. Let's see," Ricky said, reaching into a shelf behind the bar.

"Well, ordinarily I would just whoop your butt in cards like I usually do, but---"

"Girl, you must be dreaming. You better wake up and apologize."

"Anyway, Mr. 'Think Long Think Wrong,' let's play some of the games you got back there. I'll beat you no matter what we play," Angelica bragged, chuckling.

"You're lucky I like you. And you'll be even luckier if I don't smoke you on these little kid games. I'm trying to keep it cool down here and keep the heat outside, but you makin' it hard."

They played "Hands Down" and "Rock 'em Sock 'em Robots" at the bar, laughing, trash-talking and teasing one another the whole time. Ricky went upstairs to grab a bowl of his mom's tuna fish salad from the refrigerator along with some Ritz crackers.

"Man, no cracker tastes as good as Ritz. It tastes fancy and makes good stuff taste even better. Do you have more pop?" Angelica asked.

Ricky crossed to the fridge and looked back at Angelica with a mischievous smile.

"You ever heard of Cold Duck? It's like champagne or something. A guy right here in Detroit invented it."

"What do you know about champagne? You tasted it before?"

"Yup. My mom let me have a sip on New Year's. This Cold Duck is pretty popular. My uncle Bill brought it over and my mom is probably keeping it for a special occasion."

"Well, I'd say me beating you in "Hands Down" is pretty typical, I mean, special," Angelica joked.

"And, me kicking your butt with my robot was pretty special…"

"Are we gonna get in trouble if we have some?"

"We'll just have a little bit, okay," Ricky said, rushing to get two high ball glasses down from the cabinet over the bar.

"Brother, these bar stools are hard after a while."

"Go ahead and sit on the bed. It's cool," Ricky said nodding his head toward the let-out sofa bed which occupied the spot in front of the television and hi-fi.

Ricky was glad he'd spread it up and hadn't left it unmade and messy. Sometimes he slept downstairs to escape the swelter that was a Detroit summer night. Once it was 11:00 and 90 degrees outside, according to Channel 4 weatherman Sonny Eliot.

Ricky brought the drinks over to the bed where Angelica was sitting cross legged. The bright blue spread made her look as if she were levitating over an azure sea with the game "Operation" and a deck of cards floating past as debris.

"I couldn't resist," she said coyly.

"Operation" was a game of limited skill that required tweezers in a steady hand to remove tiny, comically named body parts from a patient whose nose would light up with a buzzing sound when the tweezers inevitably touched the specially rigged edges of the machine. It was challenging and fun anytime, but alcohol made the game virtually impossible to play and every little mistake seemed hilarious to the two teens.

"You ever meet Carlton's mother?" Ricky asked, already tipsy and slurring slightly.

"Yup. She's fat," said Angelica, laughing and on her way to being drunk. "That's mean. Sorry."

"She's weird, is what she is. A weirdo," Ricky declared, pausing. "This music is so groovy. It's making me drunk!"

"Me too, I think."

They laughed without even noticing they had graduated to a second glass of sparkling wine.

"Hey, let's go to the State Fair! You want to?" Angelica piped up.

"Well, it's not until a month from now, so there wouldn't be much to see if we went up there today," said Ricky, believing they were both making sense.

"I know, silly. I meant when the fair opens next month."

The Michigan State Fair was a fun, family-oriented amusement that happened at the end of every summer. The nearly 100-year-old tradition took place at 8 Mile and Woodward Avenue, near the Detroit Zoo. The colorful midway, the music, the sights and smells reminded Michiganders that they were a diverse population with farmers participating in many special events right alongside local and national recording artists. Taking place over several days, the fair was wildly popular with attendance peaking in 1966 at 1.2 million visitors. It would never be that popular again, partly due to the evolution of entertainment and leisure, but mostly due to the events that would occur later that very night in 1967.

"One time, I saw an elephant at the fair. Why was an elephant at the state fair?" Angelica asked. She tried to describe the incongruous sight to Ricky. "This big elephant is in a barn with the horses, stinking to high heaven. Next thing I know, this giant ball of doo-doo comes flying out of its butt!"

Ricky doubled over in laughter, imaging the sight.

"Nasty."

"I'll say. It was like a big ole wet brown bowling ball. We were lucky we didn't get splashed!"

Angelica's wide-eyed abhorrence made him laugh even harder.

The music was still playing when Angelica and Ricky fell asleep. Talking one minute and asleep the next, a small respite had overtaken them without warning.

Enrique awoke first with his back to Angelica, momentarily not knowing where he was or with whom. He blinked a few times to clear his eyes and stretched out his hands and legs, turning over on his back. That's when he saw her. His Angel. He took advantage of these first quiet moments of the late afternoon to stare at the sleeping girl, realizing he had never woken up beside anyone in his life, and waking up beside Angelica made him smile. And yet, he didn't feel discomfort or trepidation. He wanted to stroke her hair, but didn't. He wanted to wake her up so they could talk some more, but didn't.

Ricky began to think about his father and mother and particularly about something Gabriel Williams had told his son. "Find the one who has heart. Give your love to a woman who will have your back and will fight anyone who doesn't. A pretty woman with no heart is like a fine watch that doesn't keep time. You may like looking at it for a while, but eventually, you get tired of it being more wrong than right. You begin to understand that pretty thing is pretty useless."

Enrique bent his face near Angelica's and said in the softest whisper, "I'm going to marry you, girl."

Angelica heard him but thought she was dreaming, awakening about a minute later.

"Hi sleepy head."

"Hi."

TWENTY-SIX

"I'm hungry. You wanna go get something to eat?" asked Ricky.

"Sure, me too," Angelica said.

"Since I can't really drive with one hand, you want to take a walk? Let's go up to Greene's. I would go to the Shake 'n Spin but Gilhooley might put me to work."

Everybody loved White Castle hamburgers but there were two local establishments that ran neck and neck with them for cheap, tasty, tiny burgers. Elmer's Hamburgers on W. Chicago near Oakman Boulevard and Greene's on Wyoming and 6 Mile Road. A paper sack full of hot, delicious hamburgers could be had for about a dollar. The grilled onions, pickles and mustard made the burgers explode with flavor and Greene's was in walking distance.

As they ambled, Enrique mentioned going to Elmer's with his brother and dad, but stopped short, falling silent.

"You miss your dad, huh?" Angelica said, gently.

They walked a little ways further before he answered.

"I can barely remember his face or the sound of his voice. That makes me feel low, you know?" Ricky answered, looking straight ahead so Angelica wouldn't see the tears in his eyes. "I look at his pictures to remind me." Enrique cleared his throat and smiled weakly. "My brother Danny looks just like him, or more like him than any of the rest of us. I miss my brother, too. Weird, huh?"

"No, not at all," she said, looking up at him and squinting one eye as the late afternoon sun formed a halo around his head.

At that moment they saw a surge of about 25 people, mostly walking in the street, women and kids coming up the block towards them. Ricky shook his head slowly.

"Oh, boy."

"They do this on your block, too?"

"Um hmm. Wonder what the beef is?"

A long standing, unwritten neighborhood tradition was about to be played out somewhere up the street. When kids couldn't resolve their disagreements or parents were at odds with one another, one family, along with a horde of supporters, came up the block to "visit" the other. The "home" family was called out onto the lawn and the beef was settled with an audience of instigators, hecklers and curiosity seekers. Sometimes children were made to fight, with the crowd making sure of a fair battle by not allowing anyone not a part of the quarrel, to jump in. Parents seldom came to blows but there was much cursing, threats and name calling. Once the disagreement was settled fairly, everyone would move on, en masse, the way they came.

"I don't know, but I'm kind of glad we're missing it," Ricky said, never looking back. He mulled things over for a few seconds and said, "You can't get mad at them. You want your family to back you up. My daddy used to say loyalty goes a long way. Be loyal to your family, your country and your friends."

"Dang, your dad's dead and you can still quote him? I see my mama every day and can't remember her ever telling me anything worthwhile," Angelica exclaimed.

"She has, you know she has. You just want to give your moms a hard time. You are one of the coolest girls, coolest people, I know. How did you get that way without any help from your mom?"

Angelica's heart leapt at the compliment Enrique had paid her.

"My grandparents. They always treated me like I was something special. Maybe 'cuz I'm the oldest grandchild. I don't know. My Aunt Fannie and Uncle Ned have always been good to me, too. My mother? Well, let's just say she remains a mystery."

"She still loves you, though. You gotta admit that."

"Okay, okay, since you want to twist my arm. She does."

"Man, what time is it? It's gotta be after 7 and the sun ain't even thinking about goin' down."

"Yeah, this Daylight Savings thing is cool if you're having a good day," Angelica said, smiling slyly.

Ricky grinned in solidarity as they were coming up on Charlie's Party Store on 6 Mile Road. As usual and as always, the Prentiss brothers were posted outside the entrance to the store. The Prentiss brothers were three notorious junkies whose social largesse depended upon whether they were already high or needed to get that way. Charlie couldn't get rid of them, but somehow, he kept most of his customers. It was a strange and uneasy alliance and everyone in the neighborhood knew these siblings were more pathetic than dangerous. People gave them their spare change because they felt sorry for the young brothers or perhaps they just hoped it might keep them from being robbed.

Angelica had been in elementary school with the middle Prentiss brother and for a while, every day was a small torture with the boy pulling her hair, tripping her, pulling up her skirt or some such nonsense. The final straw came when he threw a snowball, its center loaded with a rock, raising an ugly welt near her eye. At first the sting of humiliation was only equaled by the burning injury to her face. Some of the kids on the playground pointed, laughing, while others clapped their hands over their mouths in stifled shock.

Angelica ran at the boy with her book bag raised above her head like an anvil, bringing it down on the boy's head, driving him into the snow. He was stunned and didn't move as Angelica kicked him with her snow boots, her feet flailing at any part of his body she saw. Within minutes, her classmate was in tears, rolling to and fro in the snow. Sheila and some other school mates finally subdued Angelica, pulling her back. The boy got up yelling something about Angelica not knowing he was trying to show her he liked her, which enraged Angelica.

"Well, I don't like you! Leave me alone! Don't you ever touch me again!"

The Prentiss boy never again bothered Angelica and by the time they were in junior high the next year, all three brothers were in juvenile detention and well on their way to being unpopular with the local authorities.

Ricky and Angelica had no intention of stopping at the store, but knew they wouldn't likely be able to bypass its entrance without some interaction with the trio of idiots standing on the sidewalk.

"Ay, ay, say, y'all got some change y'all can spare a brotha?" the oldest Prentiss said.

"Yeah, help us out, man. Show yo' girl you generous, Cool Breeze," the youngest brother added.

"Hi fellas. Let me get you on the way back, okay?" Ricky said only pausing his gait for a few seconds.

Angelica didn't speak as she stood a few paces beyond Ricky.

"Yeah, okay then. Take it easy, my man. See you on the flip side," one of them said.

Ricky and Angelica began to walk again, just two blocks from their destination. She was relieved the drug addled young man hadn't recognized her. Ricky looked straight ahead.

"You know we won't be coming back this way, right?"

"Yup."

"Man, those dudes are sad," Enrique said, imagining that his own brother Danny could end up like those fools.

It was a challenge, but Ricky managed to eat five Greene's hamburgers with just one hand, with an occasional napkin assist from his companion. Angelica ate three burgers herself, while enjoying the tunes coming from the jukebox in the corner inside the black and white tiled hamburger joint. There was a mother eating at a table with her two pre-teen sons who seemed to be amusing one another with their antics. In truth, the bigger one was teasing the smaller one, throwing French fries at his head when their mother wasn't looking. When the mother did take notice, the smaller boy tried to explain what had happened. Before anyone knew it, the woman slapped both boys across the mouth with the back of her hand. Ricky turned to Angelica and they both burst into laughter, burying their faces in the Formica counter.

All colored children knew the hazards that came with telling on a sibling. One had to weigh whether or not the infraction about to be reported was worth the inherent repercussions since a kid couldn't always gauge what an adult thought was important and thus exempt the "tattler" from collateral punishment. In very rare instances was a child thanked and rewarded with some trifle or sent along their way, unscathed. Generally, not only would the perpetrator of foolishness get in trouble, but also the bearer of the report. And, if the teller dared to revel in the schadenfreude visited upon their sibling, it was short lived and wiped out with a shot across the chops, Moe Howard style, or with a switch from a nearby tree.

With the sun finally giving up the sky to a smattering of stars and a full moon, Angelica and Ricky stood outside the burger joint, bellies full and not wanting the day to end.

"I don't want to go back the way we came, do you?" asked Ricky.

Angelica shook her head, reading his mind envisioning the Prentiss brothers.

"Okay, let's go down Wyoming. We can take the long way home."

"You never know who we might see," Angelica teased.

"Or who might see us," he answered, with a sidelong look.

They went into the Baskin Robbins 31 Flavors trying to decide if there was room aboard for some ice cream. The boy behind the counter touted a new flavor, "Cold Duck."

"It tastes like the real thing, y'all. Might get you drunk, even."

He was completely confused as Angelica and Ricky began to laugh uncontrollably, bolting from the store and running down the street.

TWENTY-SEVEN

As the majority of the city slept fitfully in the sticky darkness, history was being made as a shot was coming across the bow that could not be retracted. Nobody in Detroit, black or white, could have dreamed the nightmare that would consume that great city over a period of six days.

The Detroit riot began in the early morning hours of Sunday, July 23 when police raided an illegal after-hours social club on the city's West side. Instead of the expected and manageable few Negro patrons, there were more than 80 people inside. As the police awaited paddy wagons, alcohol, indignation and false bravado overtook the crowd which used bottles and rocks to overwhelm the police, pushing them into retreat.

Crowds looted every manner of store and set most of them ablaze without regard to the color of the proprietor. The firefighters were fired upon by snipers and they soon gave up any semblance of rescue or containment. When the smoke cleared, literally, there were 43 people, some white, most black, taking up residence in the county morgue. Some for televisions and furniture, some for socks and cigarettes, some due to the misfortune of proximity. A split-second decision based on bad luck, bad timing and bad judgement felled many a soul.

So many of the victims of the Detroit riots of 1967 were simply and foolishly trying to outrun bullets fired by scared, ill-trained and in some instances, blatantly racist cops, guardsmen and state troopers. Sadly, innocent victims like the four-year-old shot in the chest by a mortar shell while in her aunt's arms, as well as black men in police and firemen's uniforms, found no protection from the indiscriminate destruction of a bullet. No sanctuary to be had in the arms of a loved one or in the blue and brass of an official uniform.

So much more than just people died that week. The dreams and hopes and future of the city on the river were snuffed out. Perhaps those who threw Molotov cocktails or the incidental and random match into the stores within their neighborhoods believed someone would simply rebuild them. Why wouldn't they? The distrust and desolation swept silently and swiftly over the city like the cloud of radiation that was forewarned every Saturday afternoon at 1:00 p.m. Except, no one ducked or covered. They left. White citizens moved out of Detroit and to the suburbs in a massive migration without precedent. How were these people able to mobilize themselves and their families so quickly?

The economic slide down had a momentum of its own like snowflakes in an avalanche. And, nothing was ever the same. The Summer of Love, for those living in Detroit, Michigan, had ended abruptly in blood and ashes.

TWENTY-EIGHT

Bill Williams was cruising downtown Woodward Avenue, having just broken his hos on the track nearby. He slowed down his Cadillac and happened to glance toward the Coney Island joint near the Fox Theatre, spotting Danny through the front window. Feeling hungry, he decided to park and go inside for a bite and chat up his nephew. Bill navigated the big boat of a car into a space in front of the restaurant and hopped out.

When Bill came striding in, the air seemed to change and quicken with excitement and electricity. Other pimps and players were giving him skin as he passed by, his every step seeming to form an invisible wake pushing people to either side of him. The few hos in the place kept their eyes lowered, as if royalty were passing by. Every whore knew the chance she took by staring at Still Bill since he kept 7 bitches—no more, no less, at any given time. Whoever knew when there was a vacancy? No matter how tempting the idea of defection, it wasn't worth an ass whipping. If a ho was lucky enough and brave enough, and yes, stupid enough to try to choose Still Bill Williams, she had to break herself right then and there, giving all her money to Bill. Out of respect, even though everyone could plainly see what had taken place, Bill would have to serve notice to some unfortunate pimp that his ho had "chosen" Bill.

Danny saw Bill walking, swaying as if to a musical accompaniment, toward his table. Seeing his Uncle Bill in his element, seeing the fear and the respect he commanded, never got old for Danny.

"Hey, Uncle Billy," Danny said, with a tinge of braggadocio.

"Hey nephew, what's the haps?" Bill countered as he slid into the booth next to Danny.

"This is my friend, Dave Lizaro, but we call him Dave the Lizard," said Danny as he gestured with his head toward the young man sitting across from them.

David's family, the Lizaros, had a garage and collision shop where his dad fixed automobiles. The neon sign out front was in large capital, block letters and the "O" was ill formed and partially rounded and therefore looked like a "D." Dave had been called "Dave the Lizard" since first grade and no one had plans to call him anything different. The bigger mystery was how someone as black as he and his family were ended up with an Italian surname?

"Hey, little nigga. Your daddy owns the grease monkey joint?" Bill said, less a question than an acknowledgement.

"Yes, nice to meet you, Mr. Williams," David said, good naturedly. *Wow, Bill Williams knows my family!*

Bill laughed slightly. "Calm down, motherfucker, we ain't on a date."

Daniel shot a look over to his friend, who appeared chagrined and slightly deflated.

"Dave, he's just kidding, man. Trust me, my uncle only cracks on people he likes."

"Where the bitches at? Why you two hard legs sitting up here with no hos?" Bill asked.

"We had a couple of girls with us, but they had to go home. They were kinda young, man. They mamas came to pick them up from the Fox."

"Y'all at the review they had over there tonight?"

"Yeah, man. It was the bomb. Some dudes I know from Pershing High was performing tonight, The Dramatics. I'm telling you, Uncle Billy, these brothers is bad. The Temptations better watch theyself," Danny said.

"Man, let me hit the reefer you smokin'. Ain't nobody, no male singing group, badder and got more precision than the Temps. Little high school niggas? I don't think so," Bill said, taking out a Kool.

The grill was sizzling with frankfurters about to become the famous hot dog treat known all over Detroit as a Coney Island. A grilled kosher beef hot dog was swaddled inside a softly steamed bun, topped with a smear of mustard and slathered with fresh chili and chopped onions. The skin on the hot dog was so taut it snapped when bitten. *The only dog that bites back*, everyone liked to say.

"Ok, Unk. Mark my words, you heard it here first. We're about to swing over to the spot they stayin' at, the Algiers Motel over near Virginia Park. Some friends are meeting us over there, so we gotta get going. Good seeing you, Uncle Billy," said Daniel, signaling that he was ready to be let out of the booth.

Bill didn't move. Instead he peered over to David.

"Hey, my man, you mind giving me and my kin folk some privacy? There's a seat for you up at the counter," Bill said, indicating an empty stool with a nod of his head.

209

"Yeah, cool," said Dave the Lizard, getting up from the table.

Bill slid into the seat the boy had just occupied and was now facing Daniel.

"The Algiers, huh? That place might be a little rough for your young ass. I know some players running hos out of that place, some dope dealers too. Why don't you find something else to do tonight?"

"Nah, it's cool. My homeboys work with the Dramatics and they only there tonight. I actually want to talk to them about Ricky. You know how much he loves music and want to get into that business. Man, Ricky's smart, he knows music and I think he could be a manager or somethin'. And, by the way, the Algiers is a motel still in the lay-your-ass-down-and-get-some-sleep-business, ya dig?"

Danny laughed and Bill laughed too.

"Alright, cool," Bill said, lighting his cigarette and blowing the smoke straight up into the air. "What about you? What are you doing for money these days?"

"Oh, odds and ends. This and that," Danny said, vaguely.

This pained Bill because Danny, with the angelic face and cool demeanor, was the replica of himself. He knew if Danny didn't find something legitimate to occupy his time and free his mind up, the streets would claim him.

"Look, Young Blood, I know it's hard to believe, but I do know a few people. I can get you a job working at GM or how about at Henry Ford Hospital? I can—"

"Doing what? I ain't no square, Uncle Bill, you know that. I ain't gonna push a broom at no hospital or anywhere else. That

210

kinda shit is for squares, chumps and gumps. Let me hustle with you or somebody cool that you know," Danny implored.

Bill's eyes flashed with anger as he pulled the cigarette out of his lips and leaned forward.

"Danny, I am the first, last and only hustlin' motherfucker in this family. This is what I do, this is what I know. This is what I chose. I'll be damned if any of my brother's kids go down this road. You have choices that we didn't have. Your daddy chose the straight path and sacrificed himself for a bunch of strangers. I don't judge him. It was his choice and he's a hero. I chose the crooked path and, as much as these motherfuckers smile in my face, they want to cut my throat. You think niggas like me get to retire from this shit, man? Do something good with your life, man. Your mama and them love your ass and worry about you all the time."

Bill had calmed down and stabbed out his cigarette in the small glass ashtray on the table. Daniel had never heard him speak like that. He didn't know what to think or what to say.

"How about I think about it, okay? I could use some help. I want to go to Wayne State," said Daniel.

"I can help you with that too. Let's talk on Saturday. Where you staying at?"

"With Dave's family. Here," Daniel said, writing the Lizaro family's phone number on a napkin with a stray pencil the waitress had left behind, handing it to Bill.

"Cool," Bill said, motioning to Dave, who had never taken his eyes off the two men at the table.

Dave walked over just as Danny and Bill stood up.

"Y'all need a ride?" Bill offered.

"No, I got my wheels," Danny responded.

"What you pushin' now?"

"A VW bus," Danny replied, self-consciously, girding himself for the laughter and derision he knew was surely coming his way.

Bill laughed so hard, he almost fell.

"What the fuck?" he said, coughing, practically choking. "No wonder them bitches had they mamas pick 'em up. I wouldn't want to be seen in that hippy shit neither!"

"Well, it's paid for and girls like it. It's like a hotel on wheels," Danny said, proudly defending his unlikely whip as a pussy wagon.

"Alright, alright. Take it easy, fellas. Talk to you on the flip side," Bill said, gliding out of the restaurant.

"Damn, we are so late! I bet they are partying up a storm, man," David said, looking at his watch.

"Let's go," said Danny, flicking dollar bills onto the table for their tab.

Since they were running late, Danny and Dave decided to smoke some reefer, parking in a dark, deserted alley on a side street to get high. The effects of the marijuana and heavy food on them was like a sleeping pill as two hours passed in silent torpor.

"Shit, Dave, wake up! We musta fell asleep. It's past midnight," Danny said, disoriented and squinting at his watch. "Fuck! What we gonna do about the curfew?"

"Where the hell are we?"

"I don't know, but we gotta either get to your crib or to the Algiers."

"Let's just swing by the motel. I mean, it's a motel. We could be travelers from out of town. We should be cool."

"Or we could be shot," said Danny, starting his vehicle.

When the young men got in the vicinity of the Algiers Motel, they were surprised to see police activity—flashing red lights, lots of blue uniforms, the fire department and ambulances. They decided to park as close as they could without invoking the notice of the police and try to walk up to the motel. They drew closer, walking down Virginia Avenue with a mixture of curiosity, excitement and fear. The policemen who were monitoring the crowd that had gathered, were asking people to disperse. People in the crowd began to shout them down, asking the police what they had done to the guests of the motel, demanding to know why there was such a large police presence on their block at that hour of the night? They were obviously defying the curfew, and most of the officers seemed to be more concerned about what was happening inside the Algiers Motel than on the street in front of them. Other policemen were now bordering the increasingly riled up crowd, batons at the ready.

"What happened?" Dave asked a barefoot girl in a black mini dress with pink foam rollers in her hair.

She looked like she'd gotten out of bed to see what the commotion was about.

"I don't know, but, I heard the pigs killed some kids at that motel," she replied.

Dave looked at Danny whose eyes were already sweeping the scenery for snipers or police who wanted to be heroes. They could only pray their friends were not among the dead, but the reality was that young black lives were the most expendable resource there was. Both of them realized Bill may have saved their lives by detaining them at the Coney spot past their meet up time with their friends at the motel. Detroit had practically been burned down in the past three days with riots and looting all over the city with dozens of lives lost. The fact that they were able to gather at the Coney Island joint without a hassle, while the curfew was in effect was a gift horse in whose mouth no one wanted to peer.

Back at his home, Bill grew uneasy as the night progressed. He'd been thinking about his nephew Danny since a phone call with his partner Smoke just a half an hour earlier.

"Man, some funky shit done went down at the Algiers. I'm hearin' they mighta killed some young niggas down there. And, there was a couple of white chicks down there, maybe pros. All yo' girls wit you, man?" Smoke had asked.

This curfew was putting a major dent in business for Bill. Having all his hos at home at the same time made for a tension filled atmosphere. It was clear that they all got along best in shifts. Bill insisted that they find new ways to work during the daylight hours up until the witching hour that was the city-wide curfew. Because they were used to being up at night and asleep during the day, this turn-about made them all quite edgy. But they weren't stupid. They did not want to upset their Daddy. Bill did not like unrest in his houses, so they played nice when he was around. All his bitches had gotten home safely and by 9:30 p.m., no less!

Had Danny and his homeboy gotten off the streets in time for the 9:30 p.m. curfew or had their smart asses decided to go meet their friends at the Algiers? Bill knew he might be risking his life, but he needed to see about Danny. He changed into the squarest shirt he could find, an olive green Banlon, grabbed a black, straw stingy brim hat and walked into the living room, past Chan and two of his other girls. The girls all looked at one another as he

214

was walking out of the door. Bill stopped and turned back toward Carol and Denise standing nearby.

"How do I look?"

He had pushed the hat back on his head like a farmer might, a rube. They were confused, exchanging nervous glances, having never seen him look so silly.

Finally, "Kind of like a square, Daddy," said Chan.

"Good."

He was out of the door and sliding behind the wheel of his Mercedes Benz. Bill's Caddy was for street business and his Benz was for anything that wasn't.

The streets were deserted and Bill had to use side streets to get from the West side over to Woodward Avenue, taking forever just to crawl down from Grand River. Once he found the street, he had to try to cross it without being caught or stopped so he could make it down toward Virginia Park. It was strange seeing military vehicles on the city streets. The police and National Guardsmen seemed to be preoccupied with a couple of clusters of mostly Negroes on both sides of the street as he eased past.

When Bill was near the Algiers Motel he began searching the darkness for Danny's VW van. Snipers and police had shot out many of the street lights and the blackness enveloped the street like a spreading ink blot. He felt like he'd been tooling around far too long, and he was sweating in the heavy summer night air. *This thick ass shirt ain't helping*, he thought. The hot and humid atmosphere was like someone breathing down his neck letting him know he was on a dummy mission and his luck was about to run out. Then, he saw the van. But was Danny with it?

Bill pulled up close to the vehicle with his driver's side next to its passenger side. The window was down.

"Danny! Danny Williams!" Bill whispered loudly.

Danny's face quickly appeared in the short distance to the driver's side of the van. He leaned over toward where Bill's voice had come from, trying to see. Dave the Lizard's head popped forward out of the confusion of sleep, as if on a spring.

"It's almost 3 o'clock in the morning. What are y'all doing over here?"

In the murkiness, Danny could barely make out his uncle's features, though he could clearly see the hat perched strangely on top of his head, and the voice was unmistakable. He knew it was Bill Williams. He also knew he was about to get cussed out.

"Get the fuck out of the van and get in this car. Hurry up!" Bill said in a roaring whisper.

Within seconds both young men were in the back seat of the car.

"Get down and be quiet."

Danny and Dave slouched down into the seat, almost lying down with their shoulders touching. They were uncomfortable and slightly embarrassed, but relieved to be on their way somewhere, anywhere away from the war zone.

They had heard random gunfire that seemed close by and decided to wait it out in their vehicle. Better to stay put than to risk being a moving target. Danny and Dave had planned to be at a party all night with some drinks, reefer and girls. They planned to do what young men were prone to do on a summer night at a motel with their friends. Now, they lay quiet in the back of Bill's car, wondering about their buddy. Was he wondering where they were?

Their friend was lying dead inside the Algiers Motel at 8301 Woodward Avenue, shot in cold blood, at close range, by the Detroit police. The two white girls, two members of the singing group The Dramatics, and four other men who survived the police brutality of that evening, would bear witness to one of the most savage nights of the Detroit riots. Soon enough, the world would know the story of the events that had taken place that summer night at the Algiers Motel at Woodward and Virginia Avenues.

Three black males, teenagers, had been tortured and murdered by the police without provocation. Whatever plans, dreams or hopes those young men went into that motel with that night, had been extinguished like a finished cigarette and discarded with as little care. They were now names on a historical roster of victims killed before or during the riots that took place in Detroit in the summer of 1967.

"Do y'all have a piece?" Bill asked.

"No, I left my .22 hidden in the van," Danny answered.

"Are you holding?"

"No, we were gonna get high once we got to the spot. We figured somebody probably had some decent weed, so we smoked what we had."

"Okay, just lay low back there and stay quiet. I don't want the pigs to freak out if we get stopped. And, if we do get stopped, let me do the talking."

As the car rolled slowly down the dark side streets, Bill started to feel relieved. These two fools were so eager to get some pussy they were risking their stupid lives. He had to smile to himself.

Yes, he was in the right game, alright. These idiots were living proof of what lengths a man will go to for some trim.

Suddenly the area Bill found himself travelling through was awash in strobing red lights. He saw the police had stopped two cars in the distance.

"Shit."

He knew he couldn't do anything but keep moving toward the lights as a uniformed officer walked toward the car, neither fast nor slow. Warily, Bill held his breath and set his jaw tightly.

"Sir," the officer now at his window said, "why are you out here past curfew? Are you aware the curfew is 9:30 p.m., ordered by the Governor, until further notice? You should not be on these streets, sir."

"Well, gee, officer, I do know that for a fact, I do. I was out trying to keep an eye on my store down on Woodward Avenue. Trying to make sure it's still there and hasn't been burnt to the ground, doggone it."

Danny and Dave looked at each other in the darkness of the back seat. They were now practically on the floor. Suddenly the way Bill's hat sat on his head and the square looking threads made sense. Daniel knew Bill could pass for Italian or Greek very easily. Tonight, in this light, Bill Williams was a white man.

"Okay, well you've got to get off the streets sir or you will be subject to arrest. Do you understand?"

"Yes, officer. Thanks for all your help. I'll be on my way."

And with that, Bill began to pull away. Before he got more than a few feet the officer was beating on the trunk of the car, indicating he wanted Bill to stop. *Oh no, here we go*, Bill thought.

The policeman rather breathlessly appeared again at the window. His hand was now atop his still holstered weapon.

"Yes sir, officer?" Bill said in the same voice he'd used before. A voice that can only be described as Bill's version of a law-abiding citizen, a guy he didn't know.

The officer withdrew his hand from his service revolver and grabbed a flashlight from his belt and shone it into the back seat of the car.

"Who are these boys? What are they doing with you?"

The policeman now sounded peeved, as if he was getting the feeling wool was trying to descend over his eyes.

"Officer, these colored boys work in my store. I had them guarding the place until I could come and pick them up. I'm taking them safely to their homes," Bill explained calmly.

The officer stared into Bill's blue eyes, which by now were full of sincerity and purpose. The policeman seemed flummoxed and was getting angry.

"I just wanted to make sure they weren't holding you against your will or something. These black animals have gone crazy in this city."

Bill answered quickly to put salve on a sore point.

"No, no, officer. I appreciate your concern, but as I said, these niggers work for me. I'm taking them home."

The cloud lifted from the brow of the man in uniform and his demeanor changed. He liked that this guy was calling a spade a spade, literally. The officer nodded his head up and down, unconsciously, bobbling like a dashboard ornament.

"Goodnight, sir," he said patting the side of the car door just below the window.

"Goodnight, officer," Bill said with a jaunty wave of his hand.

Bill put his outstretched palm over the seat toward the back of his car where Danny and Dave both slapped him some skin. Bill was relieved that he hadn't been asked to get out of the car and that his square Banlon shirt and set back lid had worked their magic of deception in perception. If he'd gotten out of the car, the cop would have seen what he was wearing on his feet. Gators. Purple ones. He pulled his stingy brim Stetson from Henry the Hatter forward and down, just above his eyebrows and rolled on into the night.

TWENTY-NINE

The knocking at the door became steady, rhythmic banging that jarred awake Ana Williams and Enrique, who had jumped up and grabbed his Louisville Slugger baseball bat from under his bed. They met each other in the dark hallway.

"Stay here, Mama. Let me see what's happenin'," Ana's son said.

Dogs were barking in the distance, but the banging had ceased, perhaps because a light had been turned on inside the house. It had to be after 2:00 in the morning. Who the hell was knocking on their door at this time of night?

Ricky stood behind the door with his right hand tightly gripping the bat, left hand on the door knob.

"Who is it?" he asked, loud and hard.

"Man, it's me. Danny."

Ricky exhaled, rolling his eyes as he opened the door.

"Man, you almost got beat with this bat!" he said, letting his brother into the house.

A short horn burst pierced the night and Ricky looked toward the street to see his uncle pull off in his ride.

"Is everything okay, *mijo*?" Ana called out.

"Yeah, Mama. It's just Danny."

Mrs. Williams came quickly down the stairs to embrace her eldest son.

"What happened? Why you here so late?"

"Nothing," Danny answered. "Uncle Bill picked me up downtown and didn't want me to go back to my place on the West side cuz things is still hot over there. There's still a curfew because of the riot."

"It's okay. You stay here. This is your home, Danny. Stay as long as you want," his mother said, holding Danny's hands in hers.

"Nah, I'm just here 'til tomorrow. I gotta get back."

"I'll get some clean sheets. You go back to bed, Mama," Enrique said.

"Are you hungry, son? Do you want something to eat?" Ana asked.

"No, I'm fine. Goodnight, Mama."

"Okay," Ana said with a sigh of reluctance before going back up the staircase.

When Ricky got down to the basement with the sheets, Danny was already in his shorts. Together, they stripped off the old sheets and made the bed up with the cool, clean sheets Ricky had brought, working in silence. Danny slid underneath the covers and let out a long sigh. He closed his eyes and put his forearm across them, signaling he didn't want to talk or be questioned. He just wanted to sleep, but he could feel his brother standing nearby, staring at him.

"What, man?" he said with mild exasperation.

"What's going on with you, man? You must be in some kind of trouble to come here. What's really going on?"

Silence.

"What happened to your arm?" Danny asked, never taking his arm from his face.

"I fell. Why are you here?"

"Can't a nigga come home sometime? I told you Uncle Bill saw me and Dave the Lizard out and decided it was dangerous. We swung by Dave's and dropped him off first."

"Okay, dude, okay."

"Hey, you think Mama would like a new TV? A color TV?"

"You bet' not bring no stolen, looted shit in here, man. Mama don't want that."

"She won't know. Maybe I bought it with money from my job."

"What job you got, Danny?"

Danny sat up fast and straight like a stuck piston.

"Okay now, boy. You better watch how you talk to me. I'm the big brother, not you, nigga."

"So, what you gonna do? Fight me now? Come on, Danny."

"Naw. You just seem like you gettin' a little bit too big for your britches. I guess you the man of the house, right?"

"Like I want to be. If dad was here---"

"Oh, but he ain't. He ain't here. He went off and got killed for some damn people who don't give a damn about us."

"That's not true. He died in service to his---"

"Nigga, please! I don't see it that way and you know what? Neither do Uncle Bill. Only yo' stupid ass."

The silence hung heavy like draperies in a parlor. Danny could see his words had stung his little brother.

"Sorry, man. You ain't stupid. You doin' better than me, that's for damn sure. It's good you gonna be a lawyer. I might need you," Danny chuckled.

"Not a defense lawyer, Danny. An entertainment lawyer. For singers and actors and what not."

"Oh yeah, I forgot."

"This is my Senior year coming up in September. Then I'm going away to college. I don't like to think of Mama and Eddie and Pi-pi by themselves, Danny. They need you. How you gonna help Mama, if you're always in trouble or running from the law? Why is this outlaw shit so fascinating to you?"

"Hand me one of them Kools in my shirt pocket. The matches are in my pants."

Ricky rifled through the small pile of clothes on the floor and found what his brother had asked for. He tossed the crushed pack of cigarettes at Danny, followed by the matches. Ricky sat nearby, patiently waiting for an answer to his question and wondering what the stall was for? What yarn of criminal intrigue and street-wise mischief was Danny going to weave?

Danny took two long drags from his cigarette, turning his lips upward, head tilted back slightly, as the smoke punctuated the air.

"You remember when I broke it to you that there wasn't no Santa Claus?"

224

"Yeah. That shit was cruel and traumatic. I was so mad you showed me our presents and stuff."

Danny laughed.

"Sorry about that, man."

"That was the last Christmas Daddy was actually around for. He was on leave. I remember I had to pretend to be excited on Christmas day. But I really wanted to cry."

"You see, Ricky, when you're a kid and you believe everything, all the bullshit your parents tell you, it makes you weak in a way. They call it fantasy or preserving your innocence, but in the end it's pretty much a bunch of fuckin' lies. You can't un-know something once you find out or figure out how the world really works. When you believe in Santa Claus, there's nothing but possibilities. You pray to God, you go visit Santa down at Hudson's and you cross your fingers until Christmas day comes. You all excited and happy and grateful for whatever you get, right? It's like validation that being good works. You feel lucky and you just want to keep it up until next year. Who knows? You could get everything on that list of yours."

"Okay, I don't get it."

Danny stabbed out his cigarette in the ashtray on the floor and sat up in bed with his arms folded.

"Then you come to find out Christmas is not a crapshoot of luck and goodness…it's your parents. Oh, great, these motherfuckers! So now that I know, I'm gonna take it personally when I don't get all the shit I want. They punishing me without saying that's what they doin'."

"Wait a minute. You sound crazy. Were our parents rich? How many kids are there in our family? So, you turned to a life

225

of crime because you didn't get a pony or some shit for Christmas?" Ricky said, incredulous.

"No. What I'm saying is, I'd rather take my chances with the people and situations that let me feel like anything could happen. Things haven't already been decided, no matter what I do or how hard I try, you dig? I want to decide my own fate, rolling the dice, taking my chances. It makes life...exciting! Nobody will ever decide what I should have or what I deserve. Only me, brother, only me."

"That sounds dangerous, Danny. But, it's your life."

"That's right. And, as far as sounding crazy little brother, you ever wonder why I didn't go to Vietnam? Why I'm still here in Detroit and not across the river in Canada?"

"Probably because you have a record?"

"Naw, nigga, that ain't it. The stuff I got busted for was juvie, petty offenses. I ain't never been to jail and don't plan to go. Now, what I did do was show up to my draft date, high as hell. I was impaired enough to flunk my physical, but not enough that I could get arrested. Shit, I wasn't holdin' nothin'. What they gonna do? 4-F, baby."

He lit another cigarette and pointed to Ricky.

"That shit ain't crazy. It's smart," Danny said, pointing to his temple with the cigarette burning between his fingers. "You know what is crazy? Thinking--"

"Man, if you mention Daddy fighting for strangers one more time--"

"Thinking that yo' black ass ain't gonna be drafted or you gon' get a deferment because you in college. You done mixed up yo'

'D's' boy. *Deferment* is for rich white boys. *Draft* is for niggas and everybody else who ain't the other."

Ricky knew once his brother had his mind set on something, it would be like trying to get a bone out of a dog's mouth to get him to drop it.

"Alright, man. Try not to burn the damn house down," Ricky finally said.

He stood up and turned off the light, heading upstairs to bed. Ricky stopped at the third step.

"I love you, Danny."

"I know," his brother answered sleepily.

THIRTY

T he summer shuffled on like an injured foot inside an oversized shoe, unsteady and wincing. Angelica began to date Barry again after a month of contrite phone calls and two Hallmark greeting cards. The boy seemed to be sorry and ashamed of his loutish behavior and Angelica seemed to believe him.

The day before Labor Day, Angelica and Barry made the annual pilgrimage of so many Detroiters to the Michigan State Fair. The perilously bright and gay midway was in danger of injuring the eyes of onlookers and everyone, white and black alike, was cautious and optimistic and determined to find normalcy in that end of summer ritual. Sergio Mendes, Johnny Cash and Motown's favorite daughters, The Supremes, were the entertainment. Diana Ross and The Supremes held court for four days and though they were Detroit girls, people could scarcely believe these elegant young women were right before them onstage, poised and stunning.

Angelica and Sheila and anyone else who'd give them encouragement, used to mock Diane Ross for changing her name and pushing herself forward as the leader of the group. But seeing them in person wiped away any cynicism. Angelica was enthralled to the point of temporarily forgiving Miss Ross for the absence of original Supreme, Florence Ballard, who was no longer in the group.

Angelica and Barry went on a few more dates before school intervened, casting them back into academia and away from one another for most of the week. Angelica was excited when Barry called to ask her to accompany him to a house party on San Juan. Twin and them were Seniors at Mumford and were having a "Back to School" shindig. The invitation was an index card with the ingenuity of brevity: who, what, when and where. The entrance fee was twenty-five cents to cover pop and potato chips and three members of Mumford's football team stood sentry at the door to collect money, let people in and kick people out.

Barry and Angelica danced almost every record from the time they arrived. After about an hour or so, the lights dimmed—Twin removed some light bulbs from his mother's floor lamps—and it was time to "social" or slow drag. Because she hadn't slow danced a lot, Angelica was always slightly nervous and very conscious of the fact she had to relax enough to let a boy lead her on the dance floor.

Even though the heat and humidity had fogged up every small window ringing the basement, Barry pulled his girl close and settled into a slow, sweaty groove. Soon his hands had travelled from her mid back to the top of her buttocks, just below her waistline. It was so crowded in the basement, each couple was barely moving, mincing around the floor with truncated steps. Angelica's hair was plastered to her neck and Barry had gotten musty as his deodorant was failing. She could predict where Barry's roving digits might end up, but she didn't want to make a scene.

"Barry, can we get out of here? It's just too hot down here."

"Okay, baby," Barry said, surprisingly agreeable.

The cool night air was a relief as they made their way out of the door and down the driveway. Just then, a kid from school recognized her and waved.

"Is it still happening in there?"

"Yup, we came out cuz it was so crowded, but it's definitely a happening party," Angelica answered.

"Cool. Hey, where's Ricky?"

"Oh, um, shoot, I don't know," Angelica said warily, staring at the boy to give him a visual punch in the arm for being so indiscrete.

"Yeah, okay. See 'ya," the kid said, hurrying up the driveway.

"Like I'm supposed to keep tabs on Ricky Williams," she snorted.

"Let's go," Barry said brusquely, walking toward his car a few houses down.

Once they settled inside the car, Angelica rolled her window down a bit to cool off and dry out her damp hair.

"I'm hungry. Do you want to get something to eat or you want to go home?" Barry asked, seemingly recovered from the perceived slight.

A voice inside Angelica, strong and clear, as if she was sitting next to her own body, said, "*Go home.*"

"Okay, we can get something I guess. I'm hungry too," she said, settling back into her seat.

The night air was invigorating and felt good flowing through the windows. After a while they were riding down 8 Mile Road, toward Southfield.

"Where are we going?"

"I thought we could swing by Onassis for some Coneys."

Angelica wrinkled her nose and pushed out her lips thoughtfully.

"It's 11:00. I don't think they're open this late," she said, glancing at her Timex.

Barry looked straight ahead.

"Well, we'll see," he said drily.

Angelica was noticing their conversation inside the car became less and less with each exchange, contracting and evaporating like a drop of water in a hot skillet. *I know he's not mad because some guy asked about Enrique. That's silly. He needs to get over it and stop being such a drip.*

Barry's car swung off 8 Mile and into the parking lot of one of the many motels lining the street. Garish and brightly flashing arrows beckoned them to come inside to an oasis of free phones and television. Angelica turned to Barry, her back against her car door.

"What is this? What are you doing? I thought—"

"You thought what? That you could tease my ass all night long and I wouldn't do anything about it? I just want what's mine. You probably been giving it up to that pretty nigga, Ricky Ricardo, huh? Now, I've been more than patient," Barry said.

Before he could say anything else, Angelica flipped up the door lock and was opening the door. He grabbed her around her waist with his muscular right arm and slid her across the seat and practically into his lap.

231

"Look, girl," he said, breathing into her ear. "If you don't do what I want, I'm gonna just tell everybody you did and how'd that be? Everybody would know you're a slut."

"Let me go, you asshole!" Angelica screamed, nearly jumping across the seat, scrambling out of the car as his grip slackened.

Reaching across the bench seat to close his door, he yelled, "How you gonna get home?"

"Don't worry about it, fuck face!"

Angelica went inside the motel and Barry drove off.

"Sir, can I use your phone?" Angelica calmly asked the fat bald man at the desk.

Cigar smoke choked the air, complementing the drab interior.

"We don't have no phone for public use," he said, barely looking up at her from the Dream Book he had in front of him, contemplating what numbers to play the next day.

"Mister, I need to use a phone! I'm stuck and I need to get a ride home," she said, sobbing now.

The old guy clenched his cigar between his stained, yellowed teeth.

"Okay, okay. Jesus H. Christ!" he exclaimed, pushing the phone toward her from behind a little partition on top of his desk.

Who could she call? Who would be up this time of night or home at all on a Saturday night? It was a long shot, but she called Sheila. Mrs. Davis was not happy that she was calling so late, but Angelica said it was an emergency and Mrs. Davis listened on the extension as the girls talked. Angelica was saying Barry had gotten fresh with her and she got put out on 8 Mile Road.

"Girl, my daddy got our car. He's visiting his brother in Pontiac. Shoot, call your mama. She'll come get you."

"Can't. She's out with my Aunt Fannie. Who knows where they are? I'll just catch a cab home and just give them my piggy bank money."

"Dang, that hurts. What is the address you're at?"

Angelica inquired about her exact location with the man behind the desk. She relayed the info to Sheila.

"Okay, let me see if I can call Ricky Williams. I'm sure he'd come get you. He's listed, right?"

"No, no, no. I don't want him to know about this."

"Angelica, that's ridiculous."

"I gotta go. Thanks, anyway," Angelica said, before hanging up the old, heavy black phone. It was as old fashioned as every single thing that populated that lobby. *This place should be torn down*, Angelica thought.

"Okay, girlie. 'Ya got yer phone call. There's a bus that comes down 8 Mile and the last one is in about 40 minutes. You got car fare for the bus?"

"Yes, I've got enough money to catch the bus down to my side of town. Thanks."

Angelica pushed past a couple who had just come in, and went outside to find the sign for the bus stop. She peered down the street and could see the bus stop sign hanging from a post about half a block away. Angelica was glad she'd worn Levi's jeans instead of a dress to the party. Her legs were warm enough, but she struggled against the cool night air with just a blouse and a light sweater. She was grateful that her anger didn't preclude her from remembering to grab her sweater and purse on the way out of Barry's car. *Bastard.*

She walked the short distance to the bus stop and plopped down on the empty bench. She wanted to scream, she wanted to cry, but instead Angelica Tanner laughed and shook her head.

"This could only happen to me," she said aloud.

The minutes dragged by in seconds coated in molasses. The only thing that broke the monotony was the occasional car slowing down to offer her a ride. She politely refused each entreaty. The last one had been a bit aggressive and she finally cut him off with, "Get lost, creep!"

A car came past and made a U turn and was now coming slowly towards her. She turned her head to make sure this new lout knew she was not interested in anything he might say to her. The window rolled down and Angelica could see a man in her periphery.

"Get lost, jerk!" she shouted.

"Well, if I do that, how you gonna get home?"

Angelica recognized the voice and she'd never been so happy to hear anything in her life. She turned as Enrique pushed open the passenger door.

"Hop in, girl."

Angelica got into the car, closed the door and briefly glimpsed over at Enrique. Angelica ran her hand through her hair.

"I must look pretty crappy. I'm so embarrassed," she said, quietly.

"You're embarrassed? I'm embarrassed that I was home on a Saturday night. Alone. And now we're in *my mom's car.*"

After a beat, they both began to laugh. When the car went silent again, Ricky looked at his friend.

"What happened?"

Angelica surprised herself by telling Ricky everything that had taken place between herself and Barry, trusting him not to laugh, but to understand that she'd done nothing to cause what happened to her that night.

"I'm just glad you're okay. Can you eat? I can get you something from UT Gardens," he said, referring to the Chinese takeout place on 6 Mile Road that was open late.

"No, I just want to get home before my mom."

"Okay," he said as he turned on the radio to let some music help comfort this girl he cared so much about.

"The Big 8 CKLW Motor City Weekend!" the disembodied Johnny Mann Singers harmonized as a Motown song took over the darkness.

THIRTY-ONE

At school on Monday, Angelica gave Sheila a bear hug, whispering in her ear, "Thanks, girl." Sheila patted Angelica on the back knowingly, relieved everything had turned out alright. Breaking apart, Sheila gently pushed Angelica's left shoulder.

"Why didn't you call me yesterday?"

"I don't know. It was kind of a weird day. I mostly read and finished my book report. I went to bed early."

The school bell trilled loudly, echoing and bouncing through the halls.

"See you at lunch," Sheila said, turning toward the Biology lab, its door open and its fluorescent lights pooling onto the linoleum in the hallway. Angelica went the opposite way, darting into the crowd, trying to get to her Math class around the corner before the second bell rang.

Within a couple of days, Angelica and Sheila noticed a distinct and strange atmosphere had permeated their lunch time. Usually, the two girls would gather at the periphery of the cafeteria, looking to be a part of a happening lunch table. There was always something fun going on—gossip, jokes, plans for parties and movies, recaps of favorite TV shows—and all with Angelica at the center like a hostess at a dinner party. She paid attention to everyone and everyone paid attention to her, hoping she liked their take on the peculiar universe that was high school. Now, her usual crowd seemed to be preoccupied and, could it be? *Avoiding her.* Angelica and Sheila tossed off the bad vibes and sat down at their own table. One of the members of the varsity football team, whom Angelica knew only in passing, slid across the bench seat and came to rest directly across from her.

"Hey," the boy said.

Angelica looked at Sheila who signaled with a slight shrug of her shoulders that the boy could not possibly be talking to *her.* Angelica turned back around to face the boy.

"Hey," she said, bewildered.

The kid was kneading his hands nervously.

"Would you want to go out with me? I could take you to the drive-in, if you wanted to."

"Um, I don't even really know you. And, I'm not really dating right now."

"Oh, that's not what I heard. It's cool, though. Let me know when you're ready," the hulking boy said, getting up from the table.

Angelica and Sheila watched as the boy went back to the table where the other varsity football players sat. Several of the boys gave him skin, slapping his palm with theirs. Shockingly, one boy, who'd had his back to Angelica, turned around and blew her a kiss. They all began to laugh.

Angelica sat blinking furiously, mouth agape in confusion.

"What the heck was that all about?" Sheila queried.

Angelica was about to say she had no idea, but stopped as she began to realize that Barry had made good on his threat and must have told his friends she was a "loose" girl. Bad news, lies, and rumors travelled like lightening amongst teenagers.

"I think I know," Angelica said.

THIRTY-TWO

The whirring buzz of a lawn mower rose and fell in the distance as it trekked across the expanse of patchy green grass. Another part of the lawn hosted the gentle *chick chick chick* of a sprinkler, gratefully pretending it was not yet fall.

Barry Myers stood near home base on the baseball field behind Mumford High School. The late afternoon sun was in his eyes as he hit balls being pitched to him by one of his teammates. Most of the team had headed home while a few others, including Barry, stayed after practice to brush up on some personal challenges to better their game. There was a smattering of girls, always girls, in the bleachers nearby, cheering the boys on and chatting excitedly.

Barry tugged on the brim of his baseball cap and turned to one of the girls in the stands. He winked and blew a big bubble with the wad of gum he had tucked in his jaw. The girl giggled and waved. When Barry turned back around he saw someone walking rapidly toward him carrying a baseball bat. The sun made it hard to make out the details of the features, just a tall silhouette advancing on him, a bat over one shoulder clutched by a sinewy arm. For a second it ran through Barry's mind that the arm looked like a coiled snake.

The pitcher took a rest, putting one hand on his hip and the other up to shade his eyes. The walker never broke stride when suddenly there was a shift in the position of the clouds over the sun, revealing him to be Enrique Williams. Barry only became aware that he himself was smiling when his face ceased to do so. Enrique was not smiling. Barry considered this unexpected visit as unwelcomed as the snake would have been. Instinctively, Barry stepped back into the grass.

"Hey, what are you—"

Ricky used his bat to end the discussion before it began, striking Barry in his right shin.

"What the—" was stopped by a blow to the back of his left knee.

Now writhing on the ground with not enough hands to grab everything that was ablaze with pain, Barry began to cry.

"Stop it! Stop it!" he managed to scream. "Why you hittin' me, man?"

"You sure got a lot of questions for somebody with no teeth," Ricky said, raising the smooth wooden bat over his head.

He knew he wasn't going to hit the boy in the mouth, but Barry didn't know any such thing. He knew a kid who had lost all his teeth after accidentally being hit in the mouth with a baseball bat. The boy's mouth was a fascinatingly repulsive void from which errant food particles often launched.

"What! Wait a minute! Is this about Angelica?" Barry asked, hoping to bargain with Ricky.

Ricky raised the bat threateningly higher.

"Say her name again, nigga, I dare you. Put her name in your mouth one more time—"

"Okay! Okay!" Barry cried out, but the bat had already made contact with his left shoulder.

Barry was now curled up in the grass like a millipede that had been kicked. The girls in the bleachers had stampeded down the stairs and out of the field, books and ponytails flying. The other players, Barry's teammates, stood back, unmoving as if an enormous magnet held them in place. They could see as menacing as Ricky was, he was only interested in Barry.

"I don't know who you told them lies to, but you better track 'em down and make that shit right, you dig? Angelica Tanner is nobody's slut or ho, you asshole. You better make the announcement loud and clear or I'll be seeing you again, you dig?"

"Yes! Yes! I got it! Okay!" Barry shouted in a preemptive effort to avoid another blow.

He was looking up at Enrique, who, like a nightmare sprung to life in the daylight, turned and seemed to disappear in the ether. Barry's shoulders shook with his sobs, but it only lasted a few seconds. As if remembering where he was, he angrily shouted at his team members.

"Thanks for all the help, guys! I'm glad I mean so much to y'all!"

"Man, it was one on one! Y'all both had a bat! It was a fair fight," one of the teens said, as the small group of four boys moved toward Barry's crumpled body on the ground.

"Fine! Just help me up! I don't think I can walk," he said as a couple of the boys got each underarm to hoist him up.

Barry let out a loud yelp and the boys let him slump back to the grass.

"Yo' leg might be broke or somethin'," one of the boys said.

"Can somebody go to the office and call my mama? Please?" Barry implored.

Someone went to retrieve a pencil and a piece of loose leaf paper to write down his home phone number. Three of the boys trotted off as one was left behind to look after Barry. Silently, the kid wished he hadn't pulled babysitting duty. There was no way his friends weren't laughing at how much of a pussy Barry Myers was.

THIRTY-THREE

A kernel of an idea had been germinating inside Sheila Davis all during the summer of 1967 and came to flower in October. Sheila had decided that she was a young lady and wanted to be treated as such by her mother, the woman whose taciturn manner could peel paint off the walls. The woman whose unblinking stare could cause the hardest criminal to confess to something he didn't do.

Sheila couldn't help the fact that her mother had lost one child to inattentiveness and another simply lived too far away to visit with regularity. The truth was, she was still being treated like an elementary school kid and it had to cease. Sheila decided 17 was not too young to wear a little eyebrow pencil, rouge and lipstick. It did not make her look, as Velma would say, like a "floozy." What kind of a word was that anyway? She had proven her responsible and dependable nature dozens of times over.

Angelica and her pals had wanted to visit the Chit Chat Lounge on 12th Street, but unfortunately, the riot had burned down that idea. Even before the trouble, their parents would have likely nixed the idea of their kids going to a very adult night club specializing in soul music in a questionable neighborhood, so, Angelica cooked up a new field trip for them. She told Sheila that on Friday the 13th, she, Carlton and Ricky were going to visit a music club up on Grand River called the Grande Ballroom.

"I think it's mostly white kids, so, we should be okay, right?" Angelica wondered aloud.

Though she asked Sheila to come, Angelica had no hopes of her friend getting to go out to hear music on a Friday night. But, Sheila said she was coming with them and she was making Friday the 13th her "lucky day!" Velma Davis was sick with a very bad cold sapping her strength and causing her to spend most of the day in bed. Mr. Davis, not used to his wife needing his care, bought a portable television set at Montgomery Ward to make Velma's confinement more comfortable. Each day Sheila lost her nerve to ask her mother if she could go out with her friends on Friday night, until finally, she declared she was going to go and nobody was going to stop her. She just had to figure out how.

Between naps, Velma would complain about the doctor's edict of no cigarettes. Fortunately, relief came daily at 1:00 p.m. via Channel 9 and "Bill Kennedy's Showtime." The strains of "Just in Time" wafted through the air as former Warner Brothers contract player Bill Kennedy, appeared with a captain's cap skewed atop his head, peering over his eyeglasses with a cigarette in hand and a few scotches under his belt. Bill always had the back story and back stage gossip on every movie he showed.

Sheila had asked her friends to meet her at the end of the alley at 9:00 p.m. Mr. Davis was asleep on the couch, the television flickering softly off the walls of the living room, offering atmosphere to the soundtrack of his snoring. Mrs. Davis was asleep in their bedroom with her door closed.

Quietly, Sheila changed into a mini dress and made up her face. Staring at herself in the mirror, she decided she looked different tonight. She looked fun. She looked happy. Sheila crept down the living room stairs, stealthily, moving cartoonishly slow. Other than a few creaking stair steps trying to give her away, she made it to the landing, into the vestibule and out of the door without a sound. She opened the side gate to her backyard and latched it again in silence. Sheila ran to the back gate bordering the alley and peered over the fence. *Dark*. Maybe she was a few minutes early. She could wait.

Velma Davis awoke to an unnaturally still house. She got out of bed and put on her housecoat and slippers, wondering where she could go to sneak a cigarette this time? She had been sneaking a smoke here and there during her convalescence, even though her doctor had urged her to quit smoking and her husband had put his foot down regarding the matter. She always chuckled when she lit up and drew that first inhalation of delicious tobacco. They could say whatever they wanted, doctor and spouse, she did whatever the hell she wanted. And that, was that.

Velma eased down the stairs and into the kitchen. She found a half-crushed pack of Pall Malls in the drawer that held her extra bullets, batteries, spare change, matches and various and sundry items. She stood casually in front of the window and absentmindedly grabbed the matchbook from the drawer. As she lit her cigarette she saw something in the dark, moving in the shadows within her back yard. She pushed back the chintz curtains and peered through the window until it became clear what, or rather, who she was seeing.

Sheila stood stock still with her hands atop the gate, face directed toward the end of the alley, only three houses away. A car pulled up to the mouth of the narrow alleyway, blocking it off from anything that might want to get through. The window on the driver's side of the car rolled down. Sheila could see Carlton in the driver's seat with Angelica and Ricky in the back. Angelica, who was behind Carlton, was practically hanging out of the window. She waved at Sheila, beckoning her to come ahead.

Sheila lifted the gate's latch and instinctively latched it back without a backward glance. Finally, free! Finally, able to be unencumbered by unreasonable rules! Finally, ready to show she was a responsible young adult! Sheila walked a few brisk steps toward the waiting automobile, her eyes having adjusted to the darkness after waiting outside so long.

She heard a subtle clank behind her, and as she kept moving toward the car, she saw Carlton's window go up and her other two friends fall back into their seats as the car lurched forward, ducking down as the vehicle screeched off down the street. In its wake, leaves flew up into the air, chasing one another in a roundabout before fluttering back to the ground, exhilarated by their trip to nowhere.

"Hey!" Sheila cried out.

"Hey, my ass! Get yo'self in that house!"

Sheila whipped around to face the orange glow of the cigarette that had scared off her friends. That cigarette hung out of Velma Davis' mouth. Once the car with the trio got down the street and was heading toward the expressway, Ricky began to laugh and soon, even though she felt bad for her friend, Angelica was laughing so hard she was crying. Carlton joined in, too.

"Dang, I thought my mama was scary," Carlton said.

"She is," Ricky and Angelica said in unison, which only made them laugh that much harder.

"This is going to be a good night," Angelica said. "Maybe not for Sheila, though," she added, wiping mirthful tears from her eyes.

THIRTY-FOUR

Arriving at the front of 8952 Grand River Avenue, the teens could see young people lined up around the side of the building along Beverly Court, where the entrance was. Underneath a metal awning painted white and emblazoned with the words "Grande" in blue puffs of letters, was a set of oversized double doors painted bright yellow with a psychedelic red sunburst overlay. They found a place to park and walked up the street to stand in the queue.

Angelica knew many of the people entering The Grande Ballroom were her age or perhaps only a few years older, yet they seemed mature beyond their years, as if they were taking the opportunity to be real live grown-ups tonight. Maybe white kids grew up faster, or at least looked like they did.

As the line moved up quickly, Ricky said, "Only in Detroit would they take pride in mispronouncing Grande to make it *Gran-dee*."

"Are you sure I'll be able to get in? The poster said no age limit *and* you must be 17. Which is it?" Angelica asked, sounding worried. She did not want to spoil the evening for her friends by being denied entry to the dance hall.

"You should be okay. Pretty girls don't need I.D.," Carlton said.

Angelica smiled at Carlton.

He was right. In fact, none of them had to show identification, they just needed $2.50 to give to one of the two serious looking men at the door. Clearly not hippies like so many in the crowd, they said, "No alcohol inside" very loudly, every few seconds.

The Grande Ballroom had been open a year by this time and it was the coolest live music club in the city, even though ironically, the place had no air conditioning and was like a sauna once the bodies packed inside. The neighborhood wasn't grand, but that didn't stop white kids from the suburbs from filling it to capacity each Friday, Saturday and Sunday night. The house band was a dynamic group of Detroit rockers called MC5, as in Motor City 5, whose high energy sets were so exciting, sometimes the so-called headliners wouldn't go onstage after them.

The Grande would go on to host not only the best bands in Detroit and neighboring towns like Ann Arbor, but future rock and roll royalty and blues kings like Jeff Beck, Cream, The Who, Sly and the Family Stone, B.B. King, Howlin' Wolf, and Big Brother and the Holding Company fronted by a shaggy haired girl named Janis Joplin. At the Grande, the "e" was never silent. How could it be?

The three friends could see upon entering that everyone was headed upstairs where the band was playing loudly, shaking the walls and floor with reverb from their amplifiers. The upstairs was cavernous, like a great hall inside a Moorish castle with a large wooden dance floor. The periphery was ringed with arched portals behind soft velvet couches on which sat young people in various states of consciousness. It was almost completely dark except for the strobe lights hitting a glittery silver ball hanging from the ceiling, which lent an urgency to the undulating bodies on the dance floor while cutting through the haze of marijuana smoke. Angelica and company was fascinated.

The stage, with its proscenium like a huge yawning mouth, was where MC5 was midway through their blistering set. As the crowd was manically dancing and jumping in place, Angelica reminded herself that white kids weren't particularly good dancers, they just sort of moved like the synapses in their brains were wildly firing away. It was already insufferably hot and sticky inside the club and the night had barely gotten underway. A boy with glazed eyes was standing very close to Angelica and though no alcohol could be purchased at the Grande Ballroom, this guy had a bottle of Boone's Farm Apple Wine and offered her a swallow as a friendly gesture. Angelica just smiled and casually waved the bottle away, thinking God only knew what germs resided on his chapped lips.

Out of his peripheral view, Ricky could see a joint being passed and making its way toward him. He was wedged into place inside the crowd and couldn't move. As a girl with shoulder length chestnut colored hair and a headband made from what looked like Roman coins put the reefer to Ricky's lips, he was surprised when it was immediately taken from her hand by Carlton. Carlton slipped the joint between his lips, took a deep drag and held it before coughing spastically and giving the marijuana cigarette back to the girl.

"Wow, man. Ain't you suppose to drive us home tonight?" Ricky asked Carlton with more than a little bit of disdain.

Carlton was still stammering a reply when Ricky grabbed Angelica by the shoulders and pushed her through the dancing throng toward the stage. Carlton followed them forward, but stood slightly behind them, staring dumbly at the band onstage. Ricky and Angelica managed some ersatz dancing to the driving beat of the drummer. This was neither the place nor the audience for their usual, more "hip" dance moves.

Once the music ended and the band left the stage, the trio made their way over to the few couches they could see slung low in the darkness. Miraculously, a man and woman got up to leave and Ricky slid into the seat, pulling Angelica down with him, laughing at his brashness. Carlton chanced a look down to see if there was room for him to sit, already knowing there wasn't, but acted like he didn't care anyway. He knew at some point during the evening, sooner than later, he'd begin to feel like what he was—a third wheel.

The music started again and the crowd, which had been rustling with anticipation before the band hit the stage, now exploded in applause. This group was from England and they called themselves Cream. Ricky was tripping on the psychedelic guitar licks while Angelica wondered why even white boys from England sported Afro hair-dos? It seemed to her that people wanted to be black without the hassles, hardships and heartaches that came with the actual skin color.

Carlton couldn't understand why everyone was so entranced by the musicians from Britain when it seemed their song about brave Ulysses went on forever. He bet himself he could actually read "Ulysses" before their interminable song might end. And this was still only the very first song!

Bored, Carlton found himself squeezing through the crowd, travelling down the stairs and alighting on the first floor where it was decidedly cooler and less crowded. Ornately psychedelic posters announcing coming and past shows at the Grande assaulted his senses. They were as amazing as they were difficult to decipher.

"Pretty cool, huh?" said a petite white girl with red hair.

The girl, like a pale Pocahontas with two thick braids adorning either side of her round face, was right at his elbow.

"Yup," was all Carlton could muster.

"A guy named Gary does most of the posters. Far out, man!" she said, indicating the three most immediately in front of them.

One was the lithe figure of a nude woman, a double conjoined image, relaxed and proud of the triangular bush between her legs. Carlton quickly looked at another poster that looked like something found in a library with its scholarly 18th century boy featured prominently. Then there was the bright yellow poster advertising the weekend's events in the style of a mushroom cloud. *Explosive indeed*, Carlton thought, derisively.

The girl slipped her hand inside Carlton's and began to walk toward the exit.

"Wait, wait. Where are we going?"

He tried to let go of the girl's hand, but it was surprisingly strong and tight in its grip. The girl didn't say anything until they were outside. They walked a few feet to the alley around the side of the building.

"Don't you want to trip, man? It makes the scene so much groovier." The girl had clear blue eyes and gap-toothed smile.

She reached into the small fringed and beaded purse hanging around her neck and produced two tabs of LSD, one of which she popped into her mouth.

"Open up, Buttercup," she said with her fingers above Carlton's face, much like a human giving a dog a treat.

Carlton shocked himself by opening his mouth. She stuck out her tongue with the unspoken command that he do the same. She placed the acid on his tongue and smiled as they stared at each other for almost a full minute. Carlton wasn't sure what had happened or what was going to happen next.

The night air was dry and cool and smelled of lingering leaves burned hours earlier. The flame haired girl began to kiss Carlton and he didn't try to get away this time. He couldn't believe what was happening to him--a stranger, a white girl, had her tongue in his mouth! The girl, feeling Carlton's rising excitement, began to rub the bulge in his pants. He thought he was being rude and should take her hand away, but didn't. For a millisecond he thought of what his mother might say, but the thought flew right out of his mind as quickly as it had come.

The drug was starting to take effect because he was floating and powerless when the girl took his dick out of his pants and began to masturbate him right there in the alleyway. There were people nearby, but he didn't know nor care if they could see. The girl, very deftly pulled some wadded-up tissues out of her purse. Carlton let out a yelp when he came in her hands which had been feathered with the tissues.

A few minutes later Carlton and the girl went back into the club through the yellow and red sunburst doors, whose pattern now seemed to be spinning slowly as if in time to the music being played above. As they passed the posters on the wall, the scholar was following Carlton with his eyes. *Did he just wink? Does he know what we just did?* The "twin" girls in the other poster now beckoned with arms like serpents, hair billowing in an invisible breeze.

As they ascended the stairs, Carlton began babbling about how much fun he was having, even though he was drowned out by the music. He turned to talk to the red-haired girl again and she was gone. Just like that. Caught in the crowd, he allowed his eyes to travel all over the room, but the girl was not there. He did see Angelica and Ricky, no longer sitting but standing side by side, swaying to the music. They stopped dancing just as Carlton came to a stop in front of them. Ricky and Angelica looked at one another and then at their wide-eyed friend.

"Oh, shit," said Ricky. "What you been doin', man?"

Carlton opened his mouth and then thought better of it. Should he tell them? Would they even believe him? Both answers rolled and tumbled into a "no" like dice thrown at a craps game.

"Are you going to be able to drive, Carlton?" Angelica asked, slightly peeved. It was obvious Carlton had taken something.

At the end of the evening, Carlton surrendered his car keys to Enrique in a grand gesture.

"Home, Homes!" he exclaimed, laughing uproariously at his little joke.

They drove to Carlton's house talking excitedly about how much fun they'd had, ears ringing in the aftermath of the amplifiers. Even still, Angelica felt those kids they were with that night were far more worldly than they. Carlton seemed to have fallen prey to that worldliness.

"We're gonna say he drank some beer, okay?"

"You got that, man? You drank some beer and got a little bit drunk, okay?" Ricky said, co-opting Angelica's suggestion.

Carlton happily acquiesced to the suggestion, hoping he wouldn't be on punishment too long. He smiled to himself. That hand job was worth any punishment his parents would mete out.

Mrs. Meadows, answering the door at Carlton's house, was not happy with either Ricky or Angelica. She pulled her son into the house and fairly slammed the door in the teen's faces. Ricky and Angelica hadn't gotten off the porch before the light shut off, plunging them into the darkness. This struck the two as exceedingly funny as they lurched off the porch, crying with laughter and collapsing in a heap in the grass.

"Did you just snort?" Ricky asked, barely able to get out the words, he was laughing so hard.

Angelica's head bobbed up and down in assent as she could not speak, she was wheezing so much from their amusement. They tried to "shush" each other for fear Carlton would get in even more trouble with them cracking up over his mother's reaction. Of course, that made them heave and double over laughing even more. Once the mirth died down and they stood up, they realized they were high and dry without a ride.

"Dang, girl. I guess it's the long way home, huh?" Ricky said as they turned in the direction of Angelica's house.

THIRTY-FIVE

Officer Adam "Kaz" Kaznicki pulled his patrol car into a space at the curb, right in front of the Shake 'n Spin. Amplified music played through the speakers above the electrified sign over the door, cutting through the fading glow of the late afternoon sunshine. A neon go-go dancer in stop motion went from a twist with arms outstretched to a jump with her arms up in triumph, in three quick moves, again and again. Though plastic strips beat the air on the front of the big air conditioner over the entrance of the store, it wasn't as cool in there as it should have been, to Kaznicki's thinking. *Why is the air conditioner on in the fall, anyway?*

He could smell the fruity, assorted sweets before he could see them through the rows of plastic bins. The bulk candies had shiny metal scoopers peeking up from behind the candy counter. As he ventured further into the store, he could hear the sizzle of frying hamburgers, the *ting ting* of the stainless-steel spatula alternately flipping them and scrambling the onions on the grill, as well as kids yelling over one another just to be heard. The combination of hot dogs, burgers, French fries, ice cream, candy and loud music was a heady temptation to the average teen. *They gotta be spending a pretty penny every day with this Gilhooley guy.*

The policeman scanned the small throng at the magazine rack and then at the soda fountain looking for a familiar face, when he spotted Enrique Williams with a queue of girls taking up every seat at the worn Formica counter. So out of place was the man in his deep blue cap and uniform, that Ricky's eyes were drawn immediately to the policeman. Almost instantaneously, recognition and regret crossed Ricky's face. He needed to find a way to get from behind the counter, but, shit, the cop was looking right at him.

"Hey kid," Kaznicki said loudly, as he approached Ricky.

Ricky stopped moving and exhaled deeply, shoulders slumping slightly as if someone was pushing them down on either side. He turned fully towards the policeman.

"Yes, officer?"

"Need to talk to you. Let's go outside."

This was not a request or a suggestion. It was a veiled threat of disruption issued as a command and Ricky knew it.

"Sure," Ricky said, smiling to thwart the curiosity of the chicks at the counter as well as his boss, Mr. Gilhooley, who was within earshot.

Ricky gestured with his hands to signal to Gilhooley he needed to be relieved behind the counter. He put his index finger in the air, shaking it slightly to indicate he would only be a minute. Kaznicki and Ricky walked outside and then the short distance to the alley behind the store.

"Do you remember me, boy?" the cop asked.

"Yeah, didn't you work at the Y?" Ricky asked, though he already knew the answer. He remembered Adam Kaznicki as a coach who taught kids to play basketball at their neighborhood YMCA. He and Danny would go there every day after school. Ricky hadn't seen this man in a couple of years and he'd certainly never seen him in his cop's uniform. That wasn't all that was different about the man standing in front of him.

"Looking for your brother, Danny Williams. Know where I can find 'em?" the policeman asked.

Ricky's eyes narrowed slightly, "No, sir, I don't."

It wasn't a lie. He didn't know where his brother was. He hadn't seen Danny in about 3 months, not since the riots. Ricky was standing with his back almost touching the white washed brick of the store's rear. Adam Kaznicki stepped very close to him and leaned in, smiling. Ricky knew the smile was only a ruse. He didn't know anything and even if he did, he wasn't about to rat out his own brother.

"That brother of yours is bad news. Ricky? Right?"

Ricky just stared at him.

"Him and his friends are thieves and robbers and the Detroit Police are gonna find them. I'd hate for somethin' to happen to 'em. Why don't you make it easy on him and tell me where he is, son?" The smile was gone now.

"I told you, I don't know," Ricky replied. "I gotta get back to work," he said trying to step around the officer.

Ricky felt a hand on his chest, the fingers firmly pushing him back in a reflexive action.

"Listen you little half-breed...you and that smart-ass brother of yours is gonna end up dead or in prison anyway. I'm so sick and fucking tired of trying to help your kind and all you do is steal from good people who are trying to make somethin' of themselves and do somethin' for their families," Kaznicki spat.

Ricky's eyes were now on the officer's right hand, which was touching the butt of his service revolver, still holstered in its black leather prison at his side. Something had set this cop off and he didn't want to end up another dead nigger in an alley.

The policeman stepped back and relaxed.

"It's okay. Maybe your mama knows where her boy is. I'll bet she does. Sure. Hey, ain't she a Mexican or somethin'? The bitch better have her papers in order, 'cuz by the time we get her all sorted out with the INS, well, I guess your brother and sister will be just fine in foster homes. Have a good day." The cop turned to leave.

"Wait a minute," Ricky called out. "I swear, I don't know where Danny is. I haven't seen him since before the riot."

"See ya, kid. I'm on my way to your house."

"My brother lives on the West side. He didn't move with us when we moved here last year, okay?" Ricky said, finally.

"What street? Where does he hang out?"

"I don't know the address, but it's a gray brick house on Cherrylawn. It has green awnings over the front porch and windows. It's right off of Grand River."

Ricky noticed Kaznicki had relaxed his stance and both hands were now at his sides.

"My mother is an American from Puerto Rico. Please leave her alone, okay?" Ricky asked, trying to conceal his contempt for this disgrace to a police uniform standing in front of him.

"Thanks, boy," Officer Kaznicki said as he went back around the corner, heading towards his vehicle.

Ricky dug into his pockets for a dime to call his brother. He raced to the phone booth near the front of the store after making sure the policeman's patrol car was down the block and had turned out of sight.

Inside his patrol car, Adam Kaznicki's jaw was set like a steel trap about to be sprung. He wasn't going to radio in for back up to meet him at the house on Cherrylawn. He would go over there himself and see what the situation was and whatever happened, happened. The West side of Detroit had been his beat for years. He volunteered to coach kids to play basketball through the Police Athletic League and the YMCA was the facility they used. It had made him feel contributory and even patriotic to help the youth of that neighborhood.

Kaznicki grew up in Hamtramck, right off of Woodward Avenue, in a tight knit Polish American family. He was the baby and the one and only boy in a family of 4 older sisters. He adored his father, who had been a hard-working grocer whose business was one of the most successful amongst patrons in the Polish American enclave of Hamtramck. Alfred Kaznicki was a butcher by trade and a green grocer with an ebullient manner, loved by all in the community. He was proud of his large family, but especially of his son, Adam. How he loved that boy and the ease with which he could straddle life in the old world of his father and mother, and the new world of America and Detroit. He was an American boy, his boy.

One morning as Alfred was opening his store and expecting a meat delivery, some young men came to his back door, which he had propped open. Guns drawn, they were there to rob Mr. Kaznicki, but foolishly, they hadn't realized that his day's receipts went to the bank at the end of the night or in the very early morning. He almost always used the night deposit at Manufacturer's National Bank and only kept a small amount of bills and coins to begin the business day. The thieves netted a few cartons of cigarettes, three cases of beer and fifty dollars cash. 68-year-old Alfred Kaznicki died on the floor of his store, shot three times in the head.

The Kaznicki family was inconsolable. The funeral cortege was so large, one would have thought a dignitary had been assassinated. Adam viewed his father's remains at the funeral home before the wake, arriving early to see the body and make sure everything was in place and just right before his mother and sisters arrived. Adam kept his hand on top of his father's folded hands for a long time, his face awash in tears. It was the coldest thing he'd ever touched, like stone in the dead of winter. He knew he had to be strong for the women of his family and for his colleagues in the department who were coming to pay their respects.

Inside the quiet solitude of the church, near the alter, this is where he would say goodbye. Adam bent down to kiss his father's cheek and slowly rose up, walking a few steps to the left to inspect what remained of his dad's hair. In photographs as a young man in Krakow, his father had possessed the most beautiful, thick auburn mop. Peering over the dead man's head, he suddenly saw it--a nickel sized hole near the top left side of the back of the head, right before it met the satin pillow. Visible inside the hole was a tuft of cotton left uncamouflaged, some type of batting the mortician had used as filling like the cotton inside an aspirin bottle. His father's head resembled an egg that had the yolk blown out of both ends for Pysanky, the elaborate Ukrainian hollow egg decorating tradition. Adam quietly freaked out, shaking so badly he had to grab the edge of the casket to steady himself.

The 18-year olds who killed Mr. Kaznicki had attended the Y a couple of years earlier when Adam was a volunteer there, two colored and one Polish kid. *Was it a coincidence or had these boys targeted him and his family? Why?* It didn't matter. They paid as most criminals do—one way or another. All three culprits got life sentences and the Polish boy hung himself in prison. Kaz got transferred to a precinct on the Northwest side of Detroit in 1966, a year after his father's death.

Kaznicki pulled his patrol car onto Cherrylawn from Grand River and waited. His hand unconsciously moved over the handle of his weapon unsnapping the strip of leather that held it in place. He found his fresh pack of Lucky Strikes in the breast pocket of his uniform, pulled out a smoke, lit it up and waited.

The Williams family moved to Detroit in 1964 following Gabriel Williams' death in Vietnam. Danny struggled during that year, his Senior year, but he soon found his "level" of associates and continued to get into minor trouble with school and the law. When his father was alive, it seemed no matter where they lived, on or off the military base, trouble followed Danny. The most serious offense occurred at 15, when he broke into the house of one of their neighbors. No charges were brought, but it was a great embarrassment to his father. Gabriel was putting his life on the line for his country, for his family, trying to keep himself alive in their hearts and minds, while his teenaged son was acting a damn fool, throwing dirt on the family name.

Daniel Williams moved out of his mother's house the day he dropped out of Mackenzie High School. The family had attended the graduation ceremony of a cousin at Ford Auditorium downtown and met up afterward for a big dinner at Stanley's. As the festivities wound down and the relatives began to depart, Danny told his mother he'd see her later. He never came home. After a week of worrying and asking relatives to try to locate her son, Danny called his mother and assured her he was fine. Ana Williams realized something she'd known since Danny was about 12 years old--she was going to lose her son to the streets and she would never be able to get him back. Like a rubber ball cast onto

261

a body of water, the more she reached out, the further along and the farther away he drifted.

Kaznicki allowed a patina of sweat and common sense to overtake him as he sat down the block from the house he suspected held Danny Williams and a robbing crew. Kaz wanted to be a hero, but he also wanted to be alive to enjoy the recognition. He radioed in to dispatch his need for help in apprehending these lowlifes and assistance came in the persons of Jack McMahon and Walt Shea. The two officers had jurisdiction over this particular area and Kaznicki knew he'd better defer to them. The two patrol cars, Jack and Walt in one, the lone Kaznicki in the other, cruised closer to the house. They'd decided to go to the front door of the home and try to lure the suspects outside, if they were indeed there.

Kaznicki got out of his police car and carefully checked the side of the house, signaling to the other officers that he was going into the backyard, when he saw a large German Shepherd rushing toward the gate. The animal was on a very long leash but was able to throw himself up onto the fence. Kaz retreated back toward the front with the two other officers. Hands on weapons that were still holstered, there was now nothing to be done except go onto the porch and ring the doorbell--the element of surprise evaporating with every bark and growl of the riled-up dog.

A skinny, dark skinned black woman answered the door. Her hair hung like a curly decoration at the bottom of her head scarf. She had a cigarette between her lips, nothing in her hands.

"Can I help y'all?" she asked, narrowing the door's opening as the uniformed officers were revealed to her bloodshot eyes.

"I'm officer McMahon, this is officer Shea," Jack McMahon replied, gesturing with a slight tilt of his head toward Walt.

The woman couldn't see Shea and didn't open the door wider for a better look.

"We are looking for Daniel Williams and Kenneth Reed. We have reason to believe they reside here."

"Naw, naw. I don't know nobody name no Daniel or no Kennif. Sorry," the woman said, attempting to close the door.

Did she really believe she'd be rid of the cops that easily? McMahon put his foot in the opening between the door and jamb.

"We know they live here, lady. What's your name?" definitely a question that sounded like a demand coming from McMahon.

"My name is Deborah Pettiford and this is my house, okay? Don't nobody live here but me, okay? Now, I'm tryin' to cook dinner and it's burnin' on the stove, so—"

McMahon had pushed the door open a bit with his left elbow. He immediately noticed several things: there were at least 5 brand new console television sets up against the living room wall, their wooden tops gleaming in the dying sunlight. As he quickly gazed through the room he could see several brand-new couches, still enrobed in their plastic cocoons as well as large boxes stacked floor to ceiling. It was like a furniture warehouse.

The other thing he noticed, which was subtle and even more alarming--the dog had ceased barking and had vacated its post behind the gate at the entry to the backyard. *The only reason for the animal to cease and desist would involve persons known to it in the back of the house or in the backyard*, McMahon was thinking. The other officers, Shea and Kaznicki, had taken notice as well and drew their weapons.

"Do you have receipts for all this merchandise?" said officer McMahon, hand now atop the butt of his gun.

"Do you have a warrant, pig?" Deborah said.

Just then a male figure emerged from the back of the house, carrying a large box, which obscured his face and his view, oblivious to what was going on at the front door. The man put down the box and when he looked up, he saw Deborah staring at him wide eyed and officer McMahon halfway inside the door.

"Hey!" McMahon yelled as Kenneth Reed took off running. "Hold it!" he shouted as he and the other officers barreled into the house. Officer Shea ran toward the back of the house.

McMahon drew his gun and told Kaznicki, "I got this one! Go, go, go!"

After minor resistance, officer McMahon managed to handcuff Deborah Pettiford amid all the furniture and boxes. Shea and Kaznicki were soon in a foot pursuit of the two men who had parked a truck in the alley and were bringing boxes in through the back door. They hadn't seen the police at the front of the house. Danny and Kenny had looted several stores during the riots in July and selling the stuff had been so easy. There was no shortage of demand for the TVs and furniture they'd stolen. Once they ran out of merchandise, they decided to rob more stores to replenish their cache. In three months they'd pulled four jobs. It was easy money and no one got hurt. Hell, the shit was insured, wasn't it? Let the fat cats take the loss and get paid by the even fatter pockets of the insurance companies, they reasoned.

On the last job, the store's owner let them take the inventory in broad daylight, allowing the dude to file a bogus insurance claim saying he'd been robbed. Danny was uneasy about hearing the guy's plan because it seemed more involved and elaborate than it needed to be. Rule of thumb was, the more people involved, the messier things could become, the easier it was to get caught. It was hard to be partners with people because there had to be a certain level of trust. Danny trusted Kenny and he trusted Kenny's girlfriend Deborah because she was cool and she knew what she was—a thief. One of the best boosters in Detroit.

Running down that alley, Danny's life did not "flash" before his eyes. This life had chosen him long ago and he accepted it. He could hear his heart beating in his ears with every pump of his muscular legs. It seemed every fence he flew past had a damn dog behind it. *Does any city in America have more dogs than Detroit?* He could hear his breath escaping in short bursts through his lips. Finally he saw a yard with a swing set and no dogs. Danny didn't hear the shot that was fired into his back, he just knew his legs had stopped working. By the time officer Shea reached him, he had collapsed to the ground and was taking his last breaths.

Kaznicki had easily caught Kenny moments earlier when Kenny tripped over the untied shoe strings of his Chucks. A part of Kaznicki was glad he didn't have to kill anyone that day and he quickly holstered his gun so he wouldn't be tempted to. Kenneth Reed sat on the curb, subdued by steel handcuffs and the report from the shot that killed Danny Williams. They'd left their guns inside the truck as they were thieves after all, not killers. They'd be crazy to shoot it out with the cops. *Niggers don't win that battle.*

The sun had set over the city of Detroit and Cherrylawn Avenue was alive with activity. Neighbors poured out of their homes, some rushing from a block over to see Danny's body in the alley. The flashing red lights of half a dozen police cars cut through the darkness illuminating trees, houses and the growing crowd with every strobe. The police knew they had to be careful in how they spoke to the gathering mass. They needed to keep prying eyes as far back as possible and they had to make sure to tell key people in the throng that whatever was done, it was

265

justified. Rumors were extremely damaging and would rage through the crowd as quickly and destructively as a wind whipped wild fire.

Who knows? Maybe Danny was a hero to these people, supplying goods and services unknown. Maybe to some he was a bad egg whose time had come to be fried. Overall, everyone remained calm as the scene was recorded and handled by police and detectives. In the alley between Cherrylawn and Northlawn, officers chatted and smoked cigarettes under a streetlight's glare, when there came a shout of, "Get outta here. Get!"

A rat had walked across Danny's face and was now unceremoniously rooting around in his hair, its ass partially resting on Danny's forehead, its tail like a bridge between the young man's eyes. It ran when Kaznicki yelled and waved a Vernors bottle he'd picked up. Danny's eyes stared up into eternity, never knowing the difference. Tears welled in Kaz's eyes as he furiously blinked them back before they could descend.

It was Monday, October 30th and this was Detroit, which meant it was Devil's Night. It was a night that hooligans, mischievous kids and those who wouldn't dream of committing a crime the other 364 days of the year, waited for. Youthful vandalism, like throwing rocks at the windows of vacant buildings, gave way to fires being set in abandoned residences and stores once darkness fell. People could only hope and pray every year that they did not find themselves living next to an abandoned or empty house by the end of October.

The men on any given block, if there were enough of them and they had the guts, would patrol the street from dusk until dawn to make sure there were no infernos set on their block. And of course, the very next night, some of these very same fire starters would appear at their neighbor's doors like carefree amnesiacs singing, "Trick or Treat" for candy and pennies and apples to be dropped into their paper bags or pillow cases.

The medical examiner had finished bagging Danny's remains, Kenny and his girlfriend Deborah were on their way to jail, and the neighbors had drifted back to their homes, lest a prankster start a fire while they were preoccupied elsewhere. McMahon lingered to make sure his partner, Shea, was okay and to ride down to 1300 Beaubien with him. He'd be debriefed, as would the other officers, and placed on desk duty while the investigation ensued. Kaznicki drove to headquarters alone in his police car, staring glassy eyed at the road before him.

THIRTY-SIX

H aving heard what had happened to Danny, Bill went to find Ricky in the basement of his house, sitting on an old couch in the dark. He could hear the small muffled sounds of his nephew crying.

"It's me man," Bill called out in the dark.

He easily found his way to the couch and sat on the arm. They sat in silence for a few minutes, Bill respecting Ricky's grief. Ricky cleared his throat before he spoke.

"So you heard what happened to D-D-Daniel?" he managed, hating that hiccuppy thing that happens from crying too hard.

"Yeah, I heard."

Silence. A dankly verdant odor was noticeable but not overwhelming. *No matter how hard you try to fix up a basement, it still always has a hint of funk from the mildew,* Bill thought. *Is this shit just naturally in the air? Is it growing on the fucking walls? How much does there need to be to create that smell?* Bill resigned himself to the fact that he was sitting on a couch that was probably pulsating with fungus, fucking up his $500 suit. *Shit.*

Ricky sighed loudly, helplessly. His voice, when he finally spoke again, was low and he talked slowly.

"If only I had kept my mouth shut. That cop Kaz was asking about Danny and like an idiot, I—"

"Now, wait a minute," Bill interrupted. "You couldn't save Danny, Ricky." His hand waved in a gesture, somewhere in the darkness. "You couldn't save your brother no more than your father could save me. Some things are just destined to be, like fate or some shit. Daniel was like me, and you just like your daddy. You are a good kid, Ricky. You probably never gave Gabriel and Ana an hour of trouble."

Bill's eyes had adjusted to the lack of light and he turned to look at his nephew, who was staring straight ahead. He slid down onto the couch next to Ricky.

"Between the two of y'all, I'll lay odds that you were your mama and daddy's favorite. You know that shit is true, don't you?" Without waiting for an answer Bill said quietly, "Danny knew it too."

Now Ricky was looking at Bill in the inky dimness, blinking away the tears. He didn't want to talk about this. This admission, this guilt laden favoritism, seemed disrespectful to whatever Danny was. His brother hadn't asked to be the child without that light of favor shining on him. Danny once told Ricky he'd asked their parents who their favorite child was, and this was when there were only three kids in the family. He said he'd realized if you have to ask, it isn't you. Ricky didn't repeat this to Bill, he just tucked it away in his mind like putting a child to bed.

"Listen to me, man. Do not beat yourself up. There was nothing you could do. Shit, if Danny had a chance to get older, who knows what the fuck he could have been?" Bill said, his voice trailing off with the sudden recognition of the futility of his supposition.

Bill leaned back full into the couch. *Fuck it. I'll have to send my suit to the cleaners in the morning.* He felt his jacket breast pocket for the rectangle of the cigarette pack. He shook out a smoke, flipped the top of his gold lighter back and lit his cigarette. There was a smooth familiarity in the way he put both the lighter and cigarettes back into his jacket in one motion.

Ricky hated the smell of a lit cigarette, but enjoyed the scent of fire to the fresh tobacco when the first draw was taken. It was almost as if he could taste the scent in his mouth and throat. He could hear the faint rustling sound of tobacco and paper ablaze as Bill puffed on the cigarette yet again, the orange glow climbing up the tip.

"Ricky, I don't know if you know it, but our family is fucked up, okay? My mother's people were rich from about the time of the Civil War. They owned slaves. Yeah, it ain't just the white man who did that shit to black people. Our family did it too."

Enrique recalled hearing his mother mention something about the family and slaves to one of her friends years ago, but he was too young to understand what they were talking about.

"There are only two men I ever really respected, that's my father and your father—my brother. My daddy was the hardest working motherfucker I ever knew. He gave us everything we could ever want or need. He was a good man. Your dad was so much like him. Always doin' the right thing, followin' the rules. I knew I couldn't follow down that path myself. I had to find out who I was on my own, in my own way. Even though I know I musta hurt my parents, I know they loved me. They loved my sister Ruby, too, even though she broke their hearts worse than me."

Bill pinched out the end of his cigarette.

"What? Who is Ruby, Uncle Bill?" Ricky asked.

"My twin sister. She had green eyes and long, thick auburn hair. Ruby was a beautiful little girl. She was Gabriel's pride and joy. Man, he'd do anything for his baby sister. We couldn'a been closer. When Ruby turned 18, she…left."

"Where'd she go?"

"She passed."

"So, she died?" Ricky asked, not understanding Bill's meaning.

"No, she *passed*. She became white. She spent that summer getting ready for college and then she was gone. She left my mother a letter. Mama like to went crazy over that shit. Daddy kinda quit talking to everybody. He lost that spark of life. Hell, she was his baby girl."

"So, nobody ever saw her again?" Ricky asked, momentarily forgetting about the ache in his chest from crying over his dead brother.

Bill didn't answer right away. He put his head back on the top of the couch and looked up at the ceiling, imagining what he would see if he could see. He'd seen Ruby two years earlier in a store in Dearborn. He'd gone there to pick up a nice gown for one of his girls, and maybe a mink stole as well. As he was going into the shop, Ruby was coming out. They passed one another in the circular vacuum of the revolving door. Their eyes met--his wide and disbelieving, hers narrow and forbidding--a brief exchange that dared him to speak in recognition. Bill understood and had to stop himself from looking after her when she whirled past him, the hair standing up on his arms. He *felt* her. She was his sister and a part of him. Shocked and sad, he had to compose himself when he got inside the store.

"Naw, that fuckin' bitch ain't shit, man," Bill spat.

They sat with their own thoughts.

271

"I guess I was telling you all this shit to let you know your parents can try, you can try, but sometimes fate has the better hand whether you like it or not."

Bill knew he was talking too much. *Shit, the kid got his guts kicked out tonight. He's probably only hearing some and understanding even less,* Bill thought. He had to get back to the house because the girls would be waiting.

Bill stood up, shaking his legs to ease the wrinkles forming in his suit pants. He walked through the outer room and started back up the stairs.

He turned back and called, "Hey, your aunt Ruby, she ain't a bitch. She was a good girl who did what she had to do to make it in this world. She's *my* sister, *my* twin."

He pushed open the screen to the side door at the top of the basement stairs and stepped out into the night.

"I feel her," Bill said to himself as tears streamed down his cheeks.

THIRTY-SEVEN

Ana Torres Williams looked at her reflection in the mirror. Except for her eyes appearing smaller than usual, she thought she looked pretty good, though crying several times a day took a toll on her big brown eyes, reducing them to near slits. They were pink rimmed and squinty and she couldn't seem to open them any wider, though she tried.

She finished putting on her lipstick, puckering her lips in a pout as was habit, before reaching for a tissue to blot at the over saturation of color. Her lips seemed independently jovial and inviting, unaware of the sorrowful visage they were attendant to. Out of nowhere the tears poured from her eyes. She wiped furiously at them before she had to loan the tissue to her lips once again to hush the sobs coming forth.

Two months. Ana had last seen Danny about two months before he died. After staying at the house for a couple of days during the riot, he disappeared back into the streets. August 29th, a Tuesday night, he showed up on her doorstep. Ana was so happy to see her son, all she wanted to do was hug him and feed him sandwiches, and he didn't resist. She had questions—what was he doing for money? How was he really? What about college? Was he staying out of trouble? But she swallowed her inquiries with a glass of Faygo Red Pop because she didn't want to spoil their evening. Ana was glad Alecia and Ricky were out with the younger kids that night.

Ana and Danny sat on the living room couch, its chintz flowers happily incarcerated in plastic, watching the final episode of the popular TV series, "The Fugitive" starring David Janssen, which came on Channel 7. After years of the character Dr. Richard Kimble claiming a one-armed man had murdered his wife, he finally caught up with the perpetrator who had caused him to live on the run. It was a very exciting event the whole country was watching unfold. Just as Ana was sad to see the end of this drama she'd come to enjoy each week, she was even sadder when her son said he had to leave.

"I'll see you again pretty soon, Mami, okay?"

"Okay, *mijo*," Ana replied.

He'd said there would be a next time and soon. She took comfort in the thought of having time to talk to her son the next time he came over. Next time, she would tell him everything she was thinking and everything that kept her up at night. They hugged a little longer than usual. She was so grateful to have him within her arms, locked in her embrace. Danny seemed a little thin, but she would talk about that next time, too. Everything had gone so well, no need for a dust up from a well-meaning inquiry.

"I love you, son."

"I know, Mama," Danny said before breaking away and slipping into the night.

Next time, Ana told herself as she watched her son cross the street to his car. He could feel his mother's gaze raking across his back and he turned around.

"When you gonna let me get you a color TV, Mami?" he asked, already anticipating her reply. "You know 'The Fugitive' is in color, right?"

"I don't need no color television. What I'm gonna do with it? My TV is just fine and *The Fugitive* is over now, okay? Goodnight," she yelled out.

Danny was already in his car. He waved and was gone.

There was a soft rap on her bedroom door. The younger children most days were like scared little kittens clamoring and mewling for her attention, while her two oldest gave her a wide berth in which to grieve. Alecia and Ricky were always at the periphery, ready to catch her if she fell, but she always held herself together until she could get behind the door of her bedroom. In that sanctuary, in her safe place, she could cry for her first-born child.

"Come in."

It was Ricky who came in, warily. Ana looked at her son, so strong and tall and handsome. She silently praised and thanked God that perhaps she'd done something right with her children. Still, she wondered how her two oldest sons could be so different?

"You okay, Mami?" Ricky asked, even though he could tell she'd been crying again.

"Yes, baby, I am fine. Almost ready."

Ana dreaded going out, but it was almost Christmas and she promised her children she'd go to the Motortown Revue at the Fox Theatre. Mentally, she tried to push away the heaviness that had overtaken her body and the weariness that had invaded her soul, maliciously setting up house and calling the shots. It had been two months and she knew she needed to get out of the house.

"Uncle Bill called and said the car would be here in about 15 minutes."

Ana realized that she'd heard the trill of a ringing telephone somewhere in the distance, but as usual, she couldn't make her body move toward it. If the kids didn't pick up the phone, it didn't get answered. She couldn't muster the energy or the interest to talk to another sympathetic friend or family member whom she suspected had been betting on that proverbial other shoe to drop on Danny for years.

Even though Ana didn't understand Bill's elected profession, she understood his generosity to her and her family since Gabriel's death. No favor was too great or too small for Bill when it came to his family and she was grateful. Bill had talked to Enrique and they devised a plan to get Ana out of the house for a while to enjoy the soulful sounds of some of Motown Records' best musical groups.

It was opening night of the Motortown Review at the Fox Theatre downtown. Some of the brightest lights in the homegrown heaven of Motown would be performing: Smokey Robinson and the Miracles, the Marvelettes, Little Stevie Wonder, Marvin Gaye and Tammi Terrell, to name but a few. Ana loved music and was gradually and grudgingly giving herself permission to have a good time that evening.

The limousine arrived in front of the ornate venue on Woodward Avenue and the driver opened the doors to discharge Ana's entire clan—Ricky, Alecia, Eduardo and Pilar. The younger children sprung out of the vehicle full of excitement, having had had hot chocolate during the ride over, they could barely contain themselves. If it occurred to them that this was the same kind of car they'd been in on the way to their brother Daniel's funeral, they never let on. Thankfully, this limo was white and Ana silently praised Bill for his thoughtfulness. Ricky's two friends, Angelica and Sheila exited the car as well. Ana was surprised to come downstairs to find such fashionably dressed, polite and respectful girls sitting in her living room.

"Uncle Bill said to be in the lobby a half hour before show time," Ricky said, looking at his watch. "We're just a few minutes early."

"Is Bill meeting us? I thought—"

"I know, Mami. No, I don't think he will be here tonight. He said he wanted someone to meet us."

"*Aye, dios mio*. I can't. I don't want to meet anyone, *mijo*," Ana said.

A slender door opened just then, to what seemed like a small ante room, prompting a rush of people to run screaming toward it. There was Smokey Robinson, lead singer of The Miracles, sitting at a dressing table with a butter yellow dressing gown on. He waved to the fans and they screamed even louder before the door closed again.

"That's my man," a strong, masculine, jovial voice said somewhere nearby.

The man laughed and it sounded like a staccato burst of music—melodic and carefree. He walked a few steps and stopped in front of Ana. This man was wearing a brown cashmere coat with a snowy white neck scarf. His process undulated with shiny waves, and the man's skin was so smooth and brown, it looked like it had been painted on. Then there were his eyes, large and lively yet sleepy and sexy, bordered by glossy black eyelashes. They recognized the man: he was "Mr. Excitement," singer Jackie Wilson.

Jackie Wilson was one of the most dynamic and thrilling entertainers in the world. So stylish and athletic was he in his performances that Elvis Presley emulated him on stage. Ana and

277

Gabriel loved dancing to his songs, "Reet Petite," and "That's Why I Love You So." The memory of her husband bopping around the dance floor made her smile in spite of herself. Within seconds a crowd had gathered and were screaming, "Jackie!" and "Mr. Wilson!" Alecia, Angelica and Sheila linked arms nervously, not knowing what to do or what would happen next. Pilar asked excitedly, "Is that Elvis Presley?"

Jackie put his arms up to quiet the crowd.

"I'll be back in a few minutes and I'll be happy to sign some autographs. First I got to escort some friends to their seats." And with that, he put his hand out to Ana Williams, who was shocked and confused as she took his hand.

"Mrs. Williams? How 'ya doing, darling? Bill asked me to show you to your seats."

Of course Bill would know Jackie Wilson. *The man knows everyone in Detroit*, thought Ana. Ricky was unconsciously grinning from ear to ear as he looked at Angelica. *Yes, this just happened!* Ana and her entourage would enjoy the Motown performers from the very first row. Jackie kissed her hand before he departed and told her to have a great time at the show.

"Merry Christmas," he called out to the youngsters as he went toward the aisle, an uproar of fans in his wake.

Before the lights went down inside the Fox Theatre, Ana was gripping her oldest surviving son's hand like she didn't want to let it go. Enrique could sense her ambivalence at being out and enjoying herself, but she could hold his hand as long as she needed. *We won't worry about clapping.* Then, as the lights dimmed and the orchestra began to play, Ana patted her son's hand to signal that she was letting go, that it was finally time. Enrique looked over at his mother in the dark, clapping and clapping, looking forward, looking ahead.

THIRTY-EIGHT

1 968 rang in as usual, on a barrage of celebratory gunshots blasted into a frigid and clear night sky by city residents. There was always morbid fascination with who was the last casualty of the previous year and who, unsuspecting and unfortunate, would be the first person killed in the new year as reported by The Detroit News or The Detroit Free Press.

It would be a year of significance and consequence in world history, American history and in the history of Detroit, Michigan. In the fall the Detroit Tigers baseball team would win the World Series against the St. Louis Cardinals in 7 games. The final game, which remained scoreless until the 7th inning, would make heroes out of teammates Al Kaline, Denny McLain, Jim Northrup and Mickey Lolich. Novelty songs about the winners seemed to be on every radio station and every school kid's lips as the city tried to pull itself up out of the still smoldering wreckage of suspicion and hopelessness.

But on one particular Sunday morning, Palm Sunday, the congregation of Mount Moriah African Methodist Episcopal Church, the Tanner family church, sat teary eyed and inert in the polished wooden pews. The pastor was somberly preaching, but minds moved through the moments like bodies swimming in mucous. The incomprehensible was being recounted and every word was a weight hung on the soul before being flung overboard. Three days earlier in Memphis, Tennessee, on the balcony of a motel and surrounded by his peers, the Reverend Dr. Martin Luther King, Jr. had been shot dead. Assassinated.

The civil rights leader had travelled from his hometown of Atlanta, Georgia to try to help resolve a dispute with sanitation workers. He and his constituents had gone to Memphis to rally for a living wage for colored garbage men and a bullet to the throat was his guerdon. The segregationists would say it was apropos remuneration for a "trouble maker." With the sadness came anger. While cities like Baltimore, Washington, and Chicago, among others, erupted in flames and violence, Detroit remained calm. With the riots having happened just 9 months earlier, the wounds were still fresh and barely scabbed over during that literal gestational period, and what was there left to steal or burn, really?

Angelica sat with the old blue cloth covered hymnal in her lap knowing she would only pretend to sing if they insisted on singing. She was rooted in place by desolation and despair like an abandoned animal tethered to a tree. *There won't be any rising on the third day this time.* Palm Sunday was the day celebrated by Christians signaling the time Christ rode into Jerusalem hailed a messiah and savior by the populace, only to be killed five days later by those same people. Angelica's mouth turned down slightly as she thought of how perfectly duplicitous and joyously spineless those ancients must have been. Hadn't it been much the same for Dr. King?

Blacks and whites were shocked and outraged and there would be calls to, among other things, remember Dr. King by renaming city streets and schools nationwide after him. Sure enough, eventually his good name would adorn street signs in every ghetto in America--a visual signpost signaling that one had navigated to the wrong side of town. The schools so named generally didn't include white children as students. White parents

280

slept soundly at night knowing "those people" were pacified by having a few schools rechristened in the name of "their" leader.

62 days later, just as the nation was trying to clear its collective head and catch its breath, Senator Robert Francis Kennedy, presidential hopeful for the Democratic Party and brother of the former U.S. president who'd been assassinated in 1963, was himself assassinated. He'd been shot in the head and back by a young man from Palestine, angered by Kennedy's support of Israel. It happened in the kitchen of the Ambassador Hotel in Los Angeles, California as the senator and his entourage had come through the kitchen area to shake hands with the hotel staff as they made their way through to exit the hotel. It had been a rousing rally, crackling with hope for the future of the nation as the senator had just won the California primary.

The idea, no, the fact that this white man, a rational and conciliatory figure to the restless American people, another son from the storied Kennedy clan, could be killed in such an unskilled and brazenly unimaginative way was a foundation crumbler. The world was on tilt and might never right itself again. Martin Luther King Jr.'s death had put blacks into a state of suspended animation, held in space by a gossamer thread of hope, not wanting to believe there was no one in the second line to take King's place. The death of RFK unraveled the thread and everyone fell to earth like the kids inside the Rotor when the ride was over.

Angelica sat in the breakfast room of her house, the cheery sunshine shimmering off Liz's kitchen appliances. Liz came quietly into the kitchen and saw Angelica staring out of the single window in the room.

"Hi, honey," she said softly, not wanting to intrude on her daughter's solitude. She could tell the girl was woeful without fully seeing her face. "You okay?"

Without turning in her mother's direction, Angelica asked, "Where was God?"

Liz stiffened in her place and looked almost instinctively to the side as if her daughter was speaking to someone else in the room. *If only*, she thought.

"Angelica, you shouldn't say that," she said in a low hush like they were co-conspirators who might be overheard by unseen captors. "That's not a good question for you to ask. We don't question God."

Angelica turned to her mother who was standing in the arched doorway, her hands useless at her sides.

"Well, I'm asking the question. Where was God when Mr. Kennedy, both Mr. Kennedys needed him? Why didn't he save Dr. King? He was a good man, right? He tried to help everybody, especially colored people. Why did he let my daddy die?" she asked before she could stop herself.

Liz approached the table, pulled out one of her lime green Naugahyde chairs and sat down.

"I know it's confusing, Angelica. God doesn't consult with us when he wants to do something we might not like. He has to let us make our own mistakes and kind of let life happen to us. Some of the things that might happen are, well, bad. You understand?"

Angelica had stopped listening as soon as her mother sat down. She imagined the many Kennedy children getting the horrible news about their father, just as the King children had only two months earlier. They were all, herself included, part of a sad and exclusive club they did not want membership in. The price of inclusion was a dead dad and the accompanying grief, emptiness, and useless explanations of well-meaning strangers and family.

THIRTY-NINE

The Senior class of Francis Dodge High School were barely contained in their zeal to get out of school and begin whatever adventures life held in store for them. It wouldn't be long now. Pictures had been posed for and taken, caps and gowns in the school colors had been ordered and graduation parties were being planned. Kids and their parents were deciding who amongst their family would have the distinct honor of attending the actual graduation ceremony downtown at the Ford Auditorium.

However, the event that rattled nerves like ice cubes in a glass and gave just as much warmth and comfort, was the specter of the great celebration known as the prom. Some teens who had jobs were blessed with not having to go begging their parents to foot the bill for fancy formal attire, a limousine rental or an expensive dinner. Most kids asked their parents anyway and some proudly paid for everything, relieved that their child had made it out of the public-school system and could look forward to gainful employment someday. In many instances, these youngsters were first generation Northerners, having been born out of the South, or more impressively, the first children in their families to graduate high school.

Still other uses could be found for saved up allowances from most of the year. The proverbial hotel room for the party after the after party after the prom. The events that would, hopefully, take place at the hotel are what weighed on Enrique's heart and mind. He desperately wanted to ask Angelica to the prom. This was a once in a lifetime experience and he wanted to share it with the girl who made him laugh, the girl who knew his secrets, the girl he wanted to someday call *Mrs. Williams. Ha! Bet she doesn't know that secret!*

But his mind was drowning out what emanated from his chest with words, words in all capital letters, words that actually made sense. What good would it do for him to start up something, anything romantic with Angelica when they were both about the head off to college—she to UCLA in California and he to the University of Michigan? It made no sense! How can a long-distance relationship, if that's what they wanted to be, survive four years on opposite sides of the country? It wouldn't! Worse yet, the weariness of coping with the distance and longing would ruin their chances of being together later on.

Then there was the other thing Ricky tried to push from his mind as base and selfish. He wanted to get laid after the prom. That's what the hotel room was for, everyone knew that, and this was part of a game he was sure Angelica knew nothing about. She was a beautiful girl, a smart girl, a good girl and she would be going home after the after party, surely. She needed a nice, dull guy to go to prom with. He hated that he was so self-centered, but Angelica belonged to him and with him, no matter how long the eventuality. Ricky realized his eyebrows had practically merged together on his forehead when he looked into the mirror in the boy's lavatory. *Calm down, you think too much.*

"Hey, Ricky," the familiar voice said, and Enrique Williams looked into the mirror again as his high wattage grin came to life.

"Hey, man, who are you taking to the prom?" he asked as he met Carlton's reflection.

Ricky found he was the common denominator in many social situations since he still hung out with some of his old neighborhood and school pals from the West side of Detroit. He'd garnered about a dozen good friends in his years at Dodge High, but somehow when Ricky was out and about with one group of friends, and they encountered the "other" group, it was a festival of awkwardness--the teenagers wary of one another as they all laid claim to the nucleus that was Ricky. He himself likened it to when kids are friends but their parents and sometimes peer siblings, simply were not. Everyone was polite, but it went no further than surface pleasantries. The one thing both groups seemed to acknowledge was the centrifugal charm of Carlton Meadows, more tolerated than genuinely liked by all sides merely because Ricky seemed to care about the kid.

Ricky already knew the answer to his question. After all, Carlton had confided just days earlier that he was going to ask Loretta Beamis, a pretty and popular classmate. Though Carlton had yet to report the results, Ricky had already heard about the turndown at lunch a day earlier. The girl tempered her remarks when recounting the story to her friends because she saw Ricky sitting at the next table and she wanted him to ask her to the prom.

"Did you ever think about asking Angelica?"

Was he kidding? Was that a trick question?

"Angelica would rather stay home and watch paint dry than go with me to the prom."

They both knew it was true and Ricky smiled slightly, then tried to neutralize his expression before Carlton could see. Too late. Carlton did a double take as a matter of fact, and the second glance revealed the relaxed face of his pal, but he was sure there had been a glimmer of a smile or something he didn't like.

"Well, she's our girl, right? That's *our* girl. We don't want anything to happen to her on prom night. You know some of these guys can get a little--"

"Then why don't you take her?" Carlton asked, forehead raised expectantly.

Enrique had anticipated that question, but it didn't make the answer any easier for Carlton to hear.

"Well, I'm already going with, uh, this girl that goes to MacKenzie."

Carlton just blinked at Ricky, waiting for more information. *Since when was he dating some new girl from MacKenzie?* Ricky kept talking.

"And, we have plans after the prom. *And*, after the after party."

Carlton silently fumed. *Only pretty boy can get laid?* Maybe he wanted to do that too! Why not?

"Well, I'm probably gonna go to the after party, too. And, maybe me and my date will—"

"Your mama and daddy gonna let you spend the night at a hotel or a motel, Carlton?" Ricky interrupted, looking him dead in the face. Carlton looked down.

"Maybe," he mumbled. After a beat, "She doesn't want to go across the street with me. Angelica used to kind of like me and then she didn't," he explained. *And then she liked you*, Carlton wanted to say.

"Just ask her, brother. See what happens. Be creative when you do, okay? Gotta get to class. You coming?" Ricky asked, walking toward the door as 3 boys barreled through the entrance to the boys' bathroom, roughhousing.

He could tell they were Freshman. Had he been that small and silly? Ricky was happy to be a Senior, happy to be embarking on adulthood. He'd gotten his draft notice already and that was the only thing that gnawed on the corners of his mind. He would serve proudly, as his father had done, but he prayed secretly that he would get an educational deferment.

Carlton ascended the steps to Angelica's house that evening with a single red rose from Frank's Nursery, having given the rest of the bouquet to his mother, hoping to prime her for an entreaty to stay out all night for the prom. He had a bag of penny candy, assorted varieties, from Mr. Gilhooley's store. Carlton opened the screen door and rapped on Angelica's front door before he realized he should have just rang the doorbell.

"Stupid," he muttered to himself. He sure couldn't ring it now because he'd sound desperate and she'd be annoyed with him.

"Hi Carlton," Angelica answered the door, glancing furtively behind him, wanting Ricky to be there with him.

"Hi, can I come in?"

"Sure," Angelica said, pushing open the screen door and latching it after he stepped inside.

She led him into her living room where they sat on the couch. Angelica didn't quite know what to make of Carlton, his visit, or the items in his hands.

"Um, this is for you," Carlton said, handing her the rose with a clumsy flourish.

Though still surprised and confused, she smiled and put the ruby colored flower to her nose.

"And these are for you, too. I wasn't sure what all you like, so I got an assortment." God, he hated that he sounded so formal. *Loosen up*!

Angelica took the small bag of candy and shook it slightly as she poked her index finger around at its contents. Her brief inspection noted bright yellow wrappers enrobing Banana Splits, fragrant Chum Gum and brown taffy paddles mottled with flecks of nuts—Squirrels!

She arched her eyebrow at Carlton and as if reading her mind, he said, "Lucky guess."

In reality Ricky had silently shaken his head, "no" at practically every candy he attempted to load into the bag. Finally he took the bag from Carlton and deftly, knowingly, swept candies into it. *She doesn't need to know all of that.*

"Thanks, Carlton," said Angelica, genuinely touched at his thoughtfulness. They stared at one another in silence for several seconds.

Carlton had always liked Angelica Tanner. She was easily the most beautiful girl he'd ever seen. As he looked into her large green eyes, he recalled, unwittingly, his last visit to this house years earlier and the warm sling of shit he had between his legs by the time he got home. Carlton's face darkened at the memory. Angelica noticed his expression.

"What's the matter?"

Carlton shook his head in answer, to erase the image like a child would an Etch-a-Sketch toy.

"Nothing, nothing. Sorry. Um, I wanted to ask you something."

Oh no, not the prom! Angelica swallowed and smiled.

"Okay…"

"Do you have a date for the prom?" Carlton asked beaming proudly, knowing that a good lawyer never asks a question to which he doesn't already know the answer. He knew a couple of boys from school, both popular football players, had asked and had been turned down.

"Nope," Angelica answered, casually. Those two lunkheads who'd already asked her to the prom were turned away because she was nobody's fool. More to the point, she was nobody's ho. These boys expect their dates to go to a hotel after the prom and put out and that was not in her plans.

"Well, would you go to the prom with me?" Carlton didn't realize he was just going to blurt it out like that with no further small talk. Before Angelica could form her answer, Carlton felt himself still talking, unable to stop.

"You know Ricky is going to prom with some chick from MacKenzie, right?"

No, she didn't know it, but she remained completely nonchalant in Carlton's presence.

"So why are *you* asking me?"

"I wouldn't mind being seen with the prettiest girl in the school. And, you can trust me to get you home safely. Plus, we'll have fun. I can dance, you know."

Angelica had to laugh at how Carlton promoted himself. He packed a lot into that sell.

"Carlton, all the times we've been out, I've never seen you dance. Not even at the Grande! That's number one, and number two, my mother will let me stay out as long as I want to. I think it's your mama with the curfew!"

Angelica roared with laughter and soon Carlton joined in, despite himself.

"Okay, okay, you might be right. But I think we would have fun," Carlton said sincerely.

"So, what's your plan? Prom and then what?" she asked.

"Just the prom and the after party at the Michigan Inn. Then home."

Angelica didn't really care about the prom. She had figured Ricky would go with one of his West side girls and she wasn't excited about being a witness to that small knife in the gut. Then there was what usually came after the after party. She definitely wanted no part of that, with or without Ricky. Carlton was a safe bet. He could be fun when he wanted to be.

"Can I tell you tomorrow?"

"Sure, you bet!" Carlton said, excitedly.

Angelica rose from the couch with a little squeak as her bare legs departed from the plastic covering. They walked to the door and shyly said their goodbyes. Carlton was at the end of the driveway when he heard Angelica call his name.

"Hey Carlton! I'll go. Later, Gator."

And with that, she closed her front door. Carlton beamed as he walked toward his car.

"I won," he muttered to himself.

FORTY

Graduation week arrived with 7 days of parties, proms and all manner of social festivities. It seemed an eternity matriculating through Francis Dodge High School, and when Angelica reflected on the yearly class photos within her yearbook, she could scarcely recognize the little kid that was her, staring back in monochromed innocence. These were the candid photos in class, on teams, at games, from 1964 to 1968. The time had gone by like the snap of her fingers.

Angelica was sitting on the landing at the top of the stairs to the second floor waiting for Sheila, smiling to herself as she flipped through the pages musing, *I didn't realize I was such a social butterfly!* She ran her finger over a photo of Sheila playing field hockey. She met Sheila Davis on the first day of 3rd grade and they'd remained friends, best friends, from that day 10 years ago. It seemed impossible to go from there to here, on the cusp of womanhood, in such a brief span of time, but, here they were.

On the page featuring the ROTC, there was a dedication to those who had been swiped by the talons of Vietnam. There was a row of 12 pictures of bright faced young soldiers, not knowing that they would never have wives or families, but rather be blown up, shot up and burned up far, far from home. Far from lawns that needed watering, papers that needed delivering, girls that needed kissing and cars that needed fixing. Bobby Gogolian's picture was there, showing his teeth within his crooked smile, so glad to serve a grateful nation.

"Hey girl, sorry I'm late. Those dummies in the office said I didn't order a yearbook and you know I did, right? I made two different people look until they found my name. Stupid people make me sick," Sheila said in exasperation.

"I'm glad you got it. Now we gotta be carrying this heavy thing around for the next couple of days getting everybody to sign it," Angelica said, indicating the yearbook. "Sheesh! It's gonna be sheer luck to catch people with the swing out about to happen today. Everybody wants to just get the heck out of Dodge. Literally."

They both chuckled at Angelica's joke.

"If there's a line to get our cap and gowns, we can just run through the line, you know, take turns seeing who we want to sign our yearbooks. We just take turns. One of us stands in line while the other one gets dedications and stuff," Sheila posited.

"Girl, you are so smart! I knew there was a reason I wanted to be your friend," Angelica teased.

They headed down to the library to pick up their neatly folded gowns and tasseled mortar boards. Some kids were already walking around wearing both items, modeling for one another in their excitement. Angelica had worn her hair parted down the center and held in place by her favorite beaded headband. She wore two strands of "love beads" around her neck and a loose fitting paisley blouse under her faux suede vest with the cool fringe. A wide belt circled the slender waist of her bell bottom hip huggers. Today and today only, girls were allowed to wear pants to accommodate the swing out. One could maneuver much more easily in the back seat and on the thin ledge of the car door's window wearing slacks. Angelica knew she looked cute, no affirmations needed, but still she couldn't wait for Ricky to see her.

A few weeks earlier, he'd slid onto the aluminum bench attached to the lunchroom table and said he had a question for her. Angelica's breath caught slightly as she braced herself. Only two days earlier she'd acquiesced to Carlton's request for her to be his prom date. She could kick herself now. Why had she rushed to answer? Why had she had so little faith in Ricky? Of course he wanted her to be his date. Of course, she'd let Carlton down easy. Of course—

"Y'all want to ride with me for swing out?" he asked, looking at Angelica and then Sheila. "Y'all can sit in the back with both of you at a window. Carlton can sit up front with me. What do you think?"

"Sure!" Sheila said, eagerly.

Angelica shot her a quick, withering look.

"Well, maybe," said Angelica.

Ricky sucked his teeth.

"Girl, whatchu mean, maybe?" he grinned, showing that perfect white picket fence of a smile. "C'mon, it'll be fun. Our last hurrah together at Dodge," he cajoled.

She couldn't resist this boy, this black Indian with his glossy black hair pulled back and away from his face.

"Angelica, I even got pom poms from one of the JV cheerleaders. We're gonna be doing it up all over the city," Sheila said.

For a moment Angelica could envision her best friend tumbling out of the car window and smushed flat under an onslaught of car tires because she lost her grip on the car fooling around with a $2 pom-pom.

"Do we really need those things? We're not cheerleaders. Cheerleaders are goofy. Let's just wave."

Sheila considered this for a moment. She knew that trying to coordinate too many hand movements along with hanging on to the car's roof presented a challenge.

"Okay," she shrugged. "That's cool."

The girls ducked into the lavatory to situate their caps on their heads with the bobby pins they'd brought in their purses. There was a bit of a crowd inside the bathroom, but no matter, they found a place to put on their mortar boards, proudly letting the tassel dangle and fling itself to and fro from the small button at the center. A small golden charm was affixed to the adornment reading, "1968." Angelica tucked her headband inside her purse and with one last check in the mirror, swinging their heads in jerky starts like the Beatles, the girls decided their head gear was firmly in place and could stand up to a strong breeze.

When they came out of the bathroom, Carlton and Ricky were standing there waiting for them. The boys smiled appreciatively at the girls and Ricky, said "Let's ride, Clyde!"

Their swing out sojourn took them over to Mumford, Cooley, MacKenzie and Northwestern High Schools. It was a day of tolerance and solidarity in the act of departing from the Detroit Public School System, because any other time there was a subtle yet distinctive air of unwelcome in other neighborhoods and school districts.

"Hey y'all, I told my uncle I would swing by his crib for a minute," Ricky announced, immediately looking in his rear-view mirror to see Angelica's reaction. He caught her eyes as they rolled toward the roof of the car. She stopped herself when she saw Ricky's eyes reflected in the mirror.

"It'll only take a minute. I promise." He looked at Carlton next to him, looking out of the window. Carlton felt his jaw tighten as he imagined Bill Williams somehow humiliating him again in front of the girls.

They pulled up in front of a large brick house on Oakman Boulevard and Ricky blew his horn twice. The heavy wooden door opened and Bill emerged, swaying down the concrete steps.

"Hey, Uncle Bill!" Ricky exclaimed, exiting his car.

"Wow, man, look at you! We proud of you, Ricky," Bill said, giving Ricky some skin as they slapped palms.

Bill squinted and lowered his head to peer into the car. Carlton held his breath and threw up his hand as a wave.

Sheila, grinning and excited, said, "Hi!"

Angelica tilted her head up and back slightly, warily, forcing a smile.

"Hey," was all Bill said as he turned and grabbed Enrique's sleeve. "Let me holla at you for a minute, Homes."

They walked several yards in front of the car where the passengers couldn't hear their conversation.

Angelica wondered if Ricky knew she'd seen his uncle just the prior week when she was shopping downtown with her mother. They had just come out of J.L. Hudson's and Bill was going inside. His eyes registered recognition, which for a few seconds, gave her a strange thrill. To be recognized in public by a man like Bill Williams after only meeting him a couple of times was a big deal. He gave her the subtlest of nods with his head cocked to the side and she blinked her acknowledgement. After all, how on earth could she explain to her mother how or why she knew a man in a lime green suit? A man who was clearly a pimp.

Puffy white clouds rode slowly across a scrim of bright blue, as a gentle breeze lifted and flung the blue and white tassel on Ricky's graduation cap slightly. It was warm but not yet humid in Detroit, a perfect spring day. With Bill standing before him grinning from ear to ear, Ricky couldn't recall seeing his uncle smile like this. Ever. He knew Bill was proud of him.

"My man, you did it! Nowhere to go but up and up. University of Michigan better watch out!" Bill said, holding his right hand up again to slap five with his nephew.

"Thanks, Uncle Bill. I'm ready, you know? I'm gonna work this summer, get a little bit more money saved up and then, I'm out. But, you know, I'll be close enough if my mama needs me."

"So, what you doing tonight? Prom night?"

"Yup, at the Michigan Inn in Southfield."

Bill pointed over his shoulder with his thumb.

"I like this girl, man. She alright. She come across kind of delicate and proper, but, she frontin'. She ain't no pushover. Make her mad and she'll get in a nigga's ass!"

Ricky laughed. He knew Bill was right.

"That's what you need, Young Blood. She got your back, nephew. I know, I can tell. Don't let her get away, man. I'm calling destiny on this one," Bill said, pointing vaguely to the sky. "Y'all have fun at the prom. I got something for you."

Ricky didn't know if his uncle would pull out a wad of money or a pack of rubbers.

He said quickly, "Um, yeah. I'm not taking Angelica to the prom. Carlton is." Ricky had dropped his voice in case his friends, unlikely though it was, could hear.

"What? You kidding me, right? How the fuck—"

"Uncle Bill, you remember what happens after the prom, if you're lucky, right? It's like a rite of passage, I guess. I just didn't want that to happen with Angelica. I asked Carlton to ask her to the prom. He's a good friend to take her and not try to…you know…"

"Man, that nigga ain't shit. I'm tryin' to tell you, young 'un, but you ain't heard me. But okay, wow…he goin' to the party with the finest bitch, sorry, girl in the school? What a sacrifice. Kids!" he said, exasperated.

Bill could see he may have been too harsh with his words and hell, this was a special day for Ricky.

"Rick, I understand. I do. It's up to her anyway and she's a good girl…who digs the hell out of you."

That made Ricky smile again. Glancing back at the car, he hoped his uncle was right.

"I got something for you, or the girls do."

Bill put two fingers into the corners of his mouth and a loud shrill whistle burst forth. Soon girls, two, four, six of them, came out of his house. Ricky recognized most of them. As the women approached, he nervously glanced at the car again. All eyes were on him. Black Mary appeared on the porch, smoking a cigarette.

"Hey baby boy," she called out.

Ricky hadn't figured on such an outpouring of concentrated attention by Bill's girls. *Why aren't they working or asleep?*

As if he'd read Ricky's mind, Bill said, "These bitches supposed to be working, but I let them come back to the crib for a minute to see you, nigga. Funny how they all seemed to get back here to see yo' ass!" Bill laughed, then nodded at the cadre of women who came to surround Enrique, who was trying desperately to look cool and calm.

One by one, Chan, Eva, Carol, Denise, Sadie and Terri slipped an arm around Ricky's back, kissed him on the cheek and put money in his hands. Chan and Sadie managed to brush their lips against his ear to deposit some filthy words about what they wanted to do to him. Shocked and trying not to get a hard on, he just stared at a nearby tree and within minutes, they'd all drifted down the street in various directions, back to work. Ricky looked down and unfurled his fist to see he had $120. Bill smiled.

"Go on and get out of here. Have fun tonight," he said, heading back up to the house.

In the car, there was complete silence as Ricky put the key into the ignition. He looked at Angelica, Sheila and then Carlton in rapid succession. They all seemed to want to comment, but no one spoke.

"What?" Ricky said as he pulled away from the curb.

He couldn't stop grinning as everyone in the car burst into laughter.

FORTY-ONE

T he doorbell rang and Liz Tanner felt a giddiness surge through her body. She knew who was at the door and knew they weren't there to see her, but that was okay. Liz hadn't been able to go to her own prom because she was made to help her parents at the Santori's club down in Black Bottom. Her father tried hard to reason with her mother.

"Dee, the girl only graduates from high school once in her life. She should enjoy being a kid and having fun with her friends," he'd implored.

"Mr. and Miz Santori done planned this big party more than six months ago. Liz knew she was gonna have to help me. I can't help it if the stupid school scheduled their prom on the wrong night! Besides, good girls can get into trouble at those proms. I know what goes on."

That night was the first time Angelo and Liz had seen one another in five years—and sparks flew! *I didn't need a prom to get me into trouble*, she almost said aloud as she touched the doorknob, flinging open her front door.

"Hi, Carlton. Well, now don't you look handsome in your tuxedo? Come on in," she said, pushing the screen door open for him.

Carlton stepped into the vestibule and was shown into the living room. He wore a white carnation boutonniere pinned to his jacket lapel and held a small spray of white carnations in a clear plastic box in his hands.

"Thank you, Miss Tanner. These are for Angelica."

"Make yourself comfortable. Angelica's almost ready. I'll be right back," Liz said as she trotted back to her daughter's bedroom.

"How do I look, Mama?" Angelica asked.

She stood in the center of her room, her hands out slightly from her sides as if to say, "ta-da!" She wore a silk georgette dress as yellow as the sun, which draped to the floor. The sweetheart neckline and fitted bodice was modest yet flattering as the yellow silk met an elegant intersection of black grosgrain ribbon at her slender waist. Her long brown hair had been swept up into a chic French roll with a few ringlets spilling from the top. Angelica hardly ever wore make-up, but she had taken her time and accentuated the natural beauty of her face with subtle enhancements. In a word, she was gorgeous.

So many emotions coursed through Liz—her daughter would soon be on her own, out of state at college, experiencing life and looking like her father. She was a stunning girl.

"You look beautiful, Angelica. Just beautiful. I'm going to get my camera so I can take some pictures of you two. Carlton's here and he looks so handsome."

Angelica's eyes wanted to fly toward the ceiling, but she didn't allow them to. She kept her composure and smiled.

"I'm sure he does."

300

She would have just as soon stayed home and listened to the radio or played records in her room, but this was some kind of rite of passage that she would go along with, even though she couldn't fathom what the big deal was. She did want to see her friends all dressed up, though. And, she wanted Enrique Williams to see her and watch her have fun with her date, Carlton. She wanted him to wish he had her on *his* arm instead.

Angelica was getting a charge out of her mother's enthusiasm over the prom. *If only she was like this every day, or at least once a month.* She smiled as Carlton awkwardly slipped on her wrist corsage and put his arm around her waist as they posed in the living room. The Kodak Instamatic flashed as the little cube atop it turned clockwise with a tiny contained explosion. After a few more pictures, it was time to leave.

"You kids have fun," Liz called after them as they crossed from the sidewalk to the driveway.

Carlton opened the door for Angelica and she slid into his car. She had to admit, Carlton looked really cute and it reminded her that it wasn't too far-fetched that she'd been infatuated with him. Like a million years ago.

Once inside the Michigan Inn, they could hear the murmurs and laughter of the crowd and the excitement of the live band behind the ballroom doors as the percussion hit the walls. Carlton held out his elbow and formed a triangle for Angelica to slip her arm into. *Too late to turn back and run for home.* Angelica put her slender arm through the wool gabardine frame offered by Carlton and they glided into the ballroom.

A small crush of girls were near the entrance and they fussed over Angelica and she over each of them, telling them how pretty they looked. Boys throughout the room looked up from dance steps, conversations and cups of punch to cast approving nods and looks at Carlton and Angelica. Many wondered to themselves and some ruminated aloud about the unlikely duo.

"Lucky dog!" "Wow, she's with *Carlton Meadows*?" and "Sheesh, what's wrong with *that* picture?"

Carlton asked his date to dance and as they headed toward the dance floor, they spotted Sheila Davis trotting toward them, dragging her prom date behind her. The girls squealed and hugged each other while the boys introduced themselves.

"Look at us, girl! Can you believe it? My mom was actually happy for me to come tonight," Sheila said, incredulously.

"Shoot, mine too! I thought she was gonna tell me to stay home so *she* could go with Carlton!" Angelica exclaimed, laughing at the visual.

"Moms are weird," Sheila offered.

Sheila looked so pretty in her powder blue taffeta dress, and Angelica told her so. Angelica had gone to Sears with her and Mrs. Davis to pick it out. She'd even wandered up to the floor with the housewares to get some hot popcorn and peanuts for her and her friend to share on the ride home. Mrs. Davis, ever the adventurous driver, didn't seem to notice how the girls rolled and bounced around the back seat like tennis balls, their delicious treats showering the floor. Sheila had asked if she could go with Angelica to get her prom dress, but Angelica told her they'd already picked it up.

"Oh," said Sheila, slightly disappointed.

Angelica noticed her friend's bruised feelings and chimed, "My mother pretty much just brought it home and put it on my bed. I got home from school and there was this pretty yellow gown laying there. She's lucky I like it," Angelica chuckled, awkwardly.

The truth was Liz had taken her daughter to Winkelman's, B. Siegel, Saks Fifth Avenue and finally, a bridal shop to procure her gown. Angelica didn't want Sheila to feel bad or that her dress was any less beautiful or special. She also didn't want to entertain the unspoken question of how could a mom who did not work afford such a dress, which she wondered as well.

Carlton grabbed Angelica's hand and led her to the dance floor while she made a face at Sheila as if to say, "*Can I go home now?*" They danced to three songs in a row then stopped because Carlton was starving and wanted to get some potato chips and punch at the table set up in the corner of the room. Taking a seat at a nearby table, they put down their snacks while Carlton mopped his glistening forehead with some napkins.

"I wonder where Ricky and his date could be at?"

No sooner had he said it than they looked up to see Ricky Williams parting the crowd like a teenaged Moses. He was laughing and acknowledging every person in his sightline, his arm around a pretty girl wearing a sky blue formal matching Ricky's tux. While Ricky had his hair loose and flowing to his shoulders in shiny jet waves, the girl with him had a neat natural or afro hairdo. She looked mature and sophisticated, like she already went to college. The girl's hand was a cage on Ricky's arm begging him not to abandon her side.

Naturally, like the gravitational pull of the moon, Ricky turned and found himself looking straight into Angelica's face. Awkward. He smiled his megawatt grin at Angelica as she looked away.

"Boom, shut down," Angelica mumbled to herself.

How dare he roll into that place, all heat and fire and beauty and expect it to be business as usual between them! Was he crazy or just selfish and cruel? She knew she couldn't avoid Enrique

303

nor his date for very long because Carlton was calling and waving in their direction and they were coming over. Was this what they called "Death by a thousand paper cuts?" because that's the subtle torture she felt as she cranked her face into a fixed, fake smile.

"Hi, everybody. Hey, this is Sarah," Enrique said to the group.

The girl waved and said, "Hello."

Ricky turned to his date and asked, "You want to sit here?"

The agreeable girl no one knew said, "Sure," as they pulled up chairs.

Angelica struggled to keep her eyes from visiting Ricky while trying to configure some type of small talk for the girl. Just then, Sheila bounced over to the table, her large and uncomfortable date in tow.

"Hi, y'all. Did I already introduce y'all to Fred?"

"No," they all said.

"Well, this is Fred. He goes to my church."

"Hey, Fred," they all replied.

Angelica looked closely at Fred's face and figured out what was so strange about it. Fred was bald, but more alarmingly, he had no eyebrows or eyelashes. He apparently suffered from Alopecia, a disease that makes a person lose their hair, all of it, everywhere.

"Let's go to the ladies' room. We'll be right back," Angelica announced, giving Sarah a look that told her she wasn't invited.

The ballroom was beautifully decorated with powdery white and cobalt blue balloons bobbing along the ceiling. There was a knot of teachers gathered near the refreshments, looking square and uncomfortable and disinterested in their hormonal charges. All except the math teacher, Mr. Grier, who had focused his attention on one girl in particular on the dance floor. Sophia Longmire, a girl Carlton had asked to the prom. Of course she said "no" immediately and politely. No one knew Mr. Grier was secretly dating one of the girls in his class—the lovely Miss Longmire. They ended up getting married later that summer, but for tonight, he was surreptitiously making sure he kept an eye on her and her "date."

Dave "The Lizard" Lizaro was there with his younger sister as his date, Mike Morton brought a cute underclassman girl and Twin (who could tell which?) brought the class ho, Kitty O'Neal, or "Pretty Kitty" as she was sometimes called, who had transferred to Dodge from Mumford during her Senior year. Every girl in the room knew they most definitely had to watch their boyfriends around Kitty.

There was a lounge inside the ladies' bathroom and as the girls waited their turn to assess themselves in a full-length mirror, Angelica turned to Sheila.

"I love him, Sheila. A lot," she sighed in frustration.

Sheila grabbed Angelica's wrist, the one without the corsage, and swung her arm out slightly, as if to begin a dance.

"What? You love Carlton? You love Carlton!" Sheila whispered loudly, incredulously.

Angelica clutched Sheila's hand in a gesture that signaled for her to calm down.

"No, girl. I'm talking about Ricky. I love Ricky, and this is the first time I've said it out loud to anybody...including myself."

The air seemed to grow still as the girls stared at one another before simultaneously breaking into wide grins.

"I knew it! I knew it!" Sheila squealed.

"Well, you can calm down because I don't think he feels the same way I do. Shoot, he didn't even ask me to come to prom with him. How dumb does that make me?"

"I think you should tell him. Can't you tell he really likes you? I sure can."

"Nope. That's a waste of time. In a few months we're gonna all be at different schools, in different parts of the country. I don't want some kind of summer romance and then be all distracted and heartbroken at my new school. And, yeah, I know he likes me, but obviously it's just as a friend."

The girls primped, touched up their lipstick and hair and came back to the table. The band was just returning from their break and they began to play "Jumpin' Jack Flash" by the Rolling Stones. Carlton sprang up and grabbed Angelica by the hand and they continued to dance for more than a half hour with various couples trying to keep up with them on the dance floor. Who knew Carlton was such a skilled and energetic dancer?

Dancing, talking and laughing with her friends and classmates was exactly what Angelica needed to keep her mind and, more importantly, her eyes off of Ricky and Sarah. It turned out that Angelica and Carlton were the spark of the celebration, with Angelica making sure she threw her hands up higher and sung louder than anyone, and Carlton loved the attention. He excused himself to go to the bathroom soon after they sat back down at the table. Sheila was already sitting there with Fred, who had grown tired by the third song. Sheila was more than a little miffed and was eating cake.

"Want some?"

"Nope. I'm ready to dance some more."

Angelica couldn't help but scan the room for any sign of Enrique Williams. She didn't have to look far as he had migrated to another table with his date, yet again looking at Angelica. She smiled sweetly and waved.

"Jerk," she said under her breath.

Ricky excused himself from his date and went over to talk to the disc jockey who was spinning records in between the band's sets. This was the last interlude before the band came back and ended the night. The dee jay took off the record he was playing, "Young Girl" by the Union Gap, to a small chorus of "Heeeeey!" and put on "Shoo Be Doo Be Doo Da Day" by Stevie Wonder. Ricky knew Angelica loved that song and as the beginning chords of the clavinet filled the air, Angelica looked up to see Ricky Williams walking toward her.

"Oh boy," said Sheila, shoveling a forkful of cake into her mouth.

Ricky put his hand on Angelica's back and asked, "Do you want to dance?"

"Sure," Angelica said coolly as Ricky took her by the hand and led her out onto the dance floor. As they danced, Ricky leaned in so he could be heard.

"Are you having fun? Looks like you're the life of the party."

"I'm having a blast," Angelica said, adding a spin to her dance move.

Enrique was impressed and smiled before saying, "I had to dance with the most beautiful girl at Dodge High."

"Oh, I thought your girlfriend didn't go here."

"What? Angelica, I'm talking about you and you know it. And for the record, Sarah is not my girlfriend. You're more my..."

"Girl? Who's also a friend? Glad you're keeping things simple."

"Look, we're both here, having a great time, right?"

"Some plan on having a better time than others," Angelica said, looking Ricky squarely in the eyes.

"I'm not going to lie. I'm not planning to go home after the prom or even after the after parties. It's good that you came with Carlton, okay? It's for your own good."

"Gee, and here I was thinking my daddy was dead. I didn't know he was here at the prom," Angelica said, sarcastically.

Ricky laughed, but he could see Angelica was not amused and he stopped himself before he made her angrier.

"Is this our first fight?" Ricky said before he could take back his words.

The implication of a history and a future hung in the air, staring down at them blankly like an actor without his script. The disc jockey put on "La La (Means I Love You)" by the Delphonics. They could feel the collective eyes of Carlton and Sarah boring a hole in their direction, but instead of walking away from each other, Ricky slipped his right arm around Angelica's waist and his other arm came up to clutch her hand as they began to slow dance.

"Angelica Tanner, you're like a dessert. Chocolate and caramel, definitely nuts…whipped cream and a cherry. I'm saving my dessert for last."

There he'd said it, but did she understand what he meant?

"Well, my friend, life is short and unpredictable and that's why you eat dessert first. You never know what can happen. And, I've got your dessert. It's a sock in the nose."

Enrique loved this feisty girl and he had to laugh at how he'd just been shot down. So much for romance.

"Girl, you ain't gon' do nothin'," Ricky said, unable to contain his spreading smile.

"You better keep those eyes open and on me, 'cause you never know when it's coming," Angelica said, trying to look stern.

"That's not hard to do. Man, you Negroes are violent."

"I'm not a Negro. I'm Black now. So, say it loud, I'm Black and I'm proud."

"Okay, Jamesetta Brown. If you're still trying to deck me, I'm gonna have to hold your arms down, like this" Ricky said, encircling her arms with his.

Angelica became very aware of the weight and firmness of his arms and didn't want him to take them away or loosen his hold. They had stopped talking and Ricky was holding Angelica close in his embrace. They didn't speak again as the song moved their bodies slowly and silently. This was a moment to remember, to engrave in the heart and to cherish in the mind, because the record would soon be over and they both knew their summer would fly by and they would be saying their goodbyes.

FORTY-TWO

The morning of graduation, Angelica woke up grinning from ear to ear. It was as if she were in a movie like "Gidget" or "Where the Boys Are" and she was the teenaged star whose life was about to begin. The excitement in her house was palpable, she could hear her grandparents in the kitchen talking. The doorbell rang and after a flurry of sounds, her cousins Frankie and Lydia came running into her room.

"Good morning! Get up, sleepy head!" they exclaimed.

"Dang, don't you guys ever knock?" Angelica said, pretending to be exasperated.

Then she threw her arms wide and they jumped onto the bed and onto her.

"Aunt Liz said we could wake you up, so that's why we barged in," said Lydia.

Angelica loved her little cousins and she was going to miss them when she went off to college. She made a mental note to hang out with them more often during the summer.

"Okay, I'm awake, so you guys go play while I get dressed."

"Make sure you brush your teeth. Yuck!" Frankie said dramatically.

Angelica threw her pillow at the back of his head as he was running out of the door. Did they ever just walk? She shook her head, allowing herself to think again about the day that lay ahead. Angelica got up and stretched, half expecting cartoon bluebirds to fly in with her robe and slippers. She could smell bacon frying, its specific deliciousness wafting down the hallway, so she quickly washed her face and brushed her teeth before getting into the shower.

Enrique Williams was cleaning out his car to make it nice and comfortable for his mother to ride to the graduation. She would ride up front with Pilar in the middle, Eduardo and Alecia in back. Of course, there was plenty of room on the back seat for Pilar, but she adored her big brother and this was a special day and she'd already lobbied for the prime spot next to him.

As he used the old whisk broom to get every speck of dust or crumb of food from his seats and floor, Ricky became pensive. What would they, his family, do without him around? Eduardo, who'd be a teenager when Ricky graduated U of M, needed his advice and guidance, even though he was a good kid. Pilar confided every secret to her big brother ("I'm not telling anybody…but I'll tell you," she'd always say), and Alecia, now the oldest surviving child, needed him to give the once over to any potential suitors. After all, Ricky was still the oldest male and the man of the house by default, as it seemed he'd always been. And his poor mother Ana, she tried to be brave, but he could see in her eyes that she was missing him already.

"Damn you, Danny," he said in a voice that was barely audible.

A car navigated down his block with the windows down, music blaring, and Ricky could hear the unmistakable harmonies, that tremulous violin. It was "La La (Means I Love You)" and it made him smile. His mind hadn't stopped replaying that short time he'd had his Angel in his arms since it happened two nights ago.

When Ricky and Sarah left the prom, they went to a private party thrown by one of her classmates at the Driftwood Lounge inside the Twenty Grand nightclub, on 14th Street and Warren Avenue. The girl's parents had spared no expense for the teens to enjoy a late dinner, champagne and entertainment by none other than the Delfonics, who had been appearing there nightly. Ricky saw many of his old friends from MacKenzie High and they had a raucous time talking about the old days, who was a drop-out, who had moved away, who was in jail, who had died. His own brother, sadly, hit just about every mark but everyone was careful not to mention Danny.

When the Delfonics launched into their big hit record, Sarah, seated sideways in her chair, leaned back into Ricky's chest. He put his arm around her, but he wished Angelica could be there to hear the song played live. She would have laughed at the coincidence. Ricky shook off the daydream, slammed the heavy door to his Buick Electra 225 or *Deuce and a Quarter*, and ran up the steps and into the house to get dressed.

Francis Dodge High's graduating class of 1968 sat anxiously awaiting their ceremony to begin. To a youngster, everyone looked out into the audience to glimpse their parents and the family and friends who had come to witness this special occasion. There were a few uniformed policemen in attendance as was the norm for that type of event. A police officer doing a quick check backstage walked past the area considered the "wings," stage right. There stood a tall man in a light wool suit, standing just at the edge of the pulleys for the curtains where he could see but not be seen himself.

"Hey pal, you can't stand back here. You need to take a seat if you're not part of the ceremony," the officer barked.

The man turned slowly toward the policemen with his head cocked like he didn't quite hear what was just spoken to him or perhaps he wanted the man to repeat it, his deep navy-blue eyes flashing, serious and incredulous. The officer's eyes got wide as recognition registered rapidly.

"Oh, pardon me. I'm sorry. Sorry, sir. I didn't mean to—"

The tall man had turned away, back to the young people on the stage. The policeman stumbled away as if running from a swarm of bees, tripping over something that wasn't even in his path, but righting himself before he fell. The lights dimmed slightly, and the school orchestra began to play "Pomp and Circumstance," led by their very excited orchestra teacher, Mr. Meyers.

Angelica's family took her out to an early dinner on the sparkling green waterfront of the Detroit River to Sindbad's, one of the finest seafood restaurants in Detroit. They enjoyed the view of the waterway with yachts and sail boats preening in the sunshine, through the large wall of windows.

"I'm glad you could join us for dinner, young lady," Angelica's grandpa said to Sheila.

Hank Tanner was beyond proud of Angelica as she would be the first child in their family to go to college in three generations. For years, the auto factories and other distractions had swallowed up his family's ambition and desire to matriculate beyond high school. A decent paycheck, protection of a strong union, benefits and steady work trumped academia, for most, any day. He was happy to spend his money on this lavish dinner to celebrate his granddaughter. Hank always said, "You can't take it with you," when his wife scolded him for having loose pockets.

Sheila's parents and her big sister Francine had come to the graduation and though Liz invited them all to dinner at

Sindbad's, Velma declined, relenting only to allow Sheila to go be with her best friend. Liz promised to drop the girl back home afterward, as soon as dinner had concluded. Watching the formal exchange between the adults reminded Angelica that just because you are friends with someone, it didn't mean your parents would be friends as well. These were sovereign nations.

Driving home from the events downtown, Mrs. Davis announced to her husband and oldest child that they were not charity cases to be pitied by the Tanners. Mr. Davis, not surprisingly, said "Okay, Velma," and nothing more. Francine was quiet and angry because she wanted a free dinner at that fancy restaurant, and what was the harm in that? She decided her mother was as nutty as a fruitcake and she couldn't wait to get out of that car and back to her apartment.

FORTY-THREE

T he summer was filled with house parties and block parties with all the kids fortunate enough to be going to college, saying multiple goodbyes to everyone and everything. As promised, Angelica spent extra time with her young cousins Lydia and Frankie and her uncle Ned, happily, didn't ask her why she wanted to suddenly be around his children. He was grateful for time alone with his wife.

Angelica took the kids to River Rouge Park, the largest public park in Michigan. The 1300-acre park had three Olympic sized swimming pools that had been used in the Olympic pre-trials in 1956. A tragic incident had taken place at the park in 1967, exactly one month before the riots in Detroit. A black man was shot and killed, and his pregnant wife beaten by a bunch of wild white teenagers, so Liz had insisted Angelica take a male friend with them.

"Mama, the man got killed. The lady lived, you know."

"Take one of your buddies with you or stay home. Run the sprinkler in the front yard. Kids like that. You used to like it, too."

She'd had a good time with Carlton at the prom, surprisingly, so maybe he wasn't such a drip after all. She just had to manage his expectations when she called to ask him to come swim at the park. Angelica asked Sheila to go as well, since her cousins liked her and to make double sure that Carlton knew they weren't on a "date." But Sheila had to help her dad clean out the garage and that was an all-day process.

They swam, played freeze tag and Mother May I, and ate the tuna salad sandwiches she'd packed, along with a half dozen Sanders caramel cupcakes—her favorite. Carlton had insisted on bringing the pop and potato chips.

"You happy to be getting out of Detroit?" Carlton asked.

"Well, sort of. California is as far as I could go without dropping into the ocean," Angelica teased. "No, I just want to see new things, have new experiences. That's what college means to me. A test to see if my little wings will carry me. What about you?"

Carlton frowned slightly.

"My father says he needs me to be nearby to work at his firm so I can get my own place. I think my mother is behind everything…keeping me here so she can stay in my business," he said.

"Wayne State is a great school, Carlton. We're both only children, so you can't really blame your mom for not wanting you to go away."

"I don't see your mama trying to keep you in Detroit."

Angelica laughed out loud.

"Liz Tanner is a different animal, believe me."

"Even Ricky is going up to Ann Arbor to U of M."

"I think it's funny that all three of us want to be lawyers, don't you?" Angelica asked.

"Who knows? Maybe we'll start our own law firm. Wouldn't that be trippy? Williams, Meadows and Tanner, Attorneys at Law."

"More like Tanner and Associates," Angelica said, wryly.

They both began to laugh.

"Well whatever it is, I'm hoping we're friends for life. The Three Musketeers."

Angelica smiled.

"I'll do my part. All for one and one for all!"

FORTY-FOUR

One morning when she was about 15 years old, Angelica discovered a man, a hobo, on their front lawn. She was keeping vigil through the living room drapes with the man lazily sleeping away, when she got the idea to make him a brown bag lunch. Surely, he had to be hungry, right? A few minutes later she took the filled sack out to him, right after he'd roused himself awake, just sitting up and seemingly disoriented as to where he might be. He just blinked at her with red rimmed eyes and without a word, she handed him the food. The man thanked her several times and got up and moved on. Soon she was finding these nomads on their property a couple of times per month.

Unknowingly, Angelica had gained a reputation for kindness with boxcar vagrants who made their way across the railroad tracks and the few miles North to her house. The curb in front of her house had a crude tell-tale cat drawn on it with a red clay brick that signified to the hobo community that someone generous and kind lived there. No matter the time of year, Angelica would beckon the men to the side of the house and tell them to wait while she fixed a sack lunch for them. Usually two bologna on Wonder bread with American cheese sandwiches, an apple and a piece of cake or a cookie would be their fare. Sometimes her mother protested that her food was being wasted and she may as well feed the neighborhood dogs. Liz's largesse was minimal, and that may have been a generous assessment.

Angelica was happy to help those down on their luck. The grateful men often wandered off calling her an angel. Angelica just knew if it were her, she'd want someone to give her a bite to eat and treat her with respect. Sometimes she'd fantasize that maybe her dad was somewhere in the world and was lucky enough to be surrounded by kind strangers if he too was down in his fortunes. She'd allow herself this little illusion while making her sandwiches. In her heart, she knew her daddy was dead over in Korea. Best not to dwell on that. *He'd be proud of his girl, though, wouldn't he?*

When her mother wasn't home, a storm was threatening and Angelica grabbed her laundry basket to rescue their clean wash from the line. Angelica loved sudden summer storms and how the sky would grow deep and purple and gray as the clouds rattled their warning. When she was a little girl, she'd open the front door of her house to smell the rush of ozone charged wind through the screen, signaling the approaching rain. She'd press her body against the dusty screen door with her eyes closed. When she heard the rain commence, she would walk out onto her porch barefoot, sometimes with a bath towel over her back like a cape, secured by a safety pin at her neck. The summer wind's lash would whip the precipitation at her, but there she stood. With her cape billowing wildly, she'd spin around daring the rain to drench her, lest the gusts blew her from her concrete kingdom first.

Liz would always halt the reverie with, "Get your ass in this house! What's wrong with you?! Are you trying to get struck by lightning?"

Angelica would run past her mother and pad down the hall to her room with her mother's voice reverberating against the walls.

Angelica was hurriedly taking the laundry off the clothesline in the backyard when a man appeared in the alley at her gate. He was shabbily dressed and carried a large brown paper bag, like the hobos from the rail yard often did. He had surprised her, but she wasn't startled. The sheets whipping and flapping in the belligerent wind were more unnerving. After greeting her, the man asked to use her bathroom. Angelica knit her brows together. *He's a man and he's in the alley. Why doesn't he just pull his thing out near the garbage cans and do his business? Oh great, he wants to do number 2, doesn't he?*

The man could read her reticence and made a pleading face, gesturing with his dirty hands clasped in pantomimed prayer. Her mother did not like the men to come around and if Angelica wasn't home, Liz wouldn't even open her curtains. Sometimes the person would sit on the curb or on the grass for hours until Angelica got home and came out with a brown bag containing sustenance. Liz Tanner would often wag her finger at her daughter and tell her she could not save the world and she was foolish to try.

Angelica told the man to come inside the yard through the gate and he followed her to the side door of her house. Angelica turned on the light to the basement and directed him to use the bathroom located through the laundry room downstairs.

"Are you hungry? Do you need something to eat?" she asked.

"Yes, ma'am. That would be fine," he said as he disappeared down the stairs.

In the kitchen, Angelica switched on the radio to listen to Jay Butler on WCHB. She dug Jay, but man did she miss the night time deejay, Rockin' Robbie D. Angelica sang softly, "Oooh Robbie you got soul!" She shook her head, smiling at her not so great singing voice. The man had come up from the basement quietly, stealthily and slid up behind Angelica while she was singing and making his lunch. She smelled him before she saw him but was still not fast enough to escape his arm tightening around her neck. He told her to drop the knife on the counter.

"Mister, I don't have any money. Don't you want your lunch?" she said, realizing she sounded absurd and scared.

"No, that ain't what I'm hungry for, girlie," he said, his foul breath making her jerk a bit as he tightened his grip.

The filthy man was pressing up against her behind as she began to cry.

"You nasty bastard," she managed to say. "Let me go! Get out of my house!"

"Not 'til I get what I come for. You're gonna—" the man didn't finish his sentence as she felt him being pulled, jerked backward.

Momentarily, she too was dragged backward with her heels pressing into the linoleum floor. She'd come out of her sandals. As the man released his grip, Angelica spun around to see Ricky holding the man by his greasy hair with one hand and the other had wrenched the man's arm unnaturally high up his back as if he were trying to scratch his shoulder.

"Motherfucker, I ought to break your fucking arm!" Ricky said through clenched teeth.

Angelica had never before heard Ricky talk like this, his voice guttural and almost unrecognizable. He rushed the man down the three stairs to the side door so quickly, the man seemed to be levitating. He landed in a heap in the driveway and had the nerve to say he wasn't trying to do anything. That seemed to enrage Ricky, who flew out of the door and was on the bum in seconds, kicking him.

"This is how you treat somebody trying to help your busted ass? Get the fuck out of here and don't come back! If I see you around here again, I'll kill you. You got that?" he yelled giving the shaken, bleeding man a final kick.

Angelica moved from the screen door as Ricky came back into the house. He gently held her shoulders and searched her face.

"Are you alright? Did he hurt you?"

Before she could answer, Ricky had enveloped her in his arms, her head on his chest listening to his rapid heartbeat. She didn't know if it was her or him, but the man's sour scent lingered in the air and on both of them.

"Girl, if anything ever happened to you..." his voice trailed off as he hugged her tighter to his muscular body.

She held onto him, returning his urgent embrace.

"I'm not sure I like you saving me all the time," she lied.

They had never spoken about what Ricky had done to Barry. He didn't even know that she knew.

"You're a pretty tough chick. I just helped you out a little bit. Maybe someday you'll rescue me," Ricky said with a half-hearted chuckle.

Without a whit of shame, she cried softly on his chest. He rocked her gently back and forth while the lengthening afternoon shadows overtook the room as it began to rain.

FORTY-FIVE

For Enrique Williams, each day was somehow making it easier for him to leave home for college life. His mother let him know how proud she was of him and that it was truly okay for him to strike out on his own. She said they would be fine without him and there was no reason to feel guilty or conflicted. With this burden lifted, Ricky began to face each day full of energy, expectation and excitement. Uncle Bill had come by to slip him some money for things he might need for his dormitory room. Ricky gave the $300 to his mother to shop for him, she knew best what to get.

Ricky missed out on a few summer parties because he had to work. Mr. Gilhooley let him close up the store most nights and he was beat by the time he made it home, but he didn't mind. He'd have plenty of time to party and socialize up in Ann Arbor, and the extra money he was making would definitely come in handy. Mr. G was going to miss Ricky, as he'd never had someone so trustworthy and dependable working for him. He'd be hard to replace.

Some evenings Ricky would swing by Angelica's and just sit on her porch and talk. He always brought her a cold bottle of Faygo Red Pop, Nesbitt's Orange or a NuGrape, along with a bag of Superior Potato Chips. He tried to switch it up because he didn't want to be too predictable. As usual, neighbors sat on their porches to escape the unbearable heat inside their homes. Kids played in the street under the watchful eyes of the adults while mosquito chasers punctuated the night with their pungent smoke. The summer was half gone as it was nearing the end of July.

Angelica had propped her mother's radio from the kitchen in the front window where she could hear her favorite songs on WCHB. Across the street someone had on the baseball game, so Ernie Harwell was competing with her music. Ricky sat on the concrete steps guzzling his pop while Angelica reclined slightly in a chaise lawn chair on the porch. Neither spoke. It was as if they each were taking in the sights, sounds and smells of the waning summer of 1968. They wanted to remember everything, no matter how small, all the vestiges of home, of safety, of the familiar.

A car coming down the street signaled for the kids to move aside with a short burst from its horn, before pulling into a driveway across the street. A small chorus of salutations arose from the group of children playing where the man emerged from the vehicle, lunch pail in one hand, newspaper clutched in the other. The man threw his hand up as a wave to anyone interested and went into the house. The men and fathers on the block, the few that were in households, were factory men. They gave their blood, sweat, tears, youth, and some even their health, working themselves into early graves for one of the big three automakers. A family was faithful to the company that put bread on the table. If your daddy was a GM man, your mama drove a Cadillac, your brother a Chevy 409 and your uncle an Electra 225.

This was the good life to some, but many of these men woke up every day to the disillusionment and bitterness of dreams whose voices had grown still. Many had talent, with some wanting to sing or dance. Berry Gordy had been a factory worker himself before founding Motown Records. But so many voices had become harsh from cigarettes and alcohol. Dancing feet had become stiff and gimpy from standing on an assembly line for eight hours a day. What was left was anger, resentment and clenched fists that sometimes found their way to a wife's face or a kid's stomach. Even still, these two fatherless children wondered if something, someone was better than nothing and no one.

"My mother says girls go to college to find husbands. Is that what you plan to do?" Ricky asked out of nowhere.

"I'm going to college so I can be rich," Angelica offered, laughing.

"You coming back here when you finish or are you going to stay in L.A.? Shoot, you might quit school and become a movie star."

"You never know. If I do that, I'm gonna need a lawyer I can trust. I'll give you a call. You can wheel and deal for me, okay?"

"That's a deal, Angel."

She loved when he called her that.

"So, if girls go to college to find husbands, they gotta have marriage material, right? That's where you come in."

"Thanks for volunteering me, my friend, but I'm going to school so I can eventually travel all over the world. I want to speak a bunch of different languages, see the cool places you find in books. You need money to do that and a degree or two is how to do it."

"You ever been to Puerto Rico? I've seen some pictures in *Life* magazine and it looks so pretty. The people are pretty, too."

"My mother took us there when I was about 5 or 6 but I really don't remember too much about it. I want to go back, but this time I'll take my mom. My Spanish is *muy bueno*."

There was a ruckus coming from across the street. Apparently Willie Horton had hammered in a home run.

"Man, the Tigers are good this year," Angelica said.

Ricky nodded. He loved how well rounded she was.

"I know. I think they can win the Pennant."

"I'll go you one better. They're going to be in the Series."

"The World Series? I don't know about that."

"You wanna bet?" Angelica asked, putting out her right hand.

"Okay, what can we bet? How about $5? Can you afford to lose that much?" Ricky asked, reaching for Angelica's soft but strong hand.

"Boy, you got a bet. Save your money so you can pay up!"

She laughed and then realized they'd be far away from each other, thousands of miles, when the World Series was played in October.

Sensing what she may have been pondering, Ricky said, "Now you got an excuse to write me a letter."

"I don't need an excuse. I'll write you, okay?"

And he knew she meant it. He smiled in the dark.

"Alright. I gotta go. Isn't there a block party tomorrow afternoon on San Juan? I heard Mad Dog and the Pups are gonna be there. Their song "Hep Squeeze" is a jam!"

"Yup, and that kid Little Carl Carlton is supposed to be there, too. 'Competition Ain't Nothing' is the bomb! It's gonna be so cool...I mean live and in person! Are you going to be able to go?"

"I'm coming. Mr. G is closing a little bit early tomorrow because he's got to do something with his family. I probably won't get there until it's dark. Save a dance for me, okay?" Enrique said, getting to his feet and ambling toward the street.

"See ya. Get some sleep. Go straight home. Don't take any wooden nickels. Don't talk to strangers. Don't take any shortcuts. Only you can prevent forest fires," Angelica yelled after her friend.

As Ricky started his car, he smiled, saying to himself, "My Angel is kinda bossy. But I like it. Yeah, I do."

FORTY-SIX

C arlton threw the hard, red rubber ball against the brick on the side of his house and it bounced down to the concrete and into his gloved hand. Inside the house, Mavis Meadows felt like her nerves were on the precipice of collapse as the ball reported from the house to the ground, from the house to the ground with a *ka-thunk*, *ka-thunk*. It was so punctual and steady, she could have danced to it. Mrs. Meadows appeared at the side window, rapping loudly enough to disrupt her son's ennui.

"Son, it's getting dark, can you stop that? Can't you find something else to do, please?" she said through bared teeth only approximating a smile.

"No, Mother, I can't," was all Carlton said as the ball flew again toward the house.

She was gone from the window.

Ricky would be getting off from the Shake 'n Spin soon. Carlton figured he could go hang around and wait until Ricky finished cleaning the place up and then maybe they could head over to Belle Isle or the drag races at the White Castle in Warren. There was always plenty of action with the greasers throwing down challenges and their pimply girlfriends taking bets. It would be fun to hang out with Ricky tonight, just the two of them. How many more nights would they be allowed to do that before the summer ended and college intruded on them like some dreaded relative?

Hot and bored, Carlton went inside the house and upstairs in search of some money in his dad's chest of drawers so he could go to the Shake 'n Spin to get a hamburger and some pop. If he hurried he could get there before old man Gilhooley closed down the grill. Carlton was just about to push the bottom drawer shut with his foot, when he saw a dull glint. Moving aside some handkerchiefs and socks, his hand soon came to rest on the soulless, deep gray steel of a .38 handgun. His dad must have brought it upstairs from the cabinet in the den. He took a look behind him, checking the door for his mother.

This ain't no movie, fool. She's not going to suddenly appear at the door like an angel telling you to leave the gun where you found it, while some imaginary costumed devil resembling the very same woman tells you to take it. Suddenly, his hands were shaking ever so slightly and his heart was racing, a flush of heat creeping up his scalp. He quickly took the weapon and stuffed it in the back waist band of his blue jeans and raced from the room, down the stairs and out of the front door into the July night.

Mr. Gilhooley had already turned out half the lights in the store, a signal to potential customers that it was almost closing time and they needed to grab chips or candy or a pop from the cooler and go. No fountain service and no more record sales since people usually wanted to hear the records played first before they paid, sometimes several records at a time.

"We're about to close up, son," said Mr. Gilhooley as he methodically locked a display case full of cheap costume jewelry that the girls like to buy.

"It's me, Mr. G., it's Carlton."

"Oh, sure. Uh, Ricky's in the back. I guess you can find him alright."

The old man was worn out but was looking forward to entertaining a few of his relatives at the small party they were having, eating his wife's meatloaf and mashed potatoes, taking a good shit, and then getting into a hot bath before bed. Artemis Gilhooley railed against the ravages of old age and the affect it was having on his body. Every day he seemed to be bending closer to the ground as his body curled into itself, seemingly unable or unwilling to resist gravity. Gilhooley was in his late 50's, but looked and felt ten years older. Arthritis had gnarled his stubby hands and had given him a limp. The smallest tasks took Herculean effort until he could get "warmed up" as he liked to say, after he'd had his eggs and coffee.

Carlton went down the short narrow hallway past the toilet and into the tiny office. Ricky was just emerging from a store room whose entrance was on the opposite side of the room. He wiped the dust from his hands with a rag hanging from his belt loop.

"Hey, man!" he exclaimed, seeing Carlton.

"Hey. I see it's too late for a burger. Shit, I knew I shoulda left the house sooner," Carlton said with genuine disappointment.

Ricky smiled, "Yeah, man, you know Mr. G ain't firing up the grill for nobody once it's shut down." He checked his watch. "Okay, I can leave in about ten minutes. What do you want to do? I told Angelica we might meet her over at the block party on San Juan. They got music *and* food over there."

Carlton wrinkled up his face, but Ricky didn't notice because he was back inside the storage room. *Angelica. Why did she have to be a part of everything they did?* As Ricky came back into the room, having locked the storage room, Carlton blew air out between his lips.

"I don't know", Carlton said distractedly, "but I got something crazy to show you." Instantly he was no longer hungry, he just wanted to see Ricky's face when he pulled out the gun.

"Check it out," Carlton said, clutching the in his hand.

Ricky had been smiling, but now the smile was gone.

"What the fuck, man? Are you crazy?"

Carlton was taken aback by his friend's reaction, feeling a little embarrassed and foolish. He didn't like this familiar feeling.

"Man, put that shit away. Matter of fact…" Ricky grabbed the weapon with little effort, hitting Carlton's fingertips with the butt of the gun as he pulled it away and put it on the back edge of the desk.

"You'll get it back later. I need to find something to put it in. We could get stopped by the police and we'd be in big trouble, Carlton." Ricky just stared at him for a moment. "Man, what's wrong with you?"

Carlton thought he heard disbelief mixed with pure abhorrence in Ricky's voice.

Without waiting for an answer, Ricky turned on his heels mumbling, "Just wait here," and was gone.

Carlton had not anticipated this reaction. He sat in the old wooden chair in front of the desk, feeling as agitated and rickety as the chair. Why hadn't Ricky said Carlton was cool for having a gun? Why had he looked shocked and ashamed of him? Carlton began to get angry. *Does Enrique Williams, the kid with no father and a murderous pimp for an uncle think he's better than me?* He had some fucking nerve! Carlton picked up the gun, gripping it tightly, unconsciously, not realizing he was speaking aloud.

"That nigger better be glad I like him or else I'd—,"

He hadn't heard Mr. Gilhooley come in and what happened next would change the course of every life present in that store that night, in ways no one could have ever imagined. What happened next was a sunny day turning black with clouds, a lilting song turning into a discordant scream, an end-game chess board being flipped over by a petulant child.

Mr. Gilhooley was saying, "Hey, kid, put that down," but Carlton didn't hear the full sentence issue from Artemis Gilhooley's lips because he spun to the right, into the direction of the intrusive sounds, and pulled the trigger of the gun. The report was like a firecracker, so light and playful it seemed, a complete betrayal of the meaning of the heat and smoke coming from the barrel of the gun and the gravity of the sentence it had pronounced on Mr. Gilhooley. The old man dropped to the floor with a gunshot to the neck. The blood seemed to be gushing like water from an open faucet.

Ricky appeared at the door, startled, shocked and out of breath, however, he had the presence of mind to shout, "Stop, Carlton! It's me! Put the gun down!"

He held his hands in front of his chest in a "stop" pantomime with a brown paper bag wrinkled up between the fingers of his left hand. He knew not to ask Carlton what he'd done because he didn't know what Carlton might do next.

Mr. Gilhooley laid splayed across the floor blocking the entrance to the room. Terrible gurgling and gasping sounds were coming from his blood-spattered lips. Carlton and Ricky both knew he was dying and there was no way to save him. Shockingly, blankly, Carlton lowered the gun and shot Mr. Gilhooley in the chest.

"What the fuck are you doing?!" Ricky screamed.

He stepped over Mr. Gilhooley, slipping slightly in the spreading crimson rivulet, but righted himself on the desk's edge so he didn't fall. He snatched the gun from Carlton and put it in the brown bag he still had in his hand. He shoved the bag at Carlton.

"Let's get out of here, stupid," Ricky spit, and with those words they flew into the thick stickiness of the evening. They stopped for a moment as Ricky grabbed the bag from Carlton. "Give me the gun. I'll try to get rid of it. Get the hell out of here," Ricky said.

Rushing past the telephone booth a few yards outside the store, Ricky's eyes met those of a woman inside. He and Carlton kept moving, with Ricky determined to call the police from the next phone he came across, further down the block.

The woman in the phone booth had been talking with Ricky in the store just minutes before. Gilhooley would sometimes shoo her away if he was in a hurry to get home, but he usually tried to help. *He's okay for a white man*, she often thought, but Ricky, the kid, was a soft touch. He'd put some food in a paper bag for her when they had leftovers from the grill and sometimes he'd just give her a few candy bars. The sugar from the candy helped ease her pain when she was dope sick. Tonight, she was hoping to get a few dollars so she could get a fix and be right for a while.

The woman had been lingering at the counter when she heard the shot. For a microsecond, Ricky stared at her as if to affirm what he thought he heard. He ran past her so fast, he almost knocked her down as she ran out of the store. She was on the corner at the phone booth when she saw Carlton and Ricky run out of the Shake 'n Spin. The woman stood inside the telephone booth shaking. *Should she call the police? Who would believe a junkie? Hell, they might say she did it.* All these thoughts were jamming her brain and she didn't realize she'd already put her last dime into the phone and had dialed "O."

"Operator, can I help you?" said the tinny voice through the receiver. "Hello? This is the Operator, can I help you?"

The junkie was half way down the block and turning into the alley. The receiver from the telephone dangled, swinging back and forth like a miniature hanging man at the end of a noose.

FORTY-SEVEN

Ricky ran through multiple alleys trying to get to his house. Running in the darkness with only a few pools of street lights to illuminate his path, he sprinted over the concrete, knocking over a garbage can as a large Doberman surprised him by leaping at a fence. He barely turned sideways toward the sound and the barking shadow, but he could see the glistening of bared teeth. *That's King, Mrs. Johnson's dog. Almost home.* Sweat poured from his scalp through his hair and down his back, permeating his tee shirt and the waist of his blue jeans. A sour smell arose from his underarms as he worked them back and forth to help propel himself forward through the darkness. He knew he mustn't stop until he was safe, inside his room, inside his house.

Three houses away from his own, Ricky felt the gun fly out of the damp crumpled paper bag and hit his knee as it fell to the pavement, his right foot kicking at the weapon. It skittered with a heavy metallic sound, skipping into the shadows. *Shit!* He tried to focus his sweat stung eyes to see more clearly. He saw something dark a little bit ahead of him on the ground and he reached for it. It was a shoe. The rotten smell of garbage that had baked all day inside galvanized steel cans was punctuating the air. He thought of the time his mother made him go out to the trash to retrieve a dry-cleaning ticket she'd mistakenly thrown away. He lifted the lid of the garbage can and the inside was undulating with maggots. He'd slammed the lid down and did all he could to resist vomiting right then and there. He'd told his mother he would rather go and argue with the dry cleaners to get her belongings out. Turning around and around, he kept looking at the ground until finally he saw the gun barrel winking at him in the moonlight.

Ricky got to his own fence, hopping it rather than risk the clamor of the clanking, rusting gate and went into the house. He fell back onto his bed, replaying the night in his head, wishing it had never happened, wondering why he ran? His life as a young man on his own in college, waited for him outstretched like a beckoning hand. *That idiotic Carlton is not going to ruin my life!* Enrique vowed silently. Maybe he could call the police anonymously? No, that wasn't cool. Friends stuck together, especially in times of trouble.

But, Mr. Gilhooley! Poor Mr. G was a good man, a family man whose family was never going to talk or laugh with him again. He didn't deserve this. Damn Carlton! God, he wanted to talk to Angelica. She'd know what to do, but it was too late at night to call her or try to go to her house. Mrs. Tanner would have his head, plus what could he tell Angelica? Best to keep her out of it and she was probably still at the block party anyway. Maybe try to call Uncle Bill and tell him how bad things were and that he'd fucked up.

A slight breeze stirred the filmy curtains in his room and he could smell the dust on the tongue of the wind. Enrique had dozed off out of sheer exhaustion and he hadn't been asleep long when in the distance, perhaps in a dream, he heard sirens. He'd heard them earlier when he was running home, but they were drowned out by the rhythm of his heartbeat and his breathing echoing so loudly in his ears. They seemed to be getting closer. Louder and closer. Through the open window he heard four car doors slam and before he could rise up there was a pounding downstairs at the front door, followed by frantic doorbell ringing. He jumped to his feet, but he knew there was nowhere to go. He heard his mother call out through her bedroom window above the front porch, frightened.

"Who is there?"

"Police, ma'am. Open the door, we need to speak to you."

Ricky rushed out of his bedroom and stopped his mother as she descended the stairs in sleepy confusion.

"Wait, Mama. They want me."

When the police came inside they asked Ricky if he was Enrique Williams and did he work at the Shake 'n Spin. *Yes. Yes.*

"There was an incident tonight at that establishment and we need to talk to you. Who else is in the house?" the officer asked with his hand on the top of his service revolver.

The other officers were hyper alert, looking around the room, ready for any unexpected movements.

"My children are here," Ana Williams said.

Barely acknowledging her words, the officers focused on Ricky.

"Okay, son, we need to take you down to police headquarters to interview you. Do you have any weapons on you, boy?"

"No, um, I mean, yeah. Yeah, I do. There's a gun in the top dresser drawer."

Immediately one of the four policemen yelled, "Put your hands above your head and don't move!" Another had drawn his gun and trained it on Ricky. Mrs. Williams screamed.

"Stay back, ma'am. Keep those kids back."

By now the children were awake and had come down the stairs, terrified, crying and clutching their mother. Neighbors were gathering on their lawns and on their front porches, drawn by the red lights whirling atop the police cars.

"It's not mine. The gun is not mine," Ricky pleaded.

The two officers handcuffed Ricky as his mother wailed.

"No, no! There is some mistake! He is a good boy! He didn't do anything! You have the wrong boy! You have the wrong boy!" she fairly screamed.

"Ma'am, if you don't control yourself, we'll take you down too. Your kids will be in foster homes, split up! Is that what you want?"

"Mami, calm down. It's okay. I'm alright."

Enrique managed to find his mother's face over the policeman's blue shoulder. He looked her in her eyes.

"I didn't do anything. Mama, call my friend Carlton, Carlton Meadows. His father is a lawyer."

His brother and sister were crying loudly. Ricky had tears meeting under his chin as he was led out of his house. He could not have known that he'd never live in that house again. Like a phantom, his life disappeared after him into the night.

FORTY-EIGHT

S idney Meadows had just put his key in the lock of his front door when the door flew away from him, opening suddenly. He immediately felt the rush of refrigerated air from his brand-new Sears and Roebuck air conditioner surround his arms. His wife was practically draped over him, crying.

"What's wrong? What's wrong?" He quickly surmised that his son was the subject of this gruesome display. "Where is Carlton?" he asked.

"Oh, Sid, they took him! The police came and took our boy away," she sobbed, hugging her husband.

Sidney Meadows grabbed his wife's fleshy arms and pushed her away from his body so he could see her face.

"What the hell are you talking about, Mavis?" he snapped. He'd always imagined the day might come when the police would show up to retrieve his ridiculous wife, but not his son.

"The police came and took Carlton away, said he might have something to do with a m-m-murder!" she practically screamed.

"Calm yourself woman. That's absolutely asinine. Murder? Who's dead?"

"That man who owned the candy and record shop over there on Livernois, Mr. Gilhooley. That's his name. Gilhooley."

339

"Did they take him downtown to Beaubien? I'm sure they did," he said, answering his own question. He started moving toward the door he'd just come in. "You stay here. I'm going down to the police station."

"I'm going with you!"

"No, you stay here. I'm going to get our boy."

And with that, he was out the door.

When Mr. Meadows arrived at 1300 Beaubien, the headquarters of the Detroit Police Department, he made his way to the desk sergeant. The sergeant was a large ruddy faced man with a name badge on his left breast pocket that said "McDougal." Sidney Meadows never knew how things would play out with the Detroit police. So much had gone wrong, so publicly, last year during the riots, feelings were still raw and on the surface for the department and Sidney Meadows being a black lawyer might seem like an implied threat.

"Excuse me, officer. Sergeant McDougal, is it?" Meadows said with what he hoped was the right combination of deference and assertiveness.

The large man stared at him, eyes squinting like he was reading a barely visible headline on Mr. Meadows' forehead. He still hadn't responded.

"Sir, I am trying to locate my son, Carlton Meadows, whom I believe was brought in this evening. I'm his attorney, Sidney Meadows."

The man in uniform unselfconsciously picked his nose, wiped something on his pant leg and used the same finger to go down a ledger like sheet that was on the desk. His eyebrows joined to form a "V."

"Carlton Meadows is waiting to be booked on suspicion of homicide." He looked up with steely blue eyes. "It's going to be a while. You can wait over there," he said pointing over Sidney's shoulder.

"Sergeant, I am his attorney and insist I be allowed to see my client prior to any questioning or intake procedure," Mr. Meadows said, meeting the man's gaze.

Sergeant McDougal smiled sardonically.

"Have a seat, Counselor. I'll tell 'em you're here."

An hour later a Lieutenant Baxter came out to greet Sidney.

"Mr. Meadows, come with me. I'm Lieutenant Baxter, Homicide Division. Your son is in here," he said as they went through two heavy metal doors. "He's with his attorney, but—"

"Excuse me? That has to be some sort of mistake, Lieutenant. *I'm* his attorney," Sidney said, incredulously.

"Well you, uh, *gentlemen* can sort this out amongst yourselves," he said, barely able to contain his amusement. *How does one coon end up with two lawyers on the same damn night?*, he thought.

They came to a metal door with a small wire infused glass at its center. The officer opened the door. Mr. Meadows saw his son slouched in a metal chair, face streaked with tears, his usually neat afro uneven and matted as if he'd been asleep and not afforded a pick for his hair. Carlton's face was overtaken with a wave of joy to see his dad and then he began to wail. Sidney hadn't seen his son cry since he was a child. He hugged the young man without allowing him to stand, holding him in his arms and telling him it would all be okay, and that he was going to straighten everything out.

That's when Sid noticed the heavy set white man in the little room, whom he recognized him immediately. Harvey Hargraves never said a word, just observed the father and son moment. Harvey Hargraves was one of the most prominent attorneys in Detroit, and arguably the top criminal lawyer in the state. Mr. Meadows' heart began to beat rapidly as he released his boy's body to the chair. He was angry for he knew how Hargraves came to be there. He would play along because he didn't know what else to do.

The large man pushed himself up from the table and extended his right hand. A diamond and star sapphire centered in a heavy gold ring glinted in the unforgiving fluorescent light. It seemed embedded in the flesh of his meaty finger.

"Harvey Hargraves, Mr. Meadows. I've been retained to represent your son. I was waiting for you to arrive before I began interviewing Carlton. Because he's a minor, I'll need your written consent."

Meadows had seen Hargraves barrel through the waiting room about 30 minutes prior. They let him right in. He never looked around the waiting room, so he never noticed Sidney Meadows and it never occurred to Meadows that the man was there to represent his son. Sidney shook his head as if to clear it of thought so he could find out exactly or confirm concisely why this man was there.

"I'm sorry, yes, I know who you are. I had planned to represent my son myself, at least preliminarily."

"Practical, but not logical. Conflict of interest. There would be a greater chance—"

"Who called you?" Meadows asked, not caring if he sounded rude now. He was tired, angry, and the room smelled of stale body odor that probably never escaped, but lingered and was added to by the hour.

"Mr. Meadows, I've been retained by your wife's employer, Angelo Santori."

Your wife's employer was ever so slightly drawn out for effect. Sidney knew he was being subtly mocked. He was a lawyer looking to be a circuit court judge and yet his wife was still a common numbers runner for a mobster. A mobster who headed the largest organized criminal enterprise in Detroit. Meadows swallowed hard and when he did he felt his pride slide down his throat cradled in humiliation.

"If you'll sign these forms, I can get started. You can stay in the room while we talk," Hargraves said, sliding the two pages on the table toward Sidney.

Hargraves felt Carlton's confused eyes on him as he took a seat and brought out his fountain pen from his shirt pocket. The avuncular man smiled gently.

"Carlton, have you been read your rights?"

Carlton hesitated, and Lt. Baxter was about to say something.

"Yes," Carlton finally acknowledged. His eyes darted toward his father, whose expression he couldn't quite read. He seemed angry. Of course he was angry, ashamed, and embarrassed to have this happen in from of these white men, especially. Carlton looked down at the table.

"Do you want to speak in front of Lt. Baxter? Keep in mind you don't have to," said Hargraves.

Carlton suddenly exhaled a sob, his shoulders shaking as if in a seizure. Then, just as quickly, he seemed to compose himself.

"Okay," he said.

343

Lt. Baxter was sitting across the table from Carlton, staring him in the eye with a flinty gaze. His periphery caught every detail of the small interview room. Baxter leaned slightly forward.

"Carlton, I'm sure you'd like to go home to your family tonight. Wouldn't you, son?"

"Yes. Yes, sir," Carlton managed.

"Okay, tell me what happened tonight."

Carlton began to ramble about the minutiae of his evening, when Baxter asked firmly, "Were you at the Shake 'n Spin tonight?"

"Yes."

"What time?"

"I don't know, maybe about 8:30."

"Were you there with anybody? Did anyone see you?"

"Yeah, I mean yes, sir. My friend, Enrique Williams. I went there to see him. They were about to close. We were going to go to a block party."

"This Enrique Williams, does he work at the place?"

"Yes."

"Was there anyone else there, son?"

Sid Meadows quietly fumed. *Son? I'm the boy's father!* He was completely uncomfortable with hearing the story of what took place in front of strangers, especially a cop and another attorney. He'd wanted to talk to his son privately and together, they would figure out the best course of action against these serious accusations. Damn his meddling mother!

"Yes, the owner. I think his name is Mr. Gilhooley."

"Okay, so you're there to see your friend. There are only the three of you," Baxter stated as he put his clenched hands on the top of the table. "Who shot Mr. Gilhooley, Carlton?"

When Carlton didn't answer right away, Mr. Meadows interjected, "Just tell the truth, son. Just tell us what happened so I can take you home."

"Please, Mr. Meadows," Hargraves said, annoyed as if being circled by a gnat.

"Carlton, we have the gun and we have your friend, Enrique Williams," Lt. Baxter said.

Carlton's head popped up like a gopher out of a hole. He put his head on the table and began to sob again. None of the men moved toward Carlton. They all waited for him to speak again, but he didn't.

Lt. Baxter tried again, asking, "Who does the gun belong to, Carlton? Whose gun is that?"

"It's my dad's gun," he cried.

Mr. Meadows felt his jaw getting tight. Questions flooded his mind, but he pushed them aside to make sure he heard the answers coming from his son. Hargraves' bushy black eyebrows flew up toward the ceiling like a flock of crows.

"Carlton, who shot Mr. Gilhooley? He's dead, son."

Carlton wiped his eyes with his trembling hands. In those few seconds, in that one action, he saw himself as a prisoner. He saw himself in striped overalls like a cartoon character or a sad sack in a 1930's gangster-on-a-chain-gang movie.

"What did Ricky tell you? What did Ricky say?" he asked, shuddering as he spoke, like a child who'd been crying too long.

"Your friend isn't talking. He hasn't told us anything, which is not smart. He had the gun at his house."

"Carlton, it's always better to be the first one to tell what happened. It will be better for you in the long run," Hargraves said. "I want to help you."

"Did you kill Gilhooley, boy?"

Lt. Baxter's tone had changed. It was now impatient as if he'd looked at his watch and realized he was missing the Tigers on the radio. Carlton knew in an instant what he had to do and what he had to say.

"No sir, I didn't." His head was throbbing like it was being squeezed by giant hands. Carlton sighed heavily and paused as he prepared to change the course of his friend's life. "Ricky did."

He immediately looked up to gauge the men's reactions. His father was looking at the ceiling silently mouthing, "Thank you," presumably to God. The cop and the lawyer's expressions held fast. They were waiting for details.

"Tell us what happened, Carlton," Lt. Baxter said. "Take your time, son.

"Just tell us what happened in the store," Hargraves said.

Carlton began slowly.

"I went to the Shake 'n Spin to see Ricky. It was about time to close and I was just swinging by so we could go to this party. When I came into the store, I didn't see anybody, but the lights were on. I heard some loud talking in the back area, maybe there's an office? I don't know," he said, gaining momentum and confidence with every word, every breath, every lie. He just had to remember all the details in case he had to repeat his story or testify.

"I started to go toward where the talking was coming from, but it wasn't any of my business, so I just waited in the front. I heard a loud bang or popping sound and Ricky comes running out of the back area. He had a gun in his hand. He shoved it in a paper bag and grabbed me and said, 'Let's go.' We ran out. We stopped in the alley. I was scared. I didn't know why he killed his boss and I didn't know if he would shoot me, too. That's when I saw it was my dad's gun. I was too scared to ask him how he got it. Probably last time he came to the house."

"I *knew* you two had been I my den. I *knew* my stuff had been disturbed," Sid Meadows said. His powers of deduction and recollection were instantly regained as he imagined himself discovering the theft, but in reality he hadn't noticed anything amiss in his den, he was just relieved to hear Carlton was innocent.

"Please, Mr. Meadows," Hargraves chastised.

"Anyway, Ricky ran off, home I guess. I went home too."

"Why didn't you tell anyone? Why didn't you report the crime to the police?"

Carlton managed to squeeze out a few more tears.

"Scared," he said, shakily.

"Okay, okay, son," said Hargraves.

"This makes him an accessory after the fact," said Lt. Baxter.

"Now, wait a minute. I've stayed silent longer than I care to. My son has told you exactly what happened," Sidney interjected, emphasizing the word "exactly." He looked around the room before continuing. "He was scared shitless! This other kid is a thief, a liar and a killer! My son is the one doing the right thing here," huffed Mr. Meadows, standing and punctuating each point

347

with his index finger stabbing at the air. He was worked up and sweating.

"Yes, Lieutenant. My client is a juvenile with no criminal offenses, not even a parking ticket or loitering citation. He's told you everything. Surely you're not going to book him? He had nothing to do with this. He's a victim, too!" Hargraves implored.

Lt. Baxter looked at the two men and then at Carlton. All three were sweating and adding to the humidity and staleness of the room.

"Let me talk to this other boy again and I may need to confer with my captain to see if I can release him into the custody of his father. There's a water fountain down the hall if you need it. I'll be back."

The three people left in the room seemed to exhale all together. Carlton noticed that the air conditioning was suddenly on, humming loudly and sucking the moisture out of the small room. He saw the cobwebs vibrating with the air flow on the air conditioning unit's front panel. *They must keep it off in the summer to force people to confess,* Carlton thought. *Clever bastards.*

Carlton gave only a brief thought to what Ricky might say. He felt bad that he had to sacrifice his friend, but there was no other way to extricate himself from this mess. And, after all, it would be his word against Ricky's. His dad was a lawyer and Ricky had a known felon as a close relative. Yeah, he might make it out of this after all. Years ago, when he was about ten years old, Carlton had a friend who was always in trouble, always on punishment from his parents. Carlton used to tell him he'd get off punishment if he'd only tell his parents the truth. That boy looked Carlton dead in the eyes and said, "To tell a good lie, you have to believe it yourself." That adopted philosophy had come in handy tonight. No one would be able to wrest him from that life raft of deceit, no matter how hard they tried.

Thankfully, no one was talking. Those holding or interrogation rooms were notorious for their two-way mirrors and intercoms. Carlton looked at his lawyer, who was calmly doing paperwork. When he came upon his father's face he didn't know what he was looking at. Was the man ashamed? Angry? Humiliated? *All of the above.*

Carlton couldn't be sure how much time had passed when Lt. Baxter again came into the room. His heartbeat quickened.

"Okay, folks. Carlton Meadows is remanded into the custody—"

Carlton thought his heart was going to fly out of his mouth.

"—of Sidney Meadows. But…I want you back here tomorrow morning at 10:00 a.m. with your lawyer to give your sworn statement. I doubt there will be any charges filed, however, you are a witness. I would suggest you not discuss this with anyone—" Baxter shot Mr. Meadows a look and then looked toward Hargraves, ending with "—except your counsel. Understand?"

"Yes, sir. Yes, sir. Thank you, officer, I mean, Lieutenant."

Once outside, Carlton shook Mr. Hargraves' hand, as did his father, and they parted ways.

"See you here tomorrow at 10," Hargraves called after them, before heading to his car.

When Carlton got into the car with his father, he was relieved to be going home. The car idled as they sat for a moment. Carlton could sense his father was extremely upset.

"Boy, you lie down with dogs, you get up with fleas."

Somehow, this analogy struck Carlton as amusing and he began to chuckle. His father slapped him so hard, he busted the boy's bottom lip and cut his knuckle on Carlton's tooth. Carlton sobbed loudly, shaking in his seat.

"You, Carlton, and your mother, have indebted me to some very, very bad people. Do you even understand that?"

Carlton swallowed and recognized the metallic taste of blood going down his throat.

Carlton was almost afraid to speak, but managed.

"You mean the lawyer? Then let's just tell him forget it. You can find someone else to—"

"I can't! It's too late!"

The car lurched out of the parking space, through the parking lot and into traffic on Beaubien. Carlton wept quietly as the brightly colored lights of the still lively Woodward Avenue flashed across his face. As his father stared straight ahead, gripping the steering wheel like his hands were glued to it, Carlton turned toward his car window. He was sure his father thought he was crying because he'd been struck, but, Carlton's tears were for the lie that now lived in the world like an orphaned baby. His tears were for the searing disappointment he felt in himself for being so weak in character. And finally, his tears were for the fatherless boy he'd sacrificed when hours earlier that same boy was his best friend who'd help him or come to his defense without a second thought.

FORTY-NINE

Angelica and Liz Tanner touched down in Los Angeles around 9:00 p.m. in late August, 1968. Angelica sat at the window of the airplane and marveled at the white and amber lights dotting the landscape below. This was her first plane ride and after some nervous moments trying to identify sounds and getting used to the feeling of being aloft, Angelica relaxed. Her mother had grabbed hold of her hand during the take off.

They rode in a cab to their hotel in Beverly Hills, marveling at every sight—so different was this place from Detroit. Walking through the finely appointed lobby, Angelica whispered to her mother, "We're like the Beverly Hillbillies, Mama."

"Not quite, honey," her mother answered.

They had shipped her trunk directly to her new apartment and her car would arrive in a week. Anything else she would need, Liz said they'd purchase while she was there. The apartment was actually off campus housing and the place was divided up like a dormitory. She was sharing her living space with a girl from Kansas. They didn't yet know her name, so they referred to her as "Dorothy," as in "The Wizard of Oz."

"Dorothy" turned out to be a blonde haired, sky blue eyed girl named Susan Gordon. Susan was fun and pretty and easy to get along with. The girls devised a system by which one would let the other know that company—a boy—was present and other accommodations might need to be made. Susan began availing herself of this set up fairly quickly. Angelica, when questioned informally about her dating prospects, had to admit she was still a virgin.

"No way!" Susan exclaimed, genuinely shocked.

"Yup," Angelica replied, uncomfortably.

"Well that's no good. We gotta do something about this," Susan reasoned, sounding truly concerned as if getting her roomie deflowered was the same as treating a cold.

"No, no. It's fine. It will happen at some point, I suppose. It's only natural, right?"

"Yes, ma'am. Geez, what's wrong with the boys in Detroit?"

"Trust me, it's been attempted," Angelica said, thinking about Barry Myers. "I just have to find the right guy."

"And you will, too. I plan to find a husband in the next four years, so I gotta move kinda fast."

Angelica tittered at Susan and then thought about the last time she'd spoken to Enrique. The Detroit Tigers had won the World Series against the St. Louis Cardinals, so somebody owed her $5! *Stop it, Angelica.* It was useless to think about him, though she made her mother promise to tell her about any new developments with his trial.

When Thanksgiving break rolled around, Angelica amazed herself and her family by deciding to stay in Los Angeles. She and a handful of other students were staying in town and decided to be one another's family for Thanksgiving, having a feast at a spot called Fatburger in the heart of L.A. The hamburger joint on Western Avenue, had one of the most delicious burgers Angelica had ever put her mouth around. The place was crowded with hippies, musicians, artists, and business people. A young man with shoulder length hair struck up a conversation with Angelica and her three friends while they waited for their order. First he offered them LSD, then pot--all refused--then tickets to a show that night at the Whisky a Go Go. The Whisky was one of the most famous rock and roll clubs in the world. Of course they wanted to go!

That night on stage there was a rag tag band of hippies who looked like cowboys or vice versa, calling themselves "The Flying Burrito Brothers." Then came a tall, slender, folky-bluesy black man named Taj Mahal, like the wonder-of-the-world monument. Their tickets did not allow them to sit at a table, so, tired of standing, they left and went back to Westwood. Angelica asked to be dropped off at a small grocery store that happened to be open, so she could get some provisions for breakfast the next morning.

"Hey, aren't you in my Physics class?" a young man asked, peeking over the display of Cheerios.

He was the cute guy who only occasionally waved to her. She thought maybe he was too cool, with him being an upperclassman and all, to talk to a frosh.

"Hi, I'm Angelica Tanner."

"Cool, man. I'm Bakiri Ali. My friends call me Kiri."

For a few seconds Angelica just stared at the young man, wondering if he was trying to play a trick on her. Their class was not a lecture hall and the professor took attendance. She'd never heard that name before this moment.

"I didn't know that was your name," she said, probing slightly.

353

"Nah, my given name is Thomas Washington. But I don't go by that. That's a slave name."

"Okay," Angelica said, not knowing if she wanted to engage further with this guy.

"What are you doing out so late, Sister?"

Angelica considered herself a liberated woman and didn't know if she liked being questioned by this "Kiri" person. Who was he to question her about why she was out?

"Same as you, I guess. Picking up food for breakfast."

"Ha! I didn't mean to sound like I was giving you the third degree, Angelica. Sorry about that. No offense."

"None taken. See you in class," Angelica said, walking up to the cashier.

"Hey, Sis, let me walk you home. You live around here, right?"

Angelica hesitated, and Thomas could see her reluctance.

"I don't bite. I promise," he said good-naturedly.

"How do you know I want you knowing where I live?"

This time he laughed full throated, wiping a tear from his eye.

"Look, I'm a nice guy, talking to a nice girl in a store. I'd be happy to walk you to your door, if it's okay with you."

After they had both paid for their groceries, Thomas offered to carry hers and Angelica let him. He told her he was from Charlotte, North Carolina and he was studying Engineering. He was the youngest of six children and his siblings had all gone to college. Thomas was handsome, smart, ambitious and a real Southern gentleman. When they got to her door, he seemed disappointed that they'd reached their destination so quickly.

"Can I have your phone number? I'll give you mine, too. I just live a couple of blocks away."

Luckily, she'd just gotten her phone the previous month. She and her roommate, Susan, had to visit Pacific Bell in Santa Monica in order to secure a telephone and number. Anyone with a roommate had to go with said roommate to apply for a phone together so they would be equally responsible for the bill. It made Angelica feel very adult having phone service with an actual bill coming in the mail each month.

"Do you have a pen?" She gave him her number and refused to take his—for now.

"Goodnight," Thomas said as Angelica disappeared into the lobby of her building.

Angelica became friends with two girls from her English class who happened to be roommates. Peggy Hartley, was a tall, slender, brown skinned girl with big eyes and a huge afro. Her afro was so round and big and springy that Angelica marveled at its defiance of gravity. Peggy was quick-witted and lively and gorgeous. Her roomie was a petite girl with a cinnamon complexion named Daisy Jones. Daisy was plain, like her name, but not unattractive, just unadorned with anything special. She was sweet natured and a perfect match for Peg, as they seemed to be complete opposites. Peggy was an L.A. girl born and bred and knew every nook and cranny of the city, while Daisy was imported from Des Moines, Iowa.

"Dang, I didn't even know they had black folks in Iowa," Angelica exclaimed one day while studying with the girls in their dorm room in Dykstra Hall.

"I know! Me neither. And, she's Catholic! I didn't know black people were Catholic, did you?" Peggy echoed.

"Nope. Lucky I came to college or I'd be in the dark about a thing or two," Angelica teased, making the girls laugh.

Angelica Tanner and her friends enjoyed exploring Los Angeles, most times led by Peg, who didn't have a car, so Angelica served as livery. She marveled at the fact that L.A. was ocean, desert and mountains and with that, there wasn't much you couldn't do in or out of doors. Eventually, they visited the Griffith Observatory where "Rebel Without a Cause," one of Angelica's favorite movies, was famously filmed and got as close as they could to the magnificent and legendary Hollywood sign. Over the years of living in L.A., Angelica would never cease to be gob-smacked by its historic majesty every time she saw it peeking through the smog. Of course they walked up and down each side of Hollywood Boulevard's Walk of Fame to thrill at the names of all the movie, television and singing stars enshrined forever in the pink terrazzo and burnished brass.

Angelica and Peg ate their Christmas dinner at the Golden Bird Fried Chicken restaurant on La Cienega. Peg had touted it as the best chicken in the world and she hadn't lied. Daisy had wandered off to Des Moines to be with her family and Peg stayed in Dykstra Hall. Angelica wondered why a girl from Los Angeles didn't go home for Christmas, but Peg didn't offer an explanation and she didn't ask.

Angelica, on the other hand, had encouraged her mother to take a long wished for vacation to Hawaii with Aunt Fannie. She even met them at the airport in L.A. to wish them a bon voyage. Liz knew Angelica was reluctant to come home right then--too many memories and questions about her friend Ricky--so Liz allowed herself to go on vacation with her sister. On the way back to her apartment, Angelica put a Christmas card in the mailbox for Ricky Williams, addressed to his house in Detroit and one to Sheila Davis as well, since Sheila's last letter said she was going home for Christmas. *Next year I'll see them both*, Angelica told herself.

FIFTY

By Christmas Bakiri Ali and Angelica were seeing a lot of each other. Bakiri was very proud and strong willed, yet he was a gentleman trying hard not to be a chauvinist. His Southern upbringing gave him definite ideas on what a woman could and should do, like not take a job away from a man. After all, a man had to provide for his whole family. They debated this ridiculousness on occasion, but Angelica could not move Bakiri's barometer to modern times, ultimately agreeing to disagree.

Before Bakiri flew back to North Carolina for Christmas with his family, he took Angelica out on a special date, just the two of them, no third and fourth wheel friends. They drove up Sunset Boulevard, the gateway to everything fun in L.A., to La Brea to have dinner at the Copper Penny, a diner that was open 24 hours a day. From there they went over a few blocks to Hollywood Boulevard to the world famous Grauman's Chinese Theatre. The courtyard entrance famously had the autographs, and foot and hand impressions of Hollywood movie royalty embedded in the cement. People like Shirley Temple, Marilyn Monroe, Humphrey Bogart, Jimmy Stewart, Roy Rogers and even his horse, Trigger, just to name a few. After trying to put their own feet and hands over the small footprints and handprints and wondering why everyone seemed so little in the "old days," they went inside to see their movie.

The blockbuster action film, "Bullitt" starring Steve McQueen, had been playing to packed audiences for two months. Angelica could barely sit still in her seat as she watched McQueen's '68 Ford Mustang GT jump up and down Lombardi Street in what would become one of the most famous car chase scenes in cinematic history. She was dumbfounded that the character, Lt. Frank Bullitt, was sanctioned to roll at turbo speed through the streets of San Francisco in a muscle car.

On the ride home, Barkiri said, "Wow, you're a real gearhead. But what else would I expect from a Detroit girl, right?"

Angelica realized she was blathering away because she was nervous at the thought of Bakiri kissing her at the evening's end. She wasn't very experienced, but she sensed he would try to make a move. He'd spent the entire movie with his arm around her shoulder.

They pulled up in front of her building as a stray dog ambled across the street. Thomas had learned long ago that you never ask if you can kiss a girl, you just go for it and see what happens. He turned the motor off and slid out of the car, striding behind it to get over to Angelica's door to open it for her.

"Thank you. You're such a gentleman." Ugh, she didn't want him to think that was code for "Don't kiss me!"

Things were regressing and retreating in her imagination as they took the awkward walk to her front door. *This was a mistake*, she told herself, talking herself out of her confidence. And just then, Thomas lifted her chin up slightly with his index finger and kissed her lips. His mouth was soft, gentle and sure. She kissed him back as her doubts rolled away like a marble on a sidewalk. After a few more kisses he said goodnight.

Angelica slipped inside her apartment where Susan was sitting on the couch reading. She looked up from her volume.

"Have fun?" she said sleepily.

"Yeah. We really did."

"You kinda like him, huh?"

"Yeah, kinda," Angelica replied, smiling.

Thomas returned to Los Angeles the day after New Year's 1969. He called Angelica as soon as he got to his place, he'd missed her so.

"Hey, you want to go out Saturday night? I'll let you pick the place, okay?"

"Okay, thanks for *letting me*," Angelica said with mild sarcasm.

"Oh, I was just kidding with you, Angelica."

"And I was just kidding with you, Soul Brother," Angelica said mischievously.

She was so glad he was back. Angelica had been reading about a new rock and roll singer out of Detroit named Alice Cooper. He wore ghoulish black eye make-up that circled his eyes and seemed to crawl down his face. The *Rolling Stone* article she read in the library, by writer Lester Bangs, made the performer seem dangerous and unpredictable. Angelica had to see him for herself. When she found out he was performing at the Whisky a Go Go opening for a British band called Led Zeppelin, she could not believe her luck.

Angelica had heard a song called "Whole Lotta Love" on local rock station KABC-FM late one night while she was studying. The chunky distorted guitar riffs riding on the *chugga chugga* back beat, the shredded voice of the lead singer, the echo chamber— all these sounds combined to put her in an auditory trance. She turned up the radio every time she heard the song. The dee jay said there was an album coming out in about a week and it would be pandemonium at the Whisky show. When she breathlessly relayed all of this intel to Bakiri, he was curiously amused and though he knew almost nothing about rock music, he agreed to take Angelica to the club on the Sunset Strip.

They had chili dogs and soda pop at Pink's Hot Dogs on La Brea, a joint that would become a minor addiction for Angelica, much like Onassis Coney Island had been in Detroit. The show was standing room only as the boy named Alice and then the four Brits whipped the audience into a frenzy. Angelica would occasionally grab Bakiri's hand in a kind of dance to the music, but he seemed a bit uncomfortable, so she didn't force it.

On the ride home, Bakiri said, "You know those Zeppelins ain't doing nothing but the blues. Just adding electric guitars and fast drumming and then screamin' to it all. I get tired of seeing white folks take our music, while we don't get any recognition or credit for anything. And that first white boy—I guess he was a guy—I don't know what that was."

At first Angelica was a bit taken aback by Thomas' criticism, understanding it on some level, but still kind of shocked. Had she been so naïve in the way she was brought up and the way she heard music? It was either good or bad, not black or white. The only thing one needed to appreciate music was an open mind, open ears and an open soul. But, he was certainly entitled to his opinion. Angelica decided she might have to indulge her love for rock music sans Mr. Thomas Washington in the future.

"Don't get me wrong. It was pretty interesting, just not what I'm used to. Where I'm from folks don't really--blacks and whites, that is—don't really hang around together like that."

Angelica had forgotten Thomas was from the deep South and had grown up very differently than she had.

"It's okay. Part of college life is trying new things, right?"

"Speaking of new things, I want you to meet some people I've been getting to know on campus. Are you a member of the Afrikan Student Union?"

"Yup. I joined around Halloween. So far, I've only been to a couple of meetings and one new members thing," Angelica answered.

"You ever heard of the Black Panther Party?"

FIFTY-ONE

For the next two weeks it seemed every time Angelica and Bakiri met on campus and off, he was asking her to attend a meeting of the Black Panther Party. Angelica had read about them in *Jet Magazine* at her Aunt Fan's house. They were a group of radical and activist men and women, predominantly black, who believed in armed resistance. They had begun up in Oakland, California with the goal of protecting the black community from overzealous policemen. For a while they were heroes to that community as their outreach included a free breakfast program for underprivileged children.

Eventually though, many members became involved with murder and drug dealing, much like an organized gang. Armaments, notoriety, hubris and the invincibility of youth allowed for cracks in their organization that were filled by informants for the United States government under the marquee of J. Edgar Hoover's FBI. 1969 was the year that saw the beginning of the end of this movement as the Party members were killed, jailed or exiled.

Always open minded, Angelica figured it would not hurt to hear what they had to say. According to Bakiri, one of their schoolmates, Bunchy Carter, had started the Los Angeles chapter of the Panthers. It was rather exciting to be sitting so close to him at the meeting, which was being held in the back of a record store in Baldwin Hills, off of Crenshaw Boulevard.

Bunchy and his Deputy Chairman, John Huggins, a very handsome young man with a large afro and unruly beard, talked to the gathering about self-defense, police brutality and the futility of non-violence. They were impassioned and persuasive to many in attendance, but Angelica felt guilty because she had no interest in what they were advocating. She empathized with much of what was said, but she wasn't mad at anyone she could think of. Bakiri was shaking his head, nodding in agreement and mumbling "That's right," much like someone in church responding to the preacher's call for a response. He had relayed a few stories about growing up in North Carolina and, well, she guessed he had a reason to be mad.

As they were leaving, John said to Angelica and Bakiri, "See you at the forum on Friday, Sister. You too, Brother."

In between their recruitment rhetoric, Carter and Huggins had mentioned that UCLA was about to offer a new area of study, a department specializing in Black Studies and all students present, including members of the Afrikan Student Union, needed to attend to show their support and help with input on who would run this new department. Angelica zipped up her jacket against the January chill. It may have been Southern California but it was definitely cool enough for outerwear.

"Shoot, now I feel like I have to go to that meeting in Campbell Hall even though I really don't feel like it," Angelica said.

"Well that makes one of us. I wish I could go! I've got a test that day in Economics and I can't miss it. I want to be there so bad. You *are* going, right?"

"I feel like we got, like, a personal invitation or something. I'll go and let you know what they decide. It's going to be cool having a Black Studies department at a school like UCLA."

Angelica knew it was unlikely that she'd ever take any course in Black Studies because they had nothing to do with her major, which was Political Science. But, she understood that the student union members were laying the path for students who would come later and have the privilege to learn about the past, present and future of black people worldwide. It made Angelica feel proud, like a forbearer. She also knew she would not be joining the Black Panthers. Her family would kill her!

Angelica and Thomas ended up back on campus at the library to study. They'd been there all of ten minutes when he asked, "Can you make your hair into an afro? You can't, can you?"

Now, every time they'd been together, Bakiri couldn't keep his hands out of her hair. It was like they were starring in a shampoo commercial. He would constantly comment on how soft and silky it was. She almost laughed at him the first time he said, "You got such long, purdy hair. You should never cut it."

He sounded so countrified to her at first, but she liked how sweet and sincere he was. So now, because he might want to be a Panther, she had to somehow figure out how to make her hair reach for the sky?

"Um, I doubt it. I've never tried it. Wouldn't know where to begin, really."

"I think it would look real good on you. Just something new," he said, nonchalantly.

FIFTY-TWO

Friday, January 17, was an uncharacteristically chilly, gray day with low clouds pressing down on the horizon. Angelica had been late for her Physics exam, but her professor allowed her to take the test anyway. After she was done, she ran to the cafeteria to grab an apple and a banana to tide her over while she attended the meeting that was to begin around noon in Campbell Hall. Her friend Peg said she planned to come if she could get out of her study group.

Angelica absent-mindedly touched her hair and quickly drew back her fingers. She'd almost forgotten that Peggy had fixed her hair into an afro, or as close as they could get. Peg was like a scientist dipping her fingers into the thick green setting lotion before she twisted Angelica's hair onto foam rollers. Angelica went home and slept on the rollers in anticipation of waking up with a springy 'fro. Hope gave way to horror when she found she had something akin to Shirley Temple curls sprouting from her head. She used the red, black and green Goody afro pick with metal tines on one end and a black plastic fist on the other to diffuse her situation.

Every time she raked it through her hair, the fist seemed to be telling her, "*Hang in there and stay strong, Sister!*" That was this morning. The weather had loosened up her curls into a droopy ceiling of moppish hair. *Note to self: the afro is not for you.*

Angelica dug in her purse for the slip of paper with the exact location of the meeting. *Room 1201.* When she arrived, a few minutes after noon, she found a seat in the back of the room where she could watch for Peggy entering. There were about 200 people present, some laughing and talking quietly, others impatiently waiting to put this bit of business behind them just so they could say they were not apathetic spectators, but rather guardians of higher learning. Angelica looked around as she began to peel her banana, quietly surveying the multitude of black faces inside the dining hall.

She saw John, the guy who'd told her to come, but he didn't see her. She decided not to try to wave to him, as he might not recognize her with the outcropping of black power encircling her head. She saw that dude named Bunchy, as usual, dressed so sharp, looking more like he'd be an associate of Still Bill Williams back in Detroit, than a college student. Outward appearances aside, she understood John and Bunchy were Black Panthers who were very serious about the "movement."

A guy named Ron from another militant group called US was there and speaking to the crowd. Angelica had not experienced any other meeting like this on campus before where the atmosphere seemed so unusually tense. There was a palpable discomfort and malevolence that settled over the room like a hair shirt over injured skin. While stealthily eating her apple, she began to plan her escape. *Why is everyone so overly excited about who's going to chair the Black Studies department, anyway?* All Angelica could think about was the 120 pages of Chaucer she had to slog through. She'd made an attempt the night before, but only ended up face down on the kitchen table in a pool of drool. Susan had spent the night at one of the co-ed dorms with a guy she was seeing and wouldn't be back until Sunday.

After about two hours and countless heated exchanges, the meeting adjourned. Angelica figured she'd say "hello" to John and let him know she'd indeed come to the meeting, but after waiting around for a several minutes, she could see he was preoccupied near the entrance to the hallway. Though only a dozen or so people remained, Angelica decided to try to speak to him at another time. She mused to herself that Peggy could have come in with an orchestral fanfare and it wouldn't have disturbed the loud and acrimonious proceedings.

As she was walking down the hallway to leave Campbell Hall, Angelica heard shouting coming from directly behind her. She'd only travelled a short distance when she looked backward, along with some others in the hallway. She thought she saw someone's hand raised in the air and coming down on someone on the floor. The tangle of men in dark clothing seemed to move en masse back into the cafeteria and almost instantaneously, she heard popping sounds and screams.

Realizing it was gunfire, Angelica found her way outside quickly, pushed along by the escaping throng. She ran and kept running until she found her car in the parking lot. Deciding she was entirely too shaken to drive, she took off running, eventually stopping when she recognized her street. *Dammit! Since when are they shooting at college? This is UCLA!*

As she turned onto Hilgard toward her apartment, she heard the wail of sirens. *What had happened?* Angelica shut the door to her place and blocked out the energy of what she'd seen and heard. She paced back and forth inside her apartment trying to get calm. After about 40 minutes she gravitated toward her book of Chaucer on the kitchen table where she'd left it, heaving a sigh as she sat down. Angelica was reading when her phone rang. She hesitated, almost afraid to answer.

"Hello," she snapped.

368

"Girl, this is Peggy. Did you go to that meeting in Campbell Hall? I thought you said you were gonna--"

"Yeah, Peggy, I went."

"Guess what? You will *never* guess what happened."

Had this girl heard what Angelica just said? What was she talking about? Just then a tiny light seemed to come on in the attic of Peggy's mind.

"So, you were there, huh? Were they shooting and stuff?"

"I think so. Not at first, but, at the end of the meeting, after everybody was leaving. People were running down the hall, down the stairs. Some crazy shit went down," Angelica said, sensing Peggy's growing excitement. Peggy obviously already had the details and just wanted to drag what she could out of Angelica. She couldn't help herself.

"Girl, Bunchy Carter and John Huggins got killed! Ain't that a bitch? It's all over the news. Turn on the TV," Peggy said, excitedly.

Angelica stiffened.

"I gotta go, Peg. Let me call you later, okay? Or, how 'bout I just see you tomorrow?" she said, not wanting to be rude but needing to get the hell off of the phone.

"What? But you were there, Angelica. Oh my God, you—"

Angelica hung up the phone and pulled the plug from the wall. Sitting on her living room floor, stunned and shocked, she put her hands over her face and sobbed, the tears splashing her blue jeans like salted raindrops.

Angelica awoke to an insistent knocking on her front door.

"Shit," she exclaimed. She'd fallen asleep yet again and Chaucer was still alone in the kitchen. She hadn't eaten dinner and her head was pounding. She padded to the front door and looked into the peephole. Angelica saw Thomas, but asked, "Who's there?" anyway. Everything was off-kilter and not to be trusted.

"It's me, Bakiri."

Once inside, Bakiri tried to disguise his reaction to her appearance, but was unsuccessful.

His eyes grew large and he asked, "What's wrong with your hair...I mean what happened to...your hair?"

Angelica's hands flew up to her head, patting furiously as if putting out a small fire.

"Oh, God. I must look a mess."

Thomas grabbed her hands to still them. He knew she was still shaken by the events of the day. She was his girlfriend and he felt he needed to appear strong and impassive so she could feel free to react however she might.

"Did you see what happened?"

"No, thank God, but I heard it. What is wrong with people? This is UCLA!"

"I know, it's beyond crazy. It's unreal. I'm *soooo* glad I couldn't get to Campbell Hall. That could have been me. Shoot, you're lucky it wasn't you!"

"I was trying to hang around to speak to John Huggins, but I decided to go ahead and go home. God was with me today. He made me get the heck out of there before they started shooting up the place."

They both realized Thomas still had a tight hold on her hands and he released them.

"Sorry."

She decided not to tell Bakiri how her vanity played a part in her well-timed exodus. Come to think of it, her hair fail may have helped to save her life.

"By the way, my hair was supposed to be an afro. It looked better earlier. Well, maybe it didn't," Angelica confessed.

Bakiri let go of a light chuckle. Angelica told him to take off his blue jean jacket and sit down.

"I have to eat something. Did you eat anything? You hungry?" Angelica asked.

"I could have something if you are," Bakiri replied.

Angelica ducked into her bathroom to brush her hair down and used a rubber band to put it into a fluffy ponytail.

"There she is," Thomas said, smiling as Angelica emerged from the bathroom. He was thinking Angelica couldn't help but look beautiful. She was gorgeous, and he realized he was a fool to ask her to alter her own natural hair. She couldn't help it because she had "good" hair. It was long, thick and silky and he wanted to touch it every time he was with her. Angelica warmed up a can of Chef Boyardee Spaghetti-o's and they ate in near silence. She was exhausted and sad.

"Can we watch the news?" Bakiri asked, standing up and looking around.

"Sure, um, my TV is in my bedroom," she said indicating its doorway as she went to put the dishes in the sink.

They sat in her room and watched the news report on KABC, Channel 7. They'd made it seem as if the young men who lost their lives were mindless militants, just violent criminals disguised as students. Angelica couldn't help but think about Enrique Williams. She wondered if he knew what had happened or that she'd been so close to tragedy, so far away?

Bakiri, sitting on the floor, looked up at Angelica who was sitting on the edge of her bed crying softly. He came up to his knees in front of her and embraced her. When she drew away from him slightly, he began to kiss her face and finally her mouth. Angelica returned his kiss passionately and aggressively, surprising herself.

Thomas got up onto the bed and laid Angelica down, stretching out beside her. As he began to unbutton her blouse, she rested her hand on top of his.

"I've never done this before," she said softly, looking him in his eyes.

"Oh. Do you want me to stop? We don't have to."

Angelica sighed and pursed her lips. She'd never given much thought on how or when she would lose her virginity. She just knew somehow, someday, it would happen. She'd heard the stories of pain and blood, and yet, people kept doing it, didn't they? *Everybody wants to go to heaven, but nobody wants to die*, she thought. Tonight was as good a night as any.

"I want to," she whispered to him.

FIFTY-THREE

Angelica turned right and went West on Sunset. The first time she explored the famed boulevard it was on a lark. In Los Angeles, West will always, eventually, lead to the ocean. The ride was so scenic with its twists and turns, it was easy to get distracted. Indeed, over her years there she saw at least half a dozen cars smashed into the canyon walls, en route to the Pacific Ocean. These were people who were either speeding or got momentarily distracted by the scenery or both.

Twist, turn, twist, turn, up, down, up, and finally, she was heading down with the sparkling blue expanse of the Pacific Ocean right in front of her wind shield. A thin orange thread of smog separated the water from the azure sky, a different world to be sure. She often turned right at the Pacific Coast Highway, heading for Zuma Beach to the North. Angelica would just park and get out to walk along the beach or sit in the sand. *What is a girl from Detroit doing here?* she would allow herself to wonder. This is where the world's richest movie stars and singers lived. This is where Frankie and Annette made out.

Sometimes she would find tears running down her cheeks and she knew it was Ricky. He was the one tethered to her soul like a weight she couldn't put down. Handcuffed as surely as if they were prisoners running for their lives. How she wished he too could see the beauty of an unfathomably deep ocean sprinkled with diamonds from the glinting sun. She wished her friend could feel the sand getting cooler on his toes as he dug them deep beneath the initial gritty heat. She wanted him to smell the briny air and feel his hair whip into his eyes as he tried in vain to anticipate the fickleness of the wind. Angelica longed for him to witness the deep pink, orange and purple amazement of the Southern California sunset. She drew her knees up and laid her left cheek on the bony protrusions, encircling them with her arms. This was Ricky's dream and she was living it for the both of them.

Angelica and Thomas, who now insisted on being called Bakiri, exclusively, continued to date until school got out for the summer. During the time they were together, Angelica saw Bakiri's sweet Southern charm give way to brittle intractability as he became radicalized by his association with the Black Panther Party. The deaths of Huggins and Carter as well as arrests and raids throughout the country, fueled his transformation. Angelica thought she could accept how much he'd changed, but when he turned his focus to her, she knew their relationship could not survive.

Bakiri began to occasionally and off handedly make comments about her skin tone and say she was a "yella gal." These were thoughts and expressions she'd never encountered at home nor within her circle of friends. She had eyes and she could see that black people came in every hue from nearly white to blue black with every combination of hair color and texture. Eye colors, too! Bakiri became more and more obsessed with Angelica's hair and the fact that it was somewhat straight and could not successfully be formed into an afro. These outer trappings, facades of skin and hair which were beyond her reins, became symbolic to Bakiri. He called it "the veil of slavery," and apparently Angelica wore this imaginary and undesirable veil which could not be removed.

One day Bakiri could no longer contain his curiosity and asked Angelica if she was half white.

"There's nothing wrong with it. I'm just wondering. I mean, I saw that picture of your mother, and…"

"And what? Maybe I'm adopted." She paused for effect. "Okay, I'm not adopted. I never asked my mother a lot about my father. She would always get really upset when I did. He died in the Korean War, you know? They were really young. My mother was left to raise me all alone."

"So, she's a widow. Whoa, sorry about that."

"No, not a widow. I don't think my mother and father were ever married. It's like a poorly kept secret in my family. No wedding ring, no pictures either."

"Damn! You mean to tell me you don't know what your dad looks like?"

"Nope. I guess he looked like me. Like I said, my mother gets upset talking about him. Maybe she pretends to be pissed off so I'll shut up."

They both laughed. He couldn't imagine such a thing for a beautiful girl like her. Sure, back home, he knew a few kids whose fathers had run off or met with some kind of disaster, but that seemed par for the course in the South. This was a Northern girl. She seemed to deserve better, somehow. Bakiri began to feel guilty opining about "the veil of slavery," which he'd decided included anyone in whose face he could discern European heritage. Angelica need her veil. It was the only way she could see her father.

FIFTY-FOUR

With no clear plans for the summer and her Freshman year behind her, Angelica flew back to Detroit from Los Angeles in the summer of 1969. Most of her classmates had also gone back to their respective hometowns to again eat good home cooking, buy new clothes and sundries only to be found in their cities, and passive aggressively gloat to those not fortunate enough to go away to college.

As her plane touched down at Metropolitan Airport, she felt the excitement and anticipation she'd had when she boarded her flight gone. It was as if it had been sucked into the oxygen system of the plane and doled out to someone else. Angelica was left with an uneasiness and a mild feeling of dread. She told herself she was being ridiculous. She was home in her beloved Detroit. People were excited to see her, and she'd better not come off as "acting funny" or she would never hear the end of it. She needn't have worried, as she was able to shake off those unbidden feelings as soon as she thought about being in her own room and sleeping in her own bed and all the familiar sights, sounds and smells of her childhood home.

Sheila came to pick her up at the airport and they laughed and hugged tightly when they met. In the car, the girls chatted excitedly about what had been going on in their lives over the past year. Between them, there was never a dull moment, never a dark silence and as much as they talked, they knew there was so much more to be said. Sheila relayed how Boston wasn't quite what she'd expected.

"When you think of Boston, you think of history and freedom and liberty, right? Well it's all those things—for white people! Girl, they do not like black folks in Boston. If you ain't Irish or Italian or Catholic, you ain't nothin' to them. And everybody seems to know everybody, like a small-town mentality. They actually call the natives 'townies.'"

"Damn, no kidding?" Angelica exclaimed.

"Yup. It's kind of interesting because Boston and the surrounding areas have some of the best institutions of higher learning in the world. MIT, Harvard, Radcliffe, Northeastern, University of Massachusetts, Boston University, and a bunch more, actually. It's like the townies, the working-class folks, just tolerate all these interlopers, you know? In Boston, South Boston, there are projects that are white only and they will kill somebody who ain't white trying to move in there. The projects, girl!" Sheila said, incredulous.

"Are you going to stay there? Is it for you?" Angelica asked.

"Yeah, I'm going to stick it out. U Mass is a great school and I love the people I've met and made friends with. Plus, Boston is so pretty in the spring. Newbury Street is like a picture postcard with all the trees blooming."

Sheila pulled into Angelica's driveway. There were already three cars parked in a line, beginning near her backyard, with several cars parked along the street as well.

"Girl, look at this. Your mama got all the home folks over here waitin' to see you."

"Wow," Angelica said in true amazement. "I didn't expect this at all."

And she hadn't. Maybe Elizabeth Tanner missed her only child after all. Angelica shook her head and laughed.

With every outing and event that summer, friends and relatives wanted to know how she liked college life as if they wanted to live vicariously through her. The most fun Angelica had was going to house parties and having local and neighborhood boys realize she was now completely out of their league. *Yeah, you should have made your move before I left here.* But the reality was that no one could penetrate the fortress of friendship that was her, Ricky Williams and Carlton Meadows. The bond of the 3 Musketeers was obvious to everyone.

Only at UCLA a couple of months in 1968, many young men tried to fathom how to get Angelica's attention. One guy made the mistake of thinking she was feigning interest in sports because she was glued to the television in the student union during the 1968 World Series between the St. Louis Cardinals and her beloved Detroit Tigers. She was the only girl amongst the litter of boys. The young man asked her to go out for a burger and she agreed as long as she could watch the game. And watch she did, only allowing conversation during commercials. Angelica was not impolite, she just knew her expectations were probably different than his. She expected to be able to enjoy the game and enjoy a hamburger without much interference.

The Detroit Tigers would ultimately win the World Series in game 7, with a 4-1 victory over the Cardinals, the defending champions. The names of Mickey Lolich, Stormin' Norman Cash, Al Kaline, Mickey Stanley, Dick McAuliffe, Bill Freehan, Willie Horton, Don Wert and Jim Northrup would go down in Tigers baseball history. People would later blame St. Louis' Curt Flood for allowing two runs in the seventh inning off the bat of Jim Northrup, but Angelica knew that was hogwash. The Tigers were her team and they were scrappy underdogs who were winners. Period.

Angelica didn't talk about the Black Panther-US incident that had taken place six months earlier because she didn't want to worry her family. If anyone said they'd heard, vaguely, about this bit of trouble, she simply denied any knowledge of it, saying, "I go to class, I study hard, and I mind my own business."

As her vacation went on, she gave herself permission to think about some things. There was no way for her to be in Detroit and not try to find out what was going on with Enrique. That was her business, too, wasn't it?

ngelica stopped by the A&P to pick up two dozen Sanders caramel cupcakes for the Williams kids and a Bumpy Cake for Liz. Her mother loved the moist, chocolate frosted tea cake with tube like "bumps" of butter cream beneath chocolate icing. Angelica bought a tin of Better Made potato chips, but didn't know if the kids liked Vernors or Faygo, so she bought both.

The last stop was the ice cream parlor to get two pints of Stroh's Blue Moon ice cream, the aqua colored confection with the indescribably sumptuous flavor of sweet almond, and two pints of Superman ice cream with its swirls of magenta, yellow and cerulean blue. After paying the cashier, Angelica hurried out of the ice cream shop and got into her car, rushing to keep the ice cream from melting. She hoped Mrs. Williams wouldn't mind the sweet treats for the kids.

Pulling up to the house, a slight feeling of fear and trepidation overtook her. She had seen Ricky's mother all of three times. What if she didn't remember Angelica? What if she refused to see her because it forced her to think of her lost boy? Why had she come to this woman's home with soda, potato chips, cake and ice cream as if she was throwing her a party? *Oh Lord, what have I done? What am I doing?* Angelica thought. She felt the wetness forming under her arms. She knew the ice cream was not going to last in the summer heat, so she was forced to exit the car and walk up onto the porch.

When Ana Williams answered the door, she was even thinner than Angelica remembered. She had been so beautiful to Angelica, and now, in little more than a year, she was a faded exotic flower whose petals had begun to brown and curl. The loss of her husband and two sons had taken its toll. Her voice was the same—bright and vibrant and infused with the music of her native Puerto Rico.

"Yes?"

Ana looked at Angelica with slightly narrowed eyes, head to the side as if trying to figure out the puzzle of familiarity.

"Hi, Mrs. Williams. Do you remember me? I'm Ricky's friend, Angelica. From school?"

The curtain of recognition parted, and Ana Williams smiled and pushed open the screen door to let in the girl and her bags. Once inside the vestibule, Mrs. Williams wrapped her arms around Angelica and hugged her, rocking her gently. She broke away from Angelica and finally spoke again.

"Yes! Of course I remember you! You are Angel! My Ricky's Angel," Ana said, her hand softy clutching at the neck of her blouse as if trying to push back the emotions about to overtake her.

Angelica wanted to burst into tears hearing these beautiful words spoken in Mrs. Williams' soft, accented English. But she held herself in check, relieved that she was welcome in their home.

Angelica heard feet bouncing down the living room stairs as Mrs. Williams said, "Let me help you," reaching for a bag and the tin of chips.

Once they entered the kitchen and sat the parcels on the counter, Angelica realized how much she'd been carrying as her arms throbbed in relief. Mrs. Williams had taken the brown paper bag with the baked goods, but the bags that gave Angelica's arms the blues contained several cold bottles of pop and the pints of ice cream. She could feel the condensation softening the bottom of the paper bag and she'd gripped it even tighter.

In the doorway of the kitchen were two children, Ricky's siblings Eduardo and Pilar. Yes, they had grown in the last year, but there were subtleties. Pilar, Ricky's favorite, smiled with huge, sad eyes. She had to be about 13 now and she was a beauty. Her braided hair hung like two thick ropes down her back. Little Eduardo was all smiles, eyes barely leaving his mother's face. It was clear that he'd taken on the role of protector and man of the house at 11. He wasn't going to let Ana be sad. He was clutching a cardboard replica of the Apollo 11 space craft. Everyone was so excited that the following day the United States would be the first country to land on the lunar surface and have an astronaut walk on the moon. And, it was going to be on TV!

The two younger children chattered away as they excavated the ice cream inside the cartons with two large spoons, exclaiming, "Yummy!" or "Ooh, my favorite!" They each balanced a small bowl of ice cream in one hand and a caramel cupcake in the other. Eduardo had a caramel moustache from licking the irresistible confection before he could even sit at the table with it.

"Thank you, Angelica," they said in unison.

Mrs. Williams laughed and shook her head.

"Those two act like they have never had sweets before. And speaking of sweet, that's what you are to bring this for us. *Gracias.*"

"I'm happy to do it. Those are some good kids," she said before she caught herself. She didn't want to imply that Danny and Ricky weren't. She saw Mrs. Williams was putting the ice cream in the freezer. "Can I help you?" Angelica asked.

"No, no, *mija*. It's such a hot day and I don't want this, aah, colorful ice cream to melt."

They giggled. Angelica wondered how often Ana Williams was able to laugh? At anything.

"What do you want? Pop, chips, what?" Mrs. Williams asked.

"I'll have some Red Pop and a few of the Better Made's," Angelica answered.

Ana filled two glasses with ice cubes and topped them with the strawberry soda. She opened the potato chips and shook them into a big avocado green ceramic bowl. Ana handed the bowl to Angelica and then picked up the glasses.

"Let's go out on the back porch," she suggested.

The kids smiled as Angelica and Mrs. Williams walked past, their mouths full of goodies. As they made their way to the back porch, they went past the entryway of the living room and Angelica saw, only for an instant, an 8 by 10 framed photo of Ricky. It was his high school graduation picture, a larger color version of the one she kept in her wallet. His head was ever so slightly tilted to the right, his mouth brilliantly smiling as if he'd just told a joke. Enrique's beautiful eyes were full of hope and the knowledge that the future belonged to him and he to it.

There were assorted family portraits including a picture of Danny at about 8 years old. Even then, he had that innocent, yet mischievous look on his face, a heart breaker who broke his mother's heart. Ricky's older sister Alecia had just graduated from Wayne State University, and her photo was proudly displayed along with her degree inside a polished wooden frame. Angelica turned her face away and continued to follow Ana.

The screened in porch was shaded by elm and maple trees and was cool and inviting. After some small talk, Mrs. Williams pulled out a photo album which had been lying next to her on the glider they were sitting on. Angelica made sure not to rock back and forth on the glider, unless Mrs. Williams did, because it might seem capricious and somewhat disrespectful.

One of the very first photos was of a tall, handsome brown skinned man in an Army uniform. He had thick, wavy black hair and glossy eyebrows. She saw Danny and Enrique in the man's face.

"This is my husband. Sergeant First Class Gabriel Williams. He was so very handsome," she said wistfully, staring at the father of her children and running her index finger along the plastic covering the picture.

"Goodness, he is so good looking! You and Mr. Williams made a beautiful couple who made some beautiful children!" Angelica exclaimed.

As Ana flipped through her memories, Angelica felt the weight of this woman's loneliness. She'd lost her husband to a war America could not win, and her two sons to the streets of Detroit. Still, it was a kick seeing all the photos of a happy young couple beginning their lives together, births of children, childhood fun and frivolity, teenagers thinking they were grown. Angelica would occasionally peek at Mrs. Williams as she proudly showed off her family just to make sure she wasn't becoming morose or upset. She seemed genuinely happy and grateful to be able to share with someone, scenes from her life.

"Do your parents still live in Detroit? Are you just visiting from college and going back soon?" Ana asked.

"Yeah, I'm just visiting my mom for the summer. I didn't want to stay in L.A. and just hang around doing nothing. Los Angeles is where I go to school. UCLA. I like it pretty well. It's very different out there," Angelica said, supposing it would not be good to mention her social life in Los Angeles or that she was dating. Instead, she blurted out, "My dad is dead, too. He was killed in the Korean War. I never met him."

"Oh, no," Mrs. Williams said, followed by a *tsk*. Sympathy telegraphed through the brevity of a sound.

"I was lucky. Well, I thought I was lucky. My husband fought in that war and we lived all over. But he always come back safe. We lived our lives, raising our kids, and then here comes Vietnam," Ana said as if talking about a street walker out to entrap her man. "Gabriel was killed almost as soon as he got there. It was very quick and very strange. I barely got used to him being gone again," she trailed off, her eyes searching the air for an explanation. "I moved the kids here to Detroit. Danny was our oldest, but it was as if Ricky was. *Mi papito*. Ricky was always so smart, so sure of himself, you know?" she said with a sidelong gaze at Angelica, stopping to take a sip of her pop. "Danny, ay, Danny! He started getting into trouble when he was a child and never stopped. The army life can be hard for children."

"How is Ricky, Mrs. Williams? I miss my friend."

She had waited a polite amount of time to ask, but was not sure if she wanted to know the answer. She had so many questions for his mother.

"He is doing okay, I guess. He got into some trouble in there. He killed a man."

Angelica just stared at the woman. *Yes, that's why he was locked up. He killed Mr. G.* Ana recognized a look of condescension rolling toward her.

"Not the store man. Another man. A prisoner," she said, sighing, not sure if she wanted to recount the story to this girl.

"What? I don't understand. Why? What happened?" Angelica's voice had become a bit shrill.

"Someone tried to hurt my son and Enrique ended up killing him. It was self-defense, but still he has to go to trial. My poor baby boy. I pray so hard for him, for all my children. I want him home. My son did not kill that store man. He did not do it," Ana said, grabbing Angelica's forearm for emphasis.

As much as she cared for and about Ricky, she knew Mrs. Williams was simply repeating the mantra of every mother whose child was incarcerated. She didn't want to be cruel to Ana, but she had to ask.

"How do you know? I'm sorry, but, how do you know that?" Angelica said as she felt Mrs. Williams' hand slip away from her arm.

She turned and looked directly into Angelica's eyes.

"I know my son. He liked his job, he liked Mr. Gilhooley. My boy had such dreams and plans. There was no reason for him to do this thing. I believe that other boy, that Meadows boy, did it. He had the money and daddy is a lawyer. Do you think they are going to let *him* go to jail? One day somebody will find the truth and my Enrique will be free."

They didn't speak again for a few minutes, drinking their increasingly watery soft drinks and still crisp potato chips. The salt dissolved on Angelica's tongue as she mindlessly shoveled in a handful of chips, craving more with each empty fist. Angelica could hear Pilar and Eduardo moving around inside the house.

"Mommy, we'll be on the front porch, okay?" Eduardo called out.

386

"Okay," responded Ana, her voice reverberating sharply off the bricks climbing up the back of her house, inside the screened porch.

"Before Ricky, um, went away last summer, I went to see him a couple of times. He told me he did not want me to see him like that, Mrs. Williams. At first, I ignored what he'd said, but, I guess he meant it. I wasn't allowed to see him, even though I'd come for a visit. I didn't know what to think. I just knew he would be out of there within a few days. But the days turned into weeks and then I had to leave for school. I never heard a word about the trial or anything."

Angelica didn't mention that Carlton's family had made him inaccessible to her and other friends as well. It was all so very weird.

"There was no trial, Angel. This lawyer shows up and says he will handle everything and that Mr. Meadows asked him to represent Enrique as a favor. His Uncle Billy said to wait and let him find the lawyer for Enrique. But I told him 'no' because...well, he is not friends with the law, you know? I want my boy to have the best chance."

Ana wiped her face with her hand even though she wasn't sweating. She paused before speaking again.

"At first I am so happy to have a big shot lawyer want to help my son. They said they had evidence against Enrique and a witness, too. And the gun. They advise him to plead guilty instead of going for a whole, big trial. When I met with my son, he told me, 'Mami, I swear to the Lord, I did not do anything to Mr. G.' I believe my boy. This deal they offered, if he said he was guilty, was supposed to be for three years, maybe get out in 18 months."

Ana Torres Williams had tears in eyes that were now barely open slashes.

387

"The judge give him 8 years! I screamed, I screamed, I screamed and they took me out of the court room! The lawyer says 'Well, I tried.' I could kill him with my own hands. We are trying to appeal, but now, he is in trouble for killing this other prisoner. *Ay dios mio!*"

Angelica sat there dumbfounded. She had no idea all of this had taken place and she didn't know what to believe. It was not like Ricky to harm anyone, he was so gentle and kind and reasonable. But she knew he would defend himself and anyone he cared about without regard to circumstances or consequences. Her head was pounding, and she was confused. *Poor Mrs. Williams.* Was she just blindly defending her son, no matter what?

She'd seen women on the news, usually black women, screaming, crying, falling out and once the banks of cameras grew nearby, turning angry and defensive. They swore that their son, the murderer who was on trial, was a good kid, a misunderstood youth, etc., and hadn't done anything to anyone. Always, no matter the reputation, criminal past or witnesses. Michigan had no death penalty, but California did, and Angelica always wished these women could be strapped on their homicidal son's laps when the switch was thrown to electrocute them in tandem. *A bunch of in-denial ass bitches.* Surely Mrs. Williams wasn't one of those unfortunates?

"Mrs. Williams, please tell me what happened? What happened?" she asked earnestly.

Ana seemed to sit up taller as if she was being righted by a pulley.

"My son is a beautiful young man, a proud young man. He would not tell me everything because he wants to protect me, but I know. I know. Somebody hurt him, want to take his manhood from him. Enrique tried to fight back and ended up in the hospital."

Angelica clapped her hand over her mouth in stunned disbelief. She felt the sting of tears welling in her eyes.

"When he got better and went back, this same guy tried to do it again. Enrique beat him to death. Yes! He deserved it! Now they want to add to my son's sentence for killing this *cabron*. *Pinche puto*! They said he planned it, so it's not self-defense."

Angelica saw the fire in Ana Williams' eyes. Angelica had so many questions, but she didn't want Mrs. Williams to be further upset. This story of incarceration and death wasn't some juicy gossip about some neighbor's wayward child. No, it was Ricky. *Her* Ricky. The thought that someone had harmed him like that shook her to the core. He was the boy who cared about everyone and gave everyone, no matter how foolishly, the benefit of the doubt. She needed to calm Mrs. Williams.

"You know, I've been writing Ricky every other week since I left and have never, ever heard from him. He was one of my best friends and I just don't get it, Mrs. Williams. Did you send him my letters?" Angelica felt she was about to cry, like a little child.

"I know, *mija*, I know. You know, he sent me something for you. He must have thought you would come to see me. Wait a minute," she said, getting up.

Ana went into the house, her Chanel No. 5 perfume lingering and scenting the air. Angelica could hear the laughter of kids playing in the front along the street, the slap of tennis shoes on the pavement as they ran in a game of tag. The woman next door was hanging her wash out on the line and began to sing a spiritual song, humming most of it.

Ana reappeared with a shoe box. Angelica smiled as Mrs. Williams took her place beside her on the glider. Angelica smiled even wider as Mrs. Williams reached out to her with the box in her hands. She lifted the lid and saw letters, dozens of them surrounded by rubber bands. Angelica recognized the familiar handwriting on the envelopes as her own. The corners of her mouth trembled as the smile froze on her face. It was as if someone was taking her picture, but the process had become interminable and her smile had begun to crumble. In the imaginary picture she would have looked awkwardly posed and completely crazy.

"Do not be mad at him, *mija*. Just let him go," Ricky's mom said.

Was there such a thing as being so angry you want to cry, but can't? She looked at Mrs. Williams because she wanted to make sure this was not a joke and she wanted to look at her as she cursed her out. *What the fuck was this shit supposed to mean?* Mrs. Williams was touching her hand again and Angelica flinched.

"It is not easy for my son. Hearing from you makes it worse. *His words.* He wants to remember things like they were before, that's all. Please understand," Ana pleaded.

"Well, it was a pleasure seeing you today. I'm glad you and the kids are well. I'm going to go now," Angelica replied stiffly as she stood up to leave. She could not reach the front door fast enough. When she got to the front porch, Pilar jumped up from her lawn chair and hugged Angelica tightly, taking her aback.

"Thank you," Pilar whispered, barely audible above the raucous din of children playing.

"You're welcome, sweetie," Angelica said as they parted.

She hurried to her car parked at the curb. Angelica got into her car and pulled away without glancing back as Ricky's house and his family receded in her rear-view mirror.

FIFTY-SIX

Angelica and Sheila had gone by to visit Carlton while back in Detroit, but couldn't seem to catch him at home. His mother was vague as to whether he even lived there or not. Both girls agreed Mavis Meadows was beyond strange. Angelica left her mother's phone number, which hadn't changed, but still he didn't call. The girls laughed recalling how they'd tried to track down the elusive Mr. Meadows the summer prior, when the horrible incident had taken place.

"Déjà vu all over again," they exclaimed, quoting baseball great Yogi Berra.

When Angelica got back to school in late August, she acted as if her visit to the Williams family had never taken place. She continued to write to Ricky, thinking perhaps he'd relent and take comfort in the words of a friend. She believed he needed that friendship now more than ever. *He must be going through hell.* Angelica hoped the summer away would cool Bakiri's ardor for her as she'd decided he was not the boy for her. There was too much conflict between who he was, who he thought he had to be and who his parents wanted him to be. She let him down easy, yet it took a couple of weeks for him to understand and get the message. Years later a chance meeting with one of their classmates revealed that Thomas Washington had become a politician and had married a white woman. *Of course he had.*

For the next three years of her college life, Angelica never went back to Campbell Hall. She tried to avoid the Northeast part of UCLA's campus, if at all possible. It took everything she had not to transfer down to USC. Just 8 months after the shooting at Campbell Hall, a psychopath named Charles Manson had ordered the massacre of several people including an actress and an heiress who lived nearby in a place called Benedict Canyon, which was basically Beverly Hills. Literally right up the road and too close for comfort. Soon Angelica realized no campus was safe.

In May of 1970, four students were shot dead at Kent State University in Ohio. Two students were part of a group protesting the invasion of Cambodia as part of the Vietnam War and the other two were just passersby coming from class. Shot not by Vietnamese or Cambodians, but by the Ohio National Guard. The world was dangerous and crazy and inescapable.

Everyone back home thought she was so lucky to be going to school and living in L.A. She and Sheila used to dance around her basement looking at the old Sylvania black and white television with the foil wrapped antennae, watching "Swingin' Time" hosted by Robin Seymour on Channel 9. They watched the popular local teen dance show filmed across the river in Windsor, Ontario, religiously each afternoon after school and homework, whether they were together or not. Sometimes they'd just have to call one another to recap after the show, winded from doing the Jerk, the Mashed Potatoes or the Shing-a-ling.

Recovery was only minutes long, for immediately after "Swingin' Time" went off, they'd watch "Where the Action Is" on Channel 7. Produced by "American Bandstand" host Dick Clark and taking place in L.A., it was like a live action version of every beach party movie Angelica had ever seen. The cool camera-ready kids danced on the beach and at ski resorts, and though the show was also in glorious black and white, it seemed even more vivid and alive. Between the two shows, every popular performer of the day was shown. Los Angeles had seemed glorious and otherworldly. One could only dream of seeing it in the flesh. And here she was---hoping to get as far away from it as possible.

Angelica's Sophomore year would trundle on without any more incidents of note, except one. Her great grandmother Hattie passed away the week before Thanksgiving. She was buried at Detroit Memorial Park on a cold and rainy November day. During her trip home, Angelica had a chance meeting with an old high school friend who invited her to watch his brother play football at Michigan Stadium at the University of Michigan. Everyone in the Mid-west, particularly in the great states of Ohio and Michigan, knew what took place on the fourth Saturday of November each year. This year's exciting and breathtaking game would go down in history, showcasing the storied rivalry between the maize and blue of the University of Michigan Wolverines and the scarlet and gray of the Ohio State Buckeyes.

On that day began the "10 Year War" between legendary coach Woody Hayes of Ohio State and soon to be legendary coach Bo Schembechler of the University of Michigan. Michigan won on that brisk, cold day with a score of 24-12 in what would be one of greatest upsets in the history of college football as the Buckeyes had come to Ann Arbor unbeaten. The year prior Ohio State had demolished Michigan by a score of 50-14.

At over 100,000 fans, Angelica had never seen so many people in one place and the sound was deafening. She couldn't help but be concerned about the husky Woody Hayes running around on the side lines with no coat, a red tie and a short-sleeved shirt. *Doesn't he want to live to see another match-up?* He certainly didn't act like it, in Angelica's estimation.

Angelica was still on a high from the three parties she'd attended in Ann Arbor, celebrating the Wolverines' win, when she sat down at her mother's dining room table back at home.

"Somebody had fun last night or was it this morning?" her mother asked.

"I had so much fun. Boy, are the boys cute up at U of M. I should have gone there."

Liz Tanner shot her daughter a withering look.

"Just kidding."

Liz had made some hot Lipton tea with slices of lemon on the saucer. Angelica grabbed the Sunday paper. The headlines screamed about a massacre, the My Lai massacre, which had taken place in Vietnam in March of 1968, with pictures and details of depravity beyond her comprehension. Taking more than a year to be reported in the press, this was a story no one wanted to see the light of day. Upwards of 500 infants, children, women and elderly men were summarily slaughtered by a platoon of American soldiers, Charlie Company, led by Captain Ernest Medina and Lieutenant William Calley.

Soldiers were ordered to kill anything and everything that walked, crawled or grew. Every dwelling was burned as were the crops and livestock. However, the worst was what happened to the innocent farm people in the hamlet of My Lai. Elderly women were shot in their stomach with M-79 grenade launchers, children who could walk would crawl from beneath the dead bodies of their mothers and grandparents only to be mowed down by machine gun fire like tall grass in a field. Girls were gang raped while other children and family members watched, crying. No matter, because bullets dried every tear.

Angelica sat with her mouth hanging open, tears streaming down her face as she read one atrocity after the next. Finally, she read that one man, a helicopter pilot, Warrant Officer Hugh Thompson Jr., had the balls to try to stop the carnage. He was able to rescue about 20 women and children, giving them cover as they ran for his chopper. Angelica wanted to believe that's what her dad would have done against such mindless hatred masquerading as duty. She put her head in the crook of her arm and sobbed.

FIFTY-SEVEN

Angelica threw herself into her school work, keenly aware that she needed excellent grades if she expected to be accepted into law school at the University of Michigan. She had learned over the past three years that good study habits and discipline were the pillars on which to build a successful college career. Having so much freedom was a detriment to some of Angelica's classmates. They simply couldn't cope with the length of rope they were given in which to hang themselves. Her old roommate Susan ended up dropping out of UCLA and returning home pregnant. So much for finding that husband of hers.

Sometime during her Junior year, Angelica attracted the attention of a handsome young man from New York City. He was tall and lanky with large brown eyes and wild black hair. His name was Matthew Miller and he happened to be Jewish. She didn't know much about Jews other than what she'd read in history books. What she did know was that she loved the corned beef at Lou's Deli and she loved Jesus—definitely not in that order. Matt sat across from Angelica in the library one evening and found her such a complete distraction that he had to find a way to get her to talk to him. As he pondered what to say to her to break the ice, he peered at her over and around his Western Civilization syllabus.

"Take a picture. It lasts longer," Angelica said, looking up from her Communications Law book.

Surprised and searching for a retort, Angelica had gone back to reading as Matthew sputtered to life.

"Hi, I'm Matt. What's your name?"

Without breaking her concentration, she off-handedly replied, "Angelica."

Matthew, shot down, picked up his syllabus again and tried to focus. He gently slammed it to the heavy wooden table, startling Angelica enough to make her look up abruptly from her reading material. Her mouth hung open slightly as she blinked at the handsome young man in front of her. *What a jerk*!

"Do you want to get some coffee, Angelica?"

"No. Who are you?"

"Matt. Matthew Miller. I'm a Poli-Sci major. Senior."

"Cool. Nice to meet you *Señor* Miller. Why are you slumming at the library? I thought Seniors didn't do a lot of studying? You know, last year and all."

"Maybe some don't, but I should if I'm going to graduate with honors. At least that's the plan."

Angelica grabbed up her books and got up from her seat to leave. She waved at Mr. Miller to signal the end of their discourse.

"What about coffee? We don't have to do it today."

"I don't drink coffee, *Señor*. I'm a hot chocolate chick or didn't you notice? See ya."

Angelica was surprised at how cheeky she was with her little double entendre. She thought she was so clever.

398

The next day, Angelica finally, symbolically, sent her last letter to Enrique Williams care of Ana Williams. It had been almost three years and it was enough. She decided to free herself of a burden she had taken on willingly. She had only to think of her own mother, whom Angelica began to understand a bit. Liz Tanner's love for a fallen soldier, her father, had decimated her. Angelica could not allow her heart to become imprisoned with Ricky. Walking to the mailbox on the corner, she knew she had to cease listening to the whispers of what could have been. She had no fault or power in the matter and had to allow herself to let go, as Mrs. Williams had said.

She pressed the envelope to her lips and said, "I release you. I release me. Goodbye, my friend."

She flipped the envelope into the mail slot and walked away.

When Angelica came around the corner from her class, there was Matt standing with his book bag at his feet and two cups in his hands. He was smiling. He had a great smile, she had to admit, even through his scruffy moustache. Angelica shook her head ruefully, then laughed.

"Let me guess. Hot chocolate?"

"Yup, and it was not easy to find hot chocolate in L.A., in the summer, let me tell you."

Angelica took the steaming cup from his left hand.

"Thank you, *Señor*."

"No problem. And, you know you can call me Matt, right? I'm not Spanish, I'm Jewish, not that I couldn't be both."

"I'm just teasing you because you thought you needed to let me know you're a Senior."

"Oh, touché," he said smiling and nodding in considered agreement. "Can we sit over there?" Matt asked, indicating a nearby wooden bench. "I've got something else for you."

"Are you a masher, Mr. Miller?"

"Um, no, and that was clever alliteration, by the way."

They walked the short distance to the shady bench and sat down. Matt sat his drink on the ground and dug out a lumpy brown paper bag from his book bag. He had two warm bagels with cream cheese inside. He dug one out and handed it to Angelica.

"You like bagels? I didn't know if you wanted a schmear or not, but I got you one anyway."

"Thank you, Matt. This was nice of you to do."

"Glad to. How's your day going so far?"

"I know where I know you from," Angelica exclaimed, ignoring his inquiry. "Didn't you used to always be with this girl with long blonde hair? I used to see you guys around campus all the time."

"Oh, yeah, Jen, my ex-girlfriend."

"What happened to you two? Y'all seemed tight."

"We just…she wanted to get married. And I don't think she cared much who she was going to do that with. I'm not ready for all of that."

"I can dig it. So, are you some kind of hippie? You believe in 'free love' and all that stuff?"

Matt burst into laughter. This girl was funny and had no filter.

"Are you sure you're not a New Yorker?"

Angelica just looked at him as she bit into her bagel.

"No, I'm not a hippie. My parents pay too much in tuition for me to be a hippie. I do believe in free love, though. We should be able to explore and love whomever we want, right? They don't call it 'The Sexual Revolution' for nothing. It's crazy to have to get married in order to have sex with someone. Nutty."

"You have a good relationship with your parents?"

"Yeah, I do."

"You're not trying to shock them by associating with a black girl, are you? You want to rebel against them, 'The Establishment?'" she said, making her eyes large and taking a swallow of the rich hot chocolate for effect.

"That's funny. My parents are liberal New York Jews. They're not the establishment. Just the opposite. My parents are both writers."

"They sound interesting."

"They can be. What kind of music do you listen to? You know anything about rock and roll?"

"Dude, I'm from Detroit. I know about every kind of music, even Polka. You ever hear of Bob Seger?

"Ramblin' Gamblin' Man!" he fairly shouted, proud of his rock knowledge.

Angelica nodded.

"Lots of rock 'n roll coming out of Detroit. Grand Funk Railroad, Mitch Ryder, Alice Cooper, MC5. Most people hear Detroit and only think of Motown, you know?"

"Can I take you out, sometime?"

"You changed the subject."

"I know. I'm sorry. You are one fascinating chick."

Angelica laughed at how corny he was, yet she found him interesting.

"Glad you think so. Yeah, we can go out sometime."

"Great, can I get your number?" he asked, once again rummaging through his book bag, this time for a pen and paper.

"Okay, so don't think I'm being coy or trying to lead you on. I'm getting a new number because I'm moving. So, I don't have a phone number right now."

Matt looked disappointed and blew a bit of air out of his lips.

"Okay. When are you moving?" he asked, buckling the flaps to his pack, which seemed suddenly deflated as well.

"This weekend."

"Do you need help? I'd be happy to give you a hand," Matt offered.

"Wow, that's cool. Yeah, thanks. Are you sure?"

"Yes, of course. I wouldn't have offered if I didn't want to help out."

"But wait, don't you ride a motorcycle? I might need another car to—"

"Oh, so look who hasn't noticed me at all?!" Matt said, laughing in spite of himself. "I was offering my muscles, such as they are," he said, flexing his right bicep. "Don't worry about it. We can figure this out easy. Just tell me what day and what time."

"This coming Saturday at 8:30 a.m., if that's okay?"

"Sure, no problem."

Angelica looked at Matt with her eyebrows raised.

"Don't you need my address?"

"I know where you live," he said taking a bite of his food.

"Oh! You already know where I live! Should I be concerned?"

"Angelica, you got nothing to worry about," Matt said, wiping a dab of cream cheese off his moustache with a napkin.

FIFTY-EIGHT

Matt helped Angelica move to her place in the Valley in one trip. He was very organized and had borrowed his friend's van to help expedite things. Sweaty and exhausted, they sat atop blue milk crates that would serve as bookcases and record album storage. Angelica had dug up two glasses and fetched water for both of them from her gleaming kitchen. Matt took a sip and winced.

"Oy, the world's worst water," he said. "If I wasn't so thirsty I'd pour it back in the toilet where it belongs."

"Yeah, sorry about that. You'd think the water in L.A. would be good, ya know? I'm getting Sparkletts on Monday."

Sparkletts was a company that delivered bottled spring water to homes all over California.

"Let me tell you something. The best water is from New York City. For real," Matt said, proudly.

Angelica knew that Detroit had the best tap water, but she didn't want to argue with him.

He drained his glass of the distasteful liquid and said, "Look, I know you're probably too tired, but, I got tickets to the Troubadour on the strip. There's a great English singer named Elton John who's on his first American tour and this is his second to last night. The guy's so heavy."

"I know him, or I should say I've heard a couple of his tunes on KLOS. I love "Border Song." I'd dig making that scene. How did you score tickets?"

"I have my ways," Matt replied, eyes narrowing for effect. "I spend a lot of time up in Laurel Canyon listening to music all the time. I got a couple of good connections and they gave me the ducats."

"What time do you want me to be ready?" Angelica asked. She didn't know if it was worse riding in a hulking Chevy van or on a ridiculous motorcycle.

"I'll come around six. We can pop over to Canter's Deli for something quick before the show."

"Sounds good. Are we taking your motorcycle?"

"You know it. Dress accordingly."

Angelica had only ridden on a motorcycle once in her life and most of the scenery was viewed through thick curtains of hair as the wind plastered it to her face. She'd make sure she tied it down with a scarf tonight.

Doug Weston's Troubadour was another great rock and folk music venue on Santa Monica Boulevard in West Hollywood. The marquee wasn't as flashy and iconic as the Roxy Theatre and from the outside it actually looked like a Bavarian restaurant crossed with a movie theatre. Angelica and Matt could find no seat at any table inside the full club, so they watched from the upstairs railing. The club was full of celebrities, musicians and actors that Angelica had only seen on television or heard on the radio. The air was expectant and crackling as everyone seemed to understand they were witnessing rock and roll history. This was the fifth of six sold out nights for a bespectacled mop top piano player named Elton John. He performed "Take Me to the Pilot,"

"Border Song" and a new favorite, "Your Song" among others, with his band.

Matt put his arm around Angelica and swayed back and forth to the music. It was clear he liked her, and she didn't want to allow a false excitement to make the moment, the night, more than it was. Matthew Miller was cute and funny and *white*. Did that mean something to *them?* Maybe to people who stared at the couple and then smiled self-consciously when noticed, because they thought themselves more tolerant, but had lied. She'd seen a few old people in the deli earlier in the evening, furtively trying to look but not look at them.

When they got back to the San Fernando Valley, Angelica was so tired she could barely walk to her building. Matt had felt her leaning into him more and more as they rode back to Sherman Oaks on his bike. It had been a very long day. Matt walked her to her door and they hugged tightly. Matt still smelled like marijuana smoke. She suspected he'd indulged a couple of times that night when he'd taken two long bathroom breaks, but she couldn't be sure since some patrons inside the Troubadour had also lit up. Matt bent his head down and pulled Angelica's chin forward. He was a good kisser. She didn't mind his moustache though she thought she would. Suddenly she was awake—all over. They must have kissed for 5 minutes before saying goodnight.

Angelica slipped inside her apartment. She washed her face and stripped off all her clothes. She slid under the cool sheets of her bed, grateful that they'd had the foresight to assemble it earlier. Angelica had always wanted to sleep nude and this small experiment made her feel grown up and sexy. What a great night it had been. She prayed there would be no earthquakes or anything to send her into the street in her birthday suit. She smiled as she drifted off to sleep.

406

The first time Matt made love to Angelica was three months after they'd had their first date. In that time there was lots of passionate kisses, not-so-dry humping (her), tit sucking and congested testes (him). Matt never insisted or pressured Angelica to go any further and she appreciated that. It was obvious they were attracted to one another and they always seemed to be together.

Matt had finally moved into a house in Laurel Canyon with a friend and ex classmate who had graduated the year prior. Matt's pal, Ray Gonzalez, was a trust fund baby whose wealthy parents had provided him with a lush monthly stipend. As smart as he was, graduating Summa Cum Laude in Business Administration, he'd exhausted his enthusiasm for academia long before he'd left UCLA. Hanging out with musicians up in those rustic hills, Ray met artists of varying talents and trajectories. He was using his money to buy studio time to produce several singers and there always seemed to girls in various states of undress and druggery around. Matt would say his friend Ray was "cool" or "just grooving to his own thing" and that "thing" didn't concern him.

Angelica had anticipated the inevitable—she was going to sleep with Matt. He was so confident and mature and unlike anyone she'd ever known. Angelica ventured down to the Venice Free Clinic to get examined and was prescribed birth control pills. She'd been on the pill long enough for her body to stop menstruating and her already full breasts had gone up to a C cup. She liked the effect on Matt. Her breasts swinging free of her bra, big and supple and buoyant, always made Matt stop and stare before he could no longer control his hands or his mouth. He would look up at her rapt expression as he licked and sucked each nipple.

Angelica and Matt had spent most of their Saturday together looking for jobs, when she saw a sign at a brand-new record store on the corner of Sunset and Horn Avenue called Tower Records. She filled out the application and the manager, who seemed a bit dismissive at first, found himself caught up in the sunshine that was Angelica Tanner. Her knowledge of music was broad and wide ranging. He hired her on the spot.

Matt and Angelica celebrated with dinner at Madame Wu's Garden in Santa Monica and then headed to her apartment. Matt drove her car as Angelica was slightly drunk from a single Mai Tai.

"Damn, that drink was strong," she said, giggling.

"Woman, you are a lightweight! That drink wasn't that strong. I had to drink mine and finish yours, too! That's okay, I like that you're so sweet and innocent. Makes it more of a challenge to corrupt you a little," Matt teased.

"I feel kind of guilty that dinner cost so much. Madame Wu's isn't cheap. Did you see all those pictures of movie stars on the walls? I mean, Cary Grant and Lucille Ball!"

"We're celebrating remember? You slayed that dude in the record store. He never knew what hit him!" Matt said, proudly.

"I promised my mother I wouldn't work for the first two years of college. And now, it's year three, I got my own place and I can be more independent. Do my own thing. And why do I get the feeling you probably don't need to work?"

"Work schmurk, that's not the point. I want to be my own man. I wanna show my parents that they raised me to take care of myself just fine. I look at Ray sometimes and I think money's ruined him in a way."

"Yet, if any of his singers get a hit record, he'll make even more dough. I love how that works."

They both laughed.

"Besides," Matt teased, "work will make me a man. It'll put hair on my chest."

"Hair schmair, I'd say you got enough," Angelica said, cutting her eyes at him for being silly.

"Hey, good schmuh!" he said, smiling.

Once they were inside her apartment, Angelica decided if Matt tried to have sex with her, she would let him. God, she felt so inexperienced. She knew they couldn't continue the way they had been. It wasn't fair to either of them. Reading her signals, he stripped off all Angelica's clothes except her panties. She was glad she'd worn the new aqua blue satin underwear with an embroidered, nondescript flower over her right pelvic bone. Matt kissed her there and worked his way to both knees. He could feel Angelica tense up beneath his hands, which were resting on her upper thighs.

"Relax, baby," he said, barely audible.

Boldly, he ran his tongue along the cleft between her legs, at the outline of her labia. Angelica reflexively contracted her legs and scooted up the bed by her heels like a spider running from a lit match. Matt grabbed one of her ankles and held it gently.

"I'm not going to hurt you. Trust me," he said, pulling her back down flat on the bed.

"Sorry. I don't know why I did that. Maybe it's the alcohol. I'm shaking."

"No, you're not. But you will be."

SIXTY

S heila picked up the phone on the second ring.

"Hey girl, what's happening?" she said, instantly recognizing her friend's voice.

"Oh, the same ol' same ol'. What's shakin' in Beantown? God I still can't believe you live there."

They both laughed. Sheila talked about how miserable the weather was, cold and snowy.

"They claim Chicago is the 'Windy City,' but they're wrong. It's Boston. You come around a corner and that wind whips up off the ocean and fights you every step you take. I actually wear a ski mask to protect my face from windburn!"

"You better not go into a store with it on. You might end up surrounded by the police!" Angelica said, only half joking.

"How's your love life, girl? Okay, before you answer, I want to talk about mine first," Sheila said, suddenly breathless.

They both burst into giggles.

"Oh-kay…"

Five minutes later, Angelica had a vivid picture of her dearest friend fucking just about every man she came in contact with since landing at Logan Airport three years earlier. Was she

411

shocked? Yes. Surprised? No. Her aunt Fannie used to say the church girls and preacher's kids were always the wildest of the bunch. Sheila just proved her theory in spades. Angelica cleared her throat.

"Wow," was all she could muster.

"I know! I'm having a ball. So, how's *your* love life?"

"Well, clearly not nearly as, uh, varied as yours, I guess, but I really dig this guy I've been dating. He's a Senior. He's from New York. He's white," Angelica said, pausing.

"So what? Who cares if he's white? Don't be fooled. White dudes love black girls. We're exotic!"

"Well, my guy, Matt, is crazy about me. He's tall and skinny with crazy, wild ass hair. He's really cute."

"So, did you do it yet?"

Angelica didn't know how she felt about her naïve church mouse becoming this worldly woman who seemed to know a lot more than she did about sex.

"Um, yeah. It was intense. Have you ever had oral sex?" Angelica said, speaking so low that it took a few seconds for Sheila to realize what she'd been asked.

"Yes. Ain't it something?!"

"So, does that make us…"

"Lucky as hell! Yes, it does!"

"That's not what I was going to say. Don't you ever feel self-conscious or that it's wrong?"

"At first I did and then I realized I had to grow up. Hey, we didn't invent this stuff, it's been going on since the beginning of time. And nobody is making anybody do anything, right?"

"Yeah, you got that right. I liked it so much I couldn't wait until he did it again. I thought my head was going to explode," Angelica said, laughing at the visual.

"There's this really good book you need to get. 'Everything You Ever Wanted to Know About Sex But Were Afraid to Ask' by Dr. David Reuben. It's so eye opening. There's so much we didn't know, and this book tells you *everything*," Sheila said, stretching out the four syllables for emphasis. "Velma never told me anything about *anything*."

"And when Liz finally got around to having 'the talk' with me, I put her out of her misery by saying I already knew about them shits, you know? Man, was she relieved," Angelica said, laughing.

The two friends wished each other a Happy Thanksgiving and promised to relay salutations to their respective families.

SIXTY-ONE

Around 6 a.m. on a Tuesday morning, February 9, 1971 to be exact, Angelica was awakened by a gentle rocking of her bed, like an invisible hand was trying to rouse her. Before she could process what she was feeling, the room seemed to be jumping.

To say she was startled was to say the Titanic was merely a boat. Her heart leapt into her throat as she sprang up from her bed, immediately awake with the roiling violence of the earthquake beneath her feet. She ran to the front door. Where was she trying to go? She ran back to the kitchen and crawled under the kitchen table as pictures, bowls, glasses, and plates crashed down from the walls and cabinets as if thrown by a child abandoned to a tantrum. Once the shaking ceased, she began to hear her neighbors through her windows, crying, screaming and talking in the driveway and in the street.

"What the fuck?!" Angelica yelled out in anger and panic. She was completely shaken up. Literally.

Angelica Tanner was fortunate, as she had survived the Sylmar earthquake with only a bump on the head from a hurtling can of soup and her apartment building withstood the temblor. All told, more than 60 people lost their lives in the wake of collapsed buildings and exploding gas mains. Los Angeles was becoming a hellish version of paradise to the girl from Detroit. Sunshine and palm trees couldn't mask the foreboding she felt covering her like a gossamer web. Unwillingly and unwittingly, she became hyper vigilant—always expecting something crazy, natural or manmade, to go down.

Following the earthquake, Matt spent every night at Angelica's apartment for two weeks. It took a couple of days for her to sleep through the night. He took her to school each day and he'd wait in the library for her if he finished his classes before she did. Angelica thought it might be weird having a guy around constantly, but strangely, it wasn't. It was comfortable and comforting.

After much coercing and cajoling, Angelica agreed to spend the night with him at his place. He loved the fact that if he was at her apartment on Hazeltine Avenue, he could cruise east down Ventura Boulevard to Laurel Canyon Avenue, take a right and head up through the hills to his house. Angelica, if she had to work at Tower, would use Laurel Canyon to descend into West Hollywood, practically landing at the store's doorstep on Sunset.

Angelica seldom slept over because Ray and Matt had abandoned any pretense of cleaning up their little bachelor pad. She had to always wear sandals or tennis shoes because there was no telling what hazardous waste was on the floor. Thankfully, Matt had his own bathroom, which he kept as clean as he could for Angelica. She'd always end up washing the piles of dirty dishes littering the kitchen just so she'd have something to drink water out of if necessary. Slobs!

On an unusually warm day in early spring, Matt decided he needed a break from studying. They rode Matt's motorcycle down to the Canyon Country Store, a decades old fixture and staple of life in those parts. The store had everything a body could want from deli sandwiches to fresh flowers. They picked up sandwiches and provisions for a cozy picnic on the beach. On the way out of the store, a tall, stocky man with long, wavy brown hair and a beard was coming in.

"Hey, man!" Matt said enthusiastically.

"Hey, Brother," the man replied, stroking his beard distractedly, his intense, stormy blue eyes registering low level recognition. He looked like a lion or maybe Jesus.

"This is my old lady, Angelica. Angelica this is Jim," Matt said by way of introductions.

Jim took Angelica's left hand and kissed it before continuing on into the store. A few people threw up their hands to wave and some said, "Hi, Jim."

"*Old lady?* You're such a hippie now," Angelica said, pretending to be annoyed with Matt.

This part of L.A. was rife with supposed artists and hangers on and freaks and druggies.

"Sorry, I should have said 'girlfriend.' Same thing, though."

They mounted his motorcycle after placing their picnic goodies in a latching bin. Matt turned slightly side ways to speak.

"Did you recognize that dude?" Matt asked, grinning.

"I feel like I've seen him before. Intense," Angelica answered.

"Well, he went to UCLA, but graduated back in '65. Babe, that was Jim Morrison. Of *The Doors*. He lives right behind the store on Rothdell. He's in there all the time."

"Holy shit! I just met rock royalty! His voice is amazing."

"Tell me about it. Maybe we'll luck up and get tickets when they go back on tour."

There would be no more tours for The Doors as Jim Morrison would die in Paris at the age of 27 only a few months later.

With graduation approaching for Matt, his parents came to town for the ceremony. Angelica was nervous about meeting them even though he seemed to be sure they would love her. It was the night before his graduation from UCLA and his parents were taking the two of them to dinner at Tony's on the Pier in Redondo Beach. The couple took Angelica's car since she was wearing a flowing maxi dress, a garment not conducive to a motorcycle ride. Matt admitted to Angelica that his mother didn't approve of him riding a motorcycle.

"One less thing for her to *kvetch* about," he said.

When they arrived, Mr. and Mrs. Miller were already seated in the upstairs rotunda, with a perfect view of the setting sun over the Pacific Ocean. Matt could imagine not waiting for them downstairs was his father's idea.

"What, I shouldn't be comfortable if they already have a table ready? Don't worry, they'll find us."

"Mom, Dad, this is Angelica Tanner," Matt said, after salutations and hugs for his parents. Angelica looked beautiful, her hair was sleek in a long ponytail, her dress gently hugging her body underneath a light sweater. Each parent shook her hand politely before they sat back down to order dinner. Mrs. Miller was petite and pale under a dyed black coiffure. Mr. Miller was tall and ruddy of face with thick black curls that had begun to go gray. They were the physical opposite of one another, but had the weary shorthand of long term companionship down pat.

Angelica wanted to pretend she didn't see the look of shock in their eyes when introduced to her or their exchange of meaningful glances to one another during dinner. Did Matt not see any of this? He did not. He could barely take his eyes off his beautiful girlfriend, which likely alarmed his parents to no end. Angelica didn't know if she should be insulted at how relieved they seemed to be at her revealing her plans to move back to Michigan for law school.

Before dessert came, Angelica strategically excused herself to the ladies' room. She wanted Matt to have a chance to talk to his parents and they to him. Barbara Miller spoke first.

"Matt, honey, what are you doing? Are you angry with us? Please tell me this is a fling or—"

"Look, she seems to be a very nice girl. Not Jewish, but nice. She's smart and is making something of herself. How serious is this?" Paul Miller asked his son.

Matt pursed his lips, glancing over his shoulder to see if Angelica had emerged from the vicinity of the bathroom. He leaned forward, speaking low.

"This is exactly why I decided not to tell you she was black. I didn't want you to have any notions or bias toward her, but—"

"Matthew we are not biased. That's unfair."

"No? I guess you're only liberal in theory or on paper, then. Better yet, with your friends so you can seem better than them. More civilized."

"Don't talk to your mother like that."

"I like Angelica a lot. She's great. She's smart and beautiful and I don't know what's going to happen when she graduates next year. I want her to stay in L.A. She makes me a better person."

He could see by his folks' eyes, Angelica was in sight. Matt stood up when Angelica came back to the table, a sign of his respect and affection for her.

"Oh, goodness," she said mischievously. "Did I miss anything?"

"No, babe, you didn't. We're gonna have to leave right after dessert. Big day tomorrow."

"Did you two want to come back to the hotel for a night cap?" Barb asked.

"No, Mom, we can't. Here's your tickets before I forget," Matt said reaching into his jacket's left breast pocket to retrieve their tickets to the graduation at Pauley Pavilion.

"Well, that went well," Angelica teased as they walked along the boardwalk to the car. "You don't talk to them much, do you?"

"I talk to them enough, believe me. They like you, Angelica. They were just surprised, I think."

"You think?" Angelica laughed, mirthlessly.

She was learning that nobody, at least no one she knew, had a perfect relationship with their parents.

"I guess I didn't think they would be so weird. I'm sorry if they made you uncomfortable. They just need to get used to me being my own man." He stopped walking. "A man who loves you."

Matt bent down slightly to kiss Angelica on the lips.

"I love you, too," she whispered.

The briny smell of the ocean enveloped them as they held hands and stared out at the dark water illuminated by the lights of Palos Verdes Peninsula in the distance.

SIXTY-TWO

P eggy Hartley, Angelica's friend from UCLA, called her up to meet for dinner at the Chart House in Marina del Rey. They'd kept in contact even though Peg had graduated the year before. She hadn't seen Peg in several months and was looking forward to catching up with her.

Peggy stood up to greet her old friend. "Hey, little sister," she said excitedly, hugging Angelica and patting her on her back lightly.

"It's been too long, girl," Angelica said, taking a seat at the table.

"Don't you just love the Marina? So many great restaurants on the water," Peg mused.

"I know. Look at you! You look great. You look happy."

Peg flung her left hand out and thrummed the table. Angelica immediately noticed her diamond engagement ring.

"Oh, my God, Peggy, let me see!" she said, grabbing Peg's hand.

"Marvin proposed last Saturday night! We were at a barbeque with his family and the next thing I knew, he's down on one knee asking me to marry him. We went through a lot of stuff, but we made it, Angelica. We made it."

Peggy had kept a long-distance relationship with her fiancé while he was student up in Oakland. Those 500 miles may as well have been 5,000 for all they endured to keep their connection going. They were two kids on scholarships and work study, and it wasn't easy to find the time or money to visit one another. Peggy was the perfect person to get advice from. Angelica explained that she was torn between going back to Detroit, which seemed the right and best thing for her after graduation, and staying in Los Angeles to be with Matt.

"Well, have you two said the 'L' word yet?"

"What? Lemons? Lesbians? Leeches? Yes, we've discussed all of those and we've been very candid with one another," Angelica answered with a straight face.

Both women burst into peals of laughter. Peg was coughing because she was laughing so hard.

"Okay, okay, yes, we love each other. He's a great guy. Savvy and smart, good looking, too."

"Sounds perfect."

"Well…not quite perfect. He smokes weed. A lot of it. He doesn't crack on me because I don't, but I think he's got a problem. I don't want to be judgmental or turn him off, but I don't understand why he does it. Is it going to lead to harder drugs?"

"Not always," Peg said, hopefully.

"I worry sometimes because it seems to be so, um, prevalent where he is. You know that singer from The Doors? Jim Morrison? The one who died just last week? I met him with Matt only a few months ago. I mean, Matt is nothing like that—"

"Oh, I know you wouldn't be with some strung out guy."

"He's got this slob of a roommate, Ray, who has all these crazy hippy chicks hanging around all the time. Ray's got Matt dabbling in the music business, which is kind of par-for-the- course living up in Laurel Canyon."

"Well, is he any good? Can he make a living with it?"

"Yeah, he actually is good. He has an ear for talent and a great head for business. He knows the difference between crap and artistry. There's this one girl, waif thin, big eyes, long hair. I guess she thinks she's Twiggy, but she's got a very nice voice. Her name is Chloe, even though I call her 'Sticky.'"

Peg smiled behind her hand at her friend's clever put down.

"She's always hanging around. Man, is she scary looking."

"Wow, these people sound like characters in a play," Peggy said.

"I'd love for you to meet them. Can you come to a party in the Canyon next Saturday? Ray is giving a party and showcasing a few singers. Please, please come!"

"Gee, everybody sounds so wonderful, how can I say no?" Peg said with mild sarcasm.

"I must sound awful or they do! It's them, not me, right?" Angelica asked, laughing at how childish she sounded.

"So, how's your friend back in Michigan? Richard, wasn't it?"

She had told Peg about Ricky and the circumstances of his incarceration. Angelica made a weak attempt at continuing her laughter, but it was thin and strained.

"Ricky. I stopped writing him. I had to let go of that part of my life."

"Do you ever think of him and wonder what he's doing? What he's thinking?"

"All the time. I selfishly wonder if he's thinking about me. I know I'm terrible to think like that, but—"

"No, not at all, Angelica. I would think you were crazy if you didn't ever think of the guy, based on everything you told me about the two of you. It's more than sad. Is that why you seldom go back home?"

Angelica smiled.

"Pot, meet kettle."

Peggy nodded her head in silent agreement.

"Touché. The reason I don't go back home to Compton is that the people there don't make me feel good about myself. All they ever told me was what I wouldn't do and what I'd never be."

"Crabs in a barrel. When one gets so far up the side, another grabs on and pulls him back into the barrel."

"Exactly, and that's why I can't find my way back home, my friend. Me and Marvin got out of the barrel and we're building our own thing."

"Are you coming next Saturday? I'll write down the address for you."

"How can I refuse?" Peggy said, sliding a menu over to Angelica, genuinely happy to see her friend again.

SIXTY-THREE

Matt left out early Saturday morning from Angelica's apartment, promising her a clean house for the party. He was so sweet and cute that morning, bringing her a cup of tea and the latest *Creem* magazine before he split. She looked forward to the unrelenting poke-in-the-eye stream of consciousness diatribes that came courtesy of their rock and roll critic, Lester Bangs. Straight, no chaser from Detroit to the rest of the free world. His torrential downpour of caustic prose gave pause to those who thought they were about to rock. Perhaps not, according to Bangs.

Angelica padded into the kitchen with her empty cup and noticed a trail of ants near her sink. Dead ants. *The little bitches*, she thought. She'd gotten her apartment fumigated the day before and this was the glorious aftermath. She knew the victory was short lived because they would return. They always did. She had to smile at the notion of battling something instinctual and prehistoric and devoid of the occluding inconvenience of thought. In the epic and never-ending struggle called "man versus nature," what man failed to realize, according Angelica Tanner, was this: Mother Nature always wins. Even if she has to take you out. Man is an inconsequential nuisance, an irritant whose days are always numbered. She thought about the earthquakes, the rock slides on Pacific Coast Highway, the scorching Santa Ana winds that whipped the brush into spontaneous fires. Man insists on planning and plotting on how to tame or destroy nature to fit himself into it. But nature has no such plan. It has a primordial continuum, put in place by God. It simply adapts, adjusts, regenerates and resurges with the cruelest of efficiency.

Angelica slid open the door to her lanai and stepped outside into the morning heat. She could already feel the heaviness of the air pressing into her lungs. The infamous L.A. smog, the band of noxious orange brown pollution that sat on top of the Los Angeles basin, was already making its presence known. Angelica looked out into the courtyard where some children were playing with a large purple ball. She didn't want to think about it, but she was a little worried about Matt. Was she just a big old square because she didn't smoke pot? Was Ray really just a bad influence or was Matt gravitating toward his true nature with his fondness for weed?

Stop it! You need to go to the party and just be with your man and have a groovy time. Who knows, there might be some celebrities there. Angelica had asked for Saturday off a month ago so she'd better enjoy it. Some of her co-workers at the record store even seemed a little envious about Matt and Ray's shindig. She had to admit those two were kind of becoming a big deal among the music production set.

The outside of the house had been decorated with Christmas lights in the trees and intertwined on the porch railing extending down the stairs. Ugh, those steps, so many steps, ascending to the heavenly blue door of the house. The music was loud and so were the cheerful voices Angelica could hear cutting through the misty evening air. Matt had been hovering near the front door in the living room, waiting for his girl to arrive. Angelica came in wearing a paisley handkerchief dress and her hair encircled by a matching bandana. Her honey kissed skin glowed in the dim light as Matt gave her a long and lingering kiss.

"Hey, get a room!" Ray said, walking past. Trailing him were the skeletal remains that were Chloe.

"Eat a sandwich" Angelica said under her breath.

"What did you say, babe?"

"Nothing," Angelica replied.

That Chloe chick was a cross between a ghost, a skeleton and a dog, the way her bony frame was always lurching behind Ray. She and Angelica had had only one conversation and it was contentious to say the least. Chloe had somehow invoked the word "Negress" to describe Angelica, turning Angelica's green eyes black with rage.

"Excuse me? We're not on a plantation in the 1850's. What's wrong with you? Do I need to show you how black people from Detroit explain manners to people who don't seem to have any?"

The girl apologized profusely, not realizing how ignorant she'd sounded, nor that she was about to be broken in half by Angelica. Later, when Angelica and Matthew were alone, he tried to make the excuse that the girl was British, but Angelica shot him a look that ended that defense motion.

"Really? Is that what you came up with? If she were a time traveler, maybe, but even the English are hipper than that."

Matt, wisely, dropped the issue.

The inside of the house was more dark than light with the only real light coming from strobes placed in the living room, dining room and one bedroom. There was a weak ceiling light in the kitchen and candles loitering on the window sills. The air was thick with sweet incense and marijuana smoke. Angelica figured she was in for a contact high no matter what. As long as she could drive home, that was all she cared about.

As the evening wore on they ate chicken pate on crackers, which Matt proudly claimed to have made, and danced to the few songs that were worthy. There was a small area near the middle of the living room that could be considered a stage or performance space. A few canyon locals picked up the guitars and tambourines laying nearby and jammed. The music was rich and soulful, the lyrics thoughtful and deep, just poetry set to music, really. Angelica realized this was a "scene" or "a happening" and she got to be a part of it.

There were large, soft pillows bordering the periphery of the room and people in various states of stoned, talked and laughed. Angelica and Matt were sitting down, grooving to the music when he picked up a water pipe and lit it, breathing in the fog of pot smoke with a bubbling sound, like a kid blowing into his milk with a straw. This was the first time Matt had been bold enough to get high in front of Angelica. He coughed a bit as he exhaled and went in to kiss Angelica on the lips. Her instinct was to flinch and pull away, but she made herself remain still.

She couldn't begin to describe what his mouth tasted like. He withdrew from her and hit the pipe again, only this time he grabbed her face gently with one hand and set his mouth upon hers. He softly blew the smoke into her mouth, causing her to gasp and cough. Strangely, Angelica felt this was a challenge and she had failed it. She stared him in his eyes, daring him to try again. Angelica ended up being "shotgunned" seven times by Matt.

When Angelica roused herself, she realized she'd nodded off to sleep and Matt was no longer sitting with her. She was hungry and vaguely recalled Matt saying he was going to get them something to drink. *How long ago was that?* Should she just wait for

427

him to come back? After about five minutes, Angelica decided to make her way to the kitchen for a snack. Maybe Matt was in there. Angelica ate the last two pate crackers, surprised they were still available and praying she would not get sick from chicken livers that may have exhausted their welcome.

Angelica went to the bathroom to freshen up. Someone had peed in the bathtub. *What sense did that make?* She washed her hands and dried them on her dress. She walked back toward the bedroom, squeezing past a few couples in the hallway. Matt's room was lit by a few candles and three people sat on his bed, talking, with one softly playing a guitar. She looked inside the other bedroom which apparently was a graveyard for unfolded and unsorted laundry. She got to Ray's room and was turning back when she heard what sounded like muffled voices. A man moaning? *These freaks and hippies*, she thought. She'd seen Ray just moments earlier in the kitchen. *Who goes to someone's house and avails themselves of a bedroom during a party?* The moaning was becoming rhythmic and against her better judgement, which was definitely impaired, Angelica eased the door open.

She saw Chloe on her knees in front of Matthew. He was leaning against the closet door, his hands stroking her tangle of blonde hair. She was sucking his dick and he was moving it slowly in and out of her mouth. The slurping sounds she made got Angelica nauseated. Looking away, she saw a large book on the floor to her right. It was an oversized hard cover coffee table book of art and artists displayed at the Boston Museum of Fine Art. Angelica picked it up with both hands and came up beside the couple, wishing that Matt would open his eyes and stop her from what she was about to do.

Angelica raised the book up high and brought it down hard on the back of the girl's head. This apparently made her jaw instinctively bite down because Matt's eyes flung open as he let out a primal scream in a voice even he had never heard before. Chloe was immediately on the ground with blood all over her mouth and cheek. Angelica swung the book again and shut Matt up with a crack to the face. She actually heard a *crunch* as his nose sought understanding on the other side of his face. One hand flew to his face, the other to his gnawed penis. He flopped to the floor, writhing and yowling in agony. Angelica dropped the book on Chloe's back and walked out of the room as people began to rush toward the bedroom to see what that noise had been.

Angelica ran down the stairs, all those stairs, as fast as she could, got into her car and took off. She was so glad Peggy wasn't there. She wagered Matt or Chloe wished someone had left the big book of pictures on the coffee table where it belonged. She didn't know how she got there, but Angelica found herself in her parking space outside her apartment building. Her hands ached from gripping the steering wheel so tightly for the entire drive back home.

SIXTY-FOUR

Matt tried calling Angelica to apologize as soon as the day after the party, but only got hung up on. A week later he showed up at her job, insisting that they talk. He had a faint, yellowish green bruise on his left cheek and a small bandage over the bridge of his nose. Both eyes had deep shadows underneath where blood had recently pooled. He looked as if he'd been in a prize fight. They walked outside to the parking lot where Matt stood facing Angelica with his hands at his sides, hers were crossed under her breasts.

"Angelica, honey, I'm so sorry. Please forgive me. Give me one more chance to make this right. I—"

"Let me stop you right there. Let me guess. You love me, you don't know how this happened, you were stoned and didn't know what was happening, it was a one-time thing. How am I doing?"

"Yes! Yes! All of that. I swear."

"Listen to me, Matthew. Stop calling me, don't come to my job, don't come to my house, don't come up to the school. It's over. Please leave me alone."

And with that, Angelica turned and went back inside Tower Records. Matt stood there, lost, for about 60 seconds before he walked to his motorcycle, got on it and took off down Sunset.

Angelica wiped her tears away with some napkins left over from lunch and got back to work.

Years later Angelica would hear that Matt Miller, one of the most successful record producers in the entertainment industry, had died of an overdose of heroin at the age of 35.

When a girl in her office gasped and read the incredulous news aloud, Angelica said simply, "I knew him. We went to school together."

"Wow, what's a Hollywood big shot like him using heroin for? You just never know about people," the girl exclaimed.

"No, I guess you don't." Angelica said.

ngelica fastened her seatbelt as did her mother, Liz. The plane's engines were rumbling low and Angelica felt the tingly butterflies she always felt when she flew. Perhaps another, more tangible reason she seldom went back home during her undergraduate career? She didn't exactly hate flying, but she certainly didn't love it. She always felt flying through the air in a winged metal tube was against the laws of God and the heavens. How long would He remain magnanimous and allow them to get safely to their destination? Irrational? Perhaps.

"Everything okay?" her mother said, patting Angelica's hands which were clenched in her lap.

"I'm fine."

"Detroit is going to be small potatoes after being around the bright lights of Hollywood," her mother said.

Angelica just smiled faintly and looked out of the window as the plane taxied down the runway.

"Well, we're so proud of you, Angelica. I'm glad you're coming back to Michigan."

"I am too, Mama. I am too."

After the incident with Matt, Angelica worked until school began again. It was her Senior year and she wanted no distractions. She quit the record store and concentrated on getting out of UCLA and getting out of Los Angeles. She'd all but banned dating from her life, but did find time to hang out with friends, going to Disneyland, and even taking a road trip to San Diego to enjoy their famous zoo.

Angelica Tanner graduated with honors having accumulated a 4.0 grade point average. Her whole family, Liz, Aunt Fannie, Uncle Ned and his wife Ella, their children, her grandma and grandpa, all came to witness her big day. Angelica's mother stayed an additional week in Los Angeles as Angelica shut down her undergrad life. She gave away or sold everything in her apartment, even her car. Yes, she'd had some wonderful, vivid, memorable times in the City of Angels, but she knew it was time for her to go. She would spend the summer at home in Detroit and then move up to Ann Arbor for law school. She was ready for a new chapter in her life.

The plane ascended, tucking its landing gear away as it flew up and over the Pacific Ocean. Angelica never got used to the idea that flying out of L.A., the plane had to turn around over the water to head in the right direction. She closed her eyes. *Always the long way home.*

SIXTY-SIX

"Hey, Sheila, over here!" Angelica called out, waving a little more frantically than necessary. She mouthed "sorry" to the maître d', who was now staring directly at her. Angelica had phoned Sheila and asked her to meet up for dinner. They agreed to meet at the swanky Pontchartrain Wine Cellars on West Larned downtown, right across from Cobo Hall. With all the buildings lit up and the beautiful expanse of the Detroit River nearby, this part of the city was particularly lovely and photogenic, the setting of almost every post card sent from Detroit.

During their Senior year, Angelica, Ricky, Carlton, and Sheila spent a memorable Saturday night dancing until the wee hours of the morning at the world famous Roostertail nightclub, on the waterfront. Twin's younger sister was having a Sweet Sixteen party there and though it would normally be verboten for upperclassman to attend such an affair, no one would dare turn down an opportunity to see the elegant Roostertail, a venue that hosted famous musical acts from Motown to Hollywood and a fixture on many a post card of the city.

Right after Mrs. Davis declared her truce and liberated Sheila, she and Angelica found themselves across the river at the Hotel Viscount in Windsor, Ontario. The legal drinking age in Detroit and Windsor was 18 and though they were still minors, they were never carded. They found that pretty girls needn't worry about coming out of their purses with identification nor money for drinks as gentlemen were so generous with libations, the girls had to ask the bar to stop serving them. The evening ended with tasty and sobering Chinese food in the city's bustling Chinatown.

Being in Canada always made Angelica feel as if she were in another world, surely what she thought Europe must be like. They went from the Viscount's rooftop club to the Great Western Park on the riverfront off Ouellette Street, to gaze at the lights of their beloved and bedraggled Detroit just across the water. Windsor was vibrant, yet peaceful and calm. People were friendly and chatty and interestingly of all, they looked like Americans! Yes, Angelica realized that technically they were North Americans, but this was still a foreign country after all! By contrast, Detroit seemed a tranquil and sleepy backdrop as barges and ships glided by, their whistles blaring, their wakes disrupting the lapping waves. Angelica knew better. In truth her city was as ruthless and violent as that river.

Even the landmarks were frightening. If they drove to Canada during the day, which they had done on occasion to go horseback riding, Angelica kept her eyes riveted on the expansive Ambassador Bridge and the road across so as not to be distracted by the 352-foot-tall smoke stacks that seemed to rise out of the river, threatening to contact the bridge. They were known as the "7 Sisters" and part of Detroit Edison's power plant, however, Angelica felt they were cunning sirens designed to distract cars into plunging off the bridge. It was a 1.5-mile ride of sheer terror.

Travelling at night wasn't any better, for as they crossed the Ambassador Bridge into Canada, its red neon letters seemed to signal an invitation to the abyss of black, shimmering water underneath. There was a tunnel for those enamored of terra firma, but the truth was it was somehow worse with its yellow tiles, fluorescent lights, suspicious puddles of mysterious water that seemingly sprung up every few feet, and blaring horns from anxious fools who couldn't get out of the claustrophobic mile of tunnel fast enough. *It's 75 feet under the Detroit River for Chrissakes! What crazy people worked on this thing!*

Sheila and Angelica hugged tightly when Sheila got to the table, the two of them so cognizant of the sense of relief and accomplishment they shared having graduated from college. "Lucky" wasn't the word for what they were, and they knew it. Sheila looked good. Her once skinny body was now full and womanly. She wore her hair in a stylish afro, not too big, but not so small as to be considered a "natural." She had spent most of the summer working in Boston, coming home only days ago, a week before Angelica would be leaving for Ann Arbor.

Angelica's summer, the summer of 1972, was spent on seemingly endless cookouts with her family and even family friends she'd not seen since childhood. Her mother and grandparents bragged unabashedly about her collegiate accomplishments and her future as a law student at the University of Michigan. It amused Angelica to hear various embellishments on her accomplishments at each telling, and trying to make any corrections were fruitless.

"I should go away more often," Angelica said, sarcastically.

"Tell me about it, girl. You see I took my time getting back. I'm looking for an apartment as we speak. My parents insist on treating me like I'm still in high school. I need to have my own place so I can date and have a private life."

"My mother told me she was glad I didn't do anything foolish like get engaged while I was at school. 'Plenty of time for that' she says. You know, I never even told her about Matt? She almost never asked me if I was dating. Like if she didn't mention it, it wasn't happening, you know?"

"That's funny," Sheila replied.

"I tried to tell her about us over the phone a couple of times but my mom, shit, I think she might be prejudiced!"

Sheila laughed. Who could understand their parents?

"Did I tell you I'm up for a job at the Free Press? It's as an assistant to the editor, but if I play my cards right, I'll be a writer in no time."

"Wow, Sheila. That's terrific. I'm proud of you, girl. We need to order some wine or something to toast to the future."

"Hey, let's order some, shoot, what is this restaurant famous for?"

"Great French food and Cold Duck, baby!"

"Yes, Cold Duck. It's champagne, right?"

"I guess. Sparkling wine. It's so, so good."

"How do you know? You had it before? You've been here before?"

"I've never been here, but yeah, I've had Cold Duck."

"Oh yeah, when? With who?"

"A million years ago, girl. Typical kid stuff, you know," Angelica said, trying to punch down the picture rising up in her mind of her and Ricky in his basement on one of the best days. Ever.

"Well, I was just asking because I thought I was your drinking buddy back in school. The two of us could put a hurtin' on some Boone's Farm Apple wine."

"Hurt it? We killed it! We thought we were so grown, so sophisticated. Remember when we used to cross the bridge to 'Europe?'"

"You could not tell us that Canada was not somehow actually Europe and that we weren't international travelers," Sheila answered.

"And the Sloe Gin Fizzes those Canadian dudes used to buy for us at the Viscount. We're lucky we never had any problems getting home. But we were never *really* drunk, huh?"

"Nope. Never. And if we'd been over the line, well, hot egg rolls and egg drop soup took care of it. We always looked out for each other and nobody messed with us."

The girls drank and ate and talked and gossiped about everyone they could think of—who was married, who was pregnant and unmarried, who had what job, who'd moved away and even who had died. Eventually, the silence flung itself over them like a weighted net. There was something there, heavy and daring them to speak of it. Angelica sighed.

"Heard anything about Ricky Williams?"

"Nope, not a thing. Man, it's like he disappeared. A figment of our young imaginations," Sheila joked.

"If only," Angelica said, reaching for her wine glass.

SIXTY-SEVEN

L ife in Ann Arbor in general and at U of M Law School in particular, was wonderful. To Angelica, living in Ann Arbor was like hiding in plain sight. She was close enough to Detroit to get back for a visit every once in a while, but she had no fear of someone showing up unannounced on her doorstep because they happened to be "in the neighborhood."

Angelica was excited and engaged as a law student. She'd decided no matter how difficult it might be, she would not date anyone her first year as a 1L. She frequented parties, concerts and all things Wolverines, but remained friendly and elusive with the young men who approached her.

Her first year, Angelica took the full load of classes and marveled at how well she was suited to the study of law. She couldn't believe more people didn't pursue this age-old practice. Angelica loved how logical the tenants of ethics and legality were, delighting in things making sense, feeling like these small discoveries were easily deciphered inside her brain. Angelica quickly became a favorite of her professors, even the ones who took themselves so seriously as to treat their students as mere acolytes. This young woman could break down stodgy formalism with an incisive query or gentle ribbing humor. Where her peers tread fearfully, Angelica splashed in the puddles of discourse with big boots and her teachers respected her for it.

As a 1L Angelica was asked, after being suggested by one of her professors, to clerk for the revered and renown attorney Wynton Winslow, founding partner of the prestigious and storied Philadelphia law firm of Winslow and White. Even Angelica knew this was unprecedented and unheard of really, for a first-year student. She loved working as a summer associate in the Detroit office of Winslow and White and served the firm writing briefs, doing meticulous research and being generally indispensable. She'd never worked so hard and stayed up so late and gotten so little sleep in her life.

Angelica spent the next summer as a 2L again in Detroit as she clerked for the most respected judicial figure in Michigan, the honorable Judge Damon Keith of the U.S. District Court for the Eastern District of Michigan. Her family could not stop bragging about Angelica's plumb assignment. Judge Keith was an icon in the black community and among his peers nationally.

1974 ushered in the final year of maize and blue as Angelica entered her last year of law school at U of M. That year also brought a sea change to politics in the city of Detroit as its first black mayor, Coleman A. Young, was elected. He would serve an unprecedented 5 terms. He was a shoot-from-the-hip, take-no-prisoners, no bullshit man for whom profanity was an art form. He divided and united with his tactics to tame the city he loved and become a hero to many. Angelica's uncle bragged that they'd both served in the same company as Tuskegee Airmen, the first squadron of black fighter pilots to fly missions during the Second World War.

By 1978 Angelica had been working for three years at the prestigious firm of DuBois, Tristan and Webb in downtown Detroit. The building she worked in, a 25-story art deco tower, looked as though it were glass and marble thrown to the sky. Angelica was happy and fulfilled and soon discovered the slippery dynamics of working in the microcosm that was her office. Unwittingly but deservedly, she was the golden girl of the firm. Her reputation had preceded her and made some of her colleagues prejudge her before ever laying an eye on her. Angelica conducted herself with a quiet confidence her first year and eventually blossomed into a skilled litigator and trusted advisor to the senior partners.

Angelica had become particularly close with three other lawyers in her office. They were as different as their outward appearances, but coalesced into a monolith of ass kickers in the courtroom. They called themselves *Quadzilla!* There was the tall, lanky, freckled faced Gertrude Scherhoffer. She always had pencils, sharp and ready, sticking out of her puff of curly red hair. Her steely blue eyes were impenetrable to everyone except her friends and she cursed like a sailor. She was liberal and liberated and liked to say, "That's Ms. Sailor to you, asshole," if someone dared to try to rebuke her for her colorful repartee.

Malcolm Sandringham was as British as his name implied. Short, blond and rather rotund, he shyly enjoyed his "cheeky mates," as he referred to Angelica and the others. They often called him "Sir Malcolm" and teased him that he'd only barely been relieved from having to parade around in a powdered wig.

Then there was Angelica's favorite, Trevor Hastings. He was physically gorgeous with deep brown eyes, long black lashes and raven hair. He was tall and well-built and all types of Southern charm. He was also as gay as a floral arrangement and proud of it. He could almost immediately see all sides of an argument and peppered his conclusions with phrases like, "So, here's where my grits get cold" or "So, here's why there's no more sweet tea in that pitcher."

DuBois, Tristan and Webb was one of the largest law firms in Detroit, handling millions of dollars in corporate mergers and acquisitions, also the real estate and divorces of the wealthy scions of industry. Particularly, litigation as a result of the behavior of said wealthy scions and their naughty offspring. Quadzilla was instrumental in arguments that kept many a scandal from becoming all that was remembered about these families. Being part of a great team allowed Angelica to learn and observe without being the focus of attention all the time. It also let her know she wanted to practice Public Interest or Family Law someday where she might really be of service to people in need. As much as it pained the partners, they allowed Angelica to take on some pro-bono work to keep her interested, after all, they wanted her to be happy and remain on their side. As an opponent working with another firm, she would be formidable. Who wanted that?

Angelica had been tested when she clerked for Judge Winslow and Judge Keith. On her few forays out in the field to interview the occasional reprobate, she'd met men whose intensely vacant eyes echoed coldness and anger, even when their lips were upturned and smiling. She knew that to these hardened men, who'd been in prison more than out, she was just a chump—someone to get over on so they could get a new trial or maybe even get out of their incarceration altogether. She learned to be almost as calculating as they, not allowing her emotions to get the better of her, but rather, instead using her intellect and instincts. Yet, she was still able to talk to these felons as human beings and convey that she had compassion for them and most importantly, was not afraid of them. It was at those times her mind would flash onto Enrique Williams. Was he lost to her forever? God only knew what kind of animal he'd been turned into?

Sidney Meadows, now a judge, watched the trajectory of young Ms. Tanner's career with keen interest. He remembered she had been a friend of his son, Carlton. *Had they kept in touch?*

442

He didn't know, but he did know he needed Angelica Tanner working for his old firm, Meadows, Cohen and Lively. He'd have to figure out the best way to approach her. Perhaps Carlton could help with the introduction and maybe even persuade his old friend to make a move.

SIXTY-EIGHT

ngelica appraised herself from various angles as she looked in her bedroom mirror. She didn't want to look too conservative nor too casual for her meeting with Judge Meadows. A scoop neck, black jersey dress with a single strand of opera length pearls. She'd been invited to the London Chop House and it was pretty fancy. She was never as taken aback as when she received the telephone call from his secretary saying Judge Meadows wanted to speak with her. Why did she want to call him an asshole? She didn't even know him, having met him maybe once and that was at Dodge's graduation. Malcolm called him an "old sod" when she told her team about the call, but they told her she had to go to hear what he wanted. During her third year of law school, as she was looking at post graduate employment opportunities, she purposely put the offer from Meadows, Cohen and Lively to the side. It just didn't feel right to her.

Now she was following the maître d' to a table in a corner. *Strategic*, she mused. He probably had a lot to say and didn't want to compete with louder conversations, prying ears and the like. A slender gentleman of average height stood up as Angelica approached. *My, he's aged a lot*, Angelica thought. *But, weren't Carlton's parents already old when he was born?* The younger man next to him seemed to stop drinking his libation mid sip as if stricken. He sat the glass on the table and sprung to his feet. Carlton

444

smiled wide and moved to pull out Angelica's chair before the maître d' could and that caused a micro stand-off between the two of them. The man nodded at Angelica and turned on his heels to go back to the front of the restaurant.

Angelica was more beautiful than Carlton had remembered. Her brown hair hung in waves just below her shoulders. Her olive colored eyes were keen and smiling, along with that gorgeous mouth. Carlton decided then and there, Angelica Tanner would be his.

Carlton had grown quite handsome, and Angelica couldn't lie to herself. She once liked this guy, but that was before he went all weird and certainly before she'd met…well, she didn't need to think about that. *This is going to be interesting.* Small talk and the usual pleasantries were exchanged as Angelica looked over her menu. She only wanted ice water with her meal and made sure her tone was nonjudgmental, and her eyes were sufficiently averted from the two high ball glasses that sat in front of each of her dinner companions.

Finally, the waiter had taken their order as well as his leave, and Angelica felt this was Sidney Meadows' cue to begin his appeal. She smiled warmly and confidently, making sure to keep her expression steady and her emotions masked. She believed it was called a "poker face." When Judge Meadows invited Carlton and Angelica to dinner, he had a very definite agenda and an enticing offer for Angelica Tanner, blessed by his former firm and abetted, hopefully, by his son. Having a star like Angelica would allow them to offer more pro-bono services for a city whose citizens were clearly ailing and in need and the accompanying publicity would bode so very well for the firm. Who could resist orchestrated altruism? He'd had it on good authority that this was the work that interested Angelica. She won or helped win every case that crossed her desk. He tried to grease the wheels by talking about one of her recent victories that peers and those in the legal arena were still talking about.

The subject Judge Meadows was blathering on about was the case of a young woman named Naomi Najiri. Naomi was a 21-year-old paraplegic confined to a wheelchair from the age of 18. Her parents had emigrated to the U.S. from Iraq with her older brother five years before her birth. Through their enterprising hard work, they came to own several gas stations in Detroit and suburban Dearborn, Michigan, where they lived. One night when her parents were away enjoying a play at the Detroit Masonic Temple, their house caught fire and Naomi was trapped and killed. Her caregiver, Gracie Dec, had been unable to rescue the girl. Everyone was heartbroken by the tragedy and when the smoke cleared, literally, Mr. and Mrs. Najiri were suing the state of Michigan, the agency that provided Mrs. Dec's services and Gracie Dec as an individual for civil negligence.

Angelica and her team worked on the case in defense of Gracie Dec, pro bono. Mrs. Dec, a widow who'd emigrated from Poland with her late husband, was feisty and a fighter. It was discovered that Naomi put herself in a wheelchair after her second and more serious attempt at suicide. She'd shot herself in the chest, missing her heart but not her spine. Years of physical and psychotherapy had done Naomi a world of good, bringing her and her parents closer together. They'd modified a small bedroom off the kitchen on the ground floor of their home for her. Social services ordered that they expand her bedroom door, so she could enter and exit more easily, even though the Najiris didn't mind the teamwork of picking Naomi up while one or the other wedged the wheelchair into or out of her room.

Gracie Dec had complained to the agency she worked for as well as the Najiris that Naomi needed a larger ingress. The night she burned to death, Naomi had been using acetone to remove

446

her nail polish and threw several chemical soaked cotton balls into her wastebasket. She was still next to the basket, near her window curtains when she lit a cigarette and threw the match, not quite extinguished, into the wastebasket. *Whoosh!* A flash rose up, singeing her hand as the cigarette fell into her lap, but she didn't feel it, so panicked was she over the fire that was quickly becoming a consuming maw of flames. Why hadn't she called out to Gracie who was fixing the girl a snack in the kitchen?

By the time Gracie smelled the smoke and came to Naomi's room, the girl was engulfed in flames from the waist down and foolishly trying to smother the fire by flogging herself with bed pillows that were nearby. Gracie raced in and grabbed the handles on the back of the chair, but they burned her hands. She managed to somehow get the chair to the door trying to get Naomi out of the room. They were both screaming as Gracie attempted to pull the chair out of the room backward. The rubber on the wheels had melted and it was impossible to go any further. Naomi tried to free herself from the disintegrating chair, but she was strapped in and those straps were all but melted and seared to her body.

Gracie ran to the kitchen to get a knife to cut Naomi out of the chair, but the heat and flames and smoke were too intense when she came back to the bedroom. Gracie went back into the kitchen to call the police and then she ran outside screaming for the neighbors to help. Gracie Dec, to anyone who heard the full story, was a hero. She didn't deserve to come out of 3 weeks in a hospital burn unit to be slapped with a negligence lawsuit. Angelica Tanner, Gertrude, Malcolm and Trevor posited that Naomi Najiri could have been trying to kill herself for the third and final time. Also, her parents were at fault for not making the door wide enough for anyone to have rescued their daughter.

The Najiris, good Catholics, could never understand or come to grips with the palette of maladies suffered by their only daughter—depression, suicidal thoughts, even smoking cigarettes. The girl had shamed her family. Why make it so easy for her to escape the confines of her bedroom every day? She should feel guilty watching them pick her up to move her in and out of her room. To her parent's way of thinking, that small struggle served as a reminder to their daughter what she'd forfeited by being sinfully ungrateful. Angelica and her team got special recognition by the state for saving them from a protracted lawsuit built on a foundation of spurious charges.

During the conversation Judge Meadows hit her with the highlights and high-profile cases handled by Meadows, Cohen and Lively. He told her of their urgent need for her legal prowess. Carlton tried to chime in with the old saw of her needing to "remember the good times," but that forced banality fell flat and lead to an awkward silence. How could she remember the good times without talking about Ricky? She felt she shouldn't speak of him without some cue from the Meadows men, but none came. Surely Judge Meadows recalled the events of 10 years ago?

Angelica smiled and said, "Judge Meadows, your son doesn't even work at your firm."

A little bomb had exploded over their heads. She felt a bit mischievous by saying this, curious as to the answer.

"Well, perhaps my son is not as, uh, talented as you are my dear," the judge said, simply.

Shrapnel was raining down on Carlton and he never let his expression change. As for Angelica, she didn't care for the "my dear" at the end of the retort, but she let it pass. Condescension did not curry favor.

The judge quickly added, "Don't get me wrong. Carlton is a damn fine lawyer."

Carlton genuinely smiled, mostly because he and his father both knew this was not quite the case. Carlton had worked at his dad's firm briefly, after graduating law school. The perception, in this case it was true, that he was there only because his father had been a partner, was hard to overcome. Carlton came to see it as a way to exact sexual favors from almost every female in the office. He was transferred after several complaints were issued to the office manager. They were lucky no law suits were filed. Angelica was cutting the succulent flesh of the filet mignon in her plate and did not see the look of disgust that Judge Meadows shot his son. The smile fell from Carlton's lips like pearls from the strands of a broken necklace.

One particular indiscretion had cost Sid Meadows $5,000 and his son his job. A young woman, a leggy blonde who clerked for one of the partners, Morris Cohen, had caught Carlton's eye. She had refused his entreaties and advances over the entire summer. On her last day before going back home to Ohio, she agreed to go out for a farewell dinner with a small group of colleagues which included Carlton, who'd rented a limousine. After dinner, they hopped from bar to bar along Woodward Avenue from downtown to Highland Park. Somehow, Carlton had gotten the limo driver to drop off four of the other celebrants, save the blonde clerk, back at the office without any regard for their ability to navigate homeward. The alcohol had made the young woman chatty and quite lively—for a while. Carlton, sloppy and drunk, rolled around the expanse of the limousine like an unpinned hand grenade. He told the driver to take them across the Ambassador Bridge into Windsor, Ontario.

Carlton put his arm around the drunk girl, whose bright red bandana had fallen over one eye, and proceeded to relieve her of her panties. The girl passed out like a chloroformed hostage. Carlton cursed and tossed the pair of underwear on the floor and was soon unconscious himself. He awoke to a flurry of palms, fists, and fingernails. The woman had come to, saw her state of semi-undress and assumed the worst as Carlton yelped and tried to escape the feminine assault. They were both suddenly wide awake, sober and still inside the limo in the parking lot of the offices of Meadows, Cohen and Lively. Carlton ran inside the building, while the young woman gathered her belongings and found her car. The limousine driver sat silently, waiting for Carlton to emerge from the building. He was paid by the hour, so he was content with how lengthy the assignment had proven to be, not believing his good fortune!

Carlton ended up calling Sidney, who had to convince the clerk not to press charges. She left Detroit, Michigan with a check for $5,000 and Sidney Meadows was left to give his partners a version of the events that led to him sending his only son to the unemployment line. He even had to come up with an abridged version to silence Mavis.

SIXTY-NINE

Although Angelica had vowed not to date while in her first year of law school, somehow her grip on that promise slackened soon after it was made. A friend from her Contracts class insisted that she had the "perfect guy" for Angelica, which begged the question, "If he's so great, why aren't you with him?" Something about practically being a brother and other excuses issued forth until finally, Angelica agreed to a blind date.

The fact that they went to a nice restaurant in Southfield was a plus as far as Angelica was concerned. Maybe this guy had something going for himself. However, before the salad even made an appearance, Angelica found herself squinting at her date as she fended off one churlish remark after the next. According to him, he'd historically been used, nay, abused by money mad women who seemed to only be interested in getting the most expensive thing on the menu (a not so subtle hint as to what her dining options might be?) and stuffing their greedy guts. Angelica realized she must have looked like a deer in headlights with the silly shock of a smile across her face.

"Will you excuse me? I need to use the ladies room," Angelica said, exiting the table. She found their waitress, a very large woman, near the front of the restaurant at the bar.

"Hi, can you do me a favor?" Angelica asked the mountain of a woman.

The waitress's hands looked like two small hams, but she was so enthusiastic and attentive, Angelica knew she could be trusted with the task.

"Yes, ma'am," the woman said, smiling.

"Look, I want to go ahead and pay for my dinner, okay? Just wrap it up and hold on to it for me until I can grab it from you. I'm going to eat my salad with the guy at the table, but I want you to take the salad plates only when my food is ready to go, okay?"

"Um, sure. Is there something wrong, ma'am?"

Angelica was bringing a $20 bill out of her purse.

"No, I'm just leaving before I stab that dude at the table. Keep the change," Angelica said as she pressed the money into the woman's palm, looking around for her escape route.

"Wow, you okay? I thought I was going to have to send a search party for you."

"No, no. You know how we girls are," she said with a forced giggle.

The waitress brought the salads and Angelica ate hers slowly but picked up the pace when she saw the waitress looking intently in her direction. Soon she was at the table, picking up the salad plates with a knowing smile. Angelica didn't like that "tell" and was tempted to trip the girl as she walked away. *Is she trying to ruin my plan?*

"Oh goodness," Angelica exclaimed as she rifled through her purse. "I left my lipstick in the ladies' room. I'll be right back."

"Yeah, okay. Dinner is coming you know. Chop, chop," the fool said.

Yeah, chop, chop your fucking head off, Angelica thought. She coolly swung by the bar and picked up the brown paper bag with her food inside and silently mouthed "Thank you" to the waitress who was still highly amused by what was happening. When Angelica got outside, she realized that she'd made a colossal mistake by allowing her date to pick her up from her apartment. Stranded! She'd sublet an apartment on West Grand Boulevard for the summer, but it was so far away from where she was standing, it may as well have been in another state. She needed to find a cab or a phone booth to call one. She was so angry at herself she began to laugh.

"I am glad you are laughing, Lovely."

The voice was coming from inside the long black limousine that had slid up in front of her at the curb. Angelica looked at the rear window as it rolled all the way down and she saw a gorgeous, honey colored man. With the assistance of the restaurant marquee and street lights, she could see he had wavy, sandy blond hair and the clearest blue gray eyes. He spoke again.

"Do you need a ride? May I drop you somewhere?" the man said with a thick, sonorous Spanish accent.

"No, thank you. Get lost, man."

"I was lost until you found me, *Señiorita*."

Angelica glanced at her watch. She had to find a phone. She wanted this creep to take off and mind his own business, but she found herself with a retort aimed at him.

"Ha! *I* found *you*, huh?"

"*Sí.* I saw how you handled that boy in the restaurant and thought 'She is as powerful as she is beautiful.' And then you were gone. I raced to have my driver bring me out to follow your car. But like kismet, you are here. My heart is flying from my chest."

Angelica thawed and laughed despite herself. This guy was good.

"You sure know how to rap to a girl, don't you?"

"I do not know what this *rap* is but it is good, no?"

"You're for real, huh?"

"Yes, beautiful one, I am. Please allow me to take you home. You are lost here. Perhaps your friend is looking for you by now, yes?"

He opened the car door. Could this night get any worse? Yes! She could be raped and killed by this beautiful stranger! Angelica got in the car. After she'd given the driver directions as to the best route to reach her home, the man next to her put out his hand.

"Vincente Cruz. And, you are?"

"Angelica Tanner. Where are you from?"

"Venezuela," the man replied. "I am in Detroit to work, *sí*, to consult on the future of automobiles."

Angelica liked that he said "few-sher" for *future*.

"Are they going away? Will we be flying around instead of driving?" she asked, only half-joking.

"No, well, not soon. I am more about efficiency. No more eating up the petrol, ah, gas."

Vincente, once he heard Angelica was a fan of muscle cars, was very impressed that a girl knew so much about cars. Was this common to those who grow up in Detroit? She assured him it wasn't, and he apologized for breaking the bad news that the future of the automobile was smaller and fuel efficient.

"The Americans are distracted by the crisis with the oil and a very bad president."

"Precedent? Which bad precedent?" She was a law student and figured she knew a thing or two about legal precedents.

"No, *presidenté*, president. Mr. Nixon."

"Oh," she said, feeling a bit foolish. "Wait, who do you work for?"

"The Japanese."

"The Japs?! Man, that's a four-letter word in Detroit. I wouldn't say that too loud, sir."

Vincente laughed.

"That is clever. Nevertheless, the Japanese automobile will be smaller and better than what you have now, American and Japanese. They are always improving. Enough talk of business."

By the time they arrived in front of Angelica's building, Vincente and Angelica were deep in conversation about intraracial prejudice in Latin America. He was Venezuelan, but his mother was German. His family was every hue, eye color and hair type, according to Vincente. He understood that he was treated differently based on his skin tone alone and he was disheartened by this. Vincente Cruz was 35 years old and had been married for 10 years. He had three children, all boys. So, Angelica was quite shocked when the subject changed.

"I am in Detroit until the end of August. I don't care to visit with ladies on the street or my colleagues at the office. You are beautiful, smart and busy. I think you can be, are, mature enough to accept that I want to be with you only for the time I am here. I am asking you…to be my lover. I feel you need to experience a man, a real man and all that I know about love. Making love."

Angelica realized that she was staring at this man, her mouth agape and no words coming forth. He reached into his suit pocket and retrieved a slender white business card. He reached into the opposite side and brought out a beautiful, heavy, gold pen and wrote on the back of the card.

"*Aye, querida*, I hope you are not insulted. Be complimented. Please think on it and call me when you are ready. You will not regret it," he said, extending his hand with the card between his long fingers like a cigarette. "Pedro!" he called out as the driver got out and came around to the rear passenger side of the limo and opened the door.

Angelica took the card.

"Good night, Mr. Cruz. Thanks for driving me home," she said, sliding out of the car.

"Goodnight, lovely Angelica. Angel."

The door closed and, in a moment, he was off, heading down the block. Angelica shut the heavy vestibule door behind her and boarded the old fashioned wooden elevator with the retracting cage door. During the creaky ascent, she kept thinking about what had just happened. What did he call her? *Angel.* Only one person had permission to call her that.

That week Angelica was occupied at the law office from the time she got in until she went home. The thought of that man, his body riding hers, his lips covering her breasts, seeped into her mind like a slow leak. She found herself stuck mid-sentence when speaking to her work colleagues, her train of thought having taken leave of its rails or reading and re-reading the same passage in a law book with no understanding of what she was reading nor how much time had passed. By day five, Angelica had no choice but to pick up the phone and call Vincente.

He picked up the phone on the second ring. He immediately recognized her voice and greeted her warmly.

"Can I send my car for you?"

"No, give me your address," Angelica countered.

The address he gave was out in Grosse Pointe Shores along Lakeshore Road, where the mansions were, where the rich people lived. Angelica felt she was in over her head and maybe she should just turn around and go back down Jefferson, back to her place. This was some big girl shit, and well, she was a big girl, wasn't she? If she wasn't, they'd both know it soon enough. She found the house and pulled into the roundabout and there he was, standing on the steps. Vincente came and opened her car door for her and once she was standing, he embraced her fully, tightly. He pulled away from her and looked into her eyes, smiling.

"Thank you for coming. It is lonely out here."

Vincente showed her the house, even discovering some private alcoves he'd not seen or noticed before. The Japanese car company was renting the place for his use and apparently, money was no object. They sat in the solarium and looked out at the dark water reflecting the heavens above.

"Is this still the Detroit River or Lake St. Clair?" Angelica asked, nervously.

"I was hoping you could tell me," he answered, smiling.

457

"It's so beautiful. One day, I'm going to live like this," Angelica said, without any hint of self-consciousness.

Vincente sensed Angelica's nerves were on edge.

"Angelica, you are not a prostitute. You are not, how you say, to be used. I am direct to save time and to be clear. You are here because you want to be, as am I. There is no money, only making love to one another and spending time together. I have to trust you. Will you stay with me tonight?"

Angelica hadn't thought about the fact that this man had to trust her as much as she had to trust him. Trust that they were both of sound mind and body and those bodies wanted to have sex with each other.

"I don't know, okay?" she finally answered. "I think you want someone with more experience. I've only been with two guys in my life," she said, rising from her chair, unsure of where she was trying to go.

"You like men, no?"

"Yes, of course. I just never had a lot of opportunities…"

Now she was embarrassed and could feel her blood rising, flushing her neck.

"Hearing you say these things—you are even more beautiful to me. You are like a gift on Christmas," Vincente said excitedly. His eyes flashed a deep and dark blue as he became serious. "At the end of our time together, no man will be able to resist your sensuality. It will be your secret weapon. The art of love simply adds to beauty and brains like a rose to candlelight and fine wine."

"No man can resist me? Not even you?" she teased, crossing her arms. Was she trying to steady herself? Was she shaking?

"*Sí*, and that is how it will be until I go back to Venezuela. You can, how you say, handle me, yes?"

"I think—"

"First lesson, my love. Confidence. Nothing is sexier than this. It fits every woman if she dares to wear it."

He opened his arms and made a small gesture with his fingers. Angelica knew once in his embrace, she was captured like a butterfly in a net. She moved just outside his reach.

"I will warn you now. Do not fall in love with me, Young Heart."

He said this without guile or ego, hoping Angelica was listening to him. Angelica unfolded her arms and laughed sharply.

"Hey, Vinnie! You worry about yourself, okay? You just may fall in love with *me*."

Vincente grabbed Angelica by her arms and pulled her to him. "*Sí, Señorita. Yo ya estoy enamorado de ti.*"

SEVENTY

"S o, did you date much in law school?" Carlton was asking.

There was no way he or really anyone, would understand her first summer in law school. The summer of 1973. The summer of Vincente Cruz. She'd decided never to reveal it. To anyone. Not because she was ashamed, quite the contrary, Vincente forced her to grow up. He wanted a woman in his bed and she became just that. He treated her as his equal and what they shared that summer was for the two of them, only.

Vincente had been a glorious distraction. She worked hard at the firm and he worked hard for his employer, but they'd decided at the beginning of their affair that they would play just as hard. He wouldn't even allow Angelica to fix a meal.

"No *domestica*," he would say.

They usually ate at Giovanni's Roma Café or The Ivanhoe Café. They drank at Jacoby's German Biergarten or The Apex Bar. At times she felt she was dreaming with her eyes wide open, and she knew she would soon have to wake up. It was a true test of her maturity when it came time for Vincente to go back to South America--and she failed. She didn't want him to leave, yet she herself had to journey back to school in Ann Arbor. His glistening eyes answered the question of how much she'd meant to him and how much he'd miss their nights together. That made it easier for Angelica to let go. A moment in time to fuel her confidence and desire as a woman had slipped into a memory. What was now on the table before her and Carlton were her remarkable contributions as a lawyer and she'd allow that be the loudest note in the song she sung for him.

"No, I didn't really date in law school. I was pretty busy."

"Sounds kind of boring," Carlton said, snickering.

"No, it really wasn't. You'd be surprised, actually," Angelica countered, stopping her disobedient thoughts like a cartoon character running full speed into a suddenly materialized stop sign. "I learned a lot, studied really long and hard," she said, amused by the double entendre as she envisioned the cartoon character now being clobbered by the stop sign.

"Well, I did my internships here in the city working for my father, which is no surprise, I'm sure. It was a grind, but there were some fun times too. You never went out?"

"When I did get out, I had a ton of fun. Me and my friends went to a lot of discotheques. Some cool ones up in Southfield and over in Windsor, too. We would shut those clubs down, Jack!"

"No live music? I remember you were a fiend for live concerts."

Angelica thought it was sweet of Carlton to recall such an enduring part of her persona.

"I still read my *Creem* and *Rolling Stone* and go see some good music. You know the Michigan Palace on Bagley and Grand River downtown?"

"Yeah, it closed a couple of years ago."

"Well, that place, even when it was on its last legs, was gorgeous. Marble spires, red velvet drapes, chandeliers. Much too good for rock 'n roll!" Angelica exclaimed.

Carlton laughed as Angelica continued to speak.

"Seriously, I loved seeing concerts there. I saw David Bowie on his Diamond Dogs tour, Bob Seger and the Silver Bullet Band, and this new guy named Bruce Springsteen. A few weeks later, I'm in a bookstore and I look up and see the same guy on the cover of *Time and* on the cover of *Newsweek*. I'm talking simultaneously! I mean, how cool is that?

Carlton just sat smiling and staring at Angelica.

"You're so passionate. I love that about you."

The restaurant had lost most of its patrons by the time Carlton wound up his conversation with his old friend, his father having abandoned them after dessert. Sidney had to trust his son wouldn't say or do something stupid or irredeemably ridiculous over after dinner drinks with Angelica Tanner to torpedo the firm's opportunity.

"I guess you're dating someone, huh?" Carlton asked, sending up a trial balloon.

"Yes. I'm dating a really great guy who works for R.L. Polk. His name is Tony. Tony Hillman."

The check finally came and the waiter pretended he wasn't pissed that their table never turned over all night. *One seating, one set of diners and probably one lousy tip.* Tables generally turned over with new patrons as many as 3 times a night and the waiter was quite unhappy that these people had selfishly held their table all evening with no regard for his economic potential. Carlton laid his BankAmericard into the little tray left on the table to be retrieved by the waiter, then held out his hand to Angelica. She didn't know if he was going to shake her hand or what? Angelica took his hand as he looked her in her eyes.

"I'm glad that Tony guy is so nice. It's not going to do him a bit of good."

"**I** have messages for you, Angelica," Leamon said, sweeping into Angelica's office and slapping the small squares of pink paper down on her desk with a decided flourish.

"Wow, let me guess...Carlton Meadows," she said with mock derision.

"Looks like he's tapering off to only three times a day, so sorry to disappoint you."

They both laughed.

"It's not enough that him and his daddy browbeat me into taking this job?!" she exclaimed, facetiously.

Six months after that fateful repast with the Meadows men, she was firmly ensconced at Meadows, Cohen and Lively. The best part was that Quadzilla remained intact. Gertrude, Malcolm and Trevor all moved over to the new firm with Angelica. It wasn't that they were unhappy where they were, hell, neither was Angelica. Judge Meadows had promised Angelica she could "write your own ticket" and bring along anyone she felt was necessary for a successful transition. The other three agreed that they all together formed something akin to lightening in a bottle and who could give that up? Then there was the money. Having one's salary increased by 50% was a great incentive.

Carlton was sweetly unrelenting in his bid to be recognized by Angelica. It seemed whenever she was spending quiet time with Tony at her apartment, flowers would appear at her door, always from Carlton. At first, Tony laughed and joked that this guy wanted his girl, but soon the cards and flowers began to make Tony angry. It was a sign of disrespect, plain and simple. Angelica tried to reassure her boyfriend that Carlton was just an old friend who was reconnecting with an old friend.

Soon enough, Tony declared, "It's me or it's this dude. It's your choice."

Angelica let Tony know there was no choice to be made and that it was likely she was just being wooed professionally as she'd not yet made a decision to leave her firm. She also let Mr. Hillman know she didn't enjoy ultimatums. Within a few weeks, they split up and Angelica joined Meadows, Cohen and Lively.

One of the perks Angelica enjoyed was having a paralegal and assistant dedicated to her and her team. Leamon Bradley was a Detroit native and a mama's boy who'd grown up in the Pentecostal church. He played the organ and piano and was the youth choir director for a few years while in high school. His proud mother was a widow and her only child was her best friend who picked out her clothes, wigs and shoes. Leamon was always different and his family knew it from an early age. He had flair and style and wasn't afraid to show it. He'd been with the firm for over 10 years and loved his job, and already, he adored Angelica.

"Why don't you just tell him to get lost and leave you the hell alone?" he asked Angelica, straightening his red striped neck kerchief with the gold ring, which was adjusted with just enough slack for comfort.

Angelica looked at Leamon and noticed the kerchief matched his celebratory ruby red socks.

"Ugh, it's complicated. I like Carlton, I do—"

"Are you trying to convince me or yourself?"

"God, in junior high I actually *liked* him. He was kind of chunky, but I thought he was so cute. Then he got weird on me. Puberty? Who knows? But when we were in high school, he was around all the time. We were kind of in a clique together. It was cool though. We were cool until we were about to go off to college. Then something happened to pull everyone apart. You worked here when he was here. Do you know him and his dad very well?"

A loaded question. Literally. Leamon felt like a gun had been pointed at him and he couldn't determine how many bullets it held.

"Well, you know in 10 years you see a lot of things, but I can't say I *know them*, know them. We've never hung out in the same social circles," Leamon said, satisfied he'd dodged at least one bullet.

He'd seen how Carlton Meadows threw his weight around back when he worked there. He knew the stories about Carlton bedding every woman he could was not just gossip. Angelica was too good for that dog, but he didn't know if it was his place to make that protest. After all, she was his boss and the Meadows family were part of the firm. He decided to keep his own counsel.

Looking out of the window without focusing on anything beyond it, Angelica was deep in thought about those four teenagers from a lifetime ago. Leamon stayed respectfully silent until Angelica began to speak again, back from wherever her mind had taken her.

"Carlton is okay. He's better when he's not around his father. Sometimes with Mr. Meadows in the room, he crumbles up and blows away like…"

Dried up dog shit on the street, Leamon thought, finishing her sentence in his head.

There was a sudden rap on her office door and before Angelica could say anything, the door flew open. It was Trevor, Gertrude and Malcolm coming in and sitting informally about the office. Angelica brightened.

"It's the fist!"

They all laughed. Soon after arriving at the new law firm, they got into a conversation about how each of their specialties complemented one another: civil law, criminal law, torts law, contract law. The four of them, along with their intrepid paralegal, were the five "fingers" that comprised a fist. Leamon, thrilled to be included, was the necessary opposable thumb, Angelica was the pointed index finger, Gertrude was naturally delighted to be the middle finger. Malcolm was the next nondescript digit and Trevor coveted being the not-so-delicate pinky.

"You lived in California. Are people just crazier on the left side of the country? Do you see what's goin' on in San Francisco?" asked Trevor.

He was referring to the assassination of Mayor George Moscone and Supervisor Harvey Milk in San Francisco's City Hall by a disgruntled ex-Supervisor.

"It is completely unheard of for something like this to happen in a city like San Francisco," Malcolm added.

467

"Yeah, I hear the killer is claiming he has diminished what? *Capacity*, yes, diminished capacity because he eats sweets and terrible fast food. *That's* insanity," Angelica said, incredulously.

She was sitting on the edge of her desk among her group and though they all had offices, she'd gotten an office with a view. Angelica was careful to never be sitting at her desk when the team worked together, but rather, sitting amongst them at the table or in the library.

"What a sad bastard that asshole had to be. So full of hate. Over a job?" Gertrude exclaimed.

"You're right, he was full of hatred, but it was more than about a job. He hated Harvey Milk because he was…different," Trevor explained.

To a person, everyone in the room knew Trevor was a homosexual, but because he chose never to say much about his personal life, everyone respected his privacy. Harvey Milk was an activist for the large gay population in San Francisco and the mayor supported him.

"That guy was sick and evil, and I hope they put him *under* the jail," Leamon chimed in.

Another country, a festive one at that, heard from, Gertrude thought. Leamon believed that everyone believed he was a lover of women. Of course, no one did. This was a young black man caught between his mother's terminal expectation that her son needed nothing more than a good woman and the monolith of intolerance called "The Black Church." Very few sins were more, well, sinful, than homosexuality in the traditional black church, even though most Sundays the congregation need do no more than gaze toward the choir stand to see those not so invisible faces.

After the short meeting, Angelica began packing up her briefcase, ready for the weekend that had taken so long to arrive. She'd review some of the briefs Leamon had prepared sometime during the weekend. *My life is so exciting!* Leamon was standing in the doorway, as this was his ruse and routine every Friday evening. He didn't want to look like he was ready to jump out of his chair at 4:59 p.m. to go home, so he'd inconspicuously saunter into Angelica's view, so she could see that her dedicated assistant wanted to leave. His verbal entree was to ask if she needed anything.

"No, I'm okay. I'm getting out of here, too."

"How's your house coming along?"

Angelica smiled as if someone was asking a mother about her favorite child. She had the great fortune of buying 13 acres of land in Ann Arbor a few years prior. The derelict of a house that stood on the property had to be gutted almost to the frame and rebuilt and expanded. Happily, this is where her money went, mostly. The plan was to live there part of the year.

"Oh, you should see it. It's fabulous! It's 180 degrees from the way it started out. I've become very good at home improvement. So, if this law thing doesn't pan out…"

"Ha! No, don't quit your day job. Literally," Leamon teased. "By the way, are you going to call Carlton Meadows? I realize I'll have less to do around here once he stops calling every day and leaving messages, but I'll have to make that sacrifice."

Once their laughter died down, Angelica said, very seriously, "I think I'm going to have to tell young Mr. Meadows I will go out with him. That ought to shut him up."

469

"Hey, you know back when everything happened with you and Ricky? I tried to come see you."

Angelica's white wine spritzer had grown a bit watery inside her goblet from neglect. She wasn't much of a drinker and tonight was no exception. Carlton was on, what? His *third* drink and why was she counting? *That's what men do, right?* The music playing in the background was at just the right volume to add to the ambiance of the bar, but allowed them to talk without shouting at one another.

"You came to the house?"

"Yeah, me and Sheila came over to see you one day. This was right before I went off to school. Your mom said you weren't receiving visitors. Then we came by again the following summer when we were home from college. Same thing. I got kind of mad at her because she acted like she didn't even know us," Angelica said, searching Carlton's eyes for a glimmer of understanding of her hurt from that time. "I kept your address and wrote you a few times. Why didn't you write me back, asshole?" Angelica asked, playfully.

"I had no idea you came to visit me, and I definitely never got your letters. Sorry about that. Really, I am," he said, sounding sincere.

"I suppose your parents were trying to protect you, Carlton. I guess I can't blame them for that."

She started to say she'd written Ricky too, but something made her stop herself. She would wait until Carlton brought up the subject of Ricky and the unimaginably awful thing that had happened. The opening was for him to traverse alone.

"My dad, my mom, too, but my dad really helped me. He really showed me how much he loved me, you know? He was there when I needed him the most."

"Wow, that's pretty cool. I wish I had a dad like that." *Wow, are you drunk already?* she asked herself. *Dad like that? How about any dad at all?*

"Your dad is..."

"Dead, remember?" she said. Before Carlton could respond, she said, "He died in Korea. He was a war hero and he died before he even knew my mom was pregnant."

"That's pretty shitty. Let's toast to our fathers, wherever they may be tonight."

As she lifted her glass, Angelica realized the unintentional and careless cruelty of Carlton's remark. Hell, her daddy was a bag of bones somewhere in a foreign land and his daddy was probably plopped down in his Lazy Boy recliner with his hand shoved inside the front of his pants, feigning sleep as he prayed he wouldn't have to fuck that fat assed wife of his. The last time Angelica saw Mrs. Meadows, she looked like an open umbrella with legs.

On their third date, Angelica asked Carlton if he was dating anyone.

"Oh, no, no. I broke up with my last girl about six months ago." He paused and looked into Angelica's eyes and smiled before continuing. "It's so cool that we're both available and—"

"Have kind of found each other again, right?" Angelica said, thinking she'd finish his thought.

Carlton was actually about to say "free" but pulled that punch as Ricky in a jail cell flashed through his mind. Her response, though, was what he had been waiting for. It was like the sun was back in the sky. Indeed, Angelica felt comfort in the familiarity of Carlton. And yes, she was falling for him. He was so charming, and so attentive, and so different from when they were in high school. He seemed to have captured, finally, the confidence he lacked in his teen years. It didn't hurt that he wooed and pursued her unrelentingly, making her feel like she was the only woman in the world. Angelica told herself she must have read the situation wrong when she met with Carlton and his father months earlier. He seemed weak and almost cowed by the older man that night. Angelica had heard all the stories from her girlfriends, in high school, in college and out of it, about men in hot pursuit of the affections of a selected woman, only to discard her after winning her over. Usually that meant after sex. She always thought that was so incredibly childish and immature, saying more about the man than it did the woman. There was no way that could be Carlton Meadows' plan. He clearly liked Angelica and he didn't hesitate to let her know. What more could a girl want?

Soon, Carlton began telling Angelica how much he loved her, surprising her with his openness and vulnerability. To him, this was something that had always been there and finally, the time was right. Six months into their courtship, Carlton asked Angelica to marry him. She took a day to think on it before accepting. She didn't call her friends, relatives or co-workers for advice. She wanted to have no outside influences as she decided the rest of her life would be with one man.

"Mama? Guess what?" Angelica asked, as Liz Tanner answered her phone.

"Two calls in one week from my only child. Am I dying?"

"No more than anyone else, Mother," Angelica said, smiling at her mother's attempt at humor. She'd rung her mother up earlier in the week to see if she wanted to go shopping. Small and insignificant compared to this. "Mom, Carlton asked me to marry him!" she practically squealed, taking herself by surprise with her excitement. Liz laughed at her daughter's reaction to her own words.

"Are you happy, honey?"

"Yes, I am."

"Did you say 'yes' to him?"

"Yup, I did!"

"Then congratulations, Angelica. I'm so happy for you and Carlton."

Liz wasn't really surprised because Carlton had paid her a visit a few weeks earlier to get her blessing on their proposed union.

"I know it's traditional to ask for a girl's hand in marriage. Ask her dad, you know?" he'd begun.

Liz Tanner allowed her right eyebrow to arch up toward her scalp. She'd known Carlton's parents since they were kids together, even though they were older than she. Detroit was a big city and, in some ways, a small town where everyone seemed to be connected by blood or friendships or life events. What had the Meadows family told their son about her and Angelica?

473

"But since that's impossible, I wanted to ask your permission to marry Angelica."

"Of course! Of course! I wish you two all the happiness in the world and I hope she says 'yes!'" Liz said, hugging Carlton.

He told his plans to his own parents and got two distinctly, contrary, reactions. His father praised him with "atta boy" zeal, clapping him on the back and shaking his hand as if he'd closed a giant and profitable merger. His mother, on the other hand, burst into tears, hugging and rocking her son, asking him if he was sure he was making the right decision.

"Yes, Mother. I love her and you're gonna love her too, you'll see."

"Okay, baby, if you say so," Mavis Meadows said with as much drama as she could conjure, causing her husband to roll his eyes.

"Mama, I'm going to grab the rest of my clothes, since I'm here," Carlton said as he headed toward the basement stairs.

Mavis did her son's laundry every two weeks and she had two laundry baskets in the basement with his clean, pressed and folded clothing as well as a dozen starched and ironed shirts on hangers. Mavis turned to her husband.

"I hope that girl doesn't think I'm doing her laundry, too!"

Sidney made note of his wife's rapid recovery from her crying jag.

"Well of course not. Unlike our son, this girl is self-sufficient in every way you can imagine. Not sure why she's willing to marry Carlton, though."

Mavis began blinking so rapidly, Sid thought something had flown into her eye.

"First of all, keep your voice down," Mavis said, her hands pressing down the air in front of her. "That girl is lucky to have Carlton, he's---"

"Do you think he's told her about his various, uh, difficulties?" Sidney interrupted. "Does she know why he didn't serve in the military?"

"Plenty of kids, rich people's kids, politician's kids, get educational deferments," Mavis said, no longer blinking but staring wide eyed at her husband, afraid of what he might say next.

"Just 'cause that's what his *official* record says, doesn't mean it's true. I paid for that, remember? I paid for that bit of creativity, for the record. No pun intended."

"Yes, and just 'cause a doctor says some nonsense, that doesn't make it true either! I'll never believe that about my baby. He's fine, he's perfect, he's---"

"A sociopath. Diagnosed by the United States federal government. His saving grace is the fact that he's sterile and can't reproduce. I'll bet he didn't mentioned *that* to that girl, either."

Carlton had gone out of the side door to load his fresh clothes into the car. He locked the door and bounced up the steps into the kitchen and found his parents in the dining room.

"Hey, Dad, do you think I should ask Angelica's father for permission to marry her? Do you think he'd care if—"

Carlton's hand flew up to his face because Sidney Meadows had back handed his son. The two men stood eye to eye as Sidney rammed his finger into Carlton's chest with every word he spoke.

"Quit. Being. Stupid! You're lucky Angelica Tanner even wants you," he snarled with contempt.

Carlton bolted out of the house with his mother's voice calling after him. He got into his car and roared down the street. As he was driving home, Carlton, enraged, knew he had to calm down and forget about his old man. The old bastard should have known he was kidding. He didn't have to lay hands on him! Carlton also knew he had to make a detour. He cruised down 6 Mile Road to Woodingham and drove until he got to her house. He took a couple of deep breaths before ringing the doorbell.

How do you tell your girlfriend that after two years, it's over, just like that? He decided he'd do the "It's not you, it's me" speech and hope that she didn't make a long drawn out scene. At one time he thought he loved her, but, alas, with Angelica Tanner now within his grasp, all bets were off. *It sure has been nice having two girls to fuck without the hassle of either of them knowing about the other,* Carlton thought. Yeah, he was definitely going to miss that.

Kitty O'Neal was a nice girl, but she wasn't Angelica Tanner. God, how had he gotten so lucky? For the two of them to find each other now, seemed like an answered prayer. An exhaustive answered prayer, for in reality Carlton had put forth quite a bit of effort to pursue Angelica and appear witty and charming at the same time. It was depleting to be so damned wonderful and he was spent.

Kitty cried and cried when Carlton told her they were over. She asked all the usual questions: was there someone else? What had happened? Was there a chance for them? He lied to her, mostly. He just wanted to get out, leave her behind and begin his new life. Kitty began working herself up and threatened not to let Carlton escape the situation with civility and dignity. Only once had Kitty "acted up" and they both remember how he put down that disturbance. He choked her until she almost passed out, all the while telling her to say she was sorry and she wouldn't make him angry again, when of course, she couldn't speak actual words because her oxygen was being cut off. Kitty had been exciting and dangerous like a rollercoaster that ran backwards. But it was over.

SEVENTY-THREE

"So, are you happy, girl?" Sheila asked her friend sitting in her living room, on her brand-new couch.

Sheila was taking her time furnishing her apartment. She had a bedroom set, some bookshelves, a coffee table, a couch and a chair. That was it. Sheila thought it foolish to buy all those trappings when she'd probably be getting married soon. Well, maybe not quite soon. She wasn't even dating anyone, but there was nothing wrong with being practical, right? *Maybe one more chair...*

Angelica perked up and reached her hand out for Sheila to grasp.

"Yes, yes. Most definitely. Everything happened kind of fast, but it feels right for us, you know?"

Sheila looked into Angelica's glistening eyes. "Are...you...crying?"

"Nooo, yeah, well maybe! I'm just happy, girl. Glad I got to share with you. Tears of joy, tears of joy," Angelica said, dabbing at her eyes with her fingertips. Betrayed yet again by the waterworks. She'd cried every single day since accepting Carlton's proposal. Was it just impending wedding jitters? Fear of the unknown? The thought of fucking the same man forever? Cold feet?

Sheila thought she could cheer up Angelica.

"Well, since we're sharing good news…my editor gave me this really great assignment last week. You know that prisoners have access to educational resources, right? They're able to earn advanced degrees, even."

Angelica could feel her chest tightening. She unconsciously put her hand between her breasts as if she was trying to prevent her heart from leaping from her chest. She knew somehow, this assignment had to do with Enrique Williams.

"Right, I knew that was allowed in Michigan," Angelica answered, cautiously.

"Yeah, so how about I was able to make contact with our old pal Ricky Williams?"

"Yeah, how about that? So, what happened? How is he doing?"

"From what I can tell, he's doing okay. He got his bachelor's and he got a J.D. He's like some kind of jail house lawyer, Angelica. He helps the other inmates with their cases and appeals. Isn't that crazy?"

"It's crazy alright. Have you seen him? How does he look?"

"No, I haven't seen him yet. We are trying to arrange a meeting. Red tape, you know."

"Please tell my friend I said 'hello.' Let me know how it turns out."

"Girl, you'll be able to read it in the Free Press. It's going to be a three-part series."

"Nice. Could be a Peabody Award in your future. You never know."

"Thanks. I'm kind of looking forward to seeing old Ricky Ricardo," Sheila said, chortling. She continued, becoming serious. "God, it's been so long. It's sad how things turned out for the guy, but I think the fact that we knew each other before will help me—"

"You know, I was head over heels in love with him, right?"

"Ha! Of course! You weren't fooling anybody, and neither was he," Sheila said with a hardy laugh.

"I never could tell how he felt. I only knew how I was feeling. Ah, unrequited love!"

"Look, I know you cute and everything, but do you have to have all the men, Angelica?" Sheila sassed as she looked around at the sparse furnishings of her living room.

"Nope. Just want to be sure I got the right one."

SEVENTY-FOUR

W arden B.B. Mashburn, Jr. sat in his office waiting for his 10 a.m. appointment to arrive. He enjoyed his job, such as it was, and took it very seriously. Warden Mashburn took pride in the fact that he wasn't easily fooled, nor flattered by bullshit. It was extremely difficult to gain his confidence and trust, but he expected nothing less from the staff serving under him. He saw himself as a father figure, sometimes benevolent, sometimes autocratic, but always as balanced as he could be. He made it a point to listen to anyone he granted an audience to and reserved judgement until he'd gotten the facts.

Warden Mashburn opened a drawer in the center of his desk to retrieve a small comb and mirror. After glimpsing himself in the glass, he decided he looked just fine. No need to improve upon anything as far as he could see. Not a hair out of place. Bertrand Bradford Mashburn, Jr. was a very pale man in his late 50's with hair the color of crow's wings and a moustache to match. Staffers quietly considered how he could dye his moustache so dark without a trace of the colorant staining his ghostly skin. Even quieter still, many on his staff had decided he looked like an animated cadaver. An officer knocked on the heavy, steel reinforced door and came in when commanded.

"Have a seat, Mr. Williams," the warden said, his hand gesturing toward the wooden chair in front of his desk.

Ricky sat down.

"That will be all," Mashburn said, looking at the guard who had brought Ricky in. The guard hesitated, his eyes asking if the warden was sure. "We are fine. You may leave, Officer."

Once alone, the warden rifled through some colored papers inside a manila folder on his desk. Ricky could see his name, last, then first, along with his prisoner number on the elevated tab.

"Mr. Williams, your time with us is about to come to an end. You have been in our care and custody a total of 14 years, I believe."

"Yes, sir," Ricky forced himself to say.

The warden was talking, but not really asking him anything important. Perhaps he was just warming up. Ricky hoped whatever this meeting was, it would be over with quickly with his release date still intact. B.B. Mashburn leaned forward and folded his fingers together into a single fist atop the folder, as if he no longer had a need to refer to anything inside of it.

"You came here, Mr. Williams, because you were convicted of involuntary manslaughter. You actually pled guilty."

"Yes, sir. That was a mistake. I was ill advised by my assigned counsel. I am innocent of that crime."

"You do realize that I hear that umpteen times as day. Literally, that's what they all say. But then you killed a fellow inmate and received seven more years added onto your sentence. This was for *voluntary* manslaughter."

"Yes, sir. I killed someone who had assaulted me previously. I planned to hurt him, and I did. I'm not proud of it, but that's what happened."

The warden stared at Ricky impassively, even though he knew Ricky had done the prison, hell, the world a favor by dispatching Butch Johnson to his fiery eternal resting place. He had been a continuously bad actor and trouble maker. But the man in front of him was a trouble maker of a different stripe. He gave hope to convicts and made them believe they were robbed of fair trials or worse yet, *innocent*. Mashburn couldn't wait for this prick to get gone. The warden smiled what resembled a scowl.

"Mr. Williams, I have to say other than that single incident, you have been an exemplary prisoner."

Ricky forced himself a thin smile. *Exemplary prisoner.* That was like "Happy slave" or "Good nigger" to his ears. He knew the warden was just stating fact and using the vocabulary with which he was acquainted. One thing Ricky learned early and well, "Don't trust anyone," and he certainly didn't trust Warden B.B. Mashburn, Jr., no further than he could throw Jackson State Prison.

"Barring any violations or misconduct, you will be released in 90 days. Good luck and God speed," the warden said, finally.

He must have pressed some surreptitious button, Ricky reasoned, because the officer who had escorted him into the office was now back to take him away. Once back in his 6 by 10-foot cell, Ricky sat on his bunk and let out a tremendous sigh. Was this the hard part? Knowing the end was near? Could he move steadily forward as the horse with the carrot dangling near his nose? He had to. He hadn't gotten this far to fail now. He was only 32 years old and he'd been in prison almost half his life.

He'd finished out his teens, completed his twenties and began his thirties behind bars. All the niceties and civilized behaviors that he'd grown up with had to be put aside like a third helping of ice cream in order for him to survive inside those prison walls.

Perhaps now they could be reconsidered and reconstituted. How to fit in to society again? How to belong? Suddenly his cautious joy turned into fear and then to sadness. Sad for the boy who had died in prison and the man he now was. Ricky's scalp tingled, and his chest became tight. He willed himself to swallow hard a few times. If he began to cry, he might not be able to stop. *No, no. Can't do that.*

And what of the man Ricky had killed, arguably in self-defense, even though technically, the judge didn't quite see it that way? Did he deserve a few seconds of Ricky's contemplation? After all, he seemed to permeate everything prison had become for Ricky, like the concrete walls themselves—ever present, mountainous and inescapable. As long as he was at Jackson, there would always be an asterisk next to his name, an addendum to his story because of Butch Johnson.

Jackson, Michigan is found along I-94, running about 40 miles West of Ann Arbor and is the seat of Jackson County, so named after President Andrew Jackson. Opened in 1839, Michigan State Prison was the first in Michigan and had once been the largest walled prison in the world housing close to 6000 inmates. The foreboding prison, with concrete walls over three stories high and 12 watch towers, had been called State Prison of Southern Michigan since the mid 1930's. However, everyone in Detroit, who somehow seemed to have a family member in residence there at one time or another, called it "Jackson" or "Jackson State Prison."

Back when Enrique Williams began serving his 8-year sentence for involuntary manslaughter, he believed his stay was completely temporary. A mistake had been made. Surely someone in authority believed his story? Surely someone in power could see he was innocent? But as the time ticked by in hours, then days and soon, weeks, Ricky slowly began to panic.

484

The lights and the noise made sleep virtually impossible, but he held steadfastly to the belief that he'd soon be back home, sleeping in his own bed—the nightmare no more than a head-scratching fever dream. How long would he have to wait? When could he go home, he wondered?

The recognizable dread rose inside him like it did when he'd first learned to drive and tried to find his house in the dark. Distracted, he'd turned onto his street, but near 8 Mile, not 7 or 6 Mile, which he lived between. The confidence of a young man with his driver's license and first car gave way to a desperate ten-minute search for a familiar block of houses within the shadows and the beckoning glow of his own porch light which his mother left on each night, no matter the season. Why was it so dark? And why weren't there any porch lights on? It was as if the sliver of moon had conspired with the soft street lights to confound and confuse him. *Boy, if my friends could see me now*, he thought. *Not so cool now, huh?*

Sitting inside that cell as an 18-year-old, he had to laugh at himself. He wanted his mama. He wanted her sheltering arms to assure him he would be alright and that this part of his life could be salvaged, and he could sail off to school as if nothing ever happened. But the drab walls of his prison cell and the stretched-out hours and days told him otherwise.

A lot of people's reputations were built on legends and lies, rumor and regurgitation. You could only pray that when facing an adversary or being called out, it was for something that you could "back up." Of course, if you could make your stand successfully, then it just added to the lore. If, however, you were unsuccessful, the news would travel fast. Logic would dictate that people should then leave you alone and not "try" you, but those on the edge of cowardice always sought out someone with a compromised reputation in order to construct their own. It was a vicious cycle at times, much like the Wild West with folks calling one another out to duel only to be struck down in defense of bullshit. Really, all a man had was his name and his family's reputation.

Sometimes the reputation of one's family, good and bad, came to the fore in unexpected situations.

"Hey, you pretty motherfucker!" someone in the prison yard called out.

Somehow, Ricky knew these words were meant for him, but he kept walking. He was hoping to be able to exercise in relative peace while he was outside. He was hoping to breathe air that wasn't choked with the stench of aggressive and unwashed men. Ricky could feel the hands before they even touched him. Someone was now squeezing his left arm and he turned around.

"You know you hear me talkin' to you. You that white nigga's folk ain't you?"

Ricky didn't understand at first, but the look in the man's eyes didn't tolerate any misunderstandings or slow responses.

"I don't know what you—" Ricky began, only to have the man move into his face, spitting as he talked.

"Yeah, it's you. That nigga killed my homeboy and turned out his wife."

He was now so close, Ricky thought the man might bite him on the nose.

"I got something for pretty niggas like you. I'll see how you like to be turned out. Motherfucker!" he spat.

Ricky felt unsteady on his feet, but knew he could not show any signs of weakness. That would be tantamount to an open buffet to the starving. *Fuck!* Ricky's mind was racing. What should he do? He was no snitch—that was part of the reason he was imprisoned in the first place. It was starting, just like all the stories he'd heard about prison life.

He'd seen men in the neighborhood who had that dead, beaten-down look in their eyes, shoulders stooped, aged beyond their years, unable to even talk to anyone about what they'd experienced or seen. Then there were those who simply came out as better criminals—no rehabilitation, just a determination to never get caught again and to make everyone pay. Bill was a bit like that, wasn't he? What a fucking choice he had before him. Which one would he turn out to be? A guard yelled something, and the man let go of Ricky's arm and walked over to a group of prisoners several yards away. Ricky stared after him briefly and then went on his way. How was he going to get through this shit? *How?*

A few days later, Butch Johnson was holding court in the exercise yard as large men, benches and weights littered the South corner. The small breeze stirred and was welcomed as it pushed aside the odor of 3-day old underarms. Ricky discovered that this was the man who had verbally accosted him his first day out of lock up. He was able to slip by unnoticed, but he soon realized there was nowhere to hide on that patch of asphalt. Ricky eyed him uneasily and kept his distance even though he was close enough to hear what was being said. *No need for a nigga to get the drop on you if he doesn't have to.*

Butch, who looked about 10 years older than Ricky, was the epitome of a big bully. He was about 6'-3" tall with an impossibly large gap between his front teeth that seemed to beg for a spare tooth. He looked as if he never groomed his hair even though a plastic afro pick was perpetually on alert in his matted fur. His nose was mostly nostrils and reminded Ricky of that of a bull, as he imagined a gold ring through his septum. Butch was the

487

biggest and the loudest and he was scary. He was convicted of beating a man to death over a pack of cigarettes.

"Man, I spent some time down in Mexico. Some of them women is kind of squatty and plain, but some of them bitches is fine as hell," Butch said, laughing.

The small entourage around him joined in whether they desired to or not, but more importantly, they made sure Butch saw them laughing along with him.

"Yeah, when they get to America, they be all humble, like 'Señor, can I give you some help with the painting or fix the garage?' I lived in Texas and there's a shit load of 'em there. But then, once you get around 'em and y'all all be working together and shit, they be having an attitude and shit. They don't dig gringos and give less than a damn if you black or white. They be like, 'We don't need no motherfucking badges!', you know?"

This struck Butch as particularly funny and he bellowed loudly, his soiled work shirt shifting back and forth as his big belly shook. The group exchanged furtive glances, confused, but began to laugh as well. And then it happened.

"It's actually 'We don't need no stinking badges.'"

Butch looked over to where the voice had come from. His smile was gone like a chalk drawing swiped by an eraser. Everyone stopped laughing as if on cue and looked over at Moss, an older inmate Ricky had seen in the mess hall and around the yard.

"It's from 'The Treasure of Sierra Madre,' a great movie..." he trailed off. Realizing the imagined slight, Moss tried to chuckle, which turned into a slight smile. His eyes grew wide and then small as if he were wincing. No doubt Moss was preparing to be upbraided by Butch Johnson.

488

"Motherfucker, did I ask yo' ass anything? Who the fuck you think you talking to?" Butch asked.

To a man, no one knew what the word "rhetorical" meant, but they all knew not to answer Butch when he asked a question like that. The old man had better be smart and keep quiet. Butch was in front of Moss in just two giant strides. Butch's fist crashed into Moss's nose and as he was falling, blood spilled to the ground in huge droplets. On the way down, he caught an elbow to the side of the temple. Moss lay supine, shaking and flopping on the asphalt like a fish that had landed in a boat. He was moaning now, mumbling something not quite intelligible. Surely Butch would walk away, everyone thought. Instead, he began kicking the old man in the stomach and side. The guards in the sky post finally saw the crowd and the dust being carried on the wind and signaled to someone on the ground to break up the fight, if it could be called a fight. To Ricky, it seemed to take forever for anyone to notice or come to the old man's aid. As horrible as it was to witness, Ricky was glad it wasn't him.

Later in his cell, Ricky could not stop thinking about Moss. He was a harmless old dude who brought books and magazines around to everyone. He wouldn't hurt anyone--well, except his wife and business partner, both of whom he killed with a hammer after he found them in bed together. Worst of all, none of those clowns standing with Butch, laughing with his ass, had the balls to tell him to cool it. Shit, if he'd do that to Moss off the cuff for an innocent interjection, God only knew what he had planned for Ricky.

Bill came to visit Ricky a couple of times a month. During one particular visit he told his nephew he had to stay strong and be hard.

"And all those feelings and shit, that stuff will get you killed. Ricky, a man's got to be two people, sometimes more, in the

489

joint. You have to take all the good memories, the love and kindness and put it away for safe keeping, like a treasure in a chest. Bury that shit. Hopefully, you will be able to dig it up again someday. People will try to use that shit against you in here. Only show what you want people to see. Keep the rest to yourself. It's all still you and it's all still there, you understand? If you need to, just take them memories out and look at 'em when you're alone like a picture in a wallet. And then back to the poker face. You dig?"

Ricky said he understood.

"Cuz there ain't not one nigger in this penitentiary yo' friend. These niggas want to be you! You look different, educated, good family. They want that shit! You gotta be careful who you talk to cuz at some point you gonna have to decide 'Do I want to get stabbed in the back or do I want to get stabbed in the chest?' That's what you gotta decide, man."

Ricky blinked rapidly. He hoped his uncle had just dropped a metaphor and didn't portend his actual future demise in the joint. He wanted to tell his uncle Bill about Butch and the constant harassment and the fact that the guy seemed to have it out for Ricky because of something Bill may have done a long time ago, but he decided against it. What good would it do? He'd have to figure out what to do on his own. The heaviness of everything pushed his spirit down like a foot on a gas pedal.

But more than anything, it killed Ricky to leave his mother, bereft of her husband, without her oldest surviving son. He had promised her she had nothing to worry about and she knew this because she knew her son. His arms were thrown wide around the world since childhood, his heart was one of compassion and understanding beyond his years. He told her after Danny was killed that he would be careful. Ricky knew the world was a minefield for a young black man, especially one with talent and intelligence. He had told her above all, he would take care of her and his siblings. When she would visit him, he could barely look into her deep, sad brown eyes. He couldn't tell her the guilt he felt over Danny, he couldn't explain why, even though he was innocent, he deserved his fate.

SEVENTY-FIVE

Three months went by and except for the occasional stare down or wolf call, Butch Johnson had left Ricky Williams alone. Ricky trusted no one and remained vigilant, not allowing himself to be caught alone in places that didn't have guards, not that the guards could be trusted either. A few were clearly in congress with certain prisoners, particularly Butch. They seemed to conveniently be preoccupied when shit went down at Butch's instigation.

One afternoon right after mess, Ricky entered his cell to find Butch Johnson inside, waiting. It was startling and Ricky wanted to step back onto the block and yell loudly for help, but he didn't do that. He instinctively put his back as close to the wall as possible.

"What do you want, man? Why are you in my cell? Where's Ridley?" Ricky asked in a low monotone.

Ridley was his cellmate, a quiet guy who wore glasses.

"I told him to get lost. Grown men are gon' be talkin' up in here."

Ricky was weary. Tired of his appeal taking forever to be heard, tired of excuses and promises from his new lawyer and tired of this big asshole in front of him. He wasn't afraid of Butch.

"Get out of here, man," Ricky said with a sigh of exasperation.

"Not 'til we, uh, talk. How old are you?"

"I'm 18."

Butch licked his chapped lips suggestively and let his hand drop to his crotch. He patted at his penis like one would the head of an obedient dog.

"I like 'em young and you is a pretty motherfucker. Maybe I knock some of them pretty white teeth out yo' mouth so you can suck my dick better."

Butch slowly moved to block the cell door. There was no way Pretty Ricky was getting past him.

Ricky looked past Butch. *Where are the guards?*

"I don't know what you lookin' out there for, nigga. Ain't nobody gon' help you. Get on your knees, bitch!"

Ricky made sure he stood even taller at that moment.

"Fuck you, motherfucker!" he yelled, defiantly. "We gon' be some thumpin' motherfuckers cuz you ain't doing shit! I'll kick your ass or die trying!" Ricky exclaimed, highly agitated. His fists were up and clenched. He wanted to tear Butch apart.

Butch laughed, mirthlessly.

"Okay, Youngblood. I'll let you off this time," he said as he turned to leave. Suddenly he flung around and flew toward Ricky, knocking his body into the cinder block wall. Butch had him in a chokehold when he fell forward as he tried to maneuver the teen onto his stomach. Ricky bucked and fought, headbutting Butch and kneeing him hard in the crotch. This angered Butch and sent him into a frenzy of fists and feet. He was no longer thinking about sex with this boy, he wanted to hurt him. Bad.

Ricky awoke in the prison hospital with a broken nose, fractured eye socket and a broken arm, but with his teeth and anus intact. He was in so much pain, his tears ran down into his ears. He'd woken up in hell once again. How long could he hold off that animal, Butch Johnson? How many times would he be sent to the hospital or infirmary, and in what condition the next time? Ricky closed his eyes and prayed. He thanked God for keeping him from being raped. He asked God to deliver him from his hell on earth. What more could he ask? What more could he do? Ricky drifted off to sleep, taking note of the relative quiet of the ward as his breathing became deeper and deeper.

"Enrique Palacio Torres Williams?"

Ricky slowly opened his eyes to see two men and a nurse near the foot of his bed. He rolled his eyes then winced from the pain travelling his face. The nurse must have noticed.

"I'll get you something for the pain," she said and went out of the door.

One of the men was a guard in uniform. The other man wore slacks and a starched blue shirt. He drug a nearby chair across the shiny linoleum floor and took a seat next to Ricky's bed. Ricky closed his eyes again. He could hear papers rustling and the click of an ink pen.

"Mr. Williams, I'm Deputy Martin Crawford with the warden's office. Can you tell me what happened to you?"

Ricky sighed.

"You mean you don't know?"

"We need you tell us what happened."

"I fell in my cell. Face first, to the floor."

"Well, I'm going to stop you right there. I don't believe you, boy. Let's try again. Were you accosted or attacked?"

"Yes."

"Who did it?"

"I don't know. I think they put a bag over my head."

"Mr. Williams, there aren't bags available to prisoners and no bag was found when they found you."

"Maybe they took it with them when they left."

"So, you're telling me you don't know who attacked you?"

Ricky heard a subtle sound, a movement in the room. He opened his eyes and looked directly at the uniformed guard who glared at him stone faced.

"Nope."

Ricky was sure he saw a slight curl at the corner of the guard's lip. A smirk? A smile? Deputy Crawford drummed on his collection of forms several times.

"I can't help you if you don't want to help yourself, son."

"Do you really want to help me, sir?"

"Yes, I do," the man said earnestly.

Ricky lifted his chained right wrist.

"Then, could you have this removed? My left arm appears to be broken and I'm right handed. I need to go to the can without an assist by the nurse, okay?"

The man blew air out of his lips and shook his head.

"Fine. Fine. There's nothing I can do. I'll leave my card in case you recall something, Mr. Williams. Goodbye," Deputy Crawford said, rising from the chair.

He placed the card on the small table next to the bed. The nurse had returned with Ricky's pain medication and as the two men passed her, the guard turned back partially to look at Ricky. Ricky was filled with revulsion. He didn't snitch because, he didn't snitch. He didn't give a shit about Butch or his uniformed minion. Ricky knew he was in a universe of corruption and he could only keep to himself for so long. Butch would come after him again and he might bring his flunkies. He wouldn't likely get away again.

The nurse had administered the two yellow pills and gave him some lukewarm water to wash them down with. The medication was strong and he was dozing off to sleep again. He hoped he would remember one thing when he awoke. He had to figure out how to kill Butch Johnson.

SEVENTY-SIX

Ricky Williams placed a phone call to his mother soon after being released from the hospital. He gave her a thumbnail sketch of what had happened to him but left it vague. She'd been so worried and now she could come to see him.

"No, Mami. It's dangerous right now and my face hasn't healed. I don't want you to see me like this. I'll let you know when you can come."

"I am not afraid of those people and I don't care what you look like, *mijo*."

"Not now. Please just trust me for now, okay?"

"Soon?" his mother implored.

"Yeah, soon. I love you."

"I love you, too, *mijo*. I got the letters you sent back from your friend." There was silence on the other end of the telephone. "Enrique?"

"Yup. Good. I know she means well and everything. I mean, Angelica's the best girl I'll probably ever know, but those letters from her just make it worse for me in here."

"Son, she cares about you. You should be happy she—"

"She needs to just forget about me. Her life is… my life is… Hey, I gotta go, Mama. No more letters though, okay? I'll call you next week."

Enrique had made an appointment with Deputy Crawford. He realized it was the searing pain and the narcotics talking him into killing Butch. He wasn't a killer. That was absurd. He'd just have to find a way to get moved to another cellblock. He'd simply go through the proper channels. This type of situation couldn't be new to them. They'd know what to do.

"I want to help you son, but I need you to help me. They're not going to approve your relocation just because you don't get along with someone. This is prison. You have to figure this stuff out on your own. Now, give me the name of the convict who is harassing you and we can go from there," Deputy Crawford said, barely able to mask his impatience.

This is a total waste of time. This kid will soon be dead anyway.

"I told you already that I don't know. I don't see why you can't just move me," Ricky said, frustrated. There was no way he was going to say Butch Johnson's name.

"I'll see what we can do to make things a bit more comfortable for you. Good day, Mr. Williams." Martin Crawford sighed. *Stupid kid. Dead kid.*

Ricky was led out of the door of the office and down the corridor by a uniformed officer. Weeks passed and there was no sign of his enemy. Had they known it was him all along and locked Butch in solitary confinement? Ricky dared to hope. When he had been cleared to go back to his cell, he found his cellmate was more hyper and animated than he'd ever seen him.

"I heard what happened, man," Ridley said, sidling up to Ricky, his beady eyes peering out from his round rimmed glasses.

He reminded Enrique of a talking serpent. He wasn't in the mood to rehash the incident for Ridley's prurient entertainment. *Funny this fucker was M.I.A. when the shit went down, but now he wants to talk about what he 'heard,'* thought Ricky.

"Yeah, I got into a little scrape," Ricky offered.

"It musta been bad. You been gone for a minute."

"Yup," Ricky said, easing into his bunk. He closed his eyes.

"You hurt Butch, I guess, cuz he's still in the hospital."

Ricky's eyes tore open. He shook his head slowly, the pain medication, his last dose, couldn't abate the beating on his skull like a bongo.

"No, I don't think so."

"Uh-huh. You broke that nigga's leg."

Ricky didn't talk anymore, he just drifted off to sleep.

Ricky went about his regular duties in the prison laundry. When he first got there, he thought the rank odor of desperate and confined ball sacks along with all the other scents and their accompanying emissions would make him throw up. But, eventually, he became inured to the daily assault on his senses.

One morning Ricky was told he had a new work assignment. He was to now report to the kitchen. He didn't know if he was going to cook, serve, or clean up, but he knew the food they served was only slightly more appealing than a wad of cum stiffened socks. Ricky and two other inmates walked single file behind one of the C.O.s down one bile green painted hallway to the next.

Soon they had gone through the empty mess hall, through two metal doors, and into the kitchen. It was almost as hot back there as it was in the laundry. They stopped in front of a large white man, about 6'-4", 300 pounds. He had a straggly blonde beard and wore a blue bandana, even more deeply blue with sweat, on his bald head. He looked like a boiled pig.

"Pinky, these are your new crew members. Put 'em to work," the correctional officer barked.

Pinky turned, saying, "Follow me."

Once outfitted with faded, dingy white aprons, plastic gloves and hairnets, each of the new men were given their duties, with Ricky being the last.

"Williams! Today you gon' work behind the line," Pinky told Ricky, positioning him in the food service line.

Every bit of food was to be parsed out in an equitable manner.

"Give a man too much and the next man gon' complain. Give 'em not enough food and the line stops with a bunch of unnecessary chatter. Try to be fair," Pinky said.

"Johnson, you late," Pinky said to a prisoner who had just entered the steamy kitchen.

Holy fuck, Ricky sighed. He may have even unconsciously shaken his head back and forth in disbelief. It was Butch. *Do I need to sprout wings to get away from this nigga?* Shockingly, Butch ignored Enrique like a child no longer interested in a favorite toy, much to Ricky's relief. He still kept himself on high alert status just in case Butch redirected his attention towards him.

For a whole 21 days, they worked together without a harsh word spoken, nor menacing look passed. Pinky told Ricky to go into the storage room to get some more American cheese slices from the walk-in refrigerator. Ricky took off on his errand, only to look back for a second. He saw Pinky nod at the guard who had been standing closest to them, and that guard tilted his head slightly toward Butch. Ricky ran into the room where the massive refrigerator was and flung open the door to try to retrieve the cheese as quickly as possible. The door closed behind him. He knew Butch was going to be outside that steel door when he opened it again and he would likely get the drop on Ricky. What to do? *Think fast*, he urged himself. He grabbed a block of bologna slices that were, thankfully, still frozen. He opened the door.

"Yeah, come on out, pretty boy," Butch almost sung.

Ricky put the cheese and bologna on a steel steam table with a loud *thunk*. He didn't speak, just looked at Butch in the face, glancing once at his hands, which were empty.

"Bet you thought you got rid of me, huh, bitch? I ended up breaking my damn leg kicking yo' ass! Then, it got infected in the hospital. I had to stay on my back in that damn hospital for almost a month, 'lil nigga. That shit was actually kinda like a vacation," Butch said with a feral grin. The smile died.

"But I almost died motherfucker, and it's yo' fault," Butch yelled as he charged forward. The injury had slowed him down somewhat. Ricky sidestepped him, and the big man lost his balance, falling to his knees. "I'm getting in that ass, bitch. Ain't nobody gon' help you," he said as he was rising from the floor.

Before he could stand at his full height, while one knee was still anchored to the concrete floor, Ricky grabbed the frozen brick of bologna and swung it hard at Butch's head. Teeth, tissue and blood flew out of his face, spattering the floor. Butch blinked and pushed his hand to his face with an anguished cry. Enrique knew he had to shut him up and he had to finish him off, so he would never have to look over his shoulder again for Butch Johnson. Enrique crashed into his head again, crumpling Butch

501

closer to the floor. The next blow was delivered with such force that the frozen meat stack broke apart.

Ricky felt Butch grab at his pant leg. How was he able to do anything with his spongy and battered head jerking as it was? Ricky kicked at him, snatching his leg away. He crossed in just a few steps to the pantry shelf that held large industrial sized cans of tomatoes. He grabbed one and rammed it over and over into Butch's head until the can was bent and caved in to the point of becoming a piece of metal shrapnel. When his arms stopped moving, Ricky stared in horror at the carnage before him. Bright red blood mixed with the tomatoes and their juices spread like a small pond across the floor.

The door to the pantry burst open and the corrections officer's face went from a knowing smirk to disbelief as he realized it was Butch Johnson on the floor. He drew his weapon.

"Hands up! Don't move!" he barked.

Enrique raised his deeply cut, pulpy, swollen and bloody hands high, in shock. The officer grabbed his walkie talkie and radioed for help, giving several numeric codes to someone on the receiving end. By now the other inmates on work detail came running to the door. As the first two stopped dead in their tracks, the rest plowed into them like constricted dominoes. Someone could be heard throwing up.

Ricky was taken into custody by three C.O.s and delivered to the hospital. Although they had asked him a myriad of questions en route, he never spoke. Not because he was being defiant, but because he was in shock. The images of the smashed man swirled around in his head. And the smell. The loud, liquid scent of rust and iron that was his blood.

With his hands stitched up and bandaged, antibiotics and a tetanus shot, Ricky fell asleep, restrained once again. He was allowed three days in the hospital where he was visited by a cadre of officials trying to get answers. He told the same story at least five times. It was self-defense. Butch Johnson had attacked him. He never told anyone how things had gotten to that state between them. It made no difference anyway, especially now.

SEVENTY-SEVEN

R icky Williams was put in segregation block for 30 days with only two hours a day out of his cell for exercise and to make phone calls. He talked to his attorney, Jon "J.R." Rhysbacher, almost daily.

"Here's the deal, Rick," Jon said, followed by a huge exhalation of air. This poor kid was in the soup and there was nothing he could do.

"Your appeal is being thrown out because it is now a moot point to the court. The fact is, while you were incarcerated, justly or unjustly, your committed murder. That is not in dispute."

Enrique frowned. His palms itched from his cuts healing. He thought of all the germs on the phone receiver invading his healing wounds like an invisible army of green plastic army men.

"Okay. So, am I about to be charged?"

"Yes. You'll be indicted for voluntary manslaughter and—"

"But it was self-defense! It was him or me and it damn sure wasn't going to be me, you dig?"

"I understand that, Rick. However, nobody has come forward as a witness for you. No one has said that the two of you had an ongoing problem that would have contributed to an extenuating circumstance precipitating the event, which would have mitigated your actions."

"In English, Mr. Rhysbacher…"

"The witnesses who have been interviewed deny any precipitating, sorry, *previous* problem between you and Mr. Johnson. They are saying, and this includes the officer who was on duty in the kitchen area, that Butch didn't have any weapons or instruments that could be used as such when he entered the store room."

"That's true. He didn't need anything. He was huge! Plus, he was going to…it's still not manslaughter!"

"But Ricky, we would have to explain that brick of bologna. The supervisor said he didn't ask you to get that out of the refrigerator. It could look like premeditation. Look, it's either voluntary or involuntary manslaughter. Both carry an 8 to 15-year sentence. Unless you are willing to testify as to what happened in the past between you and Mr. Johnson, and keep in mind, you still have no witnesses to corroborate anything, you need to plead guilty."

Enrique slammed the phone into its cradle on the wall and stormed back to his cell to think. He was stuck, and he was fucked. Ironically, if he wasn't already in prison, if this had happened on the streets, it would be clear that it was self- defense and he was only trying to protect himself. But it happened in prison, so he was obviously already a criminal to begin with to anybody on the outside looking in. It didn't matter how he got there.

As the years went by, Enrique took advantage of his opportunity to educate himself and gain as much knowledge as he could. When he'd come back to the general population of the prison, he found his status elevated by the gruesome death of

Butch Johnson, friend to no one. He was David to Goliath and many inmates were grateful and showed him respect. Best of all, no one ever tried him again. This allowed Ricky to concentrate on his studies. He gained a Bachelor of Science degree and finally a Juris Doctor. He was, without irony, a jailhouse lawyer. He vowed to help other inmates with filing appeals, reviewing their cases and answering questions. Ricky knew he'd probably never actually practice law when he was released, but the State of Michigan would allow him to take the bar exam and if he passed, he might be hired by someone in a restricted capacity.

One day in the spring of 1980 while in the library, he picked up the Michigan Chronicle, the newspaper out of Detroit documenting black life and society.

"All the black folks news fit to print," he said to himself, grinning. As he flipped only a few pages, his smile dissolved as he gazed upon a picture that took up half the page. It was Angelica Tanner and Carlton Meadows. *Getting married!* He winced as if he'd been struck in the solar plexus. He stared at his old friends, sneering at Carlton's smug and smiling face. How he hated that rat bastard! And, Angelica…she had never been more beautiful, her face gorgeous, her smile radiant. There was a promise of more photos on other pages that he didn't want to see. He threw the newspaper across the table.

Enrique quickly looked over his shoulder to see if anyone had seen. Not him throwing the newspaper in a fit, but his shame. His ears, his neck, his face was tingling, burning. The girl he loved, now a woman. The girl he confided in, someone else's bride. The dearest friend he had pushed away was now in the camp of his enemy. *How did this happen?* He recalled that these two didn't even like each other when they were all teens together. Or was that another one of Carlton's deceptions?

Throughout the last dozen years, Ricky had found himself thinking less and less about Angelica Tanner. As the years wore on it was easier to put her in the past and hope that she had found someone who would treat her like the special woman she was. That hadn't happened. Carlton Meadows had no idea who Angelica was and surely, Angelica had no idea of the snake who slithered at her side. Ricky began to realize that he'd somehow thought in the smallest way possible, Angelica was waiting for him. Suspended and unmoving like a primeval bug in amber. Irrational and ridiculous, he knew. Had it not been for that sliver of hope, he wouldn't be completely crushed in this moment. *What did you expect?*

Ricky closed his eyes and rubbed his temples and began to laugh softly. In his mind he could see the tiny face of the creature in the state of suspended animation inside its amber tomb. It was him.

SEVENTY-EIGHT

S heila Davis was at her desk at the Detroit Free Press fleshing out her idea for a three-part series on higher education in the state prison system and how recidivism decreased among prisoners who took advantage of continuing education while confined. Doing her research, she got a list of names of former inmates who were out and prisoners who would soon be at the end of their sentences, who had successfully completed academic degrees. One name stuck out among the others because of the advanced degree.

"Who's going to hire this guy?" she mumbled to herself before she realized she recognized the name. *Enrique P. Torres Williams.* "That's a blast from the past," she said aloud.

Sheila read his biography, such as it was, and sure enough it was Ricky Williams. It took a few weeks, but she was granted permission to interview Ricky after first meeting with Warden Mashburn and giving assurances regarding what she was trying to do and what she wasn't. Sheila was buzzed in to the visitor's area of the prison and sat at what amounted to a picnic table inside a massive hall. There were mothers with children in tow, lawyers, friends, and spouses there to see the confined. Sheila wondered if she was considered a "friend?" She smoothed the front of her pantsuit jacket and nervously patted at her hair. She'd never been in such a place. It was loud and smelled of disinfectant.

Ricky Williams was led to where she sat. He was wearing a gray work shirt and blue dungarees. Were these his daily accoutrements or had he "dressed up" for her?

"Hello," he said.

"Hi," she said, her voice shrill and high pitched.

This made Ricky smile.

"Don't be nervous, Sheila. It's good to see you again."

Yes, his voice was a bit deeper now and his dark eyes more piercing, but Ricky looked the same as he always had. The same features, same smile, his dark hair confined to a braid past his shoulders. Sheila hadn't known what to expect, but he was still stunningly handsome. Even with the jagged scar etched into his eyebrow, nothing could compete with his physical beauty and it was beyond incongruous to see him in this place.

He told Sheila he had been reluctant to consider her offer to be interviewed initially because he didn't want to bring more unwanted attention to his family. Particularly his mother. His wary eyes waited for a response.

"But this is *positive* attention, Ricky. You're considered a success story. I've read your file."

"Success," he said flatly. "Depends on the definition and the perception, wouldn't you say?"

"I just know your story is uncommon and needs to be told. You've done a lot of good helping inmates with their appeals. You're a—

"Jailhouse lawyer," he chuckled. The first glimmer of light since they started talking. "I'm actually proud of what I've been able to do for some of the men in here. We'll see what my degrees net me when I get released."

509

"When is that?"

"Two years."

Ricky realized much to his chagrin that he'd forgotten how to talk to regular women. His ease at conversation was one of his gifts as a teen. He was aware of how stilted he sounded now. He'd been lucky enough to have a few female guards as sexual partners over the years. They didn't require much conversation, just his ability to get the job done quickly and quietly in the random office or storage room. Sheila explained how she planned to interview him, what highlights she wanted to explore and when the interviews would take place.

She was readying to leave when Ricky asked, "How did my Angel end up with the devil? Carlton Meadows?"

The question took her aback. She'd decided she wouldn't bring up Angelica unless he did. And he hadn't. Until now. Sheila laughed nervously.

"Well, I didn't see that one coming either, but they seem happy. Both of them are lawyers, ironically."

"Why is that ironic?" Ricky asked, impassively.

"It's just that...I just meant..."

"I know what you meant," he said, evenly.

"Sorry. No offense."

"None taken, and you really didn't answer my question, but it's okay. I'm not sure I need to know the answer."

"Angelica used to visit your mom sometimes. I know she did and didn't she used to write to you?"

Ricky could see a uniformed officer approaching in his periphery.

510

"Looks like our time is up, Sheila. It was good seeing you. I'll see you again soon, I hope."

The officer followed Ricky out of the hall.

Sheila realized as she drove away from the prison that half her battle would be gaining Ricky's trust and getting him to talk. About anything. Two months later the first of the series of articles began appearing in The Detroit Free Press. Angelica happened to be drinking tea and having some buttered toast in her breakfast room when she unfurled the newspaper to search for Sheila Davis' byline. Sure enough, there was her story in a separate, special edition section. She was so excited for Sheila because it meant so much to her professionally. Angelica ran her hand across the page to smooth it and she saw Ricky Williams staring out at her. She stared at the black and white and gray image for a very long time, a myriad of emotions washing over her face and inside her soul. He was real, he was alive, he was okay. When she finally got around to reading the article, she felt such pride for her friends, both of them.

"Good morning, honey. Anything good in the paper?" Carlton asked, as he always did, heading toward the refrigerator.

"Of course not. Is there ever?" she said, rolling up the paper and putting it under her arm. "Gotta get dressed."

SEVENTY-NINE

T wo weeks before Enrique was released from prison he received a message from Sheila Davis. He was puzzled by this, even though they'd talked twice in the ensuing two years since the publication of the articles. She wanted him to call her.

"Do you know why I asked you to call?" Sheila said, regretting the question almost immediately.

"Not to be rude, but no, I don't think I do."

During their interviews Ricky had told her, off the record, that he wasn't sure where he would go when he was released. He didn't want to return to his mother's house and he wasn't sure he wanted to accept the home his uncle Bill had offered him. Bill's largesse was much appreciated, but Ricky felt overwhelmed at the prospect of being responsible for a house.

"I want you to come stay with me when you get out. This is a no-strings-attached offer to say thank you for letting me tell your story."

"That's not necessary, Sheila," Ricky said, pondering what this offer meant. *Why is she doing this?*

"Look, I've gotten two promotions since that series came out. I owe it all to you. You can stay at my house until you get your bearings and get a plan of what's next for Ricky Williams. What do you say?"

"Thanks. I'll think about it."

Sheila and Ricky pulled up in front of her house after the long drive from the State Prison in Jackson. On the road Ricky made enough small talk for Sheila to realize he was simply trying to be *free*. He was looking at the sky, the trees whizzing by, the cars, even the occasional horse or cow. The machinations of the mundane seemed magnificent and extraordinary to Ricky. He didn't want the atmosphere to be awkward for Sheila, but he was determined to allow everything to bombard and overtake his senses. Sheila understood completely. She was so happy and so sad for Ricky at the same time.

"Thank you for picking me up. I could have taken a bus, though, saved you the long drive."

"Nonsense. Why wouldn't I come get you? Are you sure you don't want to stop somewhere for breakfast?"

"Can you make me breakfast? Do you know how to cook? Sorry, I didn't mean—"

"You didn't mean to assume there's nothing more to me than my good looks?" Sheila said, laughing. She was glad Ricky was laughing too.

Sheila's house was a neat brick affair with three bedrooms and one bathroom. She'd given Ricky the bedroom right at the top of the stairs. Her bedroom was at the end of the hallway. Ricky's first call was to his mother, Ana. Even though Sheila was in the kitchen, she thought she heard a great scream come from the phone on Ana's end of the conversation. Ricky explained that he wanted to take some time to get acclimated to his freedom before he saw her. It sounded like a hard sell based on all of Ricky's responses on his side of the telephone.

Ricky sat at the breakfast table with his hands on either side of his plate. He flexed his fingers every so often as if they were brand new and he was just trying them out.

Sheila looked up from her plate of eggs, grits, toast and bacon.

"What's wrong?"

"Hmm. I'm not sure I want to eat in front of you. Inside, we had to shovel that crappy food into our faces and get up and out before some nonsense started. I've lost my home training, I think."

Sheila rested her hand on one of his, "Go ahead and eat, Ricky. We're family and this ain't a tea party."

He smiled.

"Thanks." *No wonder Angelica dug this girl so much.*

Ricky spent his days at the Detroit Main Library down on Woodward Avenue and riding the city bus from downtown to the West side, up into Southfield and back again. He would get off the bus to walk around like a foreigner on exchange. One of the biggest shocks was seeing the blocks long hulk of J. L. Hudson's shuttered and empty. This was the anchor for all downtown commerce. This was once the world's tallest department store that draped itself in the world's largest flag. This was the store with childhood wonderment beaming from frosty windows at Christmas. This was the store in which a city resided, each floor more spectacular in consumer goods and services than the last.

Ricky went to the library to glean knowledge, a time capsule of all that had happened to his city and the world in the last 15 years. Sure, they got the newspaper in prison, but many times it would be cut up or marked up with black lines of censorship and Ricky couldn't be bothered with that most days. He sat with reference books, learning about portable calculators, digital watches, Video Cassette Recorders, Compact Discs, the Sony Walkman, Atari and Nintendo. He used a computer for the first time and discovered a fun time waster called "Pong" at a rundown Coney Island restaurant. This was called a "video game" and it was extremely addictive and apparently, quite old. In addition to testing his timing and dexterity, it provided non-stop amusement for the store owner watching Ricky play. He soon discovered "Space Invaders" and "Ms. Pac Man" at a pool hall. These games put the archaic "Pong" to shame and were even more addictive if that was possible.

Ricky went to his parole officer's office once a week as agreed. The P.O. told Ricky not many ex-convicts had the people looking out for them that he had. Yes, Ricky realized he was lucky and told him as much. He needed to get a driver's license among other conveniences of daily life and his P.O. would help him. A week after he'd arrived at Sheila Davis' house, Ricky had a visit from Rodney "Smoke" Peterson. He was surprised to see him in Sheila's living room. He knew Smoke was a friend, maybe the only friend, of his uncle Bill. But he'd only seen him perhaps three times in his life.

The man was dressed in a suit, but it was decidedly normal in color and cut. This was also the only time he'd seen him alone. Smoke always had a woman or two with him. The pimp game wasn't what it used to be, he surmised.

"Hey, Big Time," Smoke said to Ricky, shaking his hand vigorously.

"Hi," Ricky said.

He didn't know what to really call him, so he didn't call him anything. Just like when he was a youngster. "Smoke" seemed too impertinent and familiar, while "Rodney" or "Mr. Peterson" were fails as well. Ricky sat across from his uncle's friend.

"Well, look-a here Youngblood, your uncle Bill asked me to come see about you. You lookin' good."

"Thanks, but you didn't need to come by to check on me. I know Uncle Bill's been out of town for about a month."

"Yeah, yeah, he wished he could be here when you got out. But, he sent me in his place." Smoke grabbed the manila envelope that he'd wedged next to himself in the chair and handed it to Ricky. "That's yours. He knew you was gonna need some help when you got out. A place to stay, wheels and what not."

Ricky reached into the oversized envelope and pulled out a jangling set of keys. He looked at Smoke, puzzled.

"Okay, them the house keys for Bill's crib. The address is written on the outside of the envelope. You also got a car key there. It's parked at the house."

"I'm actually getting a new license on Friday. Wow."

"That ain't all. There's a bank book in there," Smoke said pointing at the envelope.

Ricky turned the envelope upside down and the passbook flopped into his lap.

"What's that for?" Ricky asked as he held the small ledger from Manufacturer's National Bank.

"Open it up, my man."

Ricky opened the book and found the balance and looked at Smoke, his eyes large and disbelieving.

"Fifteen thousand dollars?"

"Looks like," Smoke said, amused at Ricky's reaction.

Enrique looked out of the window for a moment. He saw some little kids riding their bikes in the street. He turned back to Smoke and shook his head.

"I can't accept this. Thank Uncle Bill and tell him—"

"Young nigga, is you crazy? Yo' ass just got out of the penitentiary. What job you got? Where yo' house at? What whip you drivin'?"

"Hey, dude—"

"Now, you listen to me. Yo' uncle cares about you, you hear? He was really fucked up behind the fact that he couldn't help you get out of that first sentence. He put money aside for you for when you got out so yo' ass wouldn't be like these other motherfuckin' ex-cons out here with nothin' and no way to get nothin'."

Smoke's voice had a little heat to it. He blinked a couple of times before he continued in his normal tone.

"He's proud of you, Folk. You survived and got educated. If he didn't have business out West, he'd be here right now. Now, you have 90 days to live in that house rent free. After that you gon' be paying him rent until you decide to move. He sold all his other houses and he kept this one 'cause he knew you wouldn't want to stay with yo' mama." Smoke waved his hand in the air, indicating Sheila's home. "You tryin' to live here? This yo' woman?"

"No, no..." Ricky said.

517

He knew Smoke was just trying to help and had stepped out of his comfort zone to do so. Uncle Bill never ceased to surprise him. He had his own rules for living but he was good to those he loved. Ricky was fortunate, and he knew it.

"There's only a handful of lawyers who would hire an ex-con to work for 'em. But we know some who are good, successful and got that kind of heart," Smoke said, pulling a white envelope from the inside breast pocket of his jacket. He handed it to Ricky.

"Thanks, man. Thank my uncle for me. I'll call him in a few days."

Ricky noticed the envelope had a woman's name, address and phone number on the outside. Ricky's eyes narrowed as he looked over at Smoke.

"Yeah, the attorneys, they info is inside. That outside info, yeah, that's my gift to you. She's a righteous bitch and she's expecting yo' call. Get them pipes cleaned out the right way. Ya dig?

"Yeah, I dig, man."

The next day, Ricky got to see his family at a small dinner at his sister Alecia's house. He'd requested of his mother to see them all outside of her house. He couldn't bring himself to go back home, to that house. Not yet. He feared the sadness he'd feel looking at the bedroom of his 18-year-old self. The kid who was about to go out and conquer the world and make his family proud. The boy who had that yellow brick road outstretched before him leading to a Technicolor life.

He took a cab to Alecia's house and trotted up the stairs to the front door. His façade of cool crumbled as soon as the door opened. His mother and two sisters stood behind the screen door like the holy trinity. They flung open the door, pulling him inside and encircled him with their arms. Everyone was crying, hugging and touching one another's faces. So long they'd waited for this day.

"*Mijo*," his mother said softly, behind a flood of tears.

"Mami," he said, kissing her face and hair.

He looked at his beautiful sisters. Alecia was tall and slender, except for her 6 months pregnant belly. She and her husband were having a second child and she looked so much like their mother, Ana. Her husband and son were in the recreation room downstairs with their brother, Eduardo. Pilar, his little star was now a young woman who'd recently gotten her master's degree. She clung to her brother as if he would disappear if she dared let go.

"Welcome home, welcome home!" she said repeatedly.

Eduardo, the youngest, was coming through the kitchen when he saw Ricky. Ricky embraced his brother, who was as tall as he was at 6 feet. He was a young man now. Their mother had confided that Eduardo had gotten a girl pregnant while in college and he had to drop out to work to pay for the baby. But this year, at 24, he'd finally graduated. His little girl was his world and he was a wonderful father.

Alecia's husband had grilled a spread of food that was fit for a king and she'd decorated the backyard with balloons and fresh flowers. Ricky was overwhelmed and couldn't help crying at times, but he felt no shame. These people loved him. He tried to forget how much of their lives he'd missed each time he looked at one of his siblings. Instead, he focused on how healthy and happy his family was. He was truly blessed.

They sat down to eat their barbequed feast at the large cloth covered picnic table in the center of the yard.

"Baby, please say the grace," Ana said to Ricky.

Ricky asked that they all join hands as he took a deep breath, closing his eyes.

"Lord, thank you for your mercy. Thank you for loving me and my family. Thank you for another chance. Bless everyone here at this table. Guide them and keep them healthy and worthy of your grace. Bless the food before us and everyone who had a hand in preparing it. In Jesus' name we pray, Amen."

When Ricky opened his eyes, he saw his mother and sisters with tears running down their faces. Alecia raised her glass of punch, indicating all should do the same.

"To Enrique!" she exclaimed.

The entire family echoed those words, lifting their glasses to Ricky. Around 11 p.m. things had wound down enough for Ricky to be on his way. He said his goodbyes and promised to visit everyone as the taxicab tooted its horn a couple of times in front of the house. Ricky slid into the back passenger's seat.

"Where to?" the swarthy man asked, wearily.

Ricky dug out the folded up white envelope from his shirt pocket and gave the driver an address. Once they'd arrived, Ricky paid his fare, tipped the man and walked up to a well-lit, tidy looking frame house. He rang the doorbell and stepped back. A woman about 25 years old answered the door. She was easily one of the most beautiful women he'd ever seen. Tall and curvy with long black hair falling to her waist. She'd said her name, but he couldn't recall it only moments later. She was mesmerizing and for a few hours, she was his.

EIGHTY

"How was your barbeque with the family?" Sheila asked.

"It was great. Everybody is all grown up now and you should see them. Everybody was so happy to see me. I didn't realize how much I missed them."

"You came in so late, I figured y'all couldn't tear yourselves away from each other."

"Yeah, hey, sorry I got in so late. I hope I didn't wake you up."

"Oh, no. I'm actually a pretty light sleeper."

"I wanted to ask you a favor," Ricky said, his tone suddenly serious.

He was leaning on the counter near the kitchen sink with his arms folded across his chest. Sheila stood in the middle of her kitchen, wearing a denim shirt and designer blue jeans. She was paying special attention to her grooming and attire with Ricky in the house.

"Okay," she said, expectantly.

"Well, you know Smoke, I mean Rodney, came by and dropped off some stuff from my uncle. I got a place to stay, a car. But I'm still not ready to take on a house just yet. Can I stay with you a few more weeks? Just until I feel more comfortable and get my game plan in check."

"Sure, of course. Please stay as long as you want."

She hoped she didn't sound too eager or desperate, but she liked having a man, this man, in the house. He had begun to relax and talk a bit more. Ricky laughed.

"You say that now…"

In the next few weeks, in the midst of passing the road and written tests for his driver's license, being interviewed by four different law firms and spending time with his mother, Ricky met two women. One was a cashier he met while shopping at Farmer Jack supermarket, a short and voluptuous girl about 28 years old, named Maxine. She wore a short, neat afro and was the color of a Hershey's chocolate bar. Ricky took her for coffee on her lunch break one day and gave her the short version of who he was. She gave him a blow job in the front seat of her car, in the store's parking lot. The idea that someone might have seen them made her so horny and excited, Ricky had to promise they would continue later that night at her apartment.

Two days later he met another woman, Belle, tall and slender and light skinned, a former catalogue model. She was walking her dog as he was taking out the trash for Sheila. The woman, about 40, struck up a conversation with Ricky because she thought he was a new neighbor. She soon discovered he was the benefactor of Sheila Davis' largesse and wanted Ricky to benefit from some time at her house as well, just not taking out the trash or other menial tasks. Enrique let both of these women know he had no interest in settling down or even being anyone's boyfriend. He wanted to fuck them with no strings attached. He wanted to do everything and anything Maxine and Belle would allow, as long as they kept one another satisfied--which he had no trouble doing. They were lively, sexy, confident women. He had but one rule. He did not stay overnight.

After being out of prison almost a month, Enrique got hired as a clerk at Steinman and Steinman, a law practice run by brothers Joel and Howard. Their office was in an old landmark building on Fenkell. These men were tough when they needed to be, but fair as well, and they expected a lot from Ricky. He knew he couldn't let them down, nor his Uncle Bill.

The night he received the good news, he'd gone to the party store to get some champagne. He wanted to toast and share the news with Sheila.

"Lady, you have been so good to me. I can never repay you, you know."

"And you won't ever have to. This has been my pleasure. I'm glad I could help you."

By the time they made it to the dregs of the bottle, they were both a little drunk.

"I think I've had champagne once in my life. I'm a lightweight," Ricky stated, completely amused at having the constitution of a toddler. Ricky looked Sheila in her eyes and smiled.

"I'm ready, Sheila."

"Ready to take on the world?" Sheila almost shouted.

"Ready to see Angelica."

Sheila seemed to sober up momentarily as if she'd been stopped by a policeman for speeding.

"Are you sure?"

"Yes. Can you give me her phone number? And don't tell her I'm gonna call, okay? She knows I've been staying with you, right?"

"Well, um, I don't know. Maybe. Probably not. I haven't told her," Sheila answered, awkwardly.

"It's cool, man. I gotta go to bed. See you in the morning" Ricky slurred.

Later that night, Ricky awoke to Sheila standing next to his bed in a robe. He could make out the protruding nipples of her breasts, underneath.

"Ricky…"

"Sheila. Hey, what are you…"

"I couldn't sleep. I thought you might want some company."

He rose up onto his elbows.

"Sheila, this is so sweet and flattering, but I'm seeing someone." She didn't need to know it was actually *two* someones. "This is probably not a good idea."

Sheila smiled faintly in the moonlight that cut across the room through gauzy curtains. After a few seconds, she turned around and headed back down the hall to her bedroom, where she latched the door. Ricky laid back down and buried his face in the yielding softness of his pillow. He felt bad, but what could he do? He had no intention of crossing that line. Before he could ruminate further, he was asleep.

EIGHTY-ONE

A ngelica sat fidgeting at her desk inside her office. It was nearing the end of the day, but she and some of her staff would be working late tonight on arguments that needed to be presented in court. The skies had turned a deep dark purple and were angrily flashing and clashing outside the window. She swiveled around in her chair and looked far off in the distance.

Detroit was her True North. Everything in her always pointed her back to the start. Even her stint in Los Angeles was her trying to check her watch without the host taking notice. She wondered how or why she hadn't run into Ricky? This was the big city with the soul of a small town, right? He seemed even more of an enigma now that he was free. But, that wasn't entirely true, because she certainly knew where Sheila lived. Why hadn't her best friend told her that Enrique Williams was staying at her house? Why did she have to hear it from a well-intentioned mutual acquaintance?

Angelica rolled a pencil around in her hands, as she struggled against the image forming in her mind. She would not allow her mind's eye to look down the path that at first seemed so bright and spacious, only to become dark and narrow. Ricky and Sheila in bed, *making love, having sex, fucking*. Her head would sneakily try to take her there, easing her in, testing her resolve and reaction.

Her hand shot out involuntarily as if she was physically putting a halt to the unwelcome image. The pencil rolled onto the floor.

Sheila was the girl who would put a candy bar into her mouth and suck it and suck it until it revealed the pitifully soggy nougat, raisins, or nuts which eventually resembled vomit. She would then proceed to suck on whatever was left until no traces of anything other than those raisins or nuts remained. Then she'd chew them open mouthed while Angelica bellowed with laughter at this puerile entertainment. Angelica wasn't laughing now. She was disgusted with all that *slow, patient, sucking*. Angelica had to stop herself.

"You are a sick bitch," she mumbled to herself.

"Um, who are you calling a bitch?" Leamon said, poking his head in the doorway.

"Don't you ever knock?" Angelica said, suddenly back to reality.

"I did, Miss Lady. You did not answer so I came in to make sure you were okay."

"Sorry. I'm fine."

"Well, since you didn't answer my question, what about this one: Do you want me to grab dinner for you?"

"Nope. Not hungry. I'm just gonna keep working. Thanks, though."

Leamon retreated and Angelica pulled a manila envelope out of one of her desk drawers. She slid the document out and stared at it. She had built her dream home, the beautiful retreat in the woods in Ann Arbor. She'd put so much of her money into the project and now she owned it free and clear--no mortgage. But, the house had become an instigator of more than a few arguments between Angelica and Carlton. He felt what was hers should be his and vice versa, regardless of the fact that she bought the property while in law school and began building on it soon after graduation.

Angelica picked up the phone and pressed a single button.

"Yup?" the voice squawked.

"Hey, can you come in here before you leave? I need a notary," Angelica said.

A few moments later Trevor came in with a ledger and a chrome stamp in hand.

"I was hoping you had changed your mind about this, Angelica. This is ill advised," Trevor said, sounding disappointed.

"It's just a house. If this helps me have peace in my life, then it's a small sacrifice," Angelica said, unconvincingly.

"Okay, it's your funeral. Go ahead and sign it."

Angelica and Trevor took care of certifying the document and she put it back in the envelope as Trevor closed her door. She felt a weight had been lifted and now she just needed to have the deed recorded and then she'd tell Carlton he owned half the house. Why did his victory feel like her defeat? Carlton would be elated. She could see him smiling at hearing the news. A smile she wanted to wipe away with a frying pan to the face.

Angelica realized her phone had been ringing, but she didn't know for how long. She remembered Leamon was gone, so she picked up the receiver.

"Hi, Angelica. Do you know who this is?"

Angelica sat straight up in her desk chair. Her heart sped up as if hit by a defibrillator. Should she play coy and make him say his name? No, she wouldn't do that to him.

"Yes, I do. How are you?"

"I'm good. Can I see you?"

Why did everything he say sound like sex?

"Sure. When do—"

"Tonight. Now."

"Okay...where—"

"There's a bar on Larned where we can talk. They have pretty good food too, if you're hungry."

"I know the place. See you in half an hour."

EIGHTY-TWO

Angelica had to laugh at her vanity. She didn't just dash out of the door to meet Enrique. She spent at least 15 minutes in the ladies' room making sure the shine was off her face, hair casually tousled and lipstick refreshed. Sure, this touch up might make her a bit late, but so what? She wanted to make an entrance, didn't she? Angelica hoped Ricky would be just as glad to see her as she him. She couldn't believe it had been almost 15 years. Angelica Meadows wore a fuchsia floral dress with a wide belt cinching her waist, gold hoop earrings and high heeled sandals. She took a deep breath as she entered the sepia toned bar. The lighting was soft and flattering and she swayed toward a man she thought she recognized.

Ricky's eyebrows went up slightly when he spotted Angelica in the dim, moody light. She was still so beautiful, but now she was womanly. Her full breasts bounced slightly against the bodice of her summer dress. Her perfect silhouette begged for his hands to run along her curves. Ricky wanted to look serious and slightly stern, but that notion collapsed like something constructed of toothpicks as he smiled at the beautiful woman.

Oh good, Angelica thought. *He's glad to see me.* Enrique was standing now, his left foot came forward and he lifted his hands slightly, palms up, arms open. Angelica almost fell into him, she'd gotten to his body so quickly. He held her tight, stroking her hair, while she felt his firm, muscular back, wide and strong. When they broke apart, Ricky instinctively grabbed her left hand with his right and lifted it in the air as if he wanted to appraise her. He twirled her around and they both laughed as they slid into either side of the booth.

"You thought I was about to bust a move, huh?" Ricky teased.

"No, I thought you wanted me to," Angelica said, beaming.

They just stared and smiled at one another, feeling the miracle of the moment. The waiter came to the table and interrupted whatever it was they were doing.

"Hi folks. Can I get you something to drink?" he said.

"What would you like, Angel?" Ricky said softly, fully aware of the effect that endearment had on the both of them.

"What did we used to drink? Boone's Farm?" she asked, playfully.

"Cold Duck was our magic potion."

The waiter, a slender college aged white kid, shifted his weight, wondering why he was so lucky to get these business types who cheated on their spouses just about every evening.

"I think we may have that. I can check."

"I'll tell you what. We'd like some champagne. Not cheap, but I'm not trying to pay the mortgage on this place, okay?" Ricky said.

"I got it, sir. The food menu is right there if you want something from the kitchen," the waiter said, indicating the laminated sheet stuck between the Heinz Ketchup and the salt shaker. He walked off.

"How are you, Ricky? I mean *really*?"

"I'm better every single day. I finally feel like it's okay to look ahead and see what's down the road. I have to say your girl Sheila, she was so good to me. You wouldn't believe it."

"Oh, I think I would," Angelica replied, trying not to sound jealous and trying to gauge what she could and could not ask. About anything. About everything.

"Yup, she made my transition so much easier. Did you happen to read those articles she wrote?"

"Sure did. They were wonderful. She did a great job. Did it help you get out sooner?"

"No, unfortunately. But it made the end easier. I guess I was the de facto representative of the prison's successful collaboration with a couple of local colleges."

"You're a success story."

That sounded weird and almost taunting. Angelica cringed inside and hoped he didn't find her comment sarcastic.

"So it would seem. A narrowly defined success," he said without bitterness.

Angelica wanted to navigate toward the light, the future.

"What have you been doing since you got out?"

"Well, do you remember my uncle, Bill?"

"Yes. Who could forget him?"

"He moved out West, but he left me well taken care of, so I could get back on my feet." He decided not to go into detail. He didn't want to seem like some kid who needed someone to take care of him. "He wanted to make sure I could focus on getting a job."

The waiter had returned with a stainless-steel ice bucket containing the wine, and two champagne flutes, which he sat on the table. The young man worked a small wire cage from over the cork, pulling it out of the bottle with a burst that sounded like a gunshot. Ricky waved toward the ice bucket.

"You can leave it there. I'll pour it. Give us about five minutes and we may order some food, okay?"

The waiter nodded and left again. Angelica noted that they didn't continue their conversation unless they were alone, as if every word and emotion was currency to be spent only on one another. Enrique poured the champagne.

"I've only had champagne twice in my life," he said.

"Guess what? Me, too," she giggled.

Ricky lifted his glass and Angelica followed suit.

"What should we toast to?" he asked.

"Your gig with the Steinman brothers. Your health and your freedom."

They lightly touched their glasses together to make a clinking sound before they both took a few sips of the wine. In all that time, they'd not stopped staring at one another, unabashedly luxuriating in each other's presence. Angelica reached out to touch Ricky's face, lightly tracing the small but noticeable scar over his eyebrow. Ricky closed his eyes for a few seconds, never a thought to moving away from her touch.

"What happened? Your mother told me a long time ago you'd gotten hurt."

Ricky knitted his brows together slightly.

"When did you see my mom?"

"Shoot, it was about a year after you got arrested. I came to visit her and the kids." She paused and considered whether she should say anything else about that day, but she couldn't help herself. "It was a really nice visit. I brought all kinds of goodies for your little brother and sister. Your mom showed me all these great pictures of your dad and then I saw the bundle of letters you returned. From me to you."

She tried to smile but couldn't quite manage it.

"Oh, yeah. Right." Ricky drank some of the sparkling beverage in his glass and sat it back down on the table. "You know, seeing you was hard enough. That last time in the courtroom was… Those letters were torture for me, Angelica. They were a reminder of how I'd fucked up my life. How life was going on without me and how you had gone on without me. At one point, your letters were all I lived for. I was experiencing life, college life, through you. Once I got sentenced the second time, I had to be realistic and let go of hoping that I'd get out or that we'd be together."

Yes, he'd said it and now she knew.

Angelica allowed his last few words to run through her and quench her like a cold drink on the hottest day of the year.

"I didn't know—"

"How could you, Angelica? I was so naïve in so many ways. I thought I knew what my life was going to be like. I couldn't have dreamed that shit up in my worst nightmare."

The waiter was suddenly back at the table. Angelica waved him away and he turned back around, rolling his eyes. *Oh, great. These two are planning to reminisce all evening sipping on that little bit of champagne.*

"Talk to me, Ricky."

533

"I'm hoping I never tell this story again in life," he sighed.

Angelica's eyes were unwavering. She was letting him know she could take it, that she wouldn't be shocked or judgmental. She never was. That was why he loved her. He looked around the inside of the bar, then at the floor, at his hands and then his gaze finally found Angelica.

"The fear, the sadness at the beginning was overwhelming. The things you see, the noise... I was afraid of what I'd see and hear daily. I thought my heart would bleed out until there was nothing but an empty, cold rock in its place. Believe me, it's easier to survive that way. As a predator. But I wanted to hold on to my humanity. A heart is more than what's in your chest, you know? I had to realize no one could help me, but me. I had to figure out how to hold on to Enrique Williams, no matter what."

He leaned forward, almost conspiratorially, his hands flat on the table. "Sitting in that prison cell, you never know who wants to kill you for nothing. It might be your last shower, your last meal. You just don't know. It's so intense. Killing that man, as much as I wish I hadn't done it, gave me something. His death saved my life. I killed the baddest nigger in Jackson."

Angelica realized he wasn't speaking of Mr. Gilhooley, but of someone else. The person who had harmed him. The one who'd garnered him additional years on his sentence.

"I could have just gone wild and acted like I was the shit. People would kill for me if I'd asked. But I didn't. I had to be responsible for this...power. I had time to think long and hard when I was in solitary confinement. Once I saw that people were moving out of my way and weren't trying to shank my ass, I had to find a way to harness this perceived power for good. I know it sounds cliché, but that's how it went down. Taking that dude's life gave me a better one, or should I say, a better existence in the joint. I thanked God every day. I served my time and got out."

Angelica stared at her friend, her long lost friend. How could she tell him that for years her young life was divided up into two parts, like modern history Before Christ and After Christ's death? Except hers was "BI," Before the Incident and "AI," After the Incident, with a bloody gash of demarcation between the two. As time went on and the years rolled by, the incident and its aftermath seemed akin to being in a car accelerating past the scene of an accident. Soon, everything that was so vivid and detailed and absolute, had gotten smaller and smaller in the rearview mirror until it was tiny and indistinguishable and gone. She learned eventually all eyes must look at the road ahead and try not to look too far out at what's looming in the distance.

Angelica's tears escaped her eyes without effort or embarrassment. She commanded her voice to be steady.

"Do you know that for the longest time, every time I went somewhere or saw something, a concert, the Pacific Ocean for the first time, the sunset, I, I…never mind. It's stupid."

"No, go ahead. Say it."

She pursed her lips and rolled her eyes for dramatic effect.

"Every time I went somewhere new or saw something new, I acted like you were with me! I pretended you and I were seeing it or experiencing it together. You were always there in my heart. I told myself I was doing whatever it was for me *and* Enrique, too."

In his eyes, Ricky felt the sting of tears that would not fall.

"Did you marry our friend Carlton for me too?" He immediately wanted to diffuse the bomb he'd thrown, but it was out there now. "I'm sorry, Angelica. I didn't mean that."

535

"Oh, yes you did," Angelica responded, stiffly.

"Your happiness is all I care about. Are you happy?"

The question had caught her off guard.

"Yes, of course," she said, wondering if she was lying. She knew she'd made an awful mistake from the moment she'd parked her car, and when she saw Ricky, it was confirmation. Enrique Williams was the love of her life and they would never be together.

"Good, good," he said, weakly.

"Whoa," Angelica said, looking at her watch. "We've been here for a couple of hours. You know, I started not to come."

"Ha! Guess what? I started not to come and I'm the one who called *you*!"

They both laughed.

"I'm glad I did, though. You?"

"Absolutely. What a miracle to see my Angel again." He paused. "Did Carlton tell you what actually happened that night in '68?"

"No, not really. He always makes like it pains him to talk or even think about that night," she said, hoping she didn't sound like she was betraying her husband.

Enrique had a strange smile on his face now.

"Then I won't either. Just know that a lie can't live forever. Your husband is not who or what you think he is. I didn't listen to Uncle Bill when he peeped Carlton's game a long time ago. He warned me that Carlton was not my friend and he was no good. And now I'm warning you. I've got to go," he said, putting two $20 bills on the table.

536

Angelica didn't know what to say or think, but Enrique was getting up. He shook his legs slightly to let his pants fall correctly to his shoes.

"Baby girl, it was good to see you."

Angelica knew he meant to walk out alone. The temperature of their interaction had suddenly changed. Was he angry at her? He bent down and kissed her gently on her cheek before leaving. Angelica's hand rose to her cheek as she thought about everything they'd said to one another. She knew she had to find a way to confront Carlton and make him tell her what really happened that July night, all those years ago.

Ricky walked a while in the rain before he retrieved his car from the parking lot. He knew he could never see Angelica again. It was what was best for the both of them.

EIGHTY-THREE

It became evident soon after they were married that there was a strangeness about Carlton, an unknowability. This concerned Angelica, but she felt she could break through whatever was weighing him down and they would become closer. He'd been so sweet and attentive when they began dating, but the endearing vulnerability he displayed at first was no more than the swinging open of a prison door. Lured inside by that promise of more moments of truth and openness, the door had closed tight behind her without a sound.

She once asked Carlton if he ever thought about Ricky or felt bad about what had happened to him and Carlton snapped, "Don't talk to me about that nigger! I'm dead serious. He will not be discussed in my damn house, Angelica."

Angelica had misread her husband's aloofness. She knew marriage could be fraught with many challenges, so she decided to "pick her spots" with him. No need to upset him over something neither of them could change.

Angelica was home from work early and relaxing, finally, in a luxurious bubble bath—a pleasure she could rarely afford chiefly because of the amount of time it took. Her large bathroom with a sitting area, had a lovely chaise lounge she mused was her fainting couch, like the ladies in the old South surely had. There was always a feeling of guilt when trying to find the time to sit in her claw foot tub because she felt she should be doing something—paperwork, cooking, cleaning up, something.

Angelica refused to get a housekeeper, even for the Ann Arbor house, though they could afford it many times over. She remembered how bitter her own mother seemed to be that her mother took time from their family and her own kids to help someone else raise theirs. Sure, it gave steady employment to her grandmother, but at what cost, ultimately, to her family?

Angelica had her eyes closed and the lights dimmed as she simmered in the warm water. She willed her overactive mind to still itself as she breathed in the sweet gardenia fragrance of her favorite bath potion. Then something about the air shifted, its continuity disturbed, making her open her eyes. Startled to see Carlton sitting on the tub's edge, she jumped forward, water sloshing over the side of the tub, onto the tile floor, and onto Carlton's pants. She instinctively grabbed her wash cloth to cover her breasts. Yes, this was her husband, but, Angelica never liked him to see her in the bath. It made her feel vulnerable and not quite on equal footing, presenting a psychological and physical disadvantage, somehow.

"Oh, sorry honey," Carlton said, smiling and wiping the foamy suds from his thigh. "I didn't mean to scare you. Why do you always cover up? You're my wife, for Chrissakes! You act like I've never seen those titties before. You're so funny sometimes."

"Sweetie, when I'm in the bathroom, I don't like to share, and I don't like an audience—unless I know that's part of the plan. This is my alone time. Do you mind?" she said, hoping the naughty reference would distract him and get him the hell out of there.

"Alright." He paused and suddenly appeared very serious. "Honey, I don't think you should try to see Ricky now that he's out of prison."

Where did that come from?

"I've already—" she began.

Before she could finish the first words in the sentence, she was seized with a cold fear, a darkness that was like a weight suddenly pinning her to the water. Her mind was screaming, "*DO NOT TELL HIM YOU'VE SEEN ENRIQUE!*" Carlton's eyebrows had gone up expectantly, anticipating what she might say.

Angelica continued, "—thought about it. It's a lot to absorb."

"Yes, it is. But this guy could be dangerous, you know? We don't know what kind of hardened criminal he's become. Shit, he's a killer! Definitely not the guy we used to know." Carlton wondered if he was overselling the situation. His wife could be stubborn and the last thing he wanted was for her to quench any lingering curiosity about Enrique by seeking him out.

"You realize he and Sheila are together, right?" she lied. A clever bit of thatch over a gaping hole she was about to tumble into. Maybe if she built up to it. "Sheila is one of my closest friends. And, Jesus, Carlton, Ricky used to be our friend. We were all so close. I feel bad, like once those prison doors closed, we shut him out of our lives. We don't know what he went through. Is it right to just continue on and just act as if—"

"Dammit, fuck him! I don't want you anywhere near his ass! He's a lowlife! He's a killer and I owe him nothing! I mean, *we* owe him nothing."

They both stared at one another, shocked at Carlton's emotional outburst. Unconsciously, Angelica pulled her now cold wash cloth up higher on her body.

"Stay away from him, Angelica."

His words sounded like a dire warning and Angelica felt the menace of Carlton's display. He was acting downright crazy and she wanted him away from her.

"Okay, Carlton. Please leave me to my lukewarm bath."

"Sure, honey," Carlton said kissing his wife on the forehead.

He turned and left the bathroom, closing the door behind him. She wanted to jump out of the water and run to lock the door. Instead she just stared at the door, sliding down into the water to take the chill off her suddenly shaking body.

Angelica had never asked Carlton about the incident at the Shake 'n Spin. They never talked about it as there was no need to bring up the painful past. She'd sat in the courtroom while her two friend's lives changed before her eyes. She was at the arraignment where Ricky's lawyer entered a plea of "Not guilty." Carlton's lawyer said the same for him. For some reason the prosecutor asked that Ricky not be granted bail, saying he was a flight risk to Canada and he even threw in that Ricky's family had a criminal history.

When he stood to be led out of the courtroom, Ricky and Angelica's eyes met and he mouthed, "Don't come here anymore" to her. Angelica walked out sad and confused and heartbroken. Her mother trying to divert her attention to getting ready for college, forbade her to visit Ricky in jail. No one seemed to understand the fog of despair enveloping her. She cried on the phone to Sheila almost every night.

As Angelica got acclimated to Los Angeles, she was unaware of the story that was unfolding between Carlton and Enrique, only hearing it later from Sheila. Carlton had been the state's witness against Ricky. Sure, he said, he'd been there at the Shake 'n Spin that night. He'd gone to visit his friend, Enrique Williams. The way Carlton told it, Ricky was robbing Mr. G and got caught in the act. The gun went off by accident, according to Ricky's lawyer, and Carlton didn't dispute it. He said he was in front of the shop waiting so he wasn't clear on what had actually transpired. Carlton said he had been disappointed to know that his trusted friend had stolen his dad's gun. He was already a thief, the state argued. From thief to murderer was a short leap.

His lawyer assured Ricky since there was no evidence of a robbery, reasonable doubt gave him a good chance with the jury. At first Ricky was looking at the jurors and the spectators every day, impassioned and imploring with his eyes. By the second week, he was staring straight ahead, dazed and far away, his mother and sister listening raptly and occasionally weeping. The troubling fact that Carlton had testified against him and that his fingerprints were on the murder weapon did not bode well. Still, he never ratted out Carlton.

Ricky was never called to the stand. In a surprise move, the jury was dismissed during the third week and Ricky pleaded guilty to involuntary manslaughter on the advice of his counsel. His lawyer had advised that since he had never been in trouble, was college bound, and was the son of a war hero, he would probably get a 3-year sentence, which the judge might suspend. The judge gave him 15 years. He would be eligible for parole in 8.

Angelica didn't know what to believe, it was at once devastating and mind boggling, making her question everything about the boy. She guessed she only thought she knew him, but perhaps she didn't know him at all. Now, years later, the questions circled her like carrion birds over a carcass. Was it Ricky or was it Carlton whom she didn't know?

EIGHTY-FOUR

Somehow the 1968 class of John Francis Dodge High School managed to skip over their 10 year reunion and decided to rectify the social faux pas with a 15 year reunion taking place in July of 1983. Angelica had gotten the invitation in the mail in April and found herself oddly excited. Sheila was going to miss the festivities due to a long-planned vacation with her mother, Velma. Even though she'd never admit it, Sheila would have been embarrassed to show up without a husband. She was so traditional sometimes. Angelica looked to the ceiling and sent up a little prayer, selfishly, that Ricky would be there.

She'd seen him only once since they met for drinks the previous summer. Angelica stopped at Big Boy's in Southfield one January evening to pick up some food and he was coming out with a woman as she was going in. It was an unexpected moment that shocked her nervous system. She barely looked at the woman who walked in front of him. They looked at one another as snow swirled in the light breeze, dusting Ricky's eyelashes. They smiled, never taking their eyes from one another.

Ricky reached out and hugged Angelica to him and said in her ear, "How are you, baby girl?"

"Really good to see you, Enrique."

He grabbed at her gloved hand in a half-hearted shake and then turned to catch up with the woman he was with.

At the reunion, Carlton insisted they hold court at their table with a few other obnoxious bores who had "done well" in their respective careers within the acceptable parameters of commerce and capitalism. Angelica had forgotten that part of the reason for reunions was the insufferable braggadocio and one-upmanship, and there was no shortage of that at their table.

The Viscount Hotel in Windsor, Ontario was a great choice for the reunion. It had definitely seen better days, but it was still quite impressive with their event being held on the 17th floor with a panoramic view of Windsor, the Detroit River and the Motor City dotting the horizon. About two dozen people, including the Meadows, had booked rooms to spend the night. Most even convinced themselves that they'd be able to "hang" at the after party that was planned in Mike Morton's suite.

Plenty of drinking and dancing went on in the first couple of hours interrupted only by a plated dinner of steak or chicken. There was a contest for which couple had been together the longest since high school, who had the most kids and who had travelled the furthest distance for the reunion. It was good to see so many old friends and acquaintances including Mike, Dave the Lizard, the twins, and Kitty O'Neal. Angelica so wished Sheila was there, so they could whisper about who was fat, who had lost their hair and how they couldn't believe they once were digging on this or that guy.

There were also some names announced in memoriam like a few boys who'd died in Vietnam, and a girl who used to always be in the girl's lavatory smoking and saying her mother was only nice to her when she was sick. She must have played sick one too many times because her mother strangled her to death. One of the bores, whose best days surely were in high school, was asking if anyone remembered a particular classmate from third period Biology? Who remembered anything as specific as that?

545

"He married this white chick, went over to 'Nam and I guess didn't see his wife and kids for a while. He spent time in the VA hospital in Germany and when he came back, his wife and them acted like they didn't know him."

"That's bizarre," Carlton commented.

"Oh, it gets worse. They were having a fight, him and his old lady, and her and his kids start calling him a nigger. Killed 'em all!"

"Holy shit!" someone at the table exclaimed.

"Can we dance, Carlton?" Angelica blurted out, not caring if she seemed rude.

"Yeah, sure, honey," he said, getting up from the table. Carlton had been drinking since they had gotten there and was unsteady on his feet at first.

"Jesus, never mind," Angelica said, about to sit back down.

"No, let's dance. I'm fine," he insisted.

Downstairs in the lobby bar, Enrique Williams was fortifying himself with liquid courage. He was never much of a drinker, so two glasses of wine had him teetering towards tipsy. He had talked himself into coming to his high school reunion, yet here he was sitting in the flattering shadows of the lobby bar. Ricky was going to ask one of the women he dated to accompany him but thought better of it when he imagined being pointed at and talked about with surreptitiously twisted mouths behind hands that would seek to shake his just to be polite. He could see in his mind's eye faces frozen yet talking through barely moving lips like ventriloquist's dummies. He quickly replaced that image with one of pretty girls waving at him, letting him know they missed him and couldn't wait to dance with him. Ricky had been an extremely popular and well liked young man, if he remembered correctly. And he remembered correctly.

Ricky downed the rest of his drink. He had to go upstairs. That's where *she* was.

"Hey, you two," Mike Morton greeted Angelica and Carlton, who were dancing.

Mike the Moron was only vaguely remembered but had obviously done well for himself. His suit was expensive, as were the two thick gold chains around his neck. His bright red hair was dyed black and with his pale skin, he looked like a movie mortician. Or Gomez Addams.

"Hey," Carlton greeted him, stopping his gyrations to shake Mike's hand.

"What are you, some kind of rapper?"

"Ha! I wish. No, my man, just a hard-working business man. Are y'all coming to the after party?"

He embraced Angelica as she replied, "Yes, sir, we'll be there."

"Alright, y'all. In a minute," Mike said as he walked off.

Angelica laughed to herself.

"What's so funny?" Carlton asked.

"Not a thing. I love Detroit!"

Where everybody is black whether they want to be or not, she wanted to add, but didn't.

Whenever Angelica would turn to a particular side while dancing and look out into the room, she saw a woman staring at her or was it Carlton she was looking at? She wasn't sure. In any case, she seemed to be more interested in them than the whole table of folks she was with.

"Carlton, who is that woman at that table right there? Don't look!"

"How the hell can I answer if I don't look?" he said, slightly peeved.

This was an act. He knew exactly who she was talking about. Kitty O'Neal was sitting there boring a hole in his back. He avoided looking her way. They'd spoken earlier when she was grabbing a smoke by the bathrooms. She was there with some girlfriends and one of the gay men she worked with. She'd asked the guy to come so she'd at least get to dance. Carlton told her he'd find a way to come to her room after Mike's party and after Angelica was asleep.

"I saw her earlier. She looks mad or something. That's Kitty O'Neal. Do you remember her? Anyway, she's probably drunk."

"Yeah, you're probably right."

The leader of the band announced they were going to "slow it down" and began playing The Delfonics' "La La (Means I Love You)." Angelica shook her head and stopped dancing.

"Okay, I'm done."

"No, let's slow drag. I don't think we've slow danced since our wedding," Carlton said, pulling his wife into his arms.

Angelica couldn't wait for the song to end so she could sit down. This was her and Ricky's song and it didn't feel right to be dancing with anyone else. Uncomfortably looking over Carlton's shoulder, she saw Ricky coming through the crowd on the dance floor, pushing past one couple after the next until he was behind Carlton.

Angelica stopped moving as did, seemingly, the air in the room. Ricky tapped Carlton on the shoulder just as he was loosening his grip on his wife to find out why she'd quit dancing. With the exception of some of the spouses and assorted guests, everyone knew that Carlton Meadows and Ricky Williams had been the best of friends in school. They also knew how the narrative had played out for Ricky. People at tables stood up to see what was about to happen while dance floor couples fell away from one another to get a better look.

"Can I cut in?" Ricky said, not quite making it sound like a question.

Carlton turned slightly to face Ricky as he grabbed his wife by the wrist.

"Hell no, nigga! Are you kidding me?"

Someone in the crowd went, "Oooh," like an instigating and immature kid in a school yard row.

"Let your wife answer, Carlton."

Ricky looked straight at Angelica's startled face and said, "Come on, Angel," putting his hand out to her.

Angelica shocked herself by taking Ricky's hand. She now had one man clutching her wrist and another holding her hand.

"Dayuuuum," someone exclaimed loudly. Likely the same fool as before.

Carlton yanked Angelica toward him.

"Get your hand off my wife, man."

"Carlton, you're hurting me."

"Or what? What you gon' do, nigga?" Enrique asked defiantly.

Carlton began to laugh sharply. "You been trying to fuck this bitch since the day you met her," Carlton said angrily.

"Carlton! Are you crazy?" Angelica said trying to twist out of his grip.

"Whoa, slow down partner. You the only bitch I see, punk ass nigga!" Ricky said loudly, his free hand clenching into a fist. If he hit this idiot, he'd be back in jail and Carlton knew it. Though he would like nothing better, neither man would get what they wanted in that moment. Ricky let go of Angelica's hand and walked out of the ballroom.

"Why? Why did you provoke him? Do you want him back in jail? What is wrong with you?!"

"Fuck him! Let's go," Carlton said, pulling Angelica toward the elevator.

"Wait a minute. We're checked in until tomorrow. My stuff is in the room. We can't just leave."

Carlton was wild eyed, his nostrils flaring and chest heaving. Was he still drunk or did this encounter sober him up like drinking a gallon of hot coffee? He paced in front of the elevator bank.

"Well, let's pack our shit, because I'm going home."

"Well, I'm not. If you want to go, be my guest. You're not going to embarrass me and ruin my night, Carlton. Go on, then."

The doors to the elevator parted and a couple stepped off. Carlton hustled inside and pressed a button.

"You get home the best way you can, then," he said as the doors closed.

He went to the parking lot and waited for Angelica. Surely, she was going to come out and appeal to his rational side and beg him to stay. After 10 minutes, he started the car and took off into the traffic on Ouellette Avenue, heading toward the tunnel to the United States.

Angelica put her head up and threw back her shoulders before she marched back into the ballroom and sat back down at the table.

"Well, that was fun," she said to no one in particular.

She felt the eyes on her, so she looked up to see people staring at her and smiling furtively when she caught their gaze. She couldn't wait to talk to Sheila. She'd be so mad she missed all the excitement. Where was Ricky? She wanted to apologize to him and ask him what madness had driven him to be so bold with her? If she let herself think about it, it was actually daring and sexy. Her head was pounding now. Angelica gathered her things and excused herself from the table.

She got into the elevator and absent-mindedly pushed the "L" button for the lobby. Perhaps her ridiculous husband was downstairs at the bar. Maybe she should get drunk. After a quick sweep of the bar and lobby, without seeing Carlton anywhere, she crossed over to the registration desk.

"Is there a guest registered by the name of Ricky, uh, Enrique Williams?"

There was.

"What room is he in?"

They told her and asked if she'd like them to ring his room?

"No thanks."

Angelica got to her room and it was dark and chilly from the cranked-up air conditioning. *Carlton really is gone.* She leaned against the door to take off her shoes.

"What a fucking night," she said to herself, traipsing through the room to reach the lamp on a side table.

She hadn't seen her night ending like this. She had booked a suite and had ordered wine for the room in case some classmates wanted to come through for conversation and a drink. The old hotel desperately needed a facelift, but her rooms were spacious with a view of the lights along the Detroit River from the balcony.

After a relaxing shower, Angelica put on her celebratory lingerie and laid on the couch, trying to fall asleep. It was 2:00 a.m. when she suddenly woke up, put on her silk robe, slid on her new slippers and decided to find Ricky. She wanted to laugh at herself because she was fully awake, no headache, no ill effects from the earlier libations. She was also fully aware of what she was about to do, but not certain of the reasons why.

Angelica opened the door to her room and there he stood. Ricky Williams had been outside her room for several minutes trying to figure out what he wanted to say to her. She let out a tiny yelp and quickly put her hand over her mouth as Ricky pushed past her and into the room.

EIGHTY-FIVE

K itty O'Neal was everything Angelica Meadows wasn't. Kitty was the neighborhood girl with a "reputation." Some of it was well deserved, but much of it was embellished by the testosterone fueled imaginings of the teenaged boys in the community. The wildest rumor was that Kitty had a "train" run on her by some of the older boys in the neighborhood. A "train" was akin to rape in that the girl was an unsuspecting attendee at a gathering where she was the only female amongst a group of males and didn't realize she was expected to have sex with one boy after another until all the boys had been serviced.

Of course, this wasn't true. Kitty never allowed more than two boys in her house at one time. Sure, she might have 4 or 5 guys over and they'd sit on the porch smoking cigarettes and drinking pop, but that was it as far as the volume of male visitors went. They sure wouldn't be having sex on her auntie's front porch! To Kitty, this rumor was ridiculous and hurtful, but she couldn't really refute it. Boys lied and tried to build their sexual reputations on her back, literally, and the girls just thought she was a nasty, fast girl. Plus, Kitty knew if there had been a train, she'd have been the conductor.

She had but a couple of rules for her teenaged life. Rule number one: don't let a bunch of niggers in your house. It could only lead to trouble. Rule number two: when asked anything, don't ever answer all the questions completely. Everybody didn't have to know everything about you because they were going to make up their own version anyway. Some girls may have called it being mysterious, but Kitty called it survival.

The facts of Kitty's life were as brittle, dark and twisted as a burnt pretzel. Her playful bravado hid the residue of a young girl's betrayal of the love she had for her father. Kitty's father had been 25 years older than her mother, who was only 21 when they'd met. O'Neal, as he was known, left his barren wife of two decades for the beautiful young woman who quickly became pregnant with Kitty. He divorced his wife and married the younger woman. Kitty was a small baby with delicate features, highlighted by her large, dark, almond shaped eyes. Her daddy called her his "Little Cricket," and he never tired of rocking her, holding her and just generally staring into the face of the miracle that God had blessed him with.

Within months, Kitty's young mother became restless and bored with the life of "an old married woman," as she put it. She was happy her old man, literally, liked to be around the baby so much because it gave her more time to go out and drink and socialize with her newfound acquaintances. Nothing O'Neal did could persuade his young wife to be a faithful family woman. She cared little for her child and even less for her husband. After about five years of putting up with her trifling ways and the many boyfriends she taunted him with, O'Neal decided to leave his wife to make a better life for his beautiful baby girl, elsewhere. He thought they would spend some time with his sister down in Atlanta and from there he and his little girl would see which way the wind would blow them. It was going to be their little adventure.

O'Neal was excited and smiling as he drove home from buying tickets downtown at the Greyhound station for himself and Kitty. Just as O'Neal turned down West Grand Boulevard, his car careened wildly, jumping the curb and slamming into a street light pole. If the heart attack hadn't sent him hurtling into eternity, the broken neck he suffered on impact with the pole surely would have.

The widow O'Neal wasted little time collecting the munificence of her veteran husband's life insurance and bought a new house for her and Kitty. But Kitty grieved so, she was a sad, morose little girl who could not understand what had happened to her beloved daddy and why she could not ever see him again. How could that be? Mrs. O'Neal caught the eye of a man named Lamar Hunicutt, someone she saw around frequently, a friend of her next-door neighbor. He was utterly smitten with the pretty little girl and her mother. Lamar moved in with them after gaining their trust and soon Kitty was smiling and laughing once more. She became comfortable and happy with the new version of her family.

Like the fate of the chirpy little insect she'd been nicknamed for, her soul was squashed underfoot as Lamar began molesting Kitty. She was so petrified of her stepfather, Kitty began to wet the bed, hoping this would sicken Lamar and make him leave her alone. But the assaults continued with that extra element adding to the shame and humiliation being piled upon her small body. Why didn't her mother notice what else was attendant to those sheets other than pee? Surely, she had to realize an 8-year-old shouldn't have blood and semen on her bedclothes. What did she think that was? Did she even notice? Wash day always found her mother in the basement humming along to the rhythm of the washing machine, seemingly oblivious.

At the age of 14, when Kitty finally got up the courage to tell her mother what had been happening to her, the woman told her to pack up her belongings and leave because she could no longer live under her roof. Her mother called her a jealous liar, a little troublemaker, and ungrateful to boot. Kitty was passed off to her aunt where she lived until she moved out on her own at 21. Her aunt never missed an opportunity to remind her that she was a virtual foundling and she should be grateful that anyone decent would have her in their house. They never talked specifically about the accusations or the circumstances that brought them together, but it was obvious that her aunt didn't believe the girl.

Kitty eventually gained the reputation of being an easy lay because sex was her way of attracting and making friends—male friends. Because of her striking good looks, boys overlooked her overripe notoriety, at least when it was convenient. They would seldom acknowledge her in the halls of Mumford High School, but rather, wait until no one was around to make their approach. The girls weren't quite as charitable and shunned her altogether. Kitty transferred to Dodge High to try to forge a new persona, but the old one followed her like a playful puppy and it wasn't long before she was making friends in the same way she always had.

As she grew into womanhood, Kitty increasingly found herself the paramour of married men and men who already had girlfriends. Kitty tried to drown out the little voice in her head telling her with each thrust, each bite, and each slap, that she somehow didn't deserve, could not have and would never have a man of her own. Her body was to be co-opted and appropriated by men who claimed to want her even though they seldom bothered to stay the night. No matter how compliant and malleable, she never moved beyond where she was found. She would ask herself, *why am I so easy to walk away from?*

And then there was Carlton Meadows. Carlton seemed different. He didn't remember Kitty from Francis Dodge High School and that was alright by her. The fact that a girl like Kitty,

Pretty Kitty, would give him, the time of day, was too flattering and earth shatteringly unbelievable for him to resist. Carlton hadn't long graduated from college when he ran into Kitty at Watt's Club Mozambique on Fenkell. She laughed at every joke, was rapt in her attentiveness to his every word. They became lovers that very night as Kitty had no time for playing coy. That was for suckers. This guy clearly had a future and she planned to be in it. Kitty didn't like men who played games and wanted to chase her around and act surprised that she liked sex. Quiet as it was kept, Kitty knew most women who were honest about sex preferred to get it out of the way early so as not to waste time flirting with or fawning over somebody who couldn't fuck.

Kitty and Carlton had a complex and savage relationship with sado-masochism playing a huge part in their attraction to one another. Once he decided he was going to marry Angelica, Carlton coldly cut Kitty off, leaving her sobbing on the kitchen floor of her apartment. To him, Angelica was like a gift he wanted to buy, but could never quite get enough money together to make the purchase. He always seemed to be a day late and a dollar short with her, and all he could do was window shop hoping nobody else got there first. He never allowed himself to think about Enrique Williams because if he had, he'd know that Ricky most assuredly had gotten there first.

Carlton believed he could be a faithful husband, though he'd not had practice as a boyfriend. Three months before he and Angelica married, while Angelica planned their wedding, the biggest social event in Detroit in years according to The Michigan Chronicle, Carlton bought Kitty a house on Detroit's West side. And the more prominent and accomplished his wife became, the more dependent Carlton was on his relationship with Kitty.

He paid most of her bills with a secret bank account and she didn't date any other men. Kitty seemed to be content with the time Carlton gave and the attention he paid, but occasionally, she would chafe at the constrictions of their relationship, especially if she happened to see Carlton and Angelica photographed at some high-toned event in the Chronicle. She had to remind herself how lucky she was. Didn't he buy her a house? No one had ever done that before. Yes, she had to wait until he could get away to be with her and yes, they seldom got to go out together, but it was a small price to pay for this type of security. Her own home!

It took a while, before Kitty felt comfortable showing Carlton her dissatisfaction with their clandestine, cloistered, almost vampiric life together. One night Kitty's emotions combusted and sprayed out like steam from a tea kettle.

"Don't think you gon' just come up in here and get my goodies for free without taking me nowhere. You think you 'spose to get a discount cause you done been to the store before?" she groused. "Come grabbin' me like I'm some bag of chips you found on top of the refrigerator."

Carlton remained calm, almost amused at her ranting.

"Kitty, you know I love you. Deliberately love you. Not as an afterthought, okay?" Carlton said as he came closer to her.

He seemed in that moment so kind and sweet, talking in a barely audible voice. His dick got hard as he thought about what was about to happen next. He couldn't help it. Carlton backhanded Kitty hard across the face. The little tortoise shell adornment in her mane flew into the wall and skittered to the floor. He grabbed her by her hair, entangling his fist in it. Carlton yanked her head back as he tore off her blouse with his other hand, buttons popping like bullets fired from a gun. He let go of her hair and rubbed her titties with his palms and pinched her nipples roughly. Kitty let out a squeal that was silenced by

558

Carlton's hand around her slender throat. He forced her to her knees as he unbuckled his pants with his right hand. His manhood was now free, hard and throbbing.

As Carlton pushed himself deeper into Kitty's mouth, he thought about his wife. She had no idea what his sexual desires and proclivities were, he hid them so well. She would be appalled at the S&M fantasies played out between himself and Kitty. He imagined her complete shock, amazement and horror as she came upon this scene, realizing, sadly, she didn't have anything on the sexually prolific Miss Kitty. He cried out as he came, thinking he was the luckiest man in the world.

EIGHTY-SIX

R icky was standing directly behind her when she closed the door. Angelica turned to face him. Should she try to get by him? Would he let her?

"Ricky, I—"

"Uh uh," he said putting his hand on the small of her back.

"Don't you—"

"No," he said in a firm whisper, not knowing or caring what she was about to say.

"But I—" Angelica began, about to stammer into an excuse as to why he needed to leave her hotel room.

"No, you don't," he whispered again, closing the small space between them as he pulled her body to him. She was warm and trembling slightly. The scent of jasmine came off her body.

"Aren't you tired of waiting? Aren't you tired of talking? Don't you want me?"

He had bent his face closer to hers and she could feel his warm breath on her face. Angelica relaxed into him, putting her hands on his face and then around his neck as she looked into his deep brown eyes.

Angelica kissed Ricky on his lips, softly at first and then again and again, each time with more urgency. Ricky's tongue explored her mouth, forbidding retreat, breaking down every excuse, every moment of separation and longing. He moaned soft and low as Angelica seared herself to his body so completely she could have passed through him and come out on the other side of him.

"Yes, yes, yes," she cried as her body began to involuntarily grind against his. She could feel his hardness pressing into her. Ricky stroked Angelica's hair, moving it behind her ears. He searched her eyes.

"Are you sure?" he asked softly, never breaking his gaze.

Stepping back, Angelica opened her robe and slipped it off. She slid the straps of her silk gown down her arms and it fell to the floor. Angelica always considered herself shy when it came to her body, but at this moment she was emboldened. Everything she had belonged to this man and she wanted him to see her. Ricky ran his hands over her breasts, lightly brushing her erect nipples. He pulled her to him again and put his left hand gently between her legs. Beckoned by her sodden panties, he slipped his thumb beneath the elastic at the top of her thigh and found her throbbing clit. He stroked it as he kissed her deeply. Angelica's legs were shaking. Ricky stopped and placed her hand on the mound protruding from his pants. She allowed her fingers to follow the shaft from the base to the tip. *Holy shit*, Angelica thought. Her heart was pounding. She'd waited so long for this moment.

Enrique led Angelica to the bed where she lay back, watching him undress. His eyes were narrow and smiling, even though his lips were not. Ricky's skin was some taut and gleaming chocolate Angelica couldn't wait to taste. His expansive chest rose atop of a stalk of muscles riding up his flat stomach. His arms were like veined pythons, lean and muscular. Angelica's lips parted, and her eyes opened a bit wider when Ricky took off his black underwear. His dick was thick, long and waving slightly as he moved. She looked back to his eyes to let him know she approved of everything feeding her sight.

Ricky reached over Angelica's hips and pulled off her soaked panties. He pulled her down the length of the bed by her ankles and motioned to her to get the pillows to make herself comfortable and give her a slight rise from the bed. Angelica closed her eyes as she felt Ricky's warm breath between her legs. He teased her with his lips and tongue as he worked his way to her clit. She wanted to explode, but she held back to let the two of them enjoy every flick of his expert tongue. She ran her hand gently through his hair as she felt her soul climbing up and up, higher and higher as her body tensed and shuddered. She cried out in a guttural yelp as she came, Ricky holding her hips until she was practically bucking against his mouth before he released her.

Ricky came up and laid next to her, his arm across her body.

"That was crazy," she said, catching her breath.

Ricky kissed her long and deep.

"I smell like you, Angel," he said, his voice rumbling and playful.

"Um, yeah, I know," she said, chuckling slightly. "Luckily, I like the way I smell."

"Good, so do I," he said. Ricky couldn't stop kissing Angelica, stroking her face and hair, caressing the curves of her body.

"Lay back. I want you to just relax," Angelica said as she kissed his chest and teased his nipples with her tongue.

She wanted to feast on every part of his body, baptizing everything she could taste with her mouth. Angelica kissed his thighs first outside and then inside, as his swollen penis raised itself, stiff and pulsating and bobbing for her attention. She ignored it. She was licking the inside of his thighs now and blowing lightly where her tongue had been, the cool tingling sensation making him dig his fingers into the bed sheet. Enrique was already moaning, and she hadn't even done anything yet! Flicking her tongue like a serpent, she licked his balls, one by one, finally bathing them gently inside her hot mouth.

Angelica rose up slightly to see Ricky's member practically begging for relief with a drop of sweet salty nectar on its tip. She licked and flicked all around and under the head of his dick until she knew they both could take her teasing no longer. She plunged her mouth down onto him using her lips and tongue to circle and suck until he was practically levitating from the bed. Ricky gently put his hands in her silky hair, urging her on to their mutual reward. After several minutes, feeling his excitement about to peak, Enrique tried to pull back and raise Angelica's head from him.

"Stop, stop, stop," he murmured, but Angelica began working her mouth even faster, gently gripping his tumescent rod, muttering, "Unh unh."

He pumped into her rhythmically, crying out, "Yes, baby, yes!" as his essence roared into her mouth.

Angelica had never before let a man, any man, do that. For the first time, the only time in her sexual experience, she made the split-second decision to swallow what he'd given. She hoped Ricky didn't think she was some kind of sex fiend. Before she could think any more, Ricky flipped her on her back and was kissing and licking her tits like they were twin mounds of whipped cream. Surely he hadn't recovered his erection that quickly? He pulled her on top of him and rested Angelica's head on his chest, encircling her with his sinewy arms. He kissed the top of her head. She looked up at him and he gave her a lingering kiss.

"Damn, girl. Shit! You blew my mind! Pun intended," he exclaimed.

"That was a first for me. It just seemed right," Angelica said, her hand resting lightly on his chest as she listened to his heart— her heart!

Ricky was massaging her temple and scalp gingerly. His hand slipped down to cup her firm round ass.

"Everything about this is right. I can't stop touching you, baby."

That small endearment breached the threshold from friendship to intimacy, as much as what they'd just experience with one another. If his uttering "baby" only moments earlier could be ascribed to an involuntary and unthinking word grab born of ecstasy, saying it again made it something real and deliberate. Ricky locked his fingers with Angelica's and kissed her hand.

"I've dreamed of making love to you so many times, Angelica. The thought, no matter how small or seemingly impossible, was always alive in my mind. And, it's not some high school or kiddie infatuation either. It's always been you, how you talk, how you look at me, how we are together, your honesty, your strength, your scent, your sexiness..." he was almost purring.

Angelica looked up into those beautiful brown eyes.

"I love you. I always have, probably from the moment I saw you on that stupid Bob-lo boat. I said to myself, 'Wow, who is that girl?' Baby, everybody else, I swear, receded into the background like special effects in a movie. It was so crazy that we became friends and you were so fun to hang out with. I had to play it cool, though. I couldn't let you know that for me, nobody compared to you. Nobody."

"Why didn't you ever ask me out, like on a for real date?"

"Trust me, once I went away, that's all I asked myself. I don't know. That's a lie, I do know. I wanted to be worthy of you. My family, I love them, but they're a different breed. They can be—"

"Are you kidding? I always dug your family. Even Uncle Bill. Please, my family is the weird one with all their secrets and lies. At least you know what's happening with your people."

"And yeah, there was something else. I had to practice first."

"Practice?"

"Yes, baby girl. I was gonna turn you out, Angelica Tanner. I was gonna make a good girl go bad!" They both laughed. "Seriously, I wanted to be your first and I wanted to have a few skills, that's all."

"Well, I'd say you've learned well, Grasshopper. But before we continue to practice on each other—"

"Oh, this ain't practice, baby."

"I'm gonna need you to wash your face," Angelica said before they both convulsed into laughter.

"Oh, I thought you loved your own scent so much?" Ricky said, barely able to speak through the guffaws.

"I do, but—"

"Yeah, you need to wash yours too. I never professed self-love."

565

They roared with laughter. This level of ease and comfort was something so many wanted to emulate with either of them, but never could. Hand in glove, they fit. Angelica got back to the bed first. 4Ricky emerged from the bathroom with his dick swollen and raised as if on a flagpole. Angelica smiled as he came down onto the bed embracing her full body. After a few soft kisses, he took her body with him to the center of the bed, handling her with one arm as if she were feather light. Enrique went to work on her breasts again, giving each his slow and undivided attention with his gently kneading hands and stiff tongue. He used his knee to bid Angelica's legs to open and when he entered her wet and throbbing hole he put his mouth on hers to feel her lips contort slightly to form an "O" as she gasped.

"Can you take it all?" he whispered.

"Yes," she said as if in a trance.

They found their rhythm immediately, urgently acquiescing to the primal call and response of their bodies. The couple made love as if there would never be another chance. They stroked each other's flesh as if they could feed their hunger through their fingertips. Angelica grabbed and playfully slapped at Ricky's muscular, round ass as he drove himself deeper into her. He whispered nasty, dirty things that made her feel free and uninhibited and sexier than she'd ever felt. He rode her body, feeling Angelica's insides tensing and quivering on top of his dick until she cried out in a powerful orgasm that shook both of them. Ricky was right behind her, pushing himself deep within her to release his seed with a low and shuddering growl.

Angelica was holding Ricky so tightly as his body jerked and then relaxed, she didn't want to let him go. When she loosened her grip, he moved close to her side, rising slightly to look her in her eyes, realizing they were both on the verge of tears. So tender was his gaze no words were needed as Angelica gently put his head on her breast, stroking his hair until she knew he was sleeping. She never took her hands from Enrique as he slept, a stolen glory to be sure, for she knew the sun would soon rise and her life with Carlton would resume. *Oh, but how?* There was now another line of demarcation for her. *Before tonight, after tonight.* She knew she loved this man and always had. It was a seed that had grown, first in the sunlight and then in the darkness, unwilling to surrender itself to logic or circumstance. No fantasy she could conjure could compare with what they had just done nor what their hearts felt. Now what?

Enrique stirred.

"That feels so good, you feel so good," he said, hugging her as best he could from his position. "I don't think I've ever woken up in bed with anyone in my life."

"You are so dramatic. You and I have slept together, you know. Literally. Don't you remember that crazy day we spent together in your basement? We got a little drunk and fell asleep. Remember?"

"Oh, yeah. No wonder I won't let anybody else take your spot. I only want to wake up to you, Angel."

He was only half kidding. The truth was, that was not an option and they both knew it. He was looking at her again. Angelica tried to be cheerful.

"Sounds like you're just running. Don't want anybody to get too close."

"You're probably right. You know me. I've never felt that way about you, though. It was comforting to know somebody outside of my family *knew* me, *cared* about me—"

"Loved you. Love you. Still. I've never stopped."

Ricky kissed the fleshy mound of one breast and laid his head back down.

"What happens now? Wait, before you say anything. I know what happened last night was a fluke, but we both know it had to happen. You're a married woman, someone who's made a name for herself and—"

"I don't care about that!"

Ricky rose up on his elbow, so his face was just above hers.

"Let me finish, baby girl. You were a good girl who grew up to be a great woman. Any man, hell, every man, would want you. I've struggled to hold on to who I am all these years while growing into my manhood, surrounded by men who were more like animals than what you'd find in the Detroit Zoo. Not all, but too many. In some ways, I'm still the boy, the person you knew, but I want you to know the man. And, I want to know the woman you've become. But we can't, can we? You're not a cheater and I don't mess with married women. Yet here we are. And it's okay. It's okay that this is all we get, you know? It's more than I ever thought possible."

"I love you, Ricky Williams."

He kissed her on her lips.

"I know, Angel. The sun'll be up soon. Let's go out on the balcony for a while."

"Hey, they have robes in the closet we can put on. Otherwise we'd have to be wearing sheets or birthday suits. Well, you would," she teased.

Ricky unlocked and slid open the glass door to the balcony. He reached for Angelica to help her over the threshold and outside. The air was surprisingly warm and humid as they stood looking at the lights of Detroit reflected in the black water of the river and the soft indigo of the pre-dawn sky. They were dreading the coming daylight like two vampires on the run.

Ricky ducked back into the room and came out again with two glasses of water. He stood behind Angelica at the railing with his arm encircling her, making sure she felt him near. The small lanai had two chairs and a café table.

"I wish you would never stop touching me. I wish we could hold back the dawn. I wish…a lot of things," Angelica sighed.

"You and me both," Ricky said, turning Angelica to face him. He looked serious. "There's something I want to ask you. I said I wouldn't say his name, but nothing can ruin last night for me. Why did you marry Carlton?"

Angelica drank all her water down in several gulps. Enrique followed suit, wishing it was something much stronger. They put their glasses on the small table and sat down. It was so still and quiet except for an occasional barge's far away horn.

"Los Angeles was beautiful but strange to me. It was like getting up close on someone you think is pretty and then you see all the wrinkles and scars and age spots and stuff. It's not horrible, but it's not what you expected. Let's just say I experienced my share of traumas while I was on the West coast. There were good times though, too. Anyway, I was disconnected from you even though I tried to keep us—"

"Don't blame this on me, Angelica."

"I'm not. Trust me, I'm not. When I got back here, Carlton seemed to be everywhere I was. He was so sweet and attentive and kind, or he seemed to be. He was like a physical reminder of the way we were. The way we all were. The four of us. But then he changed. He drinks. A lot…and I—"

"He dropped the act. He's showing the real Carlton. You're lucky you didn't have to go to prison to see it."

"Didn't I? Sorry. Figurative is no match for literal in this instance."

"I'm going to tell you what happened that day, but not right now. You know how you eat a steak or something and everything is so delicious and then the last bite is a bunch of fat and gristle? It spoils your meal because now you're trying to get your mind and your mouth to remember how good everything was up until that point. Well, this is that. I'll call you up when you're least expecting it and we'll have that conversation, okay?"

"Okay."

She wanted to tell Ricky that in her quest to be nothing like Liz Tanner, she'd allowed herself to be imprisoned by a love that she could not have. Her heart was landlocked, awaiting the flood that could only come from the man she loved. No matter how hard she tried, she remained stranded. Until now. Ricky reached across the table to put his fingers through hers. His hand was reassuringly real and warm and brought her back to the moment.

"You're going to think I'm horrible, but—"

"Never, my love. Never," Ricky said softly, looking at her delicate hand in his.

"I don't love him. I don't think I ever really did. I thought the love would kind of grow, but…ridiculous, huh?"

"Come here," Ricky said, leading Angelica around the table to stand in front of him without getting up himself.

He ran his hands over the outline of her body as she stood between his legs. Enrique opened his robe and his staff stood high and rock hard and ready for his woman. Angelica let her

570

robe fall from her body as she straddled him. They kissed, teasing each other with playful nips on the neck and earlobes. As they kissed more passionately, Ricky could feel Angelica's wetness dripping anew, down onto his thighs. He entered her, and they moved and moaned together, making love until the sun crept up from the indigo horizon.

EIGHTY-SEVEN

When Angelica got home on Sunday morning, her body was spent but she was happy in her spirit and ready to fight with her husband. She knew Carlton would be mad that she not only didn't leave with him but had the nerve to stay overnight in Canada. It could be so exhausting to fight with Carlton. He seemed to never tire of making sure he announced every slight, perceived or otherwise, and how he felt about it.

But their house in the fashionable Sherwood Forest neighborhood was closed up and quiet when she arrived. Angelica opened the drapes and went upstairs to unpack. She looked around keenly at the bedroom. The bed had not been slept in. She was relieved to be alone, so she could think about the events of the last 12 hours. She tried to make herself care about Carlton's whereabouts, but failed. How could she go on with this man now? What would she do the next time he touched her?

When Carlton came home, Angelica was napping and when he made a fuss in order to wake her up, she pretended to remain asleep. How long could she avoid him? When should she face him and what would she say? Carlton had been so angry when he tore out from the Viscount Hotel that he ended up at Kitty O'Neal's house. He let himself in and fell asleep. When she got home, he was particularly brutal with her, telling her she should have known to come home when he didn't show up at her hotel room. When she tried to explain that she believed, logically, he had spent the night with his wife, he choked her until she almost went unconscious. Once at home and finding he couldn't rouse his wife, Carlton retreated to the guest room. He decided Angelica deserved to be punished for embarrassing him. He wouldn't return to their bedroom for three weeks. *That'll teach her ass.*

A couple of weeks after the reunion, Angelica and Carlton were having dinner downtown at Carl's Chop House on Grand River Avenue. Carlton was still haunting their guest room and Angelica didn't ask why. She knew the answer and it seemed fortuitous for her. For now. Carlton was in a good mood and wanted to go to the fancy steak house for a meal with his wife. The oiled and gleaming dark wood paneling on the walls and ceiling helped muffle conversations. She waited until he'd begun to eat, moaning a bit each time he took a bite of his meat.

"It's good, honey?" she asked.

"Yes, indeed," Carlton replied.

Angelica didn't have much of an appetite, but she ate a few bites of food, mostly rearranging it on the plate. Angelica ruminated on how to broach the subject of *the incident* with Carlton. They were out in a public place, surely, he would act civil. Then she noticed her husband already had three cocktail glasses, two empty of everything but melting ice cubes, lined up like soldiers on the front line, silently warning her to stay quiet. Did she hear them saying, *"Don't start no shit, won't be no shit?"*

As unoriginal as he was unkind, this would be the perfect opportunity for him to try to humiliate her if she brought up Ricky. He'd fashion some secret sadness she'd confided to him into a rapier to run her through. Angelica didn't care. She took a deep breath.

"Carlton, what really happened that night at the Shake 'n Spin?"

Carlton was frozen in place, his fork suspended stupidly near his face. He offered a rigid half smile.

"Baby, I know you must have read about it in the Free Press back when it happened. You were at the arraignment, right? Are you trying to re-try the case or something?" he snorted with a short laugh.

She could tell he was about to get upset.

"No, I just want you to tell me the truth. Do you know we have never really talked about this? Ricky is so hurt—"

"Ricky!" Carlton roared, noticing people looking up from their meals.

He bent close to his plate trying to silo the conversation between himself and his wife.

In a low voice he said, "That motherfucker!? You're talking to me about Ricky? What happened? Seeing him at the reunion make you sentimental for old times? Well, the Three Musketeers is dead baby, and he helped kill 'em."

She decided not to press him, but she noticed he didn't answer the question. She saw Ricky's eyes when he contemplated just *talking* about what had happened. She saw how hurt he was and it tore at her soul. Was he just a sociopathic liar, feeling sorry for himself? Was he trying to play on Angelica's guilt for going on with her life? She knew she had to find out the truth, no matter who it hurt.

EIGHTY-EIGHT

Though difficult, Angelica and Ricky had agreed they would not try to see each other. It wasn't fair to either of them. They knew they had to go on with their own lives and live with their choices, the both of them. A month and a half had passed, and Angelica was feeling under the weather, appearing run down with not much of an appetite. She stared at the chicken noodle soup Leamon had picked up for her from the deli down the street. Just smelling it was making her nauseous. There was no way she was going to eat it.

"Leamon!"

She didn't care if he was going to scold her. She was certain she looked pitiful enough for him to back down. Her assistant appeared with his arms folded and shaking his head in disapproval.

"My God, you look worse by the hour. Why don't you go home?"

"Can't. I have too much to do. Would you mind getting me a Vernors? I just need a good burp."

"That's attractive."

"Hey, everyone can't look as great as I do right now and have courtly manners too," she teased.

"Be right back," Leamon said, ducking out of the door.

What would she do without Leamon? He had become her right hand. He challenged her and made her fight for her place at the table of "old boys" when necessary. It was a delicate dance being a young black woman with an "opinion" but not an "attitude." The phone in her office rang. Why was it so damned loud? Everything was getting on her nerves, she figured her period had to be right around the corner. Angelica picked up the telephone on the second ring.

"Angelica Meadows, can I help you?"

"Hello, Angel. I'll never get used to that name. I'm looking for Angelica Tanner, dammit," he kidded.

Angelica immediately brightened.

"Hi."

She didn't care if she sounded silly and girly.

"It's been hard not calling, but, I know it's for the best and it's what we agreed to. I miss you. How are you?"

"Yeah, it's been almost unbearable for me, too. I was feeling a bit sick, but I'm better just hearing your voice."

Neither of them spoke as Angelica closed her eyes and listened to Ricky breathe into the phone.

"That wasn't your cue to clam up on me, Enrique Williams."

He laughed, then paused, his voice serious.

"Look, I told you I was going to tell you what happened that night at the Shake 'n Spin, remember? After today, I hope I never have to tell this shit again. Do you have a few minutes?"

"Yes, of course. Tell me what happened, Ricky."

And he let it all out. He told her Carlton had come by right before they closed the store. He was acting weird and he had his father's gun with him. While Ricky was finishing up his cleaning duties in the front part of the store, Mr. Gilhooley went back to the office.

"I was thinking I was going to get into trouble for having that nigga in the office. That was for employees only. I was thinking about how I could explain Carlton's ass even being in there, and then I heard the shot."

Ricky told Angelica how he got the gun from Carlton after they ran out of the store.

"I slid in that man's blood. I had blood on the bottom of one of my Chucks. The police took my shoes into evidence at the police station."

Angelica wanted to be compassionate and keep Ricky talking because she knew it was unlikely they'd ever speak about the incident again. But the lawyer in her pushed forward, trying to understand what she was hearing her friend say. Angelica ran her hand from her forehead to her hair. She was so warm; the front of her hair was damp with perspiration. She grabbed a napkin to dab at her face.

"Why did you take the gun, Ricky? Why not—"

"Because I honestly thought Carlton might shoot me! It happened so fast and something told me to get that gun out of his hands. I had a brown paper bag in my hand. He dropped it in the bag or maybe I did. Anyway, it took me a long ass time to figure out why my prints would have been on that gun, whether I touched it that night or not."

"I don't understand. What do you mean?"

"One time, one of the few times I ever went to that fool's house, he was messing with his dad's gun and talking some crazy shit about his old man. I told him I don't go for guns. I don't play that shit, period. He said he was just kidding around but handed me the gun anyway to check it out. I put it right back on the shelf and left. So long story short, the police had my prints on the gun and the gun case at his house."

He realized his account of events made him seem like a gullible rube and in some ways, he had been. He told himself he didn't care if Angelica believed him or not. That was a lie. He did care. Ricky continued to talk.

"After my brother Danny got killed, it made me feel guilty, I guess. I wanted to protect anybody I cared about...my family, my friends. I thought I had time to figure out what to do."

"You were just a kid, Ricky. You were traumatized. How could you know what to do?"

"I was going to call my Uncle Bill, but I got arrested before I could talk to anybody. Me not talking to the police was a mistake, even though I knew I couldn't trust them and they wouldn't believe me anyway."

"Oh, Ricky. I wish you had said something to defend yourself. I wish you had just told them the truth."

"Well, hindsight is 20-20. I agree with you, but I was...I don't know. Mr. Meadows sent word that he was going to get me a lawyer. For free! No need to burden my mother with such a thing, he said. Mr. Meadows and my pal Carlton. Wow, was I lucky! I even felt bad about calling Carlton "The Weight." Remember that joke we had?"

"He ain't heavy, he's just Carlton," she said, humorlessly.

"Well, Carlton lied and said I shot Mr. G. I didn't, but it didn't matter. The hole was dug, and he pushed me in. His daddy piled on the dirt to bury me. I never had a chance. The bastard they got to represent me kept telling me about all the evidence against me and it would be my word against Carlton's. A respected attorney's boy versus the relative of a known hustler and brother of a dead thief. I took the plea deal."

Angelica sat there hunched over her desk, her mind reeling. Carlton Meadows, her husband, was a liar who committed perjury in open court and a murderer who allowed his friend to take the rap. He'd obviously buried the truth so deep, he had no idea what the real story was anymore—or pretended he didn't. The lawyer fell away as the friend sat there with tears of anger and sadness trailing from her eyes. Enrique could hear the muffled sound of her sobs over the line.

"I'm so, so sorry, my love," Angelica said softly. "You didn't deserve any of this. Oh, my God."

Leamon knocked on the door and opened it stealthily. Angelica grabbed a few tissues and tried to blot her face. She knew she looked a complete fright and Leamon's expressive eyes left no doubt. He put the can of pop on her desk and tipped out, but not before looking back at Angelica again as she faked a smile. He closed the door.

"You realize this injustice cannot stand, right? They don't get to just get away with ruining a man's life."

"Baby, they already got away with it. They—"

"No. They only *think* they did," Angelica said, steely. The lawyer had returned. "One question. Can you think of anybody, anyone who might have seen what happened or maybe was in the store or outside of the store when y'all left that night?"

579

"Oh, yeah. We weren't alone, the three of us. There was one customer in the store, but she was gone when we came out of the back. She heard the shot just like I did though, 'cause we looked at each other for a quick second."

"Who was it? What happened to her? Why didn't she testify or at least give a statement?"

"You remember that junkie they called Queen Helene? She was there. I don't know the answers to your other questions."

Once Angelica and Ricky got off their call, she popped the top to her soda and took a few big gulps. Almost immediately her stomach began to roil, and she bolted for the bathroom. The burp didn't come, but everything she'd eaten that day did, right into the toilet bowl.

EIGHTY-NINE

D r. Khalid Sumay shuffled some papers around his desk until he found a manila folder hiding under the small mountain of information piled there. He silently reviewed the contents of the folder, pushing his glasses up his nose with his index finger.

"Mrs. Meadows, every lab and culture have come back negative. I could have told you this over the phone, but I wanted to see you in person."

"Thanks for taking the time, Dr. Sumay. That's great news, but I still feel lousy."

"Still feeling feverish, run down and nauseated after you eat?"

"Yes. I barely even eat. When I smell the food, I want to throw up."

"Mrs. Meadows, when was your last menstrual cycle?" the doctor asked, his ink pen tapping with each word.

"Well, last month. No wait...I've been so busy...kind of expecting it to come like it always does. I guess late June?"

Why was she asking him? He had asked her! Dr. Sumay removed his glasses as if he were Clark Kent about to become Superman. The doctor smiled.

"It is now late August, Mrs. Meadows. I want to give you a blood test for pregnancy. Unless I miss my guess, you're having a baby."

He was saying something about the nurse taking her down to the lab and results in a week or so, but Angelica sat there trying to solve a math problem that was unique to her. She hadn't had her period since June, since before the reunion, *since before Enrique*. Carlton had sequestered himself in the guest room for almost a month after the reunion to prove a point and to "punish" her. If he only knew what relief that punishment had provided. When he finally came back to their bedroom, he wanted to make love to his wife as if he hadn't exiled himself. Carlton remarked how tight she felt to him and got himself all worked up by saying he missed her, missed her body and how much he knew she'd missed her man.

Yeah, she thought as he pounded away. *That pussy is extra tight because I'm not turned on, idiot! It's a desert down there, fool! And I do miss my man. You have no idea.*

Sex between them was always just average, with Carlton making excuses when he didn't satisfy his wife. As Angelica lay on her side, her husband's semen trickling down the inside of her thighs, she could only fixate on how she was going to be able to snap out of the dream she had with Enrique and wake up to accept her reality with Carlton.

Luckily, within a few days, Angelica was exhibiting signs of illness, which continued for weeks. Carlton tried to take care of her to make her feel better but joked that he didn't want his wife to throw up on him, so they could skip their usual marital activities. Funny enough, throwing up was exactly what he made her feel like doing. How long would she have to pretend that everything was alright, and Carlton Meadows wasn't a monster?

How long before she could take down Sidney and his son and make them answer for what they'd done?

NINETY

Angelica knew there were three sides to just about every story and she'd heard Carlton and Ricky's sides. Now she needed to find out the third side, hopefully, the truth. In front of her were the court records and transcripts of the trial, as well as the police file on the case with photos of the Shake 'n Spin and poor Mr. Gilhooley. There amongst the papers was another yellowing file jacket. She opened it and got the small rush of dusty air in her nostrils, reminiscent of a childhood spent at the library. There was a statement inside by someone claiming to be a witness to the crime. *It isn't signed.* Did that make it any less real?

As Angelica delved into the old files of the case against Enrique Williams, she was shocked at what she found. There were clear discrepancies in the statements of how everything went down that night. Ricky had refused to speak to the police at first and that mistake, call it youthful pride, sealed his fate.

Angelica read Carlton's statement from that night in 1968. The other statement was not from Ricky, but from the only eye witness and it was given a week after the crime. Perplexing. Angelica sat looking at the words on the papers before her. They seemed to rise up and taunt her with small bloody fingers. Tears flowed down her face and she laid her head on her forearms settled on her desk. Her assistant knocked and entered before she could respond. She simply lifted her right hand against his oncoming words, waving them away. Intuition told Leamon to leave her alone this time.

After a few moments, Angelica straightened up and grabbed some tissues nearby and blew her nose. She had to make sure she understood everything as she put the story together. There would be no turning back, and she decided she would have to tell Carlton what she was going to do. She wasn't going to work in stealth as he and his father had. Angelica could see Carlton and his father's hands in this morass as surely as if they'd left their fingerprints at a crime scene.

Enrique had unwittingly become the victim of one of the oldest plays of the criminal justice system that preys on the young, the poor, the vulnerable and especially, the Negro. They locked him up, setting an unattainable bail amount. His mother couldn't help him, she had children at home and she didn't have the money.

When Uncle Bill heard what had happened he looked at mortgaging his homes, but it would take time to apply for a loan and get approved. He'd paid for his houses cash just so he wouldn't have to answer questions like the ones that a mortgage company might ask. It was hard for a nigger to find $100,000 in loose change. When he went to inquire about his nephew's bail in person, he was suddenly surrounded by 3 uniformed officers who threatened to "find a reason" to put him in a cell with Ricky.

The lawyer came to Ricky with the plea deal and initially, he refused. He was innocent, he'd never been in trouble, he was expected at college. Those were the facts. As he languished in lock up, the visits by his counsel became less frequent and he began to lose hope. The plea deal was his only chance, according to his attorney. He gambled and lost, and the judge gave him at least 8 years in prison.

Angelica had to track down everyone involved in the case. Clearly, a cover up had taken place. Though the police seemed to turn a blind eye, the statement of events according to Helene Allen were in the file and she had read it many times over. This was clearly dereliction of duty and collusion amongst the lawyers. Hargraves had died of cancer in 1978. A bad break since he seemed to be the ringleader of the deception. Unbelievably, Ricky's lawyer came up deceased as well, having died of a stroke in Allen Nursing Home just a year ago. Angelica found it to be anything but a coincidence that he had been the protégé of one, Harvey Hargraves.

Angelica needed to find Queen Helene right away and she knew that might prove impossible. She was more than likely dead, in prison, or she may have left Detroit for all Angelica knew. She didn't want to think about it, but, there were two people alone in the spotlight of duplicity--Carlton and his father, Judge Meadows. Conspiracy, obstruction, failure to report a homicide and perjury all seemed like the right pronouncements for the Meadows men. She had to find Queen Helene.

NINETY-ONE

Q ueen Helene had heard on the street that Ricky Williams was being held for murder and Carlton Meadows was not. That couldn't be right. She talked herself into doing the brave thing, the right thing, to go to the police and tell what she'd seen. They had the wrong one locked up, as far as she could tell, and she wanted them to know it. At first the police were eager, even glad she'd come to them. But, as her tale unfolded, so clearly at odds with what Carlton had sworn to in his statement, their attitudes changed.

The cops asked her to wait in the public waiting area where she sat on the hard bench for what seemed like two hours before they called her back into the interview room. This time, when she entered, there were two men there who hadn't been present before. She recognized one as Mr. Meadows, Carlton's daddy, the lawyer. There was also a fat white man there, whom the others seemed to defer to. The policeman, Lt. Baxter, said her statement was typed up and ready for her to sign. But first, he asked her to just tell everyone in the room what she'd seen the night of Saturday, July 13, 1968.

Queen Helene looked at each man's face. When she looked at Mr. Meadows, he looked away and refused to meet her eyes. She began speaking while looking at the fat man, who was smiling, though his blank eyes let her know he was not very interested in the words coming from her mouth. He seemed almost in a daze.

She wasn't stupid. She'd noted that the timbre of the police officer's demeanor had changed, the energy in the room was electric and hostile. Helene Jacobs Allen was scared, and she needed to find a way out of the room. *Danger!* she felt herself screaming inside.

It was like the time she'd been called over into her neighbor's yard by the boy next door. He was a few years older than she, but he'd always been a friendly kid. He told her he had something to show her in his garage. Once she was inside, she saw several older boys she recognized from the neighborhood. Two were standing near the bumper of an old Cadillac, two more were near the entrance she'd just come through. The boy next door continued to talk to her in a calm, almost lilting voice.

It suddenly flashed in Helene's mind what was about to happen. *Danger!* She tried to run back out of the door, but the boy next door had grabbed her arm and she saw the sunlight scrambling out of the garage as the door came down, aided by the two teenagers near it. Helene was in the garage for two hours. The five boys raped and beat Helene until she was unconscious. When they had done all they could think to do, the boys picked her up and laid her in the alley where blood began to pool around her head and buttocks.

Helene's mother was hanging out the wash when she heard the incessant barking of a dog. When she could stand it no longer, she took off her shoe and ran toward the fence bordering the alley, her plan involving well-aimed footwear against the animal's head. The dog was standing near a pile of clothes. *People are too lazy to live,* she thought. *Why would someone just leave a pile of clothes in the middle of the alley?* As Mrs. Jacobs walked over, threatening to hurl the shoe at the still barking canine, she saw that the clothes had somebody in them. A girl. *Her daughter!*

Helene Jacobs entered the hospital with cracked ribs, a dislocated shoulder, broken fingers, a broken nose and a crushed eye socket. She remained in the hospital almost two weeks and continued her convalescence at home even longer. Understandably, she did not want to go back to school. Helene was only 11 years old when she'd been assaulted, but she spent many years afterward fighting off the looks of disgust from adults, her peers, parents of classmates, the whispers behind hands and the unearned reputation of being a "bad girl." Though she'd nearly lost her life, and most definitely lost her innocence in that musty garage that summer afternoon, she'd lost something else as valuable and irreplaceable. Her reputation-- before she'd even realized she had one or that it could be destroyed.

She and her mother moved to another part of Birmingham a few months after the incident, so Helene could start at a new school. But somehow, the story, twisted and embellished to paint her as a fast, panty dropping girl who got what she'd asked for, always found its way to her. It was almost impossible to make friends as the parents certainly did not want their daughters or sons hanging around such an obviously bad influence.

Helene dropped out of school and got a job in a textile mill by lying about her age. She also learned how to do hair from helping her mother in her basement beauty shop. The women who visited her home treated Helene like she was an object of pity or a disabled half-wit. "Bless her heart" always preceded the *tsk tsk* as the women secretly stared at her while pretending to read the latest Jet Magazine. At 18, Helene took a Greyhound bus to Detroit and never saw Birmingham, Alabama again.

The fat man spoke first.

"Where do you, uh, live, Miss, uh, Allen?"

"Right now? Well, I'm between places."

"I see, so you are homeless? A street person, as it were?" he said in his avuncular manner.

"Well I..."

"Isn't it true you are a dope fiend? A junkie?"

She didn't answer. She could see where this was heading. She only wanted to do the right thing. Gilhooley was alright for a white man and Ricky was always good to her. She knew now she'd made a mistake and she needed to get out of that room. She could smell her deteriorated scent penetrating her nostrils and she wondered if the others could too.

"So, you are just a good, upstanding citizen wanting to help the police, is that right?"

"Yes," she answered, defensively, as his statement sounded more like an accusation than a question.

"Did you come here thinking you could lie to us and get some money from the Meadows family? From Mr. Meadows here?"

"No, sir. I done came to tell what I seen and that's all."

"I done come to tell what I done seen, that's all," he mocked.

The officers laughed. Sidney Meadows did not laugh, taking offense at the mocking tone, the bullying of this defenseless black woman. He'd read the statement for himself and it sounded truer than anything his cowardly son had posited. Still, he knew her statement could not see the light of day. He had to protect his family's name and reputation.

"I've heard enough. Let this woman go on her way," he said, finally.

Helene popped out of the chair like a slice of bread in a toaster. She didn't want to sign anything, she just wanted out of that hot room. Lt. Baxter looked at the fat man, who nodded slightly.

"Okay, you can go," said Baxter.

The junior officer put the unsigned document in the file jacket and left the room.

Baxter said, "That Williams kid still isn't really talking. Just says he didn't kill anybody and that's all. Seems pretty open and shut if you ask me. It's gonna be years before that boy sees the outside of a prison cell."

All the men chortled, good naturedly, including Mr. Meadows.

NINETY-TWO

When Angelica stepped onto the porch of the cute little brick bungalow, she noticed how neat and well-manicured the yard was. She rang the doorbell and heard a muffled two note retort from behind the door. She heard the growl and then yapping from what sounded like a small dog. A woman's voice was playfully scolding the animal as an interior door closed loudly.

"Just a minute," the woman yelled.

Angelica was glad the dog had been put away. Years ago, she'd been invited to dinner by a guy she'd been dating. His parents were nice enough, but the family dog, a Yorkshire terrier, kept humping on her leg and no one seemed as alarmed as she was. After pulling the dog off of her for the third time, Angelica gently pushed him along the carpet, whereupon he turned around and bit her on the wrist. Instinctively, Angelica kicked the dog across the room like a football, where he landed on a couch. Everyone stared at her open mouthed and she herself was mortified, but not for reasons the family cared about. She was politely shown the door without dinner and her date never called again. Maybe God was looking out for her today. Nothing would stop her from getting to the truth.

The woman who answered the door was short and pleasingly plump--what people called "healthy." She was a medium brown skinned lady with deep set brown eyes. She wore a perky black wig and a blue dress. Angelica guessed she was in her mid-50s.

"Yes?" she asked.

"Mrs. Helene Allen, I'm Angelica Meadows. I called you earlier today—"

"Yes, yes, chile, come on in here," Queen Helene said, effusively.

They walked through the living room with its plastic covered furniture to the cozy kitchen and sat in two of the plastic covered chairs surrounding the Formica topped table.

"I'll bet you don't remember me, Miz Helene," Angelica began.

"Of course I do, of course I do. It's me that you probably don't recognize," she proudly exclaimed.

"Well, I'm so happy to have found you. Frankly, I thought you might be dead," Angelica said, honestly.

This must have struck Queen Helene Allen as funny because she laughed until tears rolled down her face.

"Quite the opposite. Born again is what I am, and God is good!" When she stopped laughing she looked Angelica in her eyes and said, "I been waiting to talk to you for a long, long, time."

Angelica was driving. Her movements and manner were mechanical, robotic. She had to make sure she was far away from Queen Helene's house, her neighborhood, her side of town. She drove, dream-like, until she ended up downtown crossing the bridge to Belle Isle. Because it was late autumn it was stark and cold. The great Scott Fountain with the lion statuary that frightened her so as a child was still, turned off for the impending winter. She looked out over the Detroit River which would soon enough be ice bound, watching the barges slowly making their way up the deep, green waterway. Angelica looked at the trees, bare and shivering against the wind, limbs flailing like hysterical old men. She looked up into the cloudless blue sky, finally, as if trying to remember this day, this moment, this feeling.

She opened her mouth and silently exhaled more breath than she knew she had. Then her body shuddered as the sobs became audible, louder and louder. Angelica's face was a grotesque mask of wet cheeks and bared teeth. She cried for almost ten full minutes inside her car, not knowing, or caring if anyone had seen her display of contorted emotions. She found some napkins in the glove compartment--*No one puts gloves in there*!--and wiped her face. She put her car in drive and pulled away.

Getting away with murder is more dangerous than getting caught. The unpunished perpetrator begins to see himself as invincible and invisible to the force of law. How did anyone not know? How did the universe or God make no answer for the spirit that had been released into the void? The first night Angelica saw Enrique he'd said, "a lie can't live forever." She didn't know exactly what he meant then, but now she'd been schooled.

Somehow Angelica had made it home. Her arms were as weak as noodles as she shut the door and dropped her purse to the vestibule floor. She laid down in her bed, the only place safe enough for her to think about all she had learned today. Her head was swimming, but the pillows seemed to cradle her and buffer the rampage of words and images fighting to be understood. She fell into a deep, abbreviated sleep. When she awoke, she woke up completely conscious. Not groggy or foggy, but totally alert. That fleeting and hopeful feeling that it was all a dream was immediately replaced with a crushing sadness, like a child being

594

told there would be no presents for Christmas and everything they believed in was a lie.

Queen Helene Allen told Angelica the truth about what happened that summer night in 1968 at the Shake 'n Spin. This woman, who had been a bum and a junkie, had a life before tragedy pulled her into its dark and windowless room and locked the door.

"I come to Detroit when I was about 18 years old outta Birmingham, Alabama. My parents had eight of us churren, so when I got old enough, I decided to light out on my own. Shoot, nobody was gonna miss me. One less mouth, 'ya know? I knew how to do hair and I could cook and clean, so I knew somebody would be needin' me for somethin'," she said, laughing a bit.

"Well, no sooner than I got off the Greyhound did I meet this big, red nigga at the bus station. Lawd hammercy, was he sharp as a tack. He say, 'Hey, gal, come on wit me and git you somethin' to eat.' Even helped me with my valise."

Angelica tried not to show her growing impatience as a tight smile crossed her face. *This is not what I came here for.* But, she also knew she might not get another chance to hear what happened at the Shake 'n Spin.

She smiled and inquired, "Now, who was this gentleman?"

"It was a pimp name Black Bottom Red. I guess I don't have to tell you I didn't end up cleaning no white folks house, huh?" she exclaimed with a cackle. "In no time, Red put me on the stroll. I was kind of shame at first, but then when I seen how much money I could make, I was down wit it. Red was good to me. He never, ever beat me," said Queen Helene.

Angelica held her composure, not betraying any feelings of surprise or judgment of this woman. She had been through a lot to just be sitting there today, healthy and alive.

"Well, Red got into some trouble and ended up going to jail for a 3-year bid. That was where he met Bill Williams. Bill wasn't but 'bout 18 and Red was 36 then. They became pretty tight and Red school young Bill in the game."

So that's where Still Bill Williams got his start, Angelica mused. Nobody really knew how Bill became a pimp and this information was like a primitive riddle being solved by an oracle. Helene continued.

"Red was good to me, like I say, and we ended up gettin' married. He kept our home life separate from bidness. I didn't work the track no mo', but he had a couple of hos that did. Red sent me to cosmetology school and I done real good wit that. That's how I got my name, 'Queen Helene, First Lady of Style.' I had my own 'lil shop on John R with several girls doin' hair for me."

Helene took a gander over at the counter to spy on the coffee pot that was heating up.

"When Red got out, I told him he had to go straight—it was me or the life—couldn't be both. Black Bottom Red was a good man and he turn his back on the sportin' life. Things was good for a good 'lil while," she said, her face suddenly going dim, like a candle dying.

She gestured with a flip of her hand like turning over an invisible sign.

"Are you alright, Queen?" Angelica asked, not sure the woman should try to continue. She was torn, but she knew she had to find a way to get what she'd come for. She had to know the truth. Helene cleared her throat.

"Red had money, 'ya know? *We* had money, I should say. We bought a car repair shop. Red loved a fine car and he sho' knew how to keep 'em runnin'."

By now the smell of fresh brewing coffee filled the kitchen, the white Corning percolator having done its duty. Angelica watched Queen Helene as she moved about the tidy sun streaked room, a plump and pretty woman. There was almost no trace of the wraith like stick figure she'd been when Angelica was a teen.

"Yes, God is good," she said as if she'd read Angelica's thoughts.

Angelica smiled, embarrassed. Helene came back to the table with two cups on saucers steadied by her chubby brown hands.

"We had the repair shop almost 5 years, no problems, no trouble. 'Til one day, these two dudes come in sayin' they needed they ride fixed. It was lunch time, so there wasn't but one or two guys in the shop wit Red. Nex' thing you know, they say 'this is a hole up, gimme all yo' money.' Red, he always had a special way with young folk. He tried to talk to 'em. Them niggas shot my man!"

Queen Helene clapped her hand to her mouth, tears rolling down her cheeks. After about 30 seconds she spoke again.

"They shot one of the other fellas too, but he was okay after a few days in Henry Ford Hospital. The police, they act like they didn't care about catchin' who did it. I guess some of 'em remember Red from when he was in the life, so who cares about a ex pimp gettin' popped, huh?" she said, bitterly.

Helene drank from her cup, little wisps of steam meeting her eyebrows.

She sipped, swallowed loudly and asked, "How is your coffee, hon?"

"Oh, it's fine, I'm fine. Continue, please," Angelica said, though she hadn't yet touched her cup. She hoped she didn't sound commanding by saying "continue" to Queen. This was obviously very difficult for her.

"The cops didn't care, but you know who did? Bill Williams. I don't know all the particulars, but Bill started looking for them two. He found 'em and he killed 'em. He sliced them bastards up like a Christmas ham," Queen exclaimed, exhaling as if relieved.

She fell silent as she unconsciously rubbed her ring finger, perhaps feeling the phantom weight of a thin gold band.

"You know how we do thangs here. We have to take care of our own. Nobody ratted on Bill, he just went back to his bidness. But me, well, that's somethin' else," she said putting her hand up to her forehead and closing her eyes.

She glowered as she spoke.

"I...just...fell...apart. I thought for a while, if I keep a-workin', doin' hair, I'd be okay. But comin' home, night after night to the emptiness, the darkness, the loneliness, it did me in. I stopped goin' to work and lost my bidness. I couldn't get outta bed and pretty soon I didn't even have that," she said, crying again. "For a spell I lived off the money from sellin' Red's shop, but pretty soon I got kicked out of my house. Sheriff come and put all my thangs out on the lawn. I was standin' out there with people askin' me what I was gonna do. Then when they walk away, they take some of my stuff wit 'em. Oh, yes! Huggin' me and pattin' me on the back while they tellin' they bad ass kids to pick up a lamp and a chair," she laughed, pitifully.

598

"Bill tried to help me, but I wouldn't let him. I thought I would be okay. But, I weren't okay. I got into them drugs and was lost, so lost for so long. So, I just wandered around, just another junkie lookin' for a fix and a place to lay my head. It's a wonder I didn't die out there. God sent Bill to get me cleaned up and back on my feet. I ain't never told any of this to nobody. Bill helped me when nobody else could. He would prolly not want people to know how good he is. Spoil his street rep," she whispered behind her hand.

By this time the coffee was gone from their cups. As informative as their conversation had been, and it had been that, Angelica didn't know the details of the night Mr. Gilhooley was killed. She'd just have to ask, no matter how seemingly indelicate. She consciously waited what seemed like a respectful amount of time before broaching the subject.

"Miz Helene, you know I'm a lawyer now, right? I had the chance to look at some legal documents and police records involving what happened that night back in '68 when Mr. Gilhooley was killed. Do you remember that night?" she asked gingerly.

"Yes."

It was funny and startling to hear her answer in one word after so much talk taking up more than an hour's time. Angelica decided to follow her lead and keep it simple.

"What happened? What did you see?"

"I used to go into the joint at the end of the night to get leftovers and sometimes a few bucks from Ricky. I done known 'lil Ricky his whole life. That's Bill's nephew, 'ya know. What a sweet, sweet kid. A good boy, real decent. Anyways, Gilhooley didn't really care as long as I didn't bother folks on they way into the sto'," she stopped, noticing the empty cups. "Want some mo' coffee? I'm gon' have some mo' myself," she said pouring the steaming hot brew into the little circle of leftover brown inside her cup.

Angelica waved off the refill.

"It was just about closin' time," Helene said, as she set her cup into the saucer, "when that boy Carlton come past me and into the sto'. I could see through the window that him and Ricky done went into that back office back there. Mr. G was just sweepin' the flo' when I come in. Pretty soon Ricky was back. He saw me and gave me the sign he had some food for me. While he was baggin' it up, Gilhooley goes into the office back there and no sooner than he go I hear a 'pop' and I didn't need nobody to tell me what it was. Man, I run outta there so fast—"

"Are you positive Ricky was with you when the gun went off?" Angelica asked.

"Yes, just as sure as I'm sittin' here talkin' to you. And, I told the police this, but they never asked me to testify. I run out the sto' 'cuz it was too much. Reminded me of what happened to Red."

She shook her head a few times and looked down at her hands.

Angelica sighed. *My poor Ricky. What had he been through?* His life could have been so very different. Why had it been so easy to believe Carlton's lies? She felt ashamed. She could feel the tears burning in her eyes. Helene Allen was still speaking.

"I had ran to the alley and then come back to call the police when they come runnin' through there, Ricky and Carlton, a few minutes later. Ricky took the gun from that fool to get rid of it. They both run off, but I know Ricky saw me."

Angelica felt a twinge of defensiveness when Queen pronounced Carlton a fool. But, Angelica was the fool because Carlton was…what? A sociopath and she was married to him. She shook herself to attention.

"He saw you?" Angelica asked.

"Yes. He look me right in the face and then ran."

Angelica sat there speechless. Aghast. Carlton had lied by playing the unsuspecting innocent bystander and unwitting accomplice of Enrique Williams, the cold-blooded trigger man.

Queen Helene explained that Carlton's dad had called in a favor from Angelo "The Snake" Santori. Mr. Meadows had paid for both boys' defense, except Ricky's lawyer was paid to lose his case. Angelica could see the saga playing out in front of her like a movie with the Meadows family doing all they could to keep their only child from a prison cell. Someone had to take the fall and that someone had no one of power in his corner. Ricky was so young, he probably believed he'd only be in one, two or three years max, because his silence and inaction made him an accomplice to *Carlton's* crime. Then he got the bad advice from his lawyer to plead guilty and while he was appealing, he ended up killing that guy in prison and it just put a period on things.

Through her tears Angelica asked, "Why couldn't Bill help his nephew?"

"Same reason they wouldn't let me testify—we was on the wrong side of the law. We didn't matter—and here I am the one and only eye witness! We was nothin' up against Meadows when he had Santori backin' him."

Angelica had heard of Angelo Santori over the years. He was a crime boss who had his hands in every illegal venture in Detroit, from gambling to prostitution to drugs. He sounded like bad news and someone not to be crossed or played with.

"Santori had the Detroit police department in his back pocket, at least some of 'em. Still do! We was nothin' up against them two. Meadows is just a puppet, but he still dangerous. And so is yo' daddy."

The movie stalled out on the projector and a blossom of melting colors burned through the images in Angelica's mind.

"What? Whose daddy? Queen, sorry, but I don't—"

"I know yo' mama, Liz. I used to do her hair," Queen Helene said looking in Angelica's green eyes. "Angelo Santori is yo' daddy."

Most people would find it hard to believe that a grown woman who was not an orphan, did not know the identity of her father. Angelica had asked her mother many times, intermittently during her childhood, but she could never get a wholly satisfying response. Because Liz Tanner was always simmering and about to come to a boil, it was hard to catch her at a moment that welcomed inquisition. Angelica knew she had a limited amount of time and sentences that could be used in pursuit of paternal queries. Generally, Liz would just utter a matter-of-fact panacea like response, "Your dad was white." Or, "Your dad never knew you." And, of course the subject closer, "He's dead. Why do you keep bothering me about this?" On this subject, Liz was as salty as the Dead Sea and twice as dense.

Angelica often wondered why she had no paternal grandparents or cousins seeking her out. Had the man, her father, fallen to the earth as if sprung from the head of Zeus? It was indeed odd, yet no one in her family dared cross Liz by giving up information on this mystery man. Even her grandmother, who seemed to relish agitating Liz, held the cards of Angelica's paternity close to the vest. As a young girl Angelica shared her confusion with a few friends and as with the nature of children, their attention to the subject of someone else's problems was brief and fleeting. Just another mystery of life that, if mentioned in genuine curiosity at their neighboring dinner tables, elicited a response of, "Be quiet and eat" from the adults.

The quest for familial validation sort of faded over the years with Angelica just accepting her life as it was. What good did it do to think or worry about it? It was a void to be sure, but she had to appreciate her life as it was and look forward to the life she'd have one day as a wife and mother. She hoped she'd find a man who understood and listened to her and one she would never grow tired of. Yes, she had planned to choose wisely. But things didn't always go as planned, did they?

ngelo Santori was the only son of Maria and Nicholas Santori. Nicholas was the owner of a jazz club in Paradise Valley called Nick's Four Aces. He ran one of the only clubs that served both black and white patrons and everyone got along. Nicholas Santori was also one of the few white owners of an entertainment venue in Detroit's Black Bottom. He knew the music was always the star of the show and spoke to every heart, no matter the color of the skin it was packaged in. He booked local acts like a little-known assemblyman from Ford Motor Company named John Lee Hooker, and national acts like Billy Eckstine, Pearl Bailey, Brook Benton and Dinah Washington. Mr. Santori was an immigrant from Italy who loved America and did not consider himself prejudiced. Angelo spent time doing odd jobs around the club while his three sisters weren't allowed to work at or even visit the club for that matter. Angelo could play a mean trumpet by all accounts and whatever band was playing would often let him sit in.

Angelo attended the University of Chicago and earned a Bachelor of Science degree in Finance. His dad hoped he would help with the family business and one day take over for him, however, fate intervened. Angelo graduated from college and was drafted by the United States Army about a week later and had to report to active duty in Korea after several weeks of basic training. Angelo was terrified. He thought a lot about the baby he might never know. What if that child was all that was left of him if he got killed overseas? His mother was completely distraught and took to her bed until the day he reported to boot camp. The day her Angelo left, Maria Santori collapsed no sooner than her son and husband had pulled out of the driveway. Nicholas came home from seeing Angelo off at Michigan Central Station to find his wife practically catatonic on the living room couch.

Angelo Santori was in the Army for three years, and made it back home unhurt, physically. He was not "shell shocked" as some of his comrades were, but he had definitely changed. The war had made him a different person, hardening both his heart and mind. He was no longer the carefree young man with the easy laugh and funny story. He became serious, very serious about life. Korea had seen to that. When he was over there all he could think was, *If I get out of here alive, I'm going to be the one calling the shots.* He knew he'd never again be able to work for anyone, including his own father.

While overseas Angelo found himself running a commissary of sorts. He was the go-to guy for marijuana, uppers--both were very useful for relaxing and for staying awake while on watch, respectively--and even local women for his fellow soldier's pleasure. He had won this position by beating a small time Korean gang member at cards one night outside a refugee camp they were guarding. To the gangster, Mr. Kim, most Americans looked the same, especially the white ones, but he was fascinated by Angelo's black hair and striking blue eyes. He liked the tall, lanky American and told him he could make his days easier while stationed in Pusan. It could be profitable for both Angelo and Mr. Kim, as he ran the action inside the camp.

Kim had heard that American Negroes liked marijuana, whites liked pills, and both had a weakness for Asian women. Angelo was unique as he had the ability to feel at ease with both the whites and coloreds. Soon, the prettier and younger women in the camp were servicing the American G.I.'s and the money was going to Angelo, who got forty percent. Kim kept fifty percent and gave ten to the girls, so they could help recruit their friends. It didn't sound like much, but inside a refugee camp, that ten percent paid for luxuries like extra rice, tea, sugar and cooking oil.

When Angelo got stateside, he took his money earned both legally and illegally in Korea and began his own business. Within three years, he was one of the biggest and most well-known gangsters in the Midwest, certainly the biggest in Detroit, Michigan. His empire included drugs, prostitution and gambling and he employed hundreds of people. He knew he needed a "legit" business to work from, so he bought out his father's interest in the Four Aces and had him retire. Angelo's club was the hottest night club in the city of Detroit with big name national acts appearing nightly, a chef straight from Paris, France and a wine cellar to rival anything New York City's best restaurant had to offer.

Though this was Detroit in the mid 1950's, he soon found the best way to keep the good families—The Dodges, Fords, Chryslers and Fishers and patrons of the Grosse Pointe Yacht Club--coming into his establishment from their outlaying enclaves of Grosse Pointe, Dearborn and Southfield, he would have to restrict his club to whites only. Outside of the entertainment on occasion and the kitchen staff, there were no black faces at the renamed Santori's Supper Club. He advertised it as, "Paradise in Paradise Valley." He didn't have to put too fine a point on the color restriction as word got around Black Bottom that a black man's money was no good at Santori's. This was in striking contrast to how his father had run his business, but Angelo could not risk his façade as a socially and upwardly mobile gentleman. The Negroes had plenty of other clubs to go to he'd say, including the Flame Show Bar, The Frolic, Club El Sino and the Garfield Lounge, among others.

Eventually, in the early 1960's, commerce, capitalism and mobility did what segregation and regulation could not. I-75 roared through Detroit's Paradise Valley and killed Black Bottom. This interstate became the literal and figurative passageway to "white flight." The flight became a comet as whites sprinted out of Detroit and to the suburbs after the riots. Angelo was glad his club went out that way rather than in the rubble and smoke of the riots that took the city in 1967. Perception was a good substitute for truth in his book. He'd been compensated handsomely for his property and he happily cashed the check like a giant poker chip, never looking back. Nostalgia was a table set for suckers.

Along the way, somehow, Angelo became known as "The Snake." Some believed it had to do with his crafty business acumen and still others the steely intensity of his piercing blue eyes. The truth was simple in its vulgarity. He'd been blessed with a 7-and-a-half-inch penis, which he put to good use before he got married. Angelo had many a sexual conquest and enjoyed his reputation among the ladies and envious enemies, alike.

NINETY-FOUR

Angelica was shocked at how easy it was to get Angelo's telephone number. She called Information and he was listed! The address, she was told by the Information Operator, was unpublished at the customer's request. Angelica was sitting in her office staring at the telephone for at least ten minutes, gathering up her nerve. She dialed the phone number and it rang three times before a woman answered.

"Hello?" she said with a calm expectancy, her voice going up slightly at the end of the word.

"Hello, may I please speak to Angelo, uh, Mr. Santori, please?" she hated the politeness in her voice. This bastard deserved to be cursed out in no uncertain terms.

"He's at his office. Do you want the number, or can I take a message?"

"Oh, I'll take the number, if you've got it," Angelica said, stupidly. *Of course she has it, that's why she offered!*

"Sure," the voice said.

After the woman recited the number and Angelica had written it down with her trembling hand, she thanked her and hung up.

Angelica looked down at the number, tracing over the digits with her ink pen. She wasn't sure what she should say to this man who was her father. Where and how to begin a conversation? Everyone in Detroit knew Angelo "The Snake" Santori. He was a notorious mobster. He was a crime boss. *He was her father.* Angelica picked up the receiver and calmly dialed the telephone.

"I'm here to see Mr. Angelo Santori," Angelica said to the man at the security desk.

He was a tall stocky white man with steel gray hair, a black suit, white shirt and black tie. There were several serious looking men dressed similarly, populating the lobby. The place was beautiful with its light pink marble floors, columns and cornices.

"Certainly," the man said flatly. His mouth smiled slightly, mechanically, but his eyes remained cold as they quickly swept over Angelica. "Your name, please?"

"Angelica Meadows. He's expecting me."

"Certainly," the man said again, looking down at papers on a clipboard.

A pen rolled off the top of the desk and as he caught it mid fall, Angelica glimpsed the handle of a gun resting in a holster on his side, just inside his suit jacket. This made Angelica quickly look left to right to see if anyone else had noticed or even cared. She was already nervous, but somehow, the small moment made her hyper aware, as if to say, "this is really about to happen."

"Take the elevator to the penthouse," the man said, walking her toward a bank of elevators. When the one in the middle opened up, the man stepped inside, inserted a key into the brightly polished panel of buttons and turned it. He beckoned Angelica inside with a slight wave of his free hand and then stepped out without another word. The doors closed, and the elevator ascended. Angelica was almost dizzy at this point, the adrenaline making her hands shake slightly, her heart pounding in her ears. What would be her first words to this man? Would he be pleased to meet her? Would he try to hug her, and would she let him?

When the doors of the elevator parted, Angelica stepped into a large office suite with rich teak paneling and hardwood floors with beautiful Persian rugs. There was a pretty blonde woman seated at the very large wooden desk that dominated the anteroom. There were bookcases, overstuffed leather couches and chairs, and subtle lighting from wall sconces. *This could be a law office or a high-class men's club*, Angelica thought as she allowed her mind to guess behind which door Angelo Santori might be waiting.

"Miss Meadows?" the blonde lady announced, more than asked.

"Mrs. Meadows," Angelica answered, reflexively.

"Of course, pardon me. Please come this way," the woman said moving toward Angelica.

She strode behind the secretary deliberately, trying to keep her jelly knees from betraying her. Within seconds they arrived at a large door. The woman rapped on the door twice and then opened it.

Angelo Santori stood in the middle of the room.

"Thank you, Miss Biderman. Please close the door behind you."

Once the soft click of the door penetrated the room, he spoke again, his voice tranquil and resonant.

"Hello, Angelica. I'm so pleased you've come to see me. Please have a seat," he said opening his hand toward one of the red and gold brocade chairs in front of his desk.

Angelo sat in a leather chair behind the desk, his hand cradling his chin. He smiled only slightly, warily, as if he were at the start of a chess match.

Angelica thought he was so handsome, as to be stunningly so, but in a rugged way. If he looked this good in his 50's, God only knew what he'd looked like in his 20's. His dark hair had a hint of gray at the temples, and he wore it stylishly short and slicked back from his face. Angelo had heavily lidded, clear, deep blue eyes, a patrician nose, wide mouth and deep dimples in his cheeks. His hands were slender and elegant, sporting a gold wedding band. She judged him to be slightly over 6 feet tall. His clean scent, or that of his cologne, traced the air.

Angelica swallowed hard. He was waiting for her to speak. Why did it seem as if he was more prepared for this moment than she'd been? He smiled now.

"You've grown into such a beautiful young woman, Angelica. Your mother has to be proud of you. I know I am."

Somehow, his polite sentiments made Angelica angry. How dare he act like he had the misfortune of entertaining a stranger's child with small talk.

"You look like Liz, but," he continued, "you definitely look more like me." More silence. "Not what you thought it would be like, huh?" her father asked.

She felt he was now mocking her. Angelica tried to gather her thoughts as they flew around the inside of her head like agitated birds inside an aviary. She was too angry to be embarrassed.

"What do you want, Angelica?" Angelo said, his tone changing from congenial amusement to piercing seriousness. "I know you're a lawyer, so is this business, or—"

"Why have I never met you before today?" she asked, not knowing exactly what to call him, not sure how to address the relative stranger before her.

"Liz might be better suited to answer that."

"No, you answer it, *Dad*."

"Your mother and I agreed that no good could come of me being in your life. It would be better if I stayed in the, ah, background."

"Well, you couldn't have gotten any further back. So, you just sent my mother money to support your little bastard, your little black secret?"

"No, not at all. Yes, I have supported Liz for many years, but—"

"Yeah, she's just a little country ass nigger, right? Throw some money at her and she'll keep quiet and be grateful."

"Angelica, I supported you and your mother because it was the right thing to do. You are my daughter. I had to make sure you were okay."

"Yeah, right. Next you're going to say you loved my mother and—"

"Yes! You're goddamned right I loved her."

"Your 'love' crushed her. It destroyed her and when she'd look at me, she saw you, the man she couldn't have. Do you know the emotional hell that put *me* through?"

"No, I don't and I'm sorry. Angelica, I didn't make the rules. I don't control the world."

"Oh, but you do!" Angelica almost shouted. "You *do* make the rules and you certainly controlled our world! That's why

612

someone like you can exist. And this, this," she said, waving her hands around, "is the world you've created. Here, you're God. You are untouchable. So, don't tell me there was nothing you could do to be with the woman you 'loved' so much."

Angelo's jaw set firmly as he looked straight at his daughter. He spoke with the deliberation of a priest.

"I can see where this is headed, and I can tell you, I'm not used to people raising their voices in my presence. I made a decision that I felt would be best for everyone, especially me, okay? Those were different times and a black wife and child was a battle I did not want to wage against society. I am in a profession where you have to choose how you get the public's attention. Your mother has never had to work since she had you. You've had every advantage, a life any kid would envy."

"You're talking about material things. You did that to assuage your guilt, to wash your hands clean—"

"Grow the fuck up, Angelica," he spat.

Angelica's face was suddenly hot, she felt like she'd been punched. He had risen and was now sitting on the desk's edge, long limbs straddling the corner.

"Do you think your life would have been better if you had both of your parents under the same roof? How many of your friends were better off? Do you know who I am, Angelica? Do you know what I do? I am not some factory worker or policemen." Noticing Angelica's expression and the harsh turn the conversation had taken, he said, "I haven't just let my wallet take care of you, Angelica. I've been to your plays, your glee club recitals. I sometimes used to watch you race those juvenile delinquents down at the White Castle. I was at your high school graduation and when you graduated from law school, I was there.

You have turned out more than okay and that's all I know and that's all I care about."

Angelica fought her emotions, but still, the tears fell. Angelo had to restrain himself from physically comforting his daughter. He knew it might make things worse, so he sat there looking down at his desk, so he could allow Angelica a bit of privacy to compose herself. She hurriedly wiped away the tears and cleared her throat.

"I didn't even come here for all of this." She wanted to run to the door, jump onto the elevator and get to her car. But she owed Ricky.

"I know. What do you want, Angelica?" Angelo asked for the second time.

"There was a boy when I was in high school named Enrique Williams. We were very close. He was not just my best friend, I loved him. He was smart, funny, and talented. He was going to be an entertainment lawyer. He was going to change the world."

Angelica stopped, the sadness suddenly squeezing her soul. Angelo nodded, he remembered that kid and what had happened with him and Judge Meadows' son, Carlton. He had to pull some tight strings to get the Meadows kid off, but he never got in trouble again, so what was the problem?

"I decided to look into the case myself after Ricky, Enrique, was released. He got sent to prison for manslaughter, but he didn't kill anyone. He was framed. There was a witness." Angelica was only a little afraid when she looked up into Angelo's stormy blue eyes. She couldn't read his expression. Building up her courage, she continued. "Someone ignored the eyewitness and buried her statement. A dirty lawyer framed Ricky and made him the fall guy while pretending to defend him. Ricky was innocently trying to protect his friend, Carlton, Carlton Meadows."

Cautiously, Angelo responded, "Okay, so what are you saying?"

"Carlton killed the store owner, Mr. Gilhooley. It was an accident, but he got off because of who his dad is."

Angelo shrugged his shoulders.

"And why are you telling me this? Isn't Carlton Meadows your husband?"

Angelica realized he really had been watching her life from some distant place.

"Yes. Angelo—" Angelica finally said his name and it was not lost on either of them. "He is my husband. I'm going out of my mind because Carlton was part of a frame up of my, *our* friend. I feel sick about it. I can't even look at him now that I know. I feel I need to do something. I know his father, Judge Meadows, had some powerful connections even back then. Shoot, he was just a lawyer but somehow, he was able to 'fix' this. They should both be disbarred."

Angelo managed a smile and just as quickly it was gone.

"You know I'm not the Michigan Bar Association, right? You also know I was the one who helped Sidney Meadows when his kid was in trouble, don't you? Mavis Meadows worked for me for years, running numbers. I'm sorry about your friend, but I don't see how ratting out your own husband and his father is going to change anything."

"Something has to be done," Angelica said leaning forward in her chair.

"Does it, Angelica? Why? These things happen every day. I know you're a good lawyer, very honest, but this is not one of those charity or pro bono cases. This is nothing to play with and I'm going to tell you that the Meadows family is pretty ruthless. What? Are you shocked?" he said, misreading her dawning expression.

"No, it's just that *you all know each other*. Carlton knows you're my father?" she said, crestfallen, slowly shaking her head. She already knew the answer. "He never said anything." This was unfathomable, but she couldn't escape it. *The man you believed to be dead, your father, is known by your husband! He not only knows him but has since childhood!*

"It seems there's a lot your husband hasn't told you. I'm not here to verify anything for you, but what I do have for you is advice. Leave those people alone. Angelica, you see me, you know what I am. I make no bones about it. This is my life, and this is how I choose to live. But them, they have the façade of civility and uprightness and they will do what's necessary to protect it. I say don't do it. Let it go, kid."

She could see he was concerned, but she didn't care.

"Aren't you worried about what I got on you? You're part of this too!"

The man laughed in a short burst like a gunshot.

"In a word, no. What did you call me? Untouchable? Well, everyone can be touched at one time or another, but on this one, my fingerprints are long gone. Nothing can or will be done to me. But you? You'd better watch your back if you insist on telling Carlton. He's running for the City Council and wants to be mayor someday, I hear." Angelo snorted at the thought. *Like he could take that job from Coleman Young, the most popular mayor in decades.*

"He's got a lot to lose, so does his old man. Not a smart move. Don't let emotions get you into trouble," he warned Angelica.

"I have to do it."

"No, you *want* to do it, for your friend and maybe some other reasons you're not telling me. It's not going to give him back one minute of his life." He could see she was steadfast and was not going to change her mind. Angelo, sighed. "Look, if you're really going to tell your husband or his father, make sure you have your plan in motion. Make sure you go all the way." He paused. "Never pull a gun unless you intend to use it. Otherwise it'll get turned on you, understand?"

"I have to do what I need to do to make it right," she said finally, standing up.

"So do I," Angelo said, looking at the beautiful girl who was his namesake.

Angelica drove along Livernois. She felt like she was floating in a dream state. It was amazing how the mind took over to guide a person from place to place—work, home, the doctor's office. She no more knew how she'd gotten to Dr. Samay's office than how a plane landed, but suddenly she was just there. She pulled into the lot near Dexter Boulevard and checked her watch. She was a few minutes early for her appointment to take a glucose test to make sure she wasn't a candidate for gestational diabetes. *Could this day get any more stressful?* Of course, it could. She was pregnant, and the clock was winding down on when would be the best time to tell Carlton, and there was no "best" time. *Gee, what should we talk about first? I'm going to the state's Attorney General to turn you and your father in and oh, by the way, I'm knocked up. It could be yours, but, don't bet on it.*

Damn, she'd just met her father and for all she knew she'd never see him again whether she wanted to or not, because according to him, she was putting herself in danger. Hell, a baby might be a moot point, literally. Angelica gripped the steering wheel, feeling the hard rubber under her palms as the temperature dropped inside the car. She had always been a good girl, never causing her mother a day of pain or grief. Yet here she was about to destroy Carlton's life, his family name and her own life most important of all. How could she keep quiet with all she knew? Angelo was a cool customer, but was he scared for himself? For her? What did he mean when he said, "So do I"? *He's not going to allow me to ruin him too.*

Angelica began sobbing, briefly, almost involuntarily and just as quickly she stopped. She felt bitterness now, scorching her mind, burning the back of her throat. She felt bitter toward her mother and father, and Carlton, who surely knew who her father was all this time. Carlton again for playing with Ricky's life and finally, Ricky for falling into the trap laid by the Meadows clan. But hadn't she fallen in as well? Angelica blamed Ricky for making her love him so much she'd destroy her life to save his.

The car was frosty with the chill of a Detroit November. Angelica opened the door and slid out of her car.

NINETY-FIVE

They were meeting two lawyers from Carlton's firm along with their wives at Joe Muer's Oyster House on Gratiot. The weather had abruptly become unseasonably warm by about 25 degrees. The sky was weeping softly, with distant thunder as its consolation. Angelica was glad the long awning in front of the restaurant would protect her and her dressy outfit from the elements. She took more care than usual getting ready tonight as she had not met these particular attorneys and Carlton requested that she look especially nice. He had been in such a good mood lately, Angelica hadn't found the right time to talk to him about all she'd discovered. She found herself being very measured and unemotional, yet hyper vigilant, like a soldier on watch. Angelica had to make the effort to appear normal, even though she felt anything but.

"Carlton, you should have worn your trench coat. It's not summer, no matter what the thermometer says."

"I'm okay. A little rain never hurt anybody."

Dinner was Oysters Rockefeller, Michigan Whitefish Meuniere, and Salmon with Lemon Caper Sauce. The banter had mostly been between the men, with the other wives quietly deferring to their husbands. Angelica did not want to make the women uncomfortable, once she took note of their demeanor, by talking too much about her own job. If the women had anything in common with her, it was not evident through their conversational pursuits. Angelica chalked it up as a one-and-done and hoped she'd never have to see these people again.

Carlton was in a strange humor, almost impish. He seemed to be playing devil's advocate on several topics being discussed and by the third martini, he was getting a bit imperious, turning his attention to his wife. Carlton always found ways to minimize and make light of Angelica's assistance to underprivileged clients. He found it amusing to no end and called it her "crusade."

"My beautiful wife is a very skilled attorney, you know."

Angelica looked in Carlton's direction and smiled shyly, hoping he would find something else to talk to these dregs about.

"What type of law do you practice, Angelica?" one of the women asked.

"I'm a Public Interest lawyer. I help families, poor people, immigrants, working folks who have been taken advantage of, people who—"

"Yes, my wife rattles her saber of righteous indignation against 'the man.' Don't you, honey?"

Angelica, slightly taken aback by his tone and inference, responded, "Well, I wouldn't say—"

"And, I, good people, am 'the man.' I am the establishment, the windmill that she tilts against because I represent corporations and big business. What are you, honey? A fist or something?" Carlton asked, laughing.

There were short, nervous bursts of laughter around the table, clandestine stares mate to mate and some throat clearing. Angelica was about to speak when she felt the stinging heat of tears just behind her eyes and excused herself. After a few awkward attempts to restart the conversation and rescue it from its flat tires on the side of the road, Carlton excused himself to find Angelica. She was just outside of the ladies' room.

"There you are. Honey, I was just kidding, just making a joke. That's all. Don't be mad," he said with all the sincerity of a child actor.

Angelica wiped her eyes and smiled slightly.

"I know. I'm sorry. I don't know why I'm so sensitive tonight. Go back to your guests. I'll be there in a minute."

Carlton moved back into the dining room and sat down with a chuckle. Angelica could hear him say, "She's fine. I think it's that time of the month."

A small rise of laughter hovered over their table with the ridiculous women joining in.

You crass bastard. Angelica turned into the bathroom and stared into the mirror. Not that she needed any more reasons, but sometimes she hated Carlton, plain and simple.

"What are you? A fist?" she said in a mocking whine. "Yeah, a fist to punch your fucking lights out."

She turned on the cold-water faucet and grabbed a hand towel to dampen it. *You wish it was that time of the month, Carlton,* she thought, instantly exhausted. As she put the towel under the icy stream of water, the inside of her arm just barely brushed her right breast, but the painful, fiery sensation radiated from her nipple. Angelica looked around at the door and the expanse of the bathroom and realized she was alone. She took both hands and pulled down the front of her dress and lifted her bra, freeing her swollen, throbbing breasts. The areolas were large and dark with thick veins that grew fainter as they moved up her chest.

Her tits were magnificent. Always had been. She dreaded the sensitivity she experienced every month with her period. Sometimes she could hardly bear to brush up against anything— a wash cloth, a bra, her own or her husband's hands, because of the extreme tenderness. But this was even worse. She soothed her shiny, heavily engorged breasts with the damp cloth meant for her no longer teary eyes. For weeks Angelica pushed away every unwelcomed thought about this, but she knew. She'd received the results of her pregnancy test two months ago in the mail and threw them in the trash. *Can't be. Can't be.* Angelica wasn't yet showing in any significant way, but her belly had become soft. She had to talk to Carlton and soon.

Angelica righted her clothes and came out of the bathroom just as two women were coming in. What a sight they would have beheld only moments before. She made her way back to the table and sat down, a smile affixed to her lips. Angelica noticed a fresh drink in front of her husband's plate. *His fourth?* He picked up the high ball glass and put it to his lips. The blockade of ice cubes gave way as if in a fatigued truce and the liquid, along with several frozen obstructions, came tumbling over Carlton's moustache and the sides of his mouth like a miniature avalanche. The liquor landed all over his shirt and the lapels of his suit, while the ice cubes ran across the table cloth. No one spoke for at least 30 seconds as they all tried to avert their eyes from Carlton.

Within a few days Carlton, duped by the warm weather, found himself afflicted with a nasty cold. Angelica left early in the morning to get some Tylenol and a box of Mrs. Grass Chicken Noodle Soup for him. She could vaguely feel the symptoms loitering about her as well, waiting to engulf her and lay her low. She made sure she got enough provisions for the both of them, just in case. She rubbed her slightly rounded belly as she walked purposefully through the grocery store. As pre-arranged, she met an investigator with the Attorney General's office in the produce aisle. Angelica had to make sure every lock was synchronized when she opened the door to hell for Sidney and Carlton Meadows.

At home, Carlton decided to get up once his wife left, but the false burst of energy was short lived. He tossed fitfully on the couch, turning one channel to the next on the television with the brand new remote control. Carlton smiled to himself. He liked it when Angelica took care of him. It almost made getting sick worth it. *She's lucky to have me*, he mused as the ring of the telephone pierced his thought balloon. He was not happy about having to get up to get to the phone and he made a mental note to make sure it was close by when he hung up.

"Hello?" he coughed into the receiver.

"This is doctor Sumay's office. May I please speak to Mrs. Meadows?"

"She's not here right now. This is Mr. Meadows."

"Mr. Meadows, we have the results of your wife's glucose test last week."

"Yes, you can give them to me. I'm her husband," he said a little defensively, as if someone had implied he might be a servant of some kind.

"Yes sir. No signs of gestational diabetes, so, congratulations, her pregnancy is normal. The doctor will want to see her in the next couple of weeks. Do you want to make the appointment for her now?"

Carlton slammed down the receiver so hard, his knuckles hit the table.

"That fucking cunt!" he shouted, his swelling hand still gripping the telephone.

An hour had passed when Carlton heard his wife's car in the driveway. She entered the house through the side door and went straight to the kitchen.

"Carlton?" Angelica called out. No answer. "Carlton?"

No sound but the TV. *He must have fallen asleep. Good*, she thought, watching her hand shake slightly as she put her fingers around the bottle of orange juice. She wondered if she'd done the right thing. Agent Wycoff wanted her to come to his office tomorrow during her lunch time and officially tell what she knew and bring any documents that would support her claims—as wild as they were!

"Hi, sweetie," Carlton said, startling her.

If Angelica hadn't just put down the bottle inside the refrigerator, she'd have dropped it. She whirled around to face him standing in the doorway.

"Hi, honey. Feeling better?"

Carlton walked slowly toward Angelica with a big smile. When he reached her, he put his arms around his wife and hugged her tight. Over her shoulder the expression on his face had changed to something unrecognizable, but Angelica didn't see it. Her face was buried in his shoulder and all that was visible were her sad eyes, but Carlton didn't see them.

"I'm never gonna let you go."

She tried to break the embrace after a few seconds, but he would not let her pull away.

NINETY-SIX

T he distance of a few weeks had tamped down some of the anger Angelica had for her parents for a betrayal she felt was so well orchestrated, with so many players involved. Napoleon once said that history is a bunch of lies agreed upon. Had Liz Tanner and Angelo Santori made a pact years ago to obfuscate the truth as far as their daughter was concerned, no matter what the cost? Just thinking about it made her blood rise afresh, so she took some minutes to calm back down before picking up the telephone.

Angelica called her mother up and asked her to meet for lunch. The two of them dining together outside of a family function was a rare occurrence, but Liz Tanner happily agreed to meet her daughter at Lou's Delicatessen on Six Mile Road and Roselawn. Angelica had always loved the comforting smell of the hot sliced meats, the pickles and mustard, and the feel of the red vinyl booth cushioning her body reassuringly. She would need it today.

Angelica was already sitting at the table when her mother came in. She wanted to be able to casually look at her mother, and not seem or act nervous as if something were amiss. Liz waved as she approached. She was still a beauty even though she seemed to fight against the idea ever since Angelica could recall.

"Hi, Mama," Angelica chirped as her mother sat down and leaned in for a quick hug. Only Elizabeth Tanner would wear a mink stroller to a deli.

"Love that coat," she said as her mother removed the garment and laid it in the booth next to her.

"Thanks, honey," Liz replied. "It's gotten cold enough to wear this thing already. Can you believe it? Just last week it was so mild. I think this winter is gonna have a lot of snow."

Angelica's head was swimming. What to say? Where to begin? She did not want to ambush her mother, but truth be told, she purposely invited her to this public place, to a booth near the back because she knew Liz would find it difficult to just leave or make a scene. Liz was not easily embarrassed, but still, Angelica could not predict what might happen. The friendly, but no-nonsense waitress asked them what they wanted to eat, and Liz ordered pastrami on rye with Russian dressing, while Angelica ordered a stacked corned beef sandwich on rye with extra mustard, cole slaw and a pickle. They both ordered bottles of Vernors Ginger Ale to drink.

The women talked about one another's health and home, the latter being a topic Angelica decided she did not want to go into detail about. Once the food arrived, Angelica exhaled and looked at her mother.

"Mama—" she began, as Liz's face became animated with a huge smile.

"Lilla!" she yelled.

A woman standing at the counter turned toward where the voice had come from and waved wildly at Liz. Liz waved the woman over to the table without so much as looking at her daughter's astonished face. The woman seemed to appear at their table before her mother could put her hand down.

"Girl, what are you doing here?" Liz squealed, hugging her friend who had plopped down next to her in the booth.

"Treating myself to a sandwich and an egg cream. I was getting it to go," said Lilla.

"No, no, no. Tell them to bring it to the table, I insist you eat with us. You know my daughter, Angelica?" Liz asked.

"Oh, my goodness. I have not seen you since you were about 12. You are beautiful! Oh, Liz, she's gorgeous."

"Thank you," Angelica managed to say, slightly perturbed.

As the two women began their energetic chatter, Angelica saw her opportunity drift away like a grateful survivor on a life raft. She drank her Vernors and ate her food trying to figure out how to get her mother alone again, and when. Maybe this was a blessing in disguise as Angelica needed to deal with one thing at a time. She first needed to confront her husband with the truth now that she'd put everything in place with the proper authorities. She could talk to Liz about the lie that was her life, later.

Angelica sat in her car in her driveway for over a half hour as she contemplated what she knew she had to do. Her inattentive husband hadn't looked out of the living room window to see she was home and had been for a while. *Typical.* Carlton, who had gotten home early, sat on the couch with his second bottle of Pabst Blue Ribbon beer in his hand, flipping through the TV Guide trying to figure out what he wanted to watch on television. He knew it was just an absent-minded distraction while he was waiting for his unfaithful wife to get home from work, so he could confront her. It had been almost two weeks since he answered the phone and got the news that his wife was pregnant.

Carlton had never gotten around to telling Angelica that he could not conceive children. He'd always meant to tell her…or had he? Information gleaned from his physical with the U.S. Army never led to true confessions and what good would it do to mention it now? Besides, he wanted to see how well she could lie. And, what would his parents think when they found out? He flexed his fingers. He had to control himself.

Angelica put her key into the door of their house and took a deep breath before going inside. She had to talk to Carlton immediately and not allow the pretense of sorting mail or cooking dinner or idle chatter derail her.

Carlton listened impassively as Angelica laid out what she knew about the Gilhooley murder and its aftermath. Like the flip of a switch, Carlton was suddenly on the defense, his head swinging from side to side like the pendulum of an out of rhythm grandfather clock. Left, a point was made, right, a point was made. Angelica wanted to laugh at his ridiculousness. She knew he would say anything to make her change her mind. Anything but the truth. During his tirade he said she would be stupid to tell on her dad. *Dad, huh?* Angelica's eyes narrowed.

"He said I'd be stupid to tell on *you!* You and that sinister ass father of yours. I must be stupid. Stupid to never have guessed about…everything! All those lies! Who the fuck are you, Carlton?"

Oh, so now this bitch thinks she can disrespect me. Sidestepping, Carlton tried to get back to the point, the sharpest point, the one that would do the most damage.

"How could I tell you that I knew about your father? About who he was? About what he is? That's what secrets are for, Angelica. To protect people we love."

He tried to reach for her and she pulled away, whirling around to face him again.

"Are you serious? You hypocrite. You pathetic, hypocrite! You would have let me go to my grave not knowing who my father was. A man you actually know! And what about Ricky? That's the worst lie of all. Was it okay to steal his innocence, his life, his good name, his family's reputation, his relationship with his brother and sisters? How can you sleep at night, Carlton? You are disgusting!" she spit.

As Angelica was walking away, her husband grabbed her wrist tightly, knowing he was hurting her. He got so close to her mouth, Angelica feared he was going to try to kiss her. She needn't have worried.

"No, I'll tell you what's disgusting. When your tramp of a wife fucks a faggot ass, soap droppin' ex con."

"What?"

"Yeah, since we're talking about daddies, who's the daddy of that baby you got in you?"

Angelica became completely calm, completely serene. It was as if a bright light had come on and she could see every detail of the man in front of her. The dutiful son who had impressed her with his deference to Sidney, was actually an easily cowed weakling who vaporized into the ether. A bumbling coward who disintegrated into so much dust to be kicked off a shoe. Why had she not looked harder, been more observant? She read so many sign posts as, "Well, you don't have a father, so you don't know how that dynamic works…" She mistook his spineless acquiescence as respect. Could she have been more wrong?

They were in it, Carlton and Sidney, however far it went, together. They were co-dependent co-conspirators. They were two sick fucks who deserved no mercy. All the incidents, humiliations and embarrassments that comprised the essence of Carlton Meadows had been ill remembered and colored in with the pastels of nostalgia. Chalked up to the process of growing up and out of that awkward dance called adolescence. The reality of who he was and had always been was lit up red and bold and blinking like the lights at a railroad crossing. All lights had been ignored and the train ran right over her. All the red flags had been bleached white and she'd helped pour the Clorox.

Angelica looked her husband in the eyes.

"Let me go, Carlton."

He could see by her eyes that the steel in her gaze was new and dangerous. He released her wrist.

"Get your shit and get out of this house. And don't go up to Ann Arbor either. I'll take the keys to my house there and to this one too."

Carlton wanted to pummel her, but a better idea presented itself. He knew he needed to talk to his father, fast. Sidney would surely see that this was not his fault. Sidney would see that his son could fix their problem.

ngelica was pleased her mother acquiesced to spending the remaining Thanksgiving weekend with her. The entire family had been on hand for the annual feast, taking part in the usual Tanner family rituals and shenanigans. Cousins Frankie and Lydia, now adults, spent the holiday at their respective girlfriend and boyfriend's homes. Uncle Ned had taken a spill, falling off of his porch, and found himself in a cast from his wrist to his shoulder. This would be the first Thanksgiving he would not have to lift something, get something, open or cut something. *Yes sir, even with the pain, this is way better*, he thought.

Aunt Fannie Tanner had a new boyfriend and he'd insisted she dispose of her "ottoman of delights." How did he even know about it, the other women wanted to know? Leave it to Fan to run her mouth when she had a few drinks on board. In any case, he found it juvenile, embarrassing and fairly distasteful. No longer would the women of the family convince someone's unsuspecting male companion to have a seat on that nylon covered x-ray machine just so they could gather around it nonchalantly, as he got up.

Angelica wanted to get her mother alone and isolated, so they could talk, really talk about what she'd discovered and what was going on and going wrong in her life. She didn't want to be cruel, but she was weary of the game being played for lo these many years at her expense. It was not easy to forgive.

The snow began falling about 20 miles outside of Ann Arbor as they carefully made their way along the interstate to Angelica's house. Liz was quietly thinking how convenience and progress nailed the coffin shut on Black Bottom when I-75 cut through its heart, razing businesses that were part of Detroit's history. Black history. Her history.

As they pulled up the long driveway, Angelica looked over at her mom.

"My goodness. This place is just magnificent," Liz marveled aloud.

"I know. I sometimes forget it's mine," Angelica said proudly.

And, she meant it. Sometimes she could barely believe that she lived like this. When she was little, she and her mother would go for Sunday drives in "rich" neighborhoods and imagine what kind of lives were lived behind the doors of those stately homes. Angelica didn't feel guilty that she lived far enough away that her family couldn't just suddenly drop in on her unexpectedly. The timer turned on the outside lights at dusk, illuminating the Tudor style façade as they rolled toward the circular driveway, snow crunching beneath the tires.

Angelica and Elizabeth watched television until about 11 p.m.

"Mama, remember when television used to go off? Like around midnight?"

"Yes, of course I do. Shoot, I remember when there was no TV," Liz said, one-upping her daughter.

"Remember how it would end with some guy reciting 'High Flight?'"

632

In unison they said, "Oh, I have slipped the surly bonds of Earth…"

"I kinda miss that, you know. People seemed to be more patriotic, didn't they? Once they killed John F. Kennedy, everything just went to hell in a hand basket," Elizabeth Tanner remarked, suddenly sad.

"I know, Mama. I know. I think we'd better go to bed. I'm so tired, just drained."

Elizabeth suspected Angelica was pregnant, but she wanted to give her a chance to tell her good news. Perhaps she needed some prompting.

"Is Carlton coming back tonight or this weekend or what?" Elizabeth asked.

Angelica lied, announcing to her family during dinner that her husband was away on business.

"Um, no Mama. He won't be back this weekend. Let's go to bed, okay?"

And with that, Angelica got up from the couch and began turning off the living room lights, her mother padding upstairs to her room and shutting the door. They would talk tomorrow—about everything.

The next day, the Friday after Thanksgiving, they had a nice lunch of fat turkey sandwiches--they'd brought home some of Grandma's delicious turkey—potato chips and orange juice. Angelica suggested she and her mother enjoy her indoor pool and Jacuzzi after lunch digested. The pool area was ensconced under a buttressed glass roof with heated glass walls rising from the floor to the ceiling. Outside they could see the undisturbed white powder snow, a stand of ash trees in the rear of the yard held fast to their fluffy white coats.

Angelica was thinking of how to talk to her mother about Angelo Santori and some of the other issues that took up too much space in her mind and soul. She smirked when they got into the water, her mother in the Jacuzzi and she in the pool. There was nowhere for Elizabeth Tanner to escape to. She'd end up a half-naked Popsicle in the yard if she dared try.

Elizabeth noticed the small protrusion of belly her daughter carefully tried to conceal with clumsily placed arms and hands. *Is it a secret*, she wondered? *Is something wrong with the baby or with Angelica?*

"Hey, where did you say Carlton is this weekend? I can't believe he leaves you in this big old house all alone." She hoped her daughter would step through the opening she'd just created.

Angelica knew good and well she hadn't mentioned Carlton's whereabouts to her mother or to anyone for that matter. She herself didn't know where her husband was, nor did she care.

"Mama, I asked Carlton to leave. He moved out last week," she admitted, finally.

"What?! What happened?"

"I guess it's been a long time coming. I don't know. I've been digging around some old business from back when our friend Ricky got into trouble and got sent to jail. Let's just say Carlton is not the man I thought he was. He is a corrupt, dirty bastard. He's a liar who'll do anything to protect his lies."

Elizabeth's throat tightened as if someone's hands had imperceptibly slipped gently and firmly around her neck. She didn't know if she wanted to know the details. This trail of conversation about liars and protecting lies could only lead to no good. While she was thinking of how to change the subject without seeming rude, Angelica spoke.

"Why didn't you ever tell me about Angelo Santori?"

Elizabeth Tanner's face contorted as she realized she was completely vulnerable. The hot water bubbled around her body, but she had a sudden chill so violent she shuddered.

Angelica locked eyes with her mother, determined not to speak again until her mother did.

"How did you find out? Who told you?" Liz asked, as sweat began to trickle down her face and onto her neck.

"No, no, I'm asking the questions here, Mother. Answer *my* questions."

Liz knew she was captive to the conversation and she held the currency to pay her way out of it.

"I—I—don't know. I don't know, Angelica. It just seemed better that you not know. It would be easier for everyone involved if you believed your father died in the war," Liz said, gravely.

Angelica closed her eyes for a few beats, then opened them. It was about to get loud.

"Better for who? Surely not better for me! When a kid believes something like that, there's a heaviness, a gravity that comes along with that knowledge. You're always thinking he's watching you from up in heaven like, 'I better be good because my daddy sees me, and I don't want him to be sad,'" she said in a childlike voice. "Shit, he's dead and I don't want him crying all over the place because his little girl is bad! Do you understand that, Mother?"

Liz just shook her head dumbly, sweat flinging itself from her face as if trying to escape the hostilities.

635

"Looking back, maybe it wasn't the best decision, but it was my decision. I did it to protect you from wanting to be with someone who was not going to be in your life. It was one blow, Angelica, rather than being beaten again and again when he doesn't come to your birthday party, or your play, or—"

"But he *has* been in our lives, Mama," Angelica interrupted. "Every day of my life, he's been there. He's been there pinning your arms helplessly to your sides when your daughter needed a hug. He's been there twisting the smile from your face when your daughter needed reassurance. He's been there taking up the entire whole of your heart while your only child tried to squeeze in like an uninvited guest. You cut yourself off from the joy of motherhood and the love of your kid. All this for a man. What kind of woman does that? I was there, and you missed me," Angelica gasped, choking back tears.

Angelica shook her head disdainfully. "You acted like you were embarrassed or ashamed of me. I could never figure out what I had done to you or when. Why? What happened to you to make you not love me? You can't blame that on my father."

Angelica's face was hot and flushed. She was ashamed to say out loud that her mother didn't love her. Elizabeth was sobbing softly, her splashing tears making no difference to the water surrounding her body. She always knew this day, these words of recrimination would come, and she had no defense. Everything her daughter said was true, except she did love Angelica more than anything and she had to let her know that. Liz reached out her hand and put it atop her daughter's resting on the sparkling tiles. She felt the stiffening resistance under her grasp.

"Listen to me, Angelica. I know I haven't always shown you the love I feel for you, but you have to know, I *do* love you. You are my only child. You are everything to me. I'm so ashamed at how long it took us to get to where we are now. I was, I don't

636

know, indifferent so many times when all you wanted was my love. I'm sorry, honey. I'm so sorry," Liz implored.

Angelica retracted her hand and began to stab at the small ceramic tiles with her index finger.

"So, he paid you? That's why you never had to work like the other moms I knew. That's why we had such a nice big house. You had fur coats and jewelry when my friend's moms didn't have any of that stuff. What were you, again? First generation born in the North, so you were just country and backward and easily bought, easily manipulated—"

"Stop it, Angelica! Now, I'm not putting up with that kind of talk! Yes, Angelo Santori, your father, set up a fund to take care of our needs. Is that so wrong? We knew we couldn't be together, a colored girl and a white boy. We loved each other and that's how you were conceived—in love. Blame me, if you're going to blame anybody. I let that broken heart swallow me. I was no good to anyone, including myself, but I was especially no good to you."

They sat in silence for nearly a minute.

"Angelica, I fell in love with your father so fast, I felt stunned, shell-shocked. I'd never seen or been around a guy like him. Mama and Daddy worked for Angelo's parents. Mama practically helped raise Angelo. She seemed to spend more time with his family than with us. The irony was that I got pregnant by someone she truly loved and instead of it making her love me that much more, she was, I don't know...appalled! Disgraced! She never forgave my indiscretion or got over the Santori family firing them after they found out about me and Angelo." Liz stepped out of the jacuzzi and sat on the side.

"But once you were born, she just adored you. You are the apple of that woman's eye and you know it. Maybe you just didn't

637

know some of the reasons why. Baby, I didn't want you to be like me either! For so long I felt used and useless. I guess I've been depressed for a good while. I just started seeing a therapist about 6 months ago and I'm learning who I really am and understanding all the mistakes I've made." Liz wanted to hug her daughter but knew she wouldn't allow it.

"Anyway, I want you to know that I was always so proud of how courageous and adventurous and independent you were. It was like God blessed you with a kind of completeness. You didn't seem to need my help and I was glad. I didn't want to mess you up, Angelica. I didn't know what else to do. I thank God for my family because I realize they filled in a lot of spaces for me and for you. Don't be mad that they never told you about Angelo. They kept that secret for me."

They fell silent again. Heavy words like storm clouds swirled above them as the sun was struggling to break through. Angelica looked at her mother. She had never heard her speak so much in one clip before.

"And everyone in the family is in on the lie?" she asked, already knowing the answer.

"I asked them to support my decision. You're a smart girl, Angelica. Somehow, I knew one day you'd find out or figure it out."

Angelica began to laugh.

"Well, Mama, the crazy thing is, I *am* like you. I've wasted a good bit of my life loving a man who's spent almost half of his behind bars. Someone who probably hates me for not standing by him, no matter how hard we pretend. How sick is that? I feel like I'm absolutely paralyzed in place and can't move forward

Angelica was tired, she felt old and shriveled.

"I have always, always loved Enrique Williams. I've tried to put my feelings aside and keep moving on with my life, but this thing has consumed me like a fire and now I have to deal with it, as will he," she said, rising up out of the water and onto the edge of the pool. She patted her little belly. "Carlton was a mistake."

"That baby you're carrying is for Enrique?" Elizabeth asked quietly.

"I love this baby more than my own life and I want to make sure he or she knows their father."

"Does he know about the baby?"

"No, but Carlton does."

Liz put her hand to her mouth and shook her head.

"I hate cheating and I hate cheaters yet here I am, a cheater, and knocked up at that! I know I have to tell him soon. I want Ricky to be in his child's life, even if he doesn't choose to be with me. I want you in the baby's life too, Mama."

Elizabeth began to sob again. Angelica grabbed her mother's hand to comfort her.

"By the way, I met my dad. Good looking guy," Angelica tossed off, as her mother's eyes got wide. "And yes, that's a whole 'nother conversation," Angelica said, with a wave of her hand as she began to laugh.

Elizabeth just stared at her daughter and finally began to laugh, too, her head pounding.

NINETY-EIGHT

Mike Morton pulled the plump, ornately upholstered chair out and sat down in front of the massive wooden desk and seconds later, slapped down two driver's licenses and a few scraps of paper, sliding them across the gleaming surface to Angelo Santori.

"The garbage got taken out, Boss," said Mike rather dramatically, with a slight smile.

He could tell Angelo was pleased that the job could be handled so quickly since Angelo had found out about Carlton's plan only 24 hours earlier. *Did that idiot really believe I'd let him kill my daughter?* Angelo scowled, reaching for the miscellaneous objects in front of him.

"A male and a female, huh? You ever see them before? I mean, you're in the same business," Angelo asked.

"Nope. They were semi-pro independents out of Pontiac."

"The plan was to get inside the house, suffocate Angelica and push her down the stairs? Kind of involved and weird, but it was supposed to look like an accident, I guess. That asshole probably told her they were coming to fix something inside the house. They have on uniforms?"

"Yup, they did. Some kind of blue coveralls. You could have knocked the guy over with a feather when I dropped that chick."

Angelo fingered the two slips of paper that accompanied the driver's licenses of the two unfortunate souls. One had Angelica's name and address. He didn't know what the other slip was or if it meant anything.

"Who is Kitty O'Neal?"

"Beats me, Boss," Mike said, pausing as if in thought, trying to decipher the name. "Sounds kinda familiar, but, nah, I don't know."

"A couple of busy little beavers. This Kitty O'Neal caught a break tonight."

When Mike got out of his car, the assassins hadn't yet arrived. He walked quickly up the hill from where he'd parked, the snow chomping at his boots while his labored breathing was echoing in his ears. He hastily mounded some snow into a small bank that allowed him to lay face down, concealed. He didn't have to wait long before the white van pulled up and came to a stop to the right of the long winding driveway. The front of the house could barely be seen from the street. Mike smirked to himself. People didn't realize if nobody can see the door to your house, nobody would see if something bad went down up there. Bodies could be laying everywhere, and no one would be the wiser.

Two people exited the vehicle and the male opened the back passenger door on the driver's side. He was moving his hands rapidly and deliberately, withdrawing a gun from the back seat and shoving it into his pocket. The woman crossed behind the van and came up beside the man, speaking to him with puffs of condensation hovering above her face. Mike had his scope at the ready, barely glinting in the fading daylight. This was always the moment when he wondered what the person had planned for the rest of the day, the night, their lives? Their time was up, and they had not a clue.

641

The dull and muffled crack from the silencer on his rifle sent a bullet crashing into the woman's head, a pink mist rose a short distance into the air like a shaken can of Red Pop. She dropped to the ground as if her legs had been severed with a hatchet. He shot her first because she may have screamed if her partner went down before her eyes. The remaining hit man looked startled as he turned to see his partner on the ground. Within seconds he put his hand on the weapon in his coat to draw it out, but before he could, he was lying dead beside his companion.

Mike moved briskly toward them, surveying his surroundings to make sure no one had seen or heard anything. All clear. He opened the back of the van and dragged the bodies toward the back gate. He hoisted them up one by one, flipping them roughly inside the vehicle. Shit, there was blood in the snow! Mike kicked and sprinkled new snow over the crimson expanse, containing and burying it until it was no longer visible.

It was now dark, not pitch, but dark enough that street lights and porch lights started to illuminate the area. It began to snow diamonds from the sky once again as Mike walked down to his car, finalizing the last part of the task at hand. He'd find a Marathon filling station and use the pay phone to call a tow truck. He had special people who did what was necessary without further inquiries. The van and its contents would go to a wrecking yard where it would be smashed into a cube that could be melted down. *Recycling, the wave of the future!*

Mike Morton cruised down I-94 back to Detroit, thankful that he didn't have to shuttle those two bodies in his Caprice Wagon, even though he was prepared to do just that. When he got home he would take the plywood out and put the seats back in, so the family could all go to Christmas Mass day after tomorrow. Mike turned on the radio and as always, the "Big 8" CKLW was there waiting for him. He began to sing.

I

One January morning in 1984, Helene Allen opened the back door off her kitchen to let her dog Skipper out into the yard.

"I know it's cold, baby. Do yo' bidness and I'll get you in a lil' while."

She locked the door and shuffled to her front door to get the newspaper. She put the rubber banded bundled under her arm and slammed the door.

"Lawd a mighty it's cold out there!" she exclaimed. Just a little exposure to that kind of cold could leave you chilled for hours. Her toes curled up inside her blue house slippers just thinking about it.

She slid over to the aluminum bread box on the counter and retrieved the loaf of Awrey's white bread and pushed down the lever on her toaster to brown a couple of slices for toast. The small kitchen was filled with the rich scent of the coffee she'd just percolated in her sturdy Corning coffee pot. "Old faithful" she called it as much for its reliability as for the little geyser of brown liquid that shot up into the glass knob in its top.

Once Helene got situated in her breakfast nook with her toast, plum jam, Blue Bonnet margarine and coffee, she opened The Detroit Free Press.

"Good God a mighty! Thank you! Thank you, Jesus!" she shouted.

Staring out from the newspaper, frozen in photographic shame was Carlton Meadows and Sidney Meadows. The headline shouted, "Corruption!" Between the two of them, the charges ranged from perjury and jury tampering to racketeering and second-degree murder.

"Um, um, um. How the mighty has fallen. Ain't that right, Red?" Helene said looking heavenward.

Skipper was barking and scratching at the door to be let back inside.

II

December of the same year, downtown Detroit was decorated as best as could be expected in preparation for Christmas. Of course, it was nothing like the proud, flag waving days of a bygone era when J.L. Hudson's ruled a full city block with its authoritative and venerable presence. Gone were window after window of the lovely and imaginative animatronics, colored lights and hurried shoppers being blown along Woodward Avenue by the winter wind coming off of the river. J.L. Hudson's had closed its doors mid-January of 1983, never anything like it to be seen again in Detroit or the United States.

Angelica stood looking out at the choppy and not quite frozen Detroit River from high above East Jefferson Boulevard. Surrounding her were shelves of law books, a sitting area with four leather chairs around a low maple coffee table atop a Persian rug, and a large matching wood desk with two chairs in front and hers behind it. There were framed photos of her family at the corner of the desk—her mother, father, husband and baby boy. This was her office. This was her building--all 14 stories--a present from her dad, Angelo. A gift to keep himself out of her legal cross hairs? Perhaps.

Tanner-Williams was a law firm dedicated to family law, with a specialty in reviewing and re-opening and appealing cases of people who were wrongfully convicted. The firm also helped the community with employment resources and services. Tonight, on the main level, a Christmas party was taking place for the families who lived nearby as well as those they'd helped and there would be food and music and presents for all. Santa would even be in attendance to surprise and delight the children.

There was a muffled rap on the door to her office and Angelica Williams was smiling before she even turned around to say, "Come in."

"Hi, baby. Look who came to see you!" Enrique Williams exclaimed to his wife.

He came through the door holding a beautiful little fat brown baby with sparkling brown eyes and his hair sticking up in ringlets all over his head. The little one was grinning and drooling with his arms out expectantly.

"Hi, my love! Hi, my baby! Mommy's baby, yes he is," she cooed as the little baby squealed with joy.

Angelica took baby Ricky from his father and kissed his chubby cheek, embracing her husband with her free arm. They held on to each other for a while, swaying ever so slightly. Ricky kissed his little boy's fingers and made a face, making the child laugh.

"Everybody here?" Angelica asked.

"Pretty much a full house down there. It's gonna be fun. The kids are excited to see Santa and get some presents. Your mom and my mom are here. I saw Sheila right before I came up, chatting up Leamon. Pilar is down there, and Eduardo even came with his little girl."

Another knock.

"Come in," Enrique said.

It was his sister Pilar, who had grown into a stunning young woman with wavy black hair and skin the color of coffee and cream. She'd married a police officer and he was on duty tonight, somewhere in the city.

"Hey you two! Mami asked me to come and get the baby, if it's okay? She wants little Ricky to get his picture done with Santa before it gets too crowded."

Angelica nodded and handed the baby to her after another quick kiss to his forehead.

"See you in a few minutes, Angel," Enrique said, smiling at his son.

"Now, to my other Angel. I'm so proud of you, baby. This work is so important. People are so grateful."

"Ricky, you know I couldn't do this without you. You sparked all of this. You made me see what we could do together as a team."

Ricky led his wife to the window and stood behind her, his arms wrapped around her waist, his face nuzzling her neck.

"Remember the time we took Pi-pi and Eduardo to see the Christmas decorations at Hudson's? I would have called you a liar if you had told me we wouldn't be able to do the same for our kids or our kids for theirs. You think some traditions, some touchstones will never die. But they do. They become only a shared memory that'll die with us. What's to become of our city, baby?"

"I don't know. I just don't know," Angelica said, sadly.

So much had changed and not for the better. Her hometown was in ruins in some parts with abandoned and burnt out homes dotting every city block. The beautiful and ornate architecture that graced and enchanted so many streets and neighborhoods was now no more than nuisance eyesores. Why didn't the vandals who burned things down realize they were only punching out the eyes of their own city? War torn Europe in the 1940's had nothing on Detroit right now.

Angelica's face brightened suddenly. She put Ricky's open palm on her stomach.

"You feel that? That's a future Detroiter in there," she said, laughing.

"When are we going to tell everyone?" he asked, lovingly rubbing her belly.

"Maybe tonight. We just have to make sure your Uncle Bill doesn't send us some kind of double pimped out stroller like the one he got for Ricky." They both laughed, and Ricky shook his head at the thought.

Still Bill Williams had become the thing he never thought he would—a retired pimp. Bill and Mary Williams were married in 1980 and moved to Las Vegas to begin their lives anew, never looking back. William Williams was a successful, legitimate businessman owning several dry-cleaning establishments and fast food franchises. They never visited Detroit, though they kept up with the family via mail and phone calls.

"Uncle Bill only buys the best. He's nothing if not, uh, *stylish* and we don't want to hurt his feelings." Enrique kissed his wife gently on the lips. "Let's go downstairs to the party, baby. I love you. Merry Christmas," he said.

"Merry Christmas, my love," Angelica answered.

CPSIA information can be obtained
at www.ICGtesting.com
Printed in the USA
LVOW11s2006070618
579892LV00001B/3/P